P9-AQD-243

It's the Little Things

It's the Little Things

ERICA JAMES

First published in 2008 by Orion Books
an imprint of The Orion Publishing Group Ltd
Orion House, 5 Upper Saint Martin's Lane
London WC2H 9EA

First published in Great Britain in 2009 by Orion Books

An Hachette Livre UK Company

Export Edition © Erica James 2008
UK Edition © Erica James 2009

The moral right of Erica James to be identified as
the author of this work has been asserted in accordance with
the Copyright, Designs and Patents Act of 1988.

All rights reserved. No part of this publication may be
reproduced, stored in a retrieval system, or transmitted
in any form or by any means, electronic, mechanical,
photocopying, recording, or otherwise, without the
prior permission of both the copyright owner
and the above publisher of this book.

All the characters in this book are fictitious, and any resemblance
to actual persons living or dead is purely coincidental.

A CIP catalogue record for this book is
available from the British Library.

Typeset by Deltatype Ltd, Birkenhead, Merseyside

Printed in Great Britain by Clays Ltd, St Ives plc.

The Orion Publishing Group's policy is to use papers
that are natural, renewable and recyclable products and
made from wood grown in sustainable forests. The logging
and manufacturing processes are expected to conform to
the environmental regulations of the country of origin.

www.orionbooks.co.uk

Acknowledgements

I'm grateful to many people who patiently answered my interminable questions, particularly Howard and Michelle Stringer.

Thanks must go to my neighbours who regularly come in for the strangest of questions from me.

A special thank you to the ever-creative Sara and her daughter Sophie – I knew that duck impression would come in handy one day!

Lastly, thank you to Jane Atkinson and everyone else at the Jessie May Trust which became the Kyle Morgan Trust in my book.

As ever to Edward and Samuel, with love.

But also to all who survived the Boxing Day Tsunami 2004. May we be thankful for being alive but never forget those who didn't return home or those still struggling with the loss of a loved one.

Chapter One

Doctor Chloe Hennessey had long since mastered the art of maintaining a perfectly neutral expression.

'Exactly how much bigger do you want to be, Chelsea?' she asked.

Chelsea Savage put her hands in front of her chest – a chest that looked to be about the same size as Chloe's – but before the girl could open her mouth, her mother piped up, 'She wants to be a 34GG.' A stout, blousily dressed woman in her mid-forties, Mrs Savage worked part-time behind the bar at the Fox and Feathers and was well known for her ability to stamp on any potential bar room brawls. She was also known for starting a few brawls in her time and more than lived up to her name. Not for nothing was she nicknamed The Pit Bull at the surgery.

'And you are currently what size, Chelsea?' Chloe asked her patient. She blamed the ever-increasing number of women and young girls wanting breast implants on all those makeover shows on the telly. You couldn't switch it on these days without seeing some poor woman having her body knocked into a supposedly better shape.

'She's a 34A,' chimed in Mrs Savage. 'And it's making her depressed. She's a right pain at times, let me tell you. Always mooching about the place with a face on her like a wet Sunday in Bridlington.'

Chloe kept her gaze deliberately on the sixteen-year-old girl before her. She was pretty enough in a bland, unremarkable way, but as with so many teenage girls, her face had been clumsily painted with too much make-up. 'Are you depressed, Chelsea?' she probed.

Shifting her chewing gum from one side of her mouth to the other, Chelsea nodded and twiddled with a large hooped earring. 'Now and then, yeah.'

Yes, thought Chloe. Show me a teenager who isn't.

'The thing is,' Mrs Savage butted in again, 'if she's going to make it as a model, she'll have to have them made bigger.'

Even since Chelsea had been crowned Eastbury's May Queen last year and had been paraded through the village in a canary-yellow, open-topped Smart car Mrs Savage had bragged to anyone who would listen that this was the start of things to come. Her daughter was going to be famous; she would be on the front of every magazine and tabloid you could care to mention.

'If I'm not mistaken, Mrs Savage,' Chloe said patiently, 'most catwalk models don't have a double G cup size. Quite the reverse, in fact.'

'I'm not talking about those zero-sized airheads who can't keep a meal down them,' the woman said. 'Chelsea's going to be a glamour model.' She turned to her daughter and smiled proudly at her. 'Isn't that right, love?'

Once more Chelsea nodded and twiddled with her earring. 'So what do you think, doctor? Can I have the surgery? For free, like.'

'It's a little more complicated than that, Chelsea. You see, you are only sixteen and we have to decide whether you really—'

The Pit Bull raised a heavily ringed hand and bared her teeth. 'Whoa there! End of. Absolutely end of. I'm not going to sit here and listen to any mealy-mouthed back-pedalling.'

'Mrs Savage, all I was trying to—'

'No, now you listen to me, doctor. I know my rights. Chelsea's rights too. If she's not happy with her body and it's causing her mental anguish, then she's entitled to have implants on the NHS. Now give us the forms or whatever it is we need to sign to get the ball rolling for the necessary referral and we'll be on our way; we've got an appointment at the tanning centre in ten minutes. And no offence, but if you don't mind me saying, you could do with some implants yourself. With a decent pair of hooters, you might not spend so many nights on your own.'

Great, thought Chloe. All those years of training, hard slog and sleepless nights only to wind up being verbally trashed and told how to do my job.

With afternoon surgery over, and only running a few minutes late for her home visits, Chloe slipped out unnoticed to the car park at the rear of the building before the practice manager could collar her. It was Chloe's first day back after a week away skiing in Austria, but she didn't doubt Karen could find something to nag her about. Usually it was her timekeeping. She spent far too long with the patients, she was frequently warned. The other doctors could keep to the schedule; why couldn't she?

She liked to think it was because she was a maverick, put on this earth to confound and frustrate, but actually it was because she was just plain old thorough and liked to spend time with her patients. She hated to upset her more elderly or timid patients by rudely hurrying them. There were exceptions, though. Some mistook kindness and understanding for pity and they required a much more robust bedside manner.

At the age of thirty-seven, Chloe was the youngest doctor at Eastbury Surgery, and was perhaps, as the other doctors regularly teased her, still the most idealistic. The practice had doubled in size in the last ten years due to the expansion of the village, sitting as it was within commutable distance of Manchester. Farmland that had been in the hands of Cheshire families for generations had been sold off to make way for a full range of properties, from doll's-house-size starter homes through to five-bedroomed executive dwellings that boasted saunas and under-floor heating. The latest must-have accessory to these upmarket houses was a hot tub installed in the garden.

Chloe had wanted to be a doctor ever since she could remember. Probably because her father had been one and she had considered him the cleverest and bravest man alive. But then, at six years old, you think anyone is a genius if they can cure you of a painful earache, and as for being able to look at a dead body without screaming or bursting into tears, that surely took courage beyond words. Now, of course, she knew better: it was all smoke and mirrors.

Her first home visit was only a five-minute drive away, up Chapel Hill and then onto Lark Lane. Ron Tuttle lived in one of the original sandstone farm workers' cottages. There had been a Tuttle living on Lark Lane for more than a hundred and seventy years. But not for much longer unless Ron – the last in the line of Tuttles – took better care of himself.

She parked on the road outside his cottage and, case in hand, walked up the short path that was lined with daffodils – King Alfred's; they were tough and sturdy and gave the impression of standing guard. She gave the door knocker a loud rap and adopted her most robust bedside manner. Anything less would be deemed as patronizing and give Ron cause to take his walking stick to her.

Minutes passed and she risked another go at the tarnished knocker. 'I heard you the first time,' came an angry shout from inside, as well as the sound of a lock being turned. The door opened. 'Who do you think I am, Roger-flipping-Bannister?'

'Roger Who?'

'First man to run a mile in less than four minutes. Don't you know nothing, girl?'

'I know plenty. Now can I come in or do you want me to examine your prostate here on the step?'

'Mother Teresa's love child, that's you!' he roared.

'That's an improvement on a fortnight ago when I was Harold Shipman's love child. These sweet endearments of yours will have to stop, you know, or people will talk.'

The old man's eyes glinted with a smile and leaning heavily on his walking stick, he stood aside to let her in. She noticed he had made his usual attempt to smarten himself up for her visit. She also noticed that his shirt collar looked a little looser around his neck, a sign he was still losing weight. Closing the door after her, he said, 'I never had this trouble with your father. He never gave me any lip. How is he?'

'Making hay with Mum. They're hardly ever at home these days. Whenever I call round or telephone them they're just about to go somewhere. They're like a couple of kids.'

'What would you rather they were doing? Sitting miserably at home waiting to die? Anyhow, give the doc my regards when you do see him next. Cup of tea before we get down to business?'

'Thank you, but another time perhaps.'

Ron Tuttle sniffed. 'Your father always had time for a brew.'

With the last of her visits completed, Chloe decided to nip home for an hour before evening surgery. A few of the patients she had seen that afternoon were elderly, and much of what they'd had to say to her had been gilded with nostalgic references to The Great Doctor Hennessey Senior. Chloe had no problem accepting that her father was a hard act to follow or that she would always be compared with him. Or that some people couldn't take her seriously because they remembered her as a child tearing around the village on her bike with her brother, Nick. None of this mattered to her because the vast majority of her patients were incomers and had never encountered her father or known her when she was little. There was also Dad's own testimony that spurred her on. These same patients who now claimed he could do no wrong had once upon a time complained unstintingly that he was nothing but a smooth-talking upstart who didn't know a bunion from a green stick fracture.

Dad had retired five years ago from the surgery he'd joined when he'd been Chloe's age. In those days the word of the local GP was the word of God. How different it was now, when the Savages of this world were able to demand their rights and dictate the terms of their treatment. Chloe had never intended to move back home to Eastbury, but then she'd never intended to very nearly lose her life and the man she'd thought she would marry.

When that had happened, throwing her life into turmoil, the pull of her childhood roots had seemed the answer to her crisis and as if by magic everything had slipped into place. A new GP was needed at Eastbury Surgery, and Pocket House, an end-of-terrace cottage facing the village green, came on the market. It was a stone's throw from her parents, as well as her closest friends, Dan and Sally. Thankfully nobody had dared utter the words 'It's meant to be' – had they done so, Chloe might have been tempted to give them a lethal injection – and by Easter 2005, almost four months after surviving one of the world's worst natural disasters, she'd moved from Nottingham back to Cheshire and her life had taken on a degree of normality again. As had Dan's and Sally's lives, for they, on holiday with Chloe and Paul, had also been caught up in the disaster that would for ever be known as the Boxing Day tsunami.

She locked her car and walked round to the back of the cottage. It was a beautiful March afternoon, and spring was very much in the air. Her small but cherished garden was teeming with new life. The magnolia tree, the forsythia bushes and the camellias basking in the late afternoon sun against the stone wall of the garage were all in full flower. As were the daffodils and grape hyacinths her mother had helped plant last autumn. The clocks had changed to British Summer Time at the weekend and to Chloe's great joy, the days were longer and brighter. This was her favourite time of the year, when, against all the odds, hope sprang eternally.

She let herself in and walked through to the conservatory that she'd had built onto the kitchen. It had opened up the space beautifully and she now had an airy and spacious room that gave her a view of not only the back garden, but also the village green at the front. What made it her favourite room was the wood-burning stove she'd had put into the fireplace, which the previous owners had boarded up.

With only forty-five minutes before she had to be back at work for evening surgery, she made herself a cup of coffee and checked her answerphone. The first message was from her brother apologizing for having somehow ended up with her ski gloves in his suitcase and saying he'd post them on to her.

The next message was from her mother, hoping she'd had a good holiday with Nick and his friends and reminding her that it was Dad's birthday on Friday. 'He's insisting on trying out the new recipes he learned during that cookery weekend, so be warned. See you Friday, at eight.'

The third message was from her father. 'Just to say I'm under orders from your mother to cook her favourite seafood risotto for dinner on Saturday. See you at seven.'

Her parents ran the Ministry of Misinformation. They did it effortlessly and to great effect; the one rarely knew what the other was up to.

The fourth message was from—

Chloe put down her cup of coffee and backed away from the machine as if it was about to explode. Hearing that voice – *his* voice – her insides churned. Time was, the churning would have been with lust and desire for him. Not now.

'Hi Chloe, it's Paul. Yes, I know, this is probably the last voice on earth you expected to hear again. The thing is …' The sound of rustling and a throat being cleared filled the kitchen. 'Oh, hell, I didn't think it would be so hard to do this – look, what I want to say is … I—' More throat clearing. 'I don't suppose there's any chance we could get together for a chat, could we? It would be a place and time to suit you. I'll leave that entirely for you to decide. You can contact me on my mobile. My number is—'

But Paul – *That man! That snake in the grass!* – as her mother had renamed him, had taken so long with his message, he'd run out of space on her machine. He hadn't rung back to give her the number either. He'd probably assumed that she'd received his message in full.

Which she had, loud and very clearly, exactly three weeks after they had flown home to Nottingham after that disastrous holiday on Phuket. Off work with her leg in plaster and a fractured collar bone, and numerous cuts and bruises, he'd announced that he didn't love her any more. 'Surviving the tsunami has brought it home to me that we only get one chance in this life,' he'd said. He'd gone on to give her every other possible cliché about there being no dress rehearsal, that this life was the only one on offer and that if there was a chance

6

of happiness one had to grab it with both hands. He'd even said that one day she would thank him for having the courage to leave her.

It turned out he'd been having an affair for goodness knows how long and coming so close to his own demise had sharpened his focus and helped him to make up his mind who he really wanted to be with. From then on, Paul Stratton, one-time prospective son-in-law to Jennifer and Graham Hennessey, became known as *That man! That snake in the grass!*

Now, three years and two months later, he wanted to get together for a drink and a chat.

Did he really think she'd agree to meet him?

Chapter Two

It was hair-washing night at Corner Cottage.

Neither Dan nor his son Marcus enjoyed the experience: Marcus hated getting the soapy water in his eyes and Dan hated to see his son cry. Leaning over the side of the bath, with a frog-shaped plastic watering can in his left hand and his young son's head resting against his right, Dan said, as he always did, 'I promise I won't let you go. Now close your eyes and tilt your head back. Ready?'

Marcus screwed his eyes up, gave a little shudder and braced himself. 'Cold!' he squealed as the water cascaded over his baby-soft hair, washing away the soapy bubbles. 'Cold, cold, COLD!'

'That's because we took so long. Sorry.'

'Mr Squeaky! Mr Squeaky!'

Dan reached for the flannel – called Mr Squeaky because he had once made a squeaky noise with it when he wrung it out – and gave it to Marcus, who covered his eyes with it. Dan refilled the watering can and rinsed away the last remaining bubbles.

'Job done, buddy,' Dan said with a salute. 'Another dangerous mission accomplished. Tomorrow we airlift in back-up troops and form an assault on your toenails. It's hazardous work, but we're a crack team and more than up for it.'

With his hair plastered wet and shiny against his scalp, giving him an oddly wise and noble appearance, Marcus looked doubtfully at his toes. He then smiled and offered the flannel to Dan. 'Make him squeak.'

Dan happily obliged and then suggested it was time to pull out the plug. Marcus scrambled to his feet. Ever since he'd made the mistake of sitting over the plug hole and had experienced the sensation of being sucked down that narrow dark hole, he never lingered when the water started making its hungry, gurgling exit.

There were certain smells that were as sharp and precise in Dan's memory as any photograph album that charted his existence. The smell of pipe tobacco reminded him of being a small boy and watching in wonder as his parents' gardener whittled away at a piece of wood with a penknife, magically turning it into an animal of Dan's choosing. The smell of pine air freshener took him back to the very first car he'd owned – a second-hand Ford Escort, and Camilla Dawson-Bradley. Home from school for the summer holidays, and a week after passing his driving test, he'd plucked up the courage to ask Camilla out on a date. Two years older than him, she was by far the hottest girl in the Cotswold village where he'd grown up. He spent all afternoon cleaning the car, inside and out, and then hung one of those air fresheners shaped like a pine tree from the rear-view mirror. He'd taken Camilla to watch a film, and afterwards he'd driven them somewhere remote so that he could get down to what had been on his mind ever since coming home from school.

Another smell that brought back happy memories was the aroma of aniseed. It reminded him of ouzo and Sally; of the exact moment during a soft summer night in an open-air fish restaurant in Paxos, when he'd proposed. A mess of nerves – he really didn't know how Sally would respond – he'd said he loved her and wanted to spend the rest of his life with her. He'd then presented her with a ring and asked her to marry him. Barely glancing at it, she'd reached across the table, laid her cool hand over his and fixing him with her pale grey eyes, she'd said yes. When the other diners, mostly locals, realized that something momentous had just occurred, the owner of the restaurant went round the tables filling everyone's glass so the happy couple could be toasted. Then the dancing had commenced and they didn't make it back to their villa until nearly four in the morning.

But it was the smell and touch of his freshly washed, pyjama-clad son that evoked the most intensely poignant response in Dan. It never failed to remind him that from the very first moment he had held Marcus, his whole being had undergone a dramatic change. It was as if previously he had merely been bumbling around in the chorus of his life. But suddenly he was a principal character with a whole new and scary script to learn. Even now as he thought of that day when he sat in the chair beside Sally's hospital bed with Marcus lying peacefully in his arms, his scrunched-up little face peering out at the world, Dan could recall how happy he had felt. It was a happiness he had never experienced before. And yes, he had totally lost it and cried. He could have put it down to relief and exhaustion – Sally had, after all, just gone through thirty-six hours of excruciating labour – but it was so much more than that.

He had been overwhelmed by the miracle that was the birth of his child.

It was something he still felt now. And never more so than when it was his son's bedtime.

Two and a half years old, Marcus loved bedtime. He had a finely tuned ritual of lining up his army of cuddly toys along the edge of his bed against the wall, but saving the places either side of him for his extra-special henchmen – Rory Bear and Rumpus Red Bear – before sitting bolt upright with his arms around the two large bears eagerly waiting for Dan to read to him.

Tonight, as they settled into the delights of the relentlessly Hungry Caterpillar, Dan thought of Sally. It was a quarter to seven and she probably wouldn't be home for another hour yet. She worked too hard. Yet he could never say that to her. Not when he perceived himself as having got the better end of the deal and occasionally felt guilty about it.

If, on that perfect night in Paxos somebody had told him that Sally would end up being the breadwinner of the family and he would become a house husband, he would have laughed in their face. Throw away his career? You have to be joking. He'd chew his own leg off before that happened thank you very much! Nonetheless here he was, a thirty-nine-year-old Domestic God – as Chloe called him – who enjoyed nothing more than spending his days potato painting, making pizzas, ambling down to the duck pond, and generally having fun. There hadn't been a single day when he'd regretted stepping back from his career. His old work colleagues had betted him that he'd return within six months. They'd lost the bet. His new life unquestionably had the edge on insufferably demanding clients and even more insufferably demanding senior partners of a major league accountancy firm. Every day there was some new joy to share with Marcus. There were milestone events like a first tooth coming through, a first step taken, a first word spoken, or simple pleasures like Marcus developing an amusing and obsessive taste for gherkins and wanting to eat them for breakfast, lunch and tea.

Of course, Dan couldn't very well bang on to Sally about how much fun he was having, just as there were other things he couldn't admit to her either. He would never be able to explain to Sally how vulnerable fatherhood made him feel. It had come as a huge shock to him to learn that something as pure and simple as his love for Marcus, coupled with the innate need to protect him from the world, ensured that he was an easy target for anguish. If surviving the tsunami had made him realize how fleeting the nature of life was, being a father had honed that knowledge to a lethal sharpness.

But none of this he shared with Sally. Nor did he tell her that he still occasionally woke in the middle of the night with his heart pounding and his brain terrifyingly wired to the events of Boxing Day just over three years ago. The nightmare had recently changed, though. For a long time it had been the same dream, a crystal clear replay of what had happened – the awesome, unstoppable power of the water, the deafening roar of it, the screams, and his failure. But now the dream had taken on a new and far more disturbing slant. A slant that had him stumbling breathlessly out of bed and pushing open the door of his son's room to make sure he was all right. Last night he had needed extra convincing that Marcas was safe and he had knelt on the floor listening to the steady fall and rise of his breathing, needing to quell his fear. Two hours later he'd woken up stiff and cold and had crept back to his own bed feeling vaguely foolish. Sally had stirred briefly as he'd slipped in beside her but as tempted as he was, he hadn't selfishly wrapped himself around her to steal her warmth and assurance. Instead he'd lain in the darkness on his side of the bed feeling alone and useless. What if he could never shake off the nightmare and the guilt that lay behind it? He'd been hailed a hero at the time because he'd saved the life of a five-year-old girl, but what of her brother, the small boy whom he hadn't been able to save?

'Daddy read now.'

'Sorry,' Dan said, giving himself a little wake-up shake. 'I was miles away.'

Nudging at the book on his lap, Marcus smiled. It was a smile that had the ability to stir a great tenderness in Dan. To make everything seem all right. He hung onto it.

Chapter Three

With the meter running on her fee, Sally Oliver made neat and precise notes on her legal pad, all the while being careful to nod and make the right non-judgemental noises at the appropriate moment.

Adamson v. Adamson had all the hallmarks of a long-haul flight to hell and back, and it would have little to do with the two law firms involved. Julia and Murray Adamson would ensure that this case would run and run. Sadly, Sally had seen it all before. Two opposing parties so cranked up on 'I'm right, you're wrong!' they would blind themselves to a reasonable outcome. Get real! she often wanted to say to the people who came to her hoping for the law to take away the pain and make everything right again. Get with the programme; this is going to be a nasty and bloody fight if you don't come to your senses. They were driven by the need for vengeance, of course. Rarely had a wronged wife or husband sat in that chair the other side of her desk and not wanted to exact revenge. If they couldn't physically hurt the so-called guilty party – and a few clients had tried, with varying degrees of success – they wanted the next best thing: an all-out, guns blazing, vicious attack made on the wallet of their one-time nearest and dearest.

When Sally had joined the firm of McKenzie Stuart most of her clients had been women – more often than not, the tearful, bewildered, middle-aged kind whose husbands had traded them in for younger, newer models. But now that she'd been made a partner, she headed up a department that dealt exclusively with high-value, high-profile divorce settlements. A lot of her clients were men, and not the wronged ones. As was becoming more common, many of these men were going through the breakdown of a second marriage and so were doubly keen to hold onto their assets, having already been relieved of a high percentage of them first time round.

'Experience tells me this is going to cost me, right? And I'm not just talking about your fee.'

Sally put down her pen and looked directly at her client, Murray

Adamson. A self-made man, he wouldn't be out of place on that absurd *Dragons' Den* programme. Having built up a kitchen and bathroom fitting empire and then sold it in the late nineties for a killing, he now diversified with small start-up businesses. He liked to give the impression that he was an altogether more altruistic businessman than the one he used to be. His private life wasn't such a model of success. He was fifty-one years old and newly separated from wife number two after she'd discovered he'd been cheating on her in the same way he'd cheated on wife number one. 'Yes,' Sally said frankly. 'This will be expensive. There's no point in pretending otherwise. But obviously, I'll do my best to minimise the extent of the damage.'

'And you're probably thinking, stupid man, ink barely dry on his last settlement and here he is again. Doesn't he learn?'

'You don't pay me to think like that.'

'But it's what's going through your head, isn't it?'

No, thought Sally as she listened to the traffic down on the street below. What's going through my head is I should never have agreed to meet you after normal office hours just because your busy schedule precluded an earlier appointment. She said: 'Statistics show that second marriages have a greater failure rate than first marriages.'

He gave her one of his super-strength smiles, which she recognised from when he'd originally come to her for help. Doubtless he used it to get what he wanted from women. 'I know it's no excuse,' he said, 'but I don't seem able to resist the charms of a beautiful woman. I guess I'm just a hapless romantic.'

She drew a line under her notes, snapped the lid back on her fountain pen and looked pointedly at her watch. 'Well, I have all the information I need for now,' she said. 'When I hear from the other side, I'll be in touch again. Don't hesitate to ring if there's anything you want to discuss.'

'I appreciate you sparing the time for me, Sally. It means a lot.'

She tried not to flinch. She hated male clients calling her by her Christian name. Especially the Murray Adamson type of client. She watched him uncross his legs and stand up. She stood up too and started putting her desk in order, despite there not being a thing out of place. According to Chloe she was obsessively tidy and should have therapy for it. Chloe often joked that she should be forced to live in a house that had never been cleaned or tidied, that a dose of healthy squalor would get things in perspective for her. Little did Chloe know that that was exactly what Sally had grown up with. It was why she craved her surroundings to be so clean and uncluttered.

'Can I tempt you into a drink?'

Sally looked up, but not with surprise. She would have been more shocked if a drink hadn't been suggested. 'I'm sorry,' she said. 'If I'm any later getting home I'll have a furious husband to placate. He's probably scraping a ruined meal into the bin as we speak.' Immediately she regretted what she'd said, knowing that she'd just painted Dan as the archetypal sour-faced, nagging housewife with a rolling pin in his hands and a cigarette dangling from his mouth. In all the many times she'd arrived home late Dan had never once complained or criticised her for the long hours she kept. He might remark on her lateness, but he never complained.

'Sounds like an offer of dinner would be more the mark in that case,' Murray Adamson said.

A knock at the door saved Sally from having to respond. Expecting it to be one of the cleaners doing their rounds of the offices, she was surprised to see Tom McKenzie come in. 'Oh, sorry, Sally,' he said affably, 'I didn't know you had anyone here with you.'

'That's all right,' she said, grateful for the interruption, 'your timing's perfect; we've just finished.'

The two men acknowledged each other with a hearty exchange. Murray Adamson was a highly valued client – divorce settlements were only a part of the services the firm provided for him – and consequently he always received the full anything-I-can-do-for-you? treatment.

'Can I have a quick word before you head off home?' Tom asked Sally.

'Of course. Let me just see Mr Adamson out.'

Leading the way, Sally walked him briskly along the carpeted corridor towards the deserted reception area and summoned a lift. While they waited, Murray Adamson offered his hand to her. 'I'll wait to hear from you, then.'

'Yes, I'll be in touch just as soon as I have anything to report,' she replied, not letting her hand linger in his for a moment longer than necessary.

The distant hum of a vacuum cleaner starting up coincided with the arrival of the lift and before the doors had even closed on her client she had moved away. Retracing her steps to her office, she worked the muscles of her shoulders. She was tired. She'd been awake since crazy o'clock after Marcus had woken wanting a drink.

After giving him some water, Dan had brought him into their room and slid him in bed between them. Within no time both Dan and Marcus were fast asleep again, but she'd lain wide awake, her mind already sifting through the day ahead of her. Unable to get back to sleep, she'd slipped out of bed, got dressed and quietly left for work. It was something she often did.

She found Tom perched on her desk, reading the notes she'd made during the meeting with Murray Adamson. 'It says here, in your scarily neat script, that the man's a serial womaniser and deserves to lose every penny of his ill-gotten gains.'

Sally smiled and took the legal pad out of Tom's hand. 'It says no such thing. Did you really want a word with me?'

'Of course not. Bill told me who you had coming in and since that particular client's reputation goes before him, I decided to hang about and make myself useful.'

Sally had suspected as much. As senior partners, both Bill and Tom were fifteen years older than her, and Tom – touchingly so at times – was absurdly chivalrous by nature. 'I am old enough to look after myself, you know,' she said.

'No grousing, Oliver! No climbing up onto your high horse! All I did was provide you with a convenient excuse to sneak out the back way.'

'I'll do the same for you one day.'

He smiled. 'I look forward to it.'

'And if it gives you a warm, fuzzy feeling inside, your timing really was perfect. He'd just asked me out for the obligatory drink.'

'I heard dinner mentioned.'

She laughed. 'Just how long did you have your ear pressed up against my door?'

'Long enough to know when the cavalry's required. Now why don't you go home before your husband calls the police and reports you as missing?'

The advantage of leaving so late was that the traffic out of Manchester was minimal; within no time she was on the M56. She may have physically distanced herself from work, but mentally it was always with her. It wasn't possible for her to compartmentalize it and leave it behind in her office. She loved her job. It was who she was. It defined her. But confess any of this too loudly and she would be condemned in an instant. Saying that she found work easier than being at home with her son was only slightly less of a crime in certain quarters than if she'd been hanging about school gates supplying drugs to ten-year-olds.

Some would call her heartless. Her mother for one. 'No one will ever love you,' she had flung at Sally when she was a teenager, 'for the simple reason you have a stone where your heart should be.'

When Dan had first told her he loved her, Sally's initial thought had not been to reply straight away that she loved him in return, but to picture her mother's face and say, 'See, Mum, someone does love me! You were wrong!'

She'd met Dan at Chloe's twenty-eighth birthday party in Nottingham, where Chloe was living at the time. Sally had travelled up from London for the weekend, accompanied by her then boyfriend, who'd only been on the scene for a couple of weeks. Dan had arrived at the party with Chloe's brother, but it wasn't until she had gone out to the kitchen to help Chloe organise the food – pizzas, spicy chicken legs, baked potatoes, salads – that they met properly. He was on his own, grating cheese, and when he saw her he immediately stopped what he was doing. 'Hi,' he said, 'if you're looking for Chloe, she's upstairs changing. Some clumsy idiot spilled red wine down her dress. I'm Dan, by the way.'

'I'm Sally,' she said.

'I know exactly who you are,' he'd replied. He used his hands to tick items off an imaginary list. 'You're Chloe's best friend from her university days here in Nottingham. You became friends during freshers' week and you're the one who held her hair back while she had her head down the loo after she'd drunk too much. Although she claimed she wasn't drunk but suffering from food poisoning. But that's a medical student for you. You're also the friend who shared a house with her, along with several families of mice.'

Amused, Sally said, 'I see you have the advantage over me; I know nothing about you.'

This was a lie. She'd heard a great deal about Dan Oliver over the last few months. He worked for the same firm of accountants as Chloe's older brother, Nick. Nick was currently living with Dan while he waited for contracts to be exchanged on the house he was buying. Chloe had said he was extremely good-looking and an initial impression confirmed this as being true. Sally gave him a quick appraisal. He was tall, well over six feet, with short dark hair that was already receding at his temples. He had dark, engaging eyes and an equally engaging smile. That was all on the plus side. The downside was that he was wearing faded brown cords, a green and white check shirt and a fawn pullover. His shoes were robustly countrified, perfect for kicking peasants out of the way. He looked the epitome of Home Counties chic. Not her type at all. But Chloe had said he was smart and ambitious, which was just her type.

'Really?' he said. 'You've heard nothing about me at all? Not a single word? I'm crushed. I would have hoped at the very least Chloe would have told you about my stunning good looks and my knockout charm and what a catch I am. Not to mention my way with a cheese grater. Please make my day and tell me you're here alone.'

'My new boyfriend's here with me.'

'Can you ditch him?'

There was something so persuasively forceful and proprietorial about him, Sally did as he asked.

A month after they met, Dan was moved to his firm's Manchester office and they embarked on a long-distance relationship. They did that for two years and then Sally moved north to be with him. Dan had offered to get a transfer back down to London, but Sally had long since realized that she was in need of a change. She was sick of London and wanted to get out. Work colleagues thought she was mad and accused her of throwing away her promising career by moving to Manchester, making it sound like a far-flung outpost of the universe. Some of them even said that it probably didn't matter in the long run, as she and Dan would end up marrying and starting a family, so why not throw in the towel sooner rather than later?

However, starting a family wasn't something either of them was keen to rush into. Sally had never been happier and the thought of introducing a third party to their relationship frightened her. She loved Dan so very much, she didn't trust herself to love a child as well.

As an adult, the two most spontaneous things she had done in her life were falling in love with Dan, and conceiving Marcus. Everything else had been precisely worked out, the pros and cons carefully weighed. But extreme circumstances can cause a person to act out of character, and Sally knew that their survival of the devastating events of the Boxing Day tsunami in Thailand caused her and Dan to make the most fundamentally life-changing decision of their lives. They did it that very night in the immediate aftermath of the disaster. In the darkness of the hotel room they'd been moved to – their old room had been destroyed – they'd clung to each other in exhausted and tearful shock. Whether it was from relief or a need to distract themselves from the horror of what they'd experienced, they'd begun to make love. 'We can't,' she'd said when he lifted himself on top of her. 'I don't have my—'

He'd shushed her with a kiss. 'Let's make a baby,' he'd whispered, 'otherwise none of this makes any sense.'

When Dan had climaxed inside her, she had held onto him tightly, seeing what they had just done as a desperate attempt to create a life to replace one of the many that had been swept away in the water.

Sally was ten minutes from home when her mobile rang from its cradle on the dashboard. Caller ID told her who it was and she answered the call with a smile. 'Hi, Chloe,' she said. 'How was your holiday?'

'It was fantastic. We had perfect snow conditions. I can't tell you how much I wish I was back there right now.'

'Not a good first day back at work, I presume?'

'You presume correctly. And talking of work, you do realize it's gone eight thirty, don't you?'

'Funnily enough, learning to tell the time was something I mastered when I was little. But I take your point.'

'Good. Now be prepared to be amazed. Guess who left a message for me on my answerphone. None other than Paul.'

'You're kidding me! What the hell did he have to say for himself?'

'He wants to meet up.'

'He can want it, but you won't agree, will you?'

'Of course not.'

They talked some more, promised to meet up soon and then rang off just as Sally drove past the sign for Eastbury. Her very first sighting of the village had been during the Easter holidays in her first year at Nottingham. By then she and Chloe had become firm friends and Chloe invited her to stay for the weekend. Even now Sally could remember how clean and bright and totally unreal everything had felt to her. The sun had shone from a faultless blue sky, daffodils had been in full bloom on the green, ducks had been quacking on the pond, people on horseback had trotted by on the road, and most unreal of all, Chloe's parents had been so easy-going and welcoming – the complete opposite to what Sally was used to. No one shouted during meals, no one put anyone down and certainly no one ate with their mouths wide open, or belched loudly before tossing an empty beer can across the room. When her visit was over and Chloe's father had driven her to the station for her train home to Hull, Sally had vowed that this was just the kind of place where she would one day live. Where the phone boxes weren't vandalised, where front gardens weren't home to decaying cars and picked-over motorbikes. Where bricks weren't hurled through windows and offensive messages daubed on front doors.

And here she was, she thought, as she pulled onto the drive of Corner Cottage and parked alongside Dan's Saab. She looked up at the house. Its solid, no-nonsense Victorian demeanour had always appealed to her and for six years, its ample five bedrooms, two bathrooms, conservatory and half-acre of garden had been everything and more she could have wished for in a home. It still gave her a secret thrill knowing that she owned such a house.

She let herself in at the front door, something that amused Dan because he always used the back door – the tradesman's entrance as he referred to it. Never would she admit to him that putting her key in the lock of such a substantial front door gave her a powerful sense of possession.

Chapter Four

It was Chloe's day off. She spent the morning dealing with the paperwork that had piled up while she'd been away and then tackled the
ironing and housework. Her reward for such virtuous behaviour
was to treat herself to an unhurried session at the gym she'd joined
in the New Year. The ridiculously named 'Rejoovin8' was a luxuri-
ous health and fitness centre at Cartwright Hall, the local hotel and
conference centre. It was a ten-minute drive away on the Crantsford
road and Chloe went there as often as time permitted. She'd worked
in the dining room of the hotel as a teenager, back in the days when
an all-day menu of the all-you-can-eat carvery was the restaurant's
big draw.

She'd jogged six miles on the treadmill, most of it uphill and listening to Snow Patrol on her iPod, when she caught sight of somebody
familiar coming out of the men's changing room. He spotted her
at the same time and gave her a friendly smile. Just her luck that
the best-looking guy she'd set eyes on in a long while had to keep
seeing her when the sweat was pouring off her and her face was a
most unattractive shade of beetroot. He'd started coming here the
week before she'd gone away on holiday. Or rather, that was when
she'd first noticed him. She'd decided then that he'd been a guest
at the hotel and was using the facilities during his stay. But here he
was again. Perhaps he was a rep and travelled round the country
and Cartwright Hall was one of his many regular stopovers. She
could be entirely wrong, of course. For all she knew he could live
locally and had joined the same time as she had but had previously
worked out at a different time from her. Either way, he was the
fittest guy here. And she wasn't just referring to the firm tone of his
muscles. He had a strong swimmer's body with broad shoulders,
neat waist and long legs. He looked exceptionally good in a pair
of shorts and thank the Lord he wasn't wearing one of those awful
wife-beater vests, but a normal loose-fitting T-shirt. Nor was he one
of those vain types who strutted cockily about the gym giving off the

message, 'Hey, want some of this?' and could ask only to work out while positioned in front of a mirror.

She'd vowed she'd never go out with a vain man again. She'd had enough of that with Paul. When he'd moved in with her, her small house in Nottingham had suddenly been swamped with men's toiletries, hundreds of back issues of GQ and enough suits, shirts and ties to kit out an entire shop. They'd had to have a new set of wardrobes built in the spare room to accommodate his things and even then he'd complained his suits didn't have sufficient breathing space. No, she'd had it with show ponies like Paul.

She thought of Sally's advice on the phone the other day when she'd explained about Paul ringing her. 'Don't even bother replying to him,' her friend had said firmly. Not that Chloe could, when she didn't have his number.

But would she call him if she did have his number? She wanted to say that her answer would be a firm no, yet she suspected she wouldn't be able to resist the temptation to speak to him again, to prove to him, and maybe to herself, that she had indeed moved on and consigned him to the past.

Even as she processed this thought, she knew that wasn't entirely the truth. Oh, yes, she'd moved on, but if she were really honest, she was still angry. It was an anger that burned deep within her. It filled that space in her where once there had been a tiny life just beginning to take form and shape.

One of the reasons Paul had left her was because he'd felt pressurized by her apparent need to have a baby. Unbelievable! All she'd done was mention it a couple of times and the next thing she was being accused of being desperate.

They'd been together since her twenty-eighth birthday. A friend had brought him along to her party and within seconds of being introduced someone had knocked his arm and he'd spilled a glass of red wine down her front. He'd sent her an apologetic bunch of flowers the following day, along with his telephone number. 'When you've forgiven me,' he'd written, 'perhaps you'd let me take you shopping so I can buy you a new dress to replace the one I ruined. Then afterwards we could go out for dinner with you wearing it.' Smooth as it was, what girl could have resisted such an offer?

Just like Sally and Dan, she and Paul quickly slipped into the pattern of being a couple, except in their case they didn't have any distance separating them as Paul conveniently lived a short distance away. Within ten months he'd moved in with her and Chloe's mother was beginning to crack jokes about her being too young to be a grandmother. Chloe hadn't been fooled; she'd known that her mother was itching to get her hands on a small, perfectly formed grandchild. Had things been different, her mother would have got her wish, for Paul's parting gesture, unbeknown to him, was to leave Chloe pregnant. It had been a short-lived pregnancy, though, and Chloe had told no one about it. Not her parents, not even Dan and Sally.

There had been signs before Paul's departure that perhaps all was not well, but denial makes fools of us all and Chloe had ignored the warning signs – the extra workload that kept him late at the office, the half-hearted interest in going out. She had convinced herself that he was just working too hard. Equally she convinced herself that their Christmas and New Year holiday to Phuket with Dan and Sally was going to result in a proposal from him. She hadn't been alone in this thought. Sally had been just as sure and they had exchanged many a knowing look during the long twelve-hour flight to Bangkok. 'Fifty quid says he'll present you with a ring on Christmas Day,' Sally had whispered to her. Slightly tipsy on holiday fever and too many miniatures, they'd laughed like a pair of schoolgirls and had told Dan and Paul that it was a private joke that they wouldn't appreciate.

But the joke had been on Chloe. All Christmas Day she waited for Paul to get down on one knee and present her with a ring. At bedtime she spent longer in the bathroom than normal, sure that he was in the bedroom mustering his courage to propose. Dousing herself in perfume, she smiled to herself as she pictured him rehearsing his lines. But when she finally emerged from the bathroom, he was in bed having fallen asleep whilst watching CNN. She'd been so disappointed she'd been tempted to ransack the room and present herself with the ring he'd been too tired to give her. With enormous restraint she'd held back and concluded that maybe he was waiting for New Year's Eve. Yes, that was definitely what he had in mind to do. On the stroke of midnight, down on the beach in the moonlight, he would ask her to marry him. Far more romantic than proposing on Christmas Day. Sliding into bed beside Paul and kissing his cheek, she'd thought how awful it would have been to pre-empt him and spoil the big moment.

Usually a heavy sleeper and not much of a dreamer, she woke several times in the night from the same dream, that she was on an aeroplane and being rocked by turbulence. When she roused herself fully and seeing that Paul was still sleeping soundly, she decided to go and use the hotel gym. In those days Dan had been as keen as her on working out and when she entered the gym, she saw that Dan had beaten her to it and was already pounding away on the treadmill. Sally must have told him about her wager because his gaze flickered over her left hand. He made no comment on the absence of a ring and instead said, 'Happy Boxing Day. Once again we have the place to ourselves.' She'd just warmed up when all of a sudden the world turned upside down and she was being crushed.

She gave a small start, realizing the treadmill next to her was now occupied. It was the good-looking man with the great body, and he was speaking to her. Surprise made her lose her rhythm and she stumbled. She reached out to the safety bar to keep from falling over, then took off her headphones.

'Sorry,' he apologized. 'I didn't mean to interrupt you. I just wanted to say hi, and that I missed seeing you last week. I hope you weren't ill.'

'I was away on a skiing holiday,' she said, giving her face a wipe with her hand towel. 'Do you ski?'

'Not as often as I'd like these days. I was in Austria for the New Year.'

'That's where I've just come back from.'

'Really? Where were you?'

'Obergurgl. Do you know it?'

He gave her a dazzling smile. A smile so bright it could light up half the country. It had to be adding dangerously to his carbon foot-print. 'That's exactly where I was,' he said. 'What a coincidence.'

She dabbed at her face again, surreptitiously clocking his left hand. No ring. Unless, of course, he was married but didn't wear one. Not that his marital status had anything to do with her. They were talking. *Just* talking. He is not chatting you up, she told herself firmly. I repeat, he is not chatting you up. Remember the rule: if you fancy him on first sight, you can't have him. He's out of bounds. Your head must rule over your heart.

The rule had been set in place because when Paul had left her, she'd ruthlessly set out to find a replacement. It still shamed her from the top of her head to the tip of her toes when she thought of the disastrous rebound relationships she'd hurled herself into. Any good-looking man who came her way she would pounce on. She would barely have got to know him before she was cutting rela-tionship corners and heading fast for the John Lewis wedding gift counter. When that not surprisingly scared them off, she went on the hunt again for someone to fill the void that Paul had created. Eventually she came to her senses, understanding that it wasn't Paul she wanted to replace, but the baby she had lost.

The man with the high-wattage smile was now running at the same speed as her, their pace evenly matched. She liked the look of his thick, black, curly hair bouncing on the top of his head. Very sexy.

Without doubt Laurel House was one of the most attractive properties in the village. Built in the early nineteenth century of classic Cheshire sandstone with its nearest neighbour being the squat Norman church of St Andrew, it provided endless opportunities for watercolourists and photographers alike hoping to capture the essence of idyllic village charm.

However, growing up at Laurel House had not been at all idyllic or charming. When Chloe's parents had bought the property, it had needed everything doing to it. Most of Nick and Chloe's childhood had been spent living on a building site. Knocked-down walls, cement mixers, scaffolding, gaping holes, bare wires, dust, and occasional periods of no water or electricity had all been part and parcel of putting up with Mum and Dad's labour of love. For years they'd scrimped and saved to get the house into shape and Chloe would be the first to say it had all been worth it.

Out of habit she went round to the back of the house. She heard Jennifer and Graham Hennessey before she saw them. Her mother's voice, shrill and defensive, cut through the cool evening air. 'There's no need to jump down my throat. All I was saying was that you tend to have a heavy hand when it comes to seasoning.'

'And all I said was that—'

'I know perfectly well what you said, Graham. You muttered *sotto voce* that I should jolly well mind my own business.'

'Would that be such a bad thing? Oh, hello Chloe. You're early.'

'No, Dad, I'm on time. What are you doing up that ladder when you're supposed to be cooking your birthday dinner?'

'I said exactly the same thing to him myself not ten minutes ago, Chloe. But no, he insisted on cleaning our bedroom window sill. He's quite mad.'

'I wouldn't have to if the window cleaner had done a half-decent job of it in the first place. Apparently it costs extra these days to have your sills cleaned.'

Chloe went over to where her mother was pricking out a tray of leggy seedlings on the wooden bench table. 'Hollyhocks,' her mother said to her unasked question. 'I'll give you some when I think they're strong enough to cope with your special brand of neglect.'

Having now clambered down the ladder with a bucket of water and a sponge, Chloe's father came over. He kissed her cheek. 'You look well,' he said.

'You too. Happy birthday.' She held out the present she'd brought for him. 'Seeing as you've got your hands full, shall I take it inside for you?'

'Yes, come and help me put the finishing touches to supper.'

'Keep him away from the salt!' Mum called after them. 'My blood pressure's shooting off the chart as it is.'

'I've told you a million times, there's nothing wrong with your blood pressure.'

Chloe laughed. 'Be quiet you two, or I'll have to send for the hyperbole police.'

Ever since Dad had retired and Mum had gleefully handed in her apron licence, Dad had assumed responsibility for all cooking at Laurel House. After a few false starts – a curry that nearly took the enamel off their teeth – he'd soon got the hang of it and relished showing off his growing prowess. The kitchen cupboards were bursting with every gadget known to the culinary world. There wasn't anything the current chefs on the block had that Dad didn't. Mum had been no slouch in the kitchen in her day, but she had been more of a workaday cook – roast on Sunday, cold meat and salad on Monday, shepherd's pie on Tuesday. If she ever needed to remind Dad of his place, and that he hadn't exactly invented the concept of fine cuisine, she had only to knock up one of her rich fruit cakes. Try as he might, Dad just couldn't stop the fruit from sinking to the bottom of the cake. He'd begged Mum to tell him the secret but she would smile back at him and say, 'Practice makes perfect, dear.'

Looking at them now as they sat in the dining room with the evening sun pouring in through the window, Chloe thought how for all their silly bickering, she envied them their marriage. They were happy. After more than forty years of marriage, they were still happy and dashing about like a couple of twenty-something pleasure seekers. She had trouble keeping up with their hectic lifestyle; they were always out. Their days were filled with visits to National Trust properties, gardens, galleries, exhibitions and evening classes. Then there were the weekends away, the coach tours, and the holidays abroad. Cheap flights and the internet had really opened up the world of travel to them.

They lived so differently these days. All those years when they'd been doing up the house, they'd obsessively watched every penny they spent. Family holidays had been restricted to one a year during the month of August and the fortnight was usually spent soggily somewhere in the Lake District or Scotland. Nothing had been thrown in the bin that couldn't be rehashed into something useful or sent off for some charity or other. Milk bottle tops were carefully washed and saved for guide dogs, old books sent to far-flung places where such things were hard to come by, and ditto for shoes and spectacles. Whenever Chloe had grown out of something, it was immediately taken apart and the material used for making a selection of patchwork skirts and dresses. She'd had a technicolour dreamcoat long before Andrew Lloyd Webber made Joseph's so famous. Mum's most legendary recycling venture was to cut up an old pair of unwanted gingham curtains and make three holiday outfits – a skirt for Chloe, and two pairs of shorts for Nick and Dad. Buried deep in the family archives was photographic evidence that it really did happen and wasn't a nightmarish figment of their imagination. Nick joked that he was still in therapy trying to overcome the horror of walking through Ambleside with everyone staring at him. 'But they cost me nothing at all to make,' had been Mum's defensive cry.

'*How much*?' had been Chloe and her brother's favourite catchphrase, mimicking their parents' horror over the cost of trainers, school blazers, or the price of a cup of tea in a motorway service station. '*How much*? It's the one cup I'm buying, not the entire tea plantation!'

But ever since they'd experienced the genuine fear that Chloe had died in the tsunami, their relief that she'd survived had altered their outlook. Life was for living, was their new creed. They still cared about helping others, but they now cared about themselves too. They'd decided that since death really was just around the next corner – an odd thing for a GP to come to terms with so late in life – they would make up for lost time and thoroughly enjoy themselves.

'If I tell you something, will you promise not to overreact,' Chloe said while her father was cutting her a slice of lemon tart – the top was perfectly caramelized.

'I've never overreacted in my life,' said her mother indignantly.

Dad snorted. But before they could sidetrack the conversation, Chloe hurriedly said, 'While I was away, Paul left a message on my answerphone.'

Both of her parents stared at her.

'And what did that snake in the grass want?' Mum's voice was low and tightly controlled.

'He wants to meet up for a chat.'

'Do you think you will?'

'Of course she won't, Graham! She's got far more sense than that.'

'Actually,' said Chloe, 'if he hadn't rambled on and got cut off before leaving me his number, I think I would have called him. What harm would it do, anyway?'

It was difficult to gauge who was more shocked, Chloe's parents, or Chloe herself. It was all very well thinking such a thought, but saying it out loud was a different matter altogether.

Chapter Five

Dan had learned very quickly that dealing with the hierarchy of
Eastbury village's nursery mafia was not so different from locking
horns with an office full of Machiavellian careerists. The trick, as
he'd mastered back in the workplace, was to steer one's own course
and keep well away from troublemakers. To this end, he ensured that
for the three mornings a week that Marcus attended nursery, they
arrived with seconds to spare; time enough only for Marcus to shrug
off his coat and give Dan a hurried kiss goodbye. The pick-up was
timed with equal SAS-like precision. Get it wrong and Dan could so
easily be accosted by one of the Mumzillas. The ones to watch were
Diane Davenport, Annette Bayley and Sandra McPhearson, or Lardy
McFierce as Dan thought of her. She was a grisly bossy-boots of a
woman who had aspirations of one day ruling the universe. She'd
near enough conquered all aspects of running the village and had no
qualms when it came to bullying people into doing her bidding.

Thank goodness he had such a great ally in Rosie Peach. She
was married to Dave the local builder and their son, Charlie, was
Marcus's best friend, if such a thing was possible at two and a half
years old. Rosie was as determined as Dan was to keep a healthy
distance between her and the Mumzillas. Her reluctance not to get
too involved was often remarked upon. Just as Dan's was. 'Come
along now, Daniel,' Lardy McFierce had once said to him, 'we're
not going to have you excusing yourself on the pretext of being a
helpless man. There's plenty you can get stuck in with.' Who'd have
thought that sending a child to nursery would entail so much work
on the part of a parent? The fundraising and social events seemed
never ending.

Before Marcus had progressed to nursery, there had been a brief
period of Mother and Toddlering to get through and when Dan had
rolled up with Marcus for his first session in the village hall, the
reaction towards him had been divided. Those who knew him – he
and Sally had been living in the village for some years – had treated

him as nothing more than a novelty in their midst. They'd made a big fuss of him, finding it 'cute' that a man should want to be with his son and had predictably made all the expected jokes about him being at risk with so much oestrogen in the air. But those who didn't know him were wary. He'd caught them watching him, observing his every move, especially if he got too near one of their own children. If they'd stood outside Corner Cottage bearing placards accusing him of being a kiddie fiddler, their message could not have been clearer.

Nobody had ever come right out and said it to their faces, but both Dan and Sally knew that the general consensus in the village was that they had some kind of weird metropolitan marriage going on. The probable conclusion was that Sally wore the trousers and he couldn't possibly be a real man. It didn't bother him that aspersions were being cast on his manhood, but it annoyed Sally. 'Anyone would think we were still living in the dark ages,' she complained. 'Plenty of couples do what we do. Role reversal is hardly pioneering stuff.'

It was exactly what he'd told her when her maternity leave had been coming to an end. Their original plan had been that when Sally returned to work, they would employ the services of a nanny to look after Marcus. But the reality of that situation, of leaving his son with someone who had no real connection with him, appalled Dan. Had Sally not been so desperate to return to work, he might have hinted that she stay home and take care of Marcus. But that was out of the question.

In the months after Marcus's birth, Sally had suffered a debilitating period of postnatal depression. Dan had been powerless to help her, other than on a wholly practical level, and had managed to take some paternity leave. He'd assumed the lion's share of care for Marcus and it was during this time that he'd begun to think it simply wasn't in him to trust anybody else with his son. Once that seed of doubt had taken root, the next logical thought had been for him to suggest to Sally that he should take a more long-term break from his career and be at home with Marcus. Already consumed with guilt that she hadn't been able to cope, Sally wouldn't listen to him, but when Dan showed no sign of giving up on the idea, she started to give it some serious thought. They looked at it every which way. Did they want to take the reduction in income? Would it be the best thing for Marcus? Did they want to be considered as oddities? Would Dan feel emasculated? Would it affect their marriage? Would they be treated as social outcasts? On and on they went until eventually they came full circle and decided there was only one way to find out; they would give it a go.

Once the decision had been made and Sally knew exactly when she'd be returning to work, the depression that had shadowed her for so many months lifted. It was all the evidence Dan needed to know that they were doing the right thing.

He hadn't done the right thing today, though. Here he was, waiting for Marcus with time to spare and all because Rosie had a cold and wasn't feeling too well and he'd offered to pick up Charlie for her. Strangely, when he was responsible for a child other than Marcus, he was extra diligent. It was the same when he had Charlie in the car with them – he drove extra carefully. He didn't know why that was, because no one, absolutely no one, was more precious to him than Marcus.

However, his diligence in this instance had been a big mistake. For there was Lardy McFierce bearing down on him, all five feet four inches of her, shaped like a barrage balloon. What was it this time? A request for everyone to pitch in for a bake sale to raise funds for some new equipment? Or was there a new petition that needed signing? The last one had been to get rid of the sandpit in the beer garden of the Fox and Feathers on the grounds that it was a health hazard. Or perhaps it was something more personal. Maybe Marcus had been singled out as the latest source of nits.

'Ah, Daniel, there you are,' she said. Other than his mother, Lardy McFierce was the only person to call him by his full first name. 'I was hoping to catch you. May I have a little word?'

Around them, mothers stopped their conversations and pricked up their ears. They all knew that a 'little word' from the lips of Lardy McFierce was no such thing. He clocked the mixture of glances – sympathy, curiosity, but mostly relief that it wasn't one of them on the receiving end of a potential ticking off – and cracked a smile. 'Sure,' he said. 'Why don't we step outside?' Giving her no time to respond, he pushed open the double doors and led the way, telling himself that nits weren't anything to be ashamed of. It happened in the best of families. 'What can I help you with?' he asked when she'd waddled down the steps and caught up with him.

'Now, Daniel, I don't want you to take this the wrong way and I'm only saying it for Marcus's own good. Which I'm sure you'll agree is of paramount importance.'

Every one of Dan's senses was on immediate full alert. If he wasn't mistaken Lardy McFierce was about to criticise his son. He loaded an imaginary shotgun and prepared to take aim. 'Go on,' he said.

'Annette was there at the time and she was as shocked as I was.'

He gave the trigger a delicate squeeze. Go ahead, make my day.

'We both clearly heard Marcus say it.'

'Say what?'

'He called Rupert a butt-face.'

Ker-boom! Lardy McFierce's brain exploded and splattered against the wall behind them.

How he'd kept a straight face, Dan didn't know. *Butt-face!* That's my boy!

'Daddy, you're smiling.'

'Too right I am,' Dan said, unlocking the back door at Corner Cottage. Marcus looked up at him, his eyebrows drawn in a comical suffer-the-silly-old-fool attitude. In fact, Dan hadn't stopped grinning all the way home. He'd shared the latest Lardy McFierce anecdote with Rosie when he'd dropped Charlie off and Rosie had had a hard job not bursting out laughing in front of the boys. Goodness knows where Marcus had picked up the expression, but it suited Lardy's pug-faced brat of a child perfectly.

Inside the house, the telephone was ringing. It took Dan a moment to recognize who was at the other end. He hadn't heard from Andy Hope in a long time. They'd been at Durham University together, had kept in touch sporadically over the years, but inevitably the friendship had run its course. 'Andy, how are you?'

'I'm fine. But I wish I was calling under better circumstances. Do you remember Derek Lockley?'

The years having been rolled back sufficiently now, Dan could picture Derek quite clearly. Del Boy, they used to call him. Thin, wiry bloke, ran the university rock-climbing club. Could scale a wall in seconds flat. Got busted for climbing into the wrong girl's room. He'd been drunk and got his new girlfriend's halls of residence mixed up. 'I remember him well,' Dan said. 'What's he up to these days?'

'I'm sorry to be the bearer of bad news, but he's dead. He committed suicide. His family's already held the funeral, a small private affair, but there's to be a memorial service for him. I'm ringing round the old gang to see who can go. I think we should, don't you?'

Shocked, Dan agreed straight away that he'd make sure he could attend. It didn't seem right to indulge in any trivial what-are-you-doing-now? banter after that and with the date of the memorial service written on the kitchen calendar, Dan rang off.

To Dan's knowledge, Derek was the first of his contemporaries to die. Not merely to be brushed by it. But to really cop it. To be no more. It was a chilling thought.

Chapter Six

Two weeks after receiving Paul's message on her answerphone, Chloe came home from evening surgery to find he'd left her another. This time he'd managed to include his mobile number.

She pressed the replay button and listened to his voice again. 'Hi, Chloe, Paul here. Knowing how unreliable these machines can be, I'm assuming you didn't get my last message. Anyway, I'd really like to see you. I know that might surprise you, but life's full of surprises, isn't it? So how about it? I'm in your area next week as it happens.' He then went on to give his mobile number.

Two things occurred to Chloe as she considered his message. This time his voice had none of the hesitancy of before; he sounded more in control of himself. Also, he evidently presumed that the reason she hadn't phoned him back was because she hadn't received his message. How typical of Paul. It probably wouldn't have entered his head that she hadn't rung him because she believed he was the lowest of the low.

She wrote down his number and went upstairs to gather her gym things. An hour on the treadmill would give her some thinking time. She needed to think how she was going to respond.

The gym was busy, and there, already on the treadmill next to the one she always used, was He of the Dark Curly Hair. Despite having run alongside each other on several occasions now, they'd never got beyond the pleasantries that most people exchanged when working out and so she still didn't even know his name. Not that she needed to know his name, rank or number. It was no hardship being in the presence of such an attractive hunk of a man and not knowing a thing about him. No hardship at all.

He gave her a friendly smile as she approached. 'Hi,' he said, his hair bouncing away on his head. 'I thought you weren't joining us tonight. Good day?'

'Not bad,' she said, keying in her running programme on the

machine and setting off with a gentle warm-up jog. 'How about you?'

'Busy. Crazily so. Fortunately it's my day off tomorrow.'

'Snap,' she said, noticing that he'd run nearly four miles and was hardly out of breath. 'Mine too.'

'Doing anything special?'

'Nothing planned. You?'

'No plans yet.'

When he didn't say anything else, she increased her speed and wondered what kind of work he did. But no way would she ask him. That was a big no-no. It was as bad a cliché as asking if he came here often. Moreover it might give out the wrong signal. Ask too many questions and he'd assume she was coming on to him. You had to be so careful in these situations. Life was so much easier when you had a partner; you could talk happily to a member of the opposite sex without ever worrying that your words might be misconstrued. Being single at her age was a minefield. It was so easy to be viewed as a predator. A desperate predator at that, whose body clock was demanding to have her eggs fertilized *NOW!* The thought made her think of Paul, which in turn sent a direct message to her legs to run faster. Within no time she'd matched her speed to He of the Dark Curly Hair and then her competitive streak kicked in and she was pushing herself to outpace him. As a child she'd never been able to let her brother outdo her, physically or mentally, and it was a trait she'd never shaken off. Even an eye test at the opticians was a competitive event for her – she wasn't going to let those tiny letters at the bottom of the chart get the better of her.

Out of the corner of her eye she was aware that He of the Dark Curly Hair was slowing his speed now. When he'd got it to a cooling-down walking pace, he turned to her. 'I was wondering,' he said, 'given that you mentioned you had no plans for tomorrow, whether you might be free to have lunch with me? Or maybe you'd rather play safe and settle for a drink only?'

It was the thoughtful politeness of his invitation that she found so appealing.

Four days had passed since Andy Hope had telephoned with the news about Derek Lockley's death and Dan hadn't slept properly since. Every night he kept being jarred awake by the same horrific dream. He'd even cried out last night and woken Sally. 'What is it?' she'd asked, straightening the tangled duvet that he'd been thrashing around in. 'Are you feeling unwell?' She'd put a hand to his fore-head, just as he did with Marcus whenever his face was flushed and he seemed feverish. 'You do seem rather hot.'

'It's nothing,' he'd said. 'I'll just get myself a glass of water. Go back to sleep.'

Now once again he was lying awake unable to sleep, his mind racing irrationally. Powerless to stop himself, and being careful not to disturb Sally, he went and checked on Marcus. Like his mother, he was fast asleep, his face nestled into the furry belly of one of his teddies.

Not wanting to go back to bed, not when he knew sleep would continue to elude him, Dan went downstairs to make himself a drink. While he waited for the kettle to boil he stared at his reflection in the window. His hair was on end and he looked shot to hell and back. What was happening to him? Why, after all this time, was he still dreaming of something that had happened more than three years ago? Not only that, why were the dreams getting worse? And why couldn't he share what he was going through with Sally? What was holding him back?

Oh, he knew what was holding him back all right. It was because he was ashamed of the gut-wrenching fear he still carried around with him. He felt diminished by it. Less of a man. Certainly not the man Sally and Marcus needed in their lives.

Or the man his parents had brought him up to be.

Dan's father came from hardy Gloucestershire stock that looked danger square in the eye and ordered it to bugger off or else! One of Ronald Oliver's most notorious acts of heroism was to have seen off a gang of robbers in the middle of the night. The three men had got as far as the stairs, armed with rope and knives to tie up their victims, when they found themselves staring up into the business end of a double-barrelled shotgun. 'I taught those thugs a lesson they won't forget in a hurry,' Ronald Oliver, respected Justice of the Peace, was quoted as saying in the local paper the following week. He was very much of the 'hang 'em high' school of thought when it came to law and order.

Glynis Oliver, Dan's mother, was of similar plucky stock and spoke proudly of her own father who had survived countless un-speakable atrocities at the hands of the Japanese during the Second World War. He may have returned home starved to skin and bone and half out of his mind, but by God, he's shown those Japs a thing or two about survival.

Little wonder then that Dan had always felt that he didn't quite live up to expectation. What did he have to offer the family annals? Other than being brave enough to defy convention and be led by his heart? His biggest act of defiance had been to marry Sally. To say that Sally was not quite the wife Ronald and Glynis Oliver had had in mind for their son and heir would be a huge understatement. Yet despite it all – her council estate upbringing, her comprehensive and redbrick university education – they politely accepted Sally into the fold and boasted about her to their friends. 'Such a pretty and clever girl,' they said, 'and she makes Daniel so happy. What more could a parent want?'

Actually, a grandchild was what his parents wanted next. Preferably two, three or maybe four to make up for their own deficit in that particular area. Ronald Oliver may well have been an expert marksman with a gun in his hand, but following several visits to a Harley Street specialist he'd been discreetly informed that he was firing a few too many blanks and the ones that did hold an explosive charge were missing their target. So that was that: Daniel Ronald Oliver was the best they could manage.

Give them their due, his parents were suitably pleased when Marcus made his entrance into the world and they descended upon Corner Cottage a week after his birth in their Land Rover Discovery with a boot full of gifts. They were mostly ancient toys and musty-smelling clothes from Dan's own babyhood, including his antique christening gown, which had been handed down from two previous generations. History and tradition aside, it was a discoloured mangy affair that looked fit only for the dustbin. Which was exactly where it did end up when Sally was feeling particularly down one day.

Not surprisingly his parents had been horrified at the prospect of Dan taking time out from his career to stay at home and look after Marcus. They'd heard of such goings on, just as they'd heard of transsexuals and a woman making it to the boardroom, but it was hardly natural, was it? Natural in their book was sending their only son off to boarding school just as soon as it suited them and never showing an ounce of emotion. Least of all allowing him to show anything that resembled a genuine emotion.

The night of Boxing Day 2004, when Dan had eventually found a telephone that worked and called home to his parents to let them know he and Sally were all right – he'd said nothing about what they'd actually experienced – Ronald and Glynis's reaction had been predictably muted. 'Right,' his father had said, 'jolly good. Yes, that's good. Well done. Looks pretty ropy there from the pictures we've seen on the news. Shall I pass you over to your mother?'

Pretty ropy. Yeah, that about summed up the situation. That's what you get when an undersea earthquake releases the equivalent energy of twenty-three thousand Hiroshima-sized atomic bombs and triggers a series of tsunamis that wipe out the lives of a quarter of a million men, women and children.

He shuddered at the thought of all those deaths. In particular, the death of one small boy who had been the same age as Marcus was now.

'Dan?'

He spun round. Sally was standing in the doorway, her turquoise silk dressing gown tied loosely around her waist. Her short, dark hair was attractively tousled, giving her face a vulnerable softness that she so rarely allowed others to see.

'I'm sorry,' he said, thinking how lovely she looked in the half-light, knowing also that she wasn't wearing anything under that delicate layer of silk. 'Did I wake you?'

'Not really. Work things on my mind. You know what I'm like; I can't fully let go.' She came over to him and placed a mug next to the one he'd already put a teabag in.

He put his arm around her, held her close. I know the feeling, he thought, wishing he had something as commonplace as work on his mind.

37

Chapter Seven

It was a beautifully sunny day. A perfect day for having lunch with a perfectly good-looking man. A man whose name Chloe still didn't know.

Incredibly they'd parted last night at the gym without having exchanged this all-important piece of information about each other. They'd got as far as establishing where and when they'd meet, when he'd reached into his running shorts' pocket and pulled out a mobile phone – he must have had it switched to silent and vibrate mode because she certainly hadn't heard it. He'd put it to his ear and stepped off the treadmill. 'Tomorrow,' he'd mouthed at her, his expression anxious. And then he was gone, off like a rocket towards the changing rooms as if his life depended upon it. Only bad news could have had provoked such a reaction, she'd concluded. Or perhaps he was a fireman and had got the call to go tearing off to the fire station?

Now, as she gave her appearance one last check in the mirror – her long blonde hair was satisfyingly sleek and shiny and her blue eyes enhanced with a light touch of mascara – she selfishly hoped that whatever bad news he had been on the receiving end of wouldn't prevent him meeting her for lunch.

Not that this lunch was going to be anything special, she told herself, gathering up her bag and keys and imagining what he might look like in proper clothes. It would be just two gym buddies having a bite to eat together on their day off.

Jeans. She'd bet a king's ransom that he'd look great in jeans, the denim all nicely moulded to those taut muscular thighs of his ...

No, it was nothing to get too excited about.

With an open-necked shirt revealing a glimpse of chest hair ...

Definitely nothing to get ahead of oneself over and think where it might lead. Absolutely no need at all.

She was almost out of the door when the telephone rang. Leave it, she told herself. Let the answerphone pick it up.

But what if it was Paul?

Even more reason to leave it!

When she'd got back from the gym last night, she'd been sufficiently buoyed up to take the plunge and dial the number Paul had left for her. Only to find herself having a one-to-one with his voicemail.

She picked up the receiver, adopting a confident and breezy manner. 'Oh, hi Dad,' she said with a mixture of let-down and relief. 'I can't chat for long; I'm just on my way out. What can I do for you?'

'Oh, not to worry, we knew it was your day off and thought we'd invite you to lunch, that's all. Going somewhere nice?'

'Just the Bells of Peover.'

'You've got a good day for it. What are you doing for the Easter weekend, by the way?'

'I haven't got as far as that. I suspect I'll be on call, though. Are you and Mum around or are you off on some jolly caper?'

'No, we're here. Any ... any news from you know who?'

'Are you referring to Paul, Dad? Because if you are, can we speak about him another time?'

'Of course. We just want to know that he's not causing you any more distress.'

Hearing the concern in her father's voice, Chloe said, 'I know, Dad, and if it makes you feel any better, I'm meeting a very nice man for lunch. A man who isn't Paul.'

'Well, in that case, have fun. Shall I tell your mother?'

Chloe laughed. 'Why not? It'll give her something new to get her teeth into. Byee.'

She arrived at the Bells of Peover exactly on time and after a quick scan of the pub's interior went back outside, deciding it was warm enough to sit at one of the tables that offered a good view of St Oswald's church directly opposite.

Okay, so he wasn't here yet. No need to panic. No need to think she'd been stood up.

Ten minutes later and studying the menu with intense concentration, she was still reassuring herself with the same advice.

Twenty minutes later, after being asked for the second time if she was ready to order, she sipped her glass of tomato juice and tried hard not to look like a pathetic loser who had been stood up. She rummaged in her bag in search of the most face-saving device known to mankind – you were never alone with a mobile phone in your hand!

She'd made two phone calls last night; one to Paul and then one to Sally. She hadn't mentioned anything about Paul to her friend but she did tell her all about He of the Dark Curly Hair. *Appalling situation*, she texted, *I think I've been stood up! Please advise.*

Sally's response came back almost at once: *The rat! No worries. We'll track him down and make him pay!*

Smiling to herself, Chloe felt a shadow fall across her. She glanced up, straight into the handsome face of her date.

'I'm so unbelievably sorry,' he said. 'Are you very angry with me?'

Angry, she thought, taking the whole of him in. Every stunning six feet plus inches of him. How could anyone be angry with someone who looked so head-turningly good? The jeans were just as she'd pictured, as was the open-necked shirt – it was a blue and white check affair that was doing ridiculous things to his sky-blue eyes.

'I swear I'm not always so unreliable,' he said when she hadn't replied, 'but something came up that I had to deal with and, of course, being the idiot I am, I hadn't thought to give you a contact number yesterday. May I?'

She moved her bag from the wooden bench seat so he could sit down next to her. 'It's not only phone numbers we should have exchanged,' she said, putting her mobile away. 'I don't even know your name. What do you think, shall we continue with the ambiguity?'

He smiled. Lovely straight white teeth flashed back at her. 'I realized that oversight when I left you last night.' He held out his hand. 'Let's do this properly. My name's Seth Hawthorne and I'm really pleased you didn't leave before I got here.'

'Hello, Seth,' she said, taking his hand with a small flush of self-consciousness. 'I'm Chloe Hennessey.'

'Are you ready to order now?' The young waitress who had previously been pestering Chloe was back at the table again. She gave a more than interested glance in Seth's direction. Frankly, Chloe didn't blame the girl.

'I think we need a little longer,' Chloe said to the waitress, passing Seth a copy of the menu.

'No, I already know what I want,' he said. 'You first, Chloe.'

'I'll have the ploughman's and a small glass of the house Chardonnay.'

40

'Ditto on the ploughman's. And I'll have a Budweiser, please.'

'We seem to have similar tastes in quite a few things,' he said when they were alone. But then he cringed. 'I'm sorry, that sounded like the lamest of chat-up lines, didn't it? Can you pretend I never said it?'

'Pretend you never said what?'

He smiled. 'Thanks. And thanks for waiting for me.'

'It was a close run thing. Five minutes more and you wouldn't have found me here. My best friend and I were just deciding what we'd do to punish you for standing me up.'

He looked about them at the surrounding tables. 'Your best friend's here?'

'No. We were texting each other.'

'Ah, and what conclusion had you reached?'

'Luckily for you, you appeared in the nick of time.'

Their food and drinks arrived and after a brief flurry of activity, during which Chloe was aware of the waitress stealing another not-so-subtle glance at Seth, they were alone again. 'You left the gym in such a hurry last night,' she said. 'Was everything okay?'

His expression became serious. 'Yes, sorry about that, but I had to go.'

'That's okay,' she said lightly, wishing he'd expand. 'I had this sudden picture of you being a fireman and having to dash heroically off to the fire station for an emergency.'

'A fireman, that's a new one on me. Do you think I look like one?'

'You have the right build.'

'Ah, so a case of if the stereotype fits? Should I take that as a compliment? I know women have a bit of a thing about firemen. Never understood it myself. But maybe that's because I'm not a woman.'

'I'm a woman and if I'm honest, I don't understand the attraction either. Not really my sort. I'm not into uniforms and an excess of bare-chested posing for calendars.'

'And your sort would be?'

'Any man who can make me laugh,' she said.

'In that case, knock, knock?'

'Who's there?'

'A very short man who can't reach the bell.'

She laughed. 'That's terrible.'

'I know. So tell me what you do when you're not at the gym and making me feel totally inadequate. You can run some, can't you?'

Trying not to enjoy the flattery of his remark too much, she said, 'I'm a GP, just as my father was. He's retired now and I work at the practice where he worked for many years.'

'And where's that?'

'Where I live, in Eastbury. How about you? We've established you don't put out fires for a living, so what do you do?'

'What do you think I do?' He was smiling, yet there was something behind that smile. Was he teasing her? Or was he testing her? Rooting out any hidden prejudices she might have.

'I don't think you're a teacher,' she said, deciding to play along. 'Teachers have enough holiday allowance as it is without having a midweek day off as well.'

'I could be a supply teacher. But I'm not, so that's one guess gone. Four left.'

'Hey, you never said there was a limit on guesses. Give me a clue.'

He picked up a stick of celery from his plate and waved the leafy end of it at her. 'Smart girl like you, you don't need any clues.'

Her competitive spirit roused, she put her mind fully to the matter. 'Accountant,' she said, recalling how at a particularly tedious dinner party Dan had once pretended to be an actor in preference to admitting he was an accountant.

'Three guesses left. And because I'm in a good mood, I'll rule out law and medicine for you.'

'Mm ... you run your own business? Something in computers? IT?'

'No, I work for a big organization. That's two guesses left.'

'Got it! You're a policeman.'

'One guess left.'

A buzzing noise went off from inside Chloe's handbag.

'That's probably your friend wanting to know if I actually had the decency to turn up. I'll leave you to answer it while I go in search of the facilities.'

Chloe watched him walk away, then flipped open her mobile. '*Well?*' Sally had texted. '*Has he arrived or do I buy a staple gun on way home?*'

'*He's here. All OK.*' Chloe quickly tapped in. '*Speak tonight!*'

'*Not home till late,*' came back Sally's lightning-fast reply. '*Speak tomorrow.*'

Chloe returned her mobile to her bag, disappointed. She couldn't remember when she'd last spent an evening with Sally, just the two of them having a good old-fashioned gossip. She probably saw more of Dan these days than she did Sally.

'What's the verdict, then? Has your friend forgiven me or am I going to have to watch my back?'

'A staple gun was mentioned,' Chloe said as Seth resumed his seat next to her. 'But you'll be glad to know I've held her off.'

'She sounds like a good friend, someone who cares about you.'

'You're right. Sally and I have known each other since university. Her husband, Dan, is also a good friend. The three of us are very close. Especially so since—' Chloe stopped herself short. Why go into all that? It was hardly an appropriate subject to discuss on a first date. If indeed this was a 'first date' situation.

'Since what?' he asked, turning to face her.

'It's nothing. Really.' She reached for her glass of wine and took a long, distracting sip.

'Is that my cue to back off?' he asked.

'It might be better if you did. It would be a shame to spoil such a pleasant lunch by getting too serious. I wouldn't want you to get the wrong idea about me, that I'm a world-class misery.'

'I'd rather know the real you by discussing what's important to you.'

It could have sounded an appallingly cheesy line, but his tone was soft and sincere. She lowered her glass and studied his expression for any sign of artifice.

'Perhaps you're doing yourself a disservice,' he pressed, 'as well as underestimating what might be of interest to me.'

Bingo! 'I've worked it out. Human behaviour's your thing. You're a psychologist, aren't you? A therapist?'

'And that,' he said, mimicking the noise of a game-show hooter, 'was your last guess. Sloppy work, seeing as we'd already ruled out medicine.'

She smiled. 'Look, it's no big deal. The reason Dan, Sally and I are especially close is because we shared what is commonly known as an extreme situation.'

'What was it?'

'We were spending Christmas on Phuket and got caught up in the Boxing Day tsunami.'

'How caught up?'

'We thought we were going to die.'

He stared at her thoughtfully. 'That sounds like a seriously major

43

big deal to me. And not something you can easily shake off. If ever.'

'The part of it I know I'll never forget is how Dan and I tried to save this little boy—' She stopped herself short, realizing again that she was telling him far more than she'd intended to. 'I'm sorry,' she said. 'But I did warn you that I'd end up depressing you.'

'Please don't apologize. What happened to the little boy?'

'He died.'

'But at least you tried to save him. That's what's important in a situation like that.'

'I don't think Dan would agree with you.'

'I'm sorry, I didn't mean to trivialize what you'd gone through. Tell me what happened.'

'You really want to know?'

'Yes.'

'It started for Dan and me when we were working out in the hotel gym. We were the only ones in there and when the first wave hit, the building collapsed around us like a pack of cards. When the water started to recede, taking us with it, we desperately held onto each other. We both had the same thought: if we were going to die, we'd die together. Not alone. Then we were thrown against a tree and we clung to it for all we were worth. We both went from accepting we were about to die, to thinking, to hell with that, we were going to do all we could to survive!

'When the water had receded to a safe distance, we let go and then a woman who ran the hotel crèche came running and screaming to us for help. The crèche had been destroyed and somewhere in the wreckage were her two children – she'd brought them to work with her that morning, something she'd never done before. By now I knew I'd broken my leg and was as good as useless, but Dan was brilliant. He found one of the children and got her out, but the other, the little girl's brother, was stuck further under the rubble. We needed more help but the hotel had been badly hit and there was chaos all around us. Then everyone started to yell that another wave was coming. People were running and climbing up onto roofs, trees, anything that had survived the first wave. Even the mother whose second child we were trying to save had run for safety. It was clear that the second wave was bigger and more powerful than the first and I tried to drag Dan away, but he wouldn't listen. He was convinced he could free the boy. Amazingly he did; he managed to shift the slab of concrete that had the boy pinned beneath it, but it was too late. The wave hit us with such a force, we were smashed against God knows what. I remember a fishing boat being tossed into the air, right over our heads.'

She blinked and stared into the distance. 'Dan was devastated that he hadn't been able to save that little boy. His body was found washed up onto the shore the next day. He was so young, about the same age as Dan and Sally's son is now.' She reached for her drink. 'Are you sure you're not some kind of a therapist? This is the most I've said about what happened in ages.'

He shook his head. 'People say I'm a good listener. What about Sally? Where was she when the waves hit?'

'It was awful for her. And Paul.'

'Paul?'

'He was my boyfriend at the time. They were both still fast asleep in bed when the first wave hit. They woke to the sound of crashing glass. Both Sally and Paul said it was as if they'd suddenly been thrown inside a washing machine. At least I had Dan with me when that first wave came in; they were both on their own. Even though they weren't badly hurt, just really shaken up with superficial cuts and bruises, I often think it must have been worse for them because they were alone.'

She drained her glass. 'Well then,' she said in a forced upbeat voice, 'now that I've thoroughly spoiled the moment, say something to cheer us both up.'

He took a moment before speaking. 'I don't know whether it would cheer you up, but I know it would me. Can I see you again? And not just at the gym.'

Chapter Eight

The Easter weekend was not going well for Sally.

It was Saturday morning, she had a thumping headache and whilst she was happy that Dan had driven to the supermarket in Crantsford to do the shopping on his own – a chore she hated with a passion – she was not quite so pleased that he'd left Marcus behind with the promise that she would take him to feed the ducks. As a result, for the last ten minutes Marcus had been waddling excitedly about the kitchen wearing a pair of yellow Marigold gloves on his feet – at trick Dan had taught him – and quacking loudly.

'We'll go in a minute,' she told him. 'Mummy's just got something very important to do.' Before Marcus had been born Sally had despised those parents who referred to themselves in the third person, but somewhere along the line she had fallen into the same linguistic trap. 'I know!' she said brightly, assuming a tone that suggested she'd discovered how to bring about world peace, 'why don't you watch one of your favourite DVDs?'

As if sensing he was being conned, Marcus considered her proposition. 'With a dink and bicksies?' he bargained.

She agreed all too readily. 'Yes, with a drink and biscuits,' she corrected him.

Once she had him set up in the playroom happily watching *Finding Nemo*, still wearing his Marigolds, she went into the study and switched on her laptop. She'd promised Dan she wouldn't work this weekend, but this wasn't really work; it was an article for the Law Society's *Gazette* and she had to send them a copy of it by the end of next week. Of the three thousand words they were expecting of her, she'd only managed to write a hundred and fifty.

She hadn't got as far as opening the relevant document when the telephone rang on the desk. Her body stiffened when she heard the voice at the other end: it was her brother, Terry. She doubted he was calling to shower Easter greetings upon her.

'Thought you might like to know,' he said gruffly and without preamble, 'Mum's been told she needs an operation.'

'What kind of operation?' Sally asked.

'One of her hips is done in. She needs it replacing.'

'Is she in a lot of pain?'

'What the bleeding hell do you think? The doc's told her she's to go on a waiting list and we all know what that means. She'll be dead and buried before she sees hair or hide of a new hip.'

'Why have you rung me, Terry?' she asked, knowing all too well why he had. The only time Terry or her mother phoned was when they were in need of something. The last call had been to ask if she could see her way to helping Terry make a down payment on a new car so that he could get a taxi business started. She'd ended up parting with the best part of two thousand quid and, surprise, surprise, the taxi business had never got off the ground. Before that it had been money for a new three-piece suite for her mother. And before that, there had been a washing machine that needed replacing. There was always some urgent financial crisis that only Sally could solve and they knew they could always rely on her, for the simple fact they knew the hold they had over her. Basically, she paid Terry and her mother to keep out of her life. They were an untidy reminder of the person she had once been.

'We thought you would want to help,' Terry said in answer to her question. 'It is our mum, when all's said and done. Family is family.'

'What are you asking me specifically, Terry?'

He snorted. 'That's you all over, isn't it? You like to make us beg, don't you? 'Course, I could just tell Mum that she'll have to wait and put up with the pain because you were too high and bloody mighty to help.'

'You want me to pay for her to go privately, is that it?'

'Oh, Brain of Britain finally gets it!'

'There's no need for sarcasm, Terry. Exactly how long has the doctor told Mum she'll have to wait if she has the operation done on the NHS?'

'I don't know specifics. Probably more than a year is likely. Eighteen months maybe.'

With so much sitting on the sofa watching daytime telly and stuffing herself on junk food, it was a wonder that Kath Wilson had worn out any of her joints, never mind her hip. Her jaw, maybe. Sally had no idea what the cost of a private operation would be, but she guessed it would be more than she could hide from Dan. In the past she had underplayed the money she had handed over to her family, but this amount would be nigh on impossible to conceal and she briefly speculated how she would be able to get round it. The deception, as slight as it was, struck a particular chord with her. How many times had she explained to her clients that when it came to financial matters, they weren't ever to think of hiding anything from her? The hypocrisy left her with a disagreeable sensation.

'It's probably best if I talk it over with Mum,' Sally said, thinking that she wouldn't put it beyond her family to pull a fast one on her. She bent down to her briefcase for her diary and flicked through the pages. 'Tell Mum I could manage a visit next weekend.'

'And while I'm about it, I'll get the bunting out, shall I?'

'Do what you like; it makes no odds to me. How's Janice?' Sally added in a futile attempt to establish some kind of family accord.

'She's fine. Why?'

'It seems a perfectly natural question to me. She is my sister-in-law.'

There was no question of Terry returning the courtesy and asking after Dan or Marcus. The last time he had referred to Dan was to imply there was something abnormal about a bloke sponging off his wife and staying at home to bring up a kid. No matter that Terry regularly sponged off taxpayers and stayed at home with his feet up in front of the television.

The call didn't go on for much longer. It was nearly a year since Sally had last seen her mother. The visits over to Hull were not happy occasions and were best kept to a minimum. All her mother and Terry were ever interested in was The Bank of Sally Oliver, a bank that was open all hours and never charged a penny of interest.

She put her diary away and returned her attention to her laptop.

She was so absorbed in what she was doing, Sally didn't hear Dan arrive back. She only knew he was home when she heard him say, 'I thought you weren't doing any work this weekend?'

Not wanting to lose her train of thought, she finished typing the sentence she'd had in her head – a particularly good sentence in her opinion – and glanced up. 'This doesn't count as work,' she said, her gaze sliding back to the screen of her laptop. Perhaps better not to use 'the yardstick of equality' twice in two consecutive paragraphs. 'Do you remember me mentioning I was asked to do a piece for the Law Society's *Gazette*, it's—'

'How long have you been here, *not working*?' he interrupted her.

She caught the uncharacteristic sharpness in his voice and forced herself to look away from the screen to where Dan was standing in the doorway and staring at the collection of opened law books on her desk. 'No more than a few minutes,' she said.

He frowned and she knew he didn't believe her.

'OK, a bit longer than a few minutes,' she conceded.

Still he didn't say anything. Then he turned his back on her and disappeared. I should go after him, she thought. But she didn't. Why should she have to apologize for what she was doing? Didn't he understand how important it was to her? Didn't he appreciate how little time there was in the day to get everything done? It was all right for him, he had nothing more pressing to do than—

She stopped herself from going any further.

Minutes later she heard Marcus quacking loudly and then his shrill voice calling out to her – 'Bye Mummy!' – followed by the sound of the back door slamming. She went to the window that overlooked the front garden. With Marcus sitting on his shoulders, Dan appeared from round the side of the house. She could see a clear plastic bag of crumbled bread in Marcus's hands. *Damn!* She'd forgotten all about those bloody ducks.

She went back to her desk and laptop. But try as she might, she couldn't concentrate. She'd lost her thread and her head was thumping with renewed vigour. She saved and closed the document and switched off the laptop. Rattled, she considered Dan's reaction to her working. She would have preferred it if they'd had an all-out blazing row, but that wasn't Dan's style. He went quiet. Not a sulking, brooding quiet, but a stiff-upper-lip quiet. She knew it was the way he'd been brought up. In contrast, she'd been raised in an environment where it was a matter of honour to fight one's corner, the louder and more vociferously the better. When she'd left Hull to go to university in Nottingham, she'd realized the street fighter in her would have to be tamed. Discreet manipulation was her new modus operandi.

But now and again the old Sally Wilson – the Sally who had been suppressed – wanted to break out and scream like a fishwife. This was one such moment. She wanted to yell at Dan and tell him never, *ever*, to turn his back on her again. The closest she had come to showing her true colours and really letting rip had been in the months after Marcus was born.

Postnatal depression was not something she had remotely pre-pared herself for. Not when she hadn't truly believed in such a thing. Yes, she'd read about it in the magazines and books that were supposed to prepare her for motherhood, but she'd flicked past those pages, dismissing them as irrelevant and intended for somebody else. Somebody not as strong and resourceful as her. She, after all, would never succumb to such a weak indulgence. Pulling oneself up by the proverbial bootstraps was all one had to do, surely?

What a shock she'd had. She'd been unable to get out of bed some days, lying there in tears, her body too leaden to move. The dark hopelessness of it all had seemed insurmountable.

It had started when she'd been unable to breastfeed Marcus. She hadn't been like those pregnant women she had met at the antenatal clinic, the type who practically hissed with evangelical zeal when it came to breastfeeding. No, she'd been one of those amateur expectant mothers who thought she'd give it a go, despite deep down feeling distinctly squeamish about the whole thing. But admit that in public and you'd be treated worse than a teenage single mother who confessed to deliberately smoking to minimize the size of her unborn child so she could have a less painful labour.

Perhaps it was the knowledge that she had failed so spectacularly at something that really did the damage. Failure was not a concept with which she was familiar, yet suddenly she was staring it right in the eye. She battled it for as long as she could, convinced that there was no reason an intelligent woman like her couldn't do what came naturally. But then Chloe – as her GP – stepped in, saying Marcus's weight wasn't increasing as it should, and that there was no shame in admitting defeat. Chloe had been so kind and caring with her, and in the end she had gently taken Sally in her arms one day and explained that she was suffering from postnatal depression and that it was time to do something about it. By getting it out in the open, Sally had hoped that the worst would be over. She was wrong. Things got a lot worse before they got better.

Poor Dan would come home from work most days to be confronted by a demon from hell. When she wasn't having a go at him – after all, it was his big idea to have a baby! – she was bawling her eyes out because she'd spent the day trying to soothe a fractious Marcus. Naturally, the second Dan lifted Marcus out of his cot and lay him on his shoulder, the screaming stopped and Marcus fell asleep, exhausted. 'How did you do that?' Sally would demand of Dan, both grateful and furious. 'Show me what you did!' Such was the poor state of her mind she began to suspect that there was a conspiracy going on: Marcus was being deliberately difficult to show the world what a terrible mother she was.

During those desperate weeks and months, Dan's patience was endless and when he took extended paternity leave to help her she wept for days on end with shame and relief. Thinking now how good Dan had been with her, Sally felt guilty for thinking badly of him earlier.

To make amends, she decided to make lunch. They'd have a proper lunch in the conservatory with a bottle of wine and napkins. The whole kit and caboodle. Hopefully Dan would see it as a peace offering and forgive her.

Her good intentions were all for nothing.

Dan and Marcus returned with fish and chips from the chip shop in the village. 'It was Marcus's suggestion,' Dan said. 'Sorry if we've spoiled your plans.'

'You don't sound particularly sorry,' Sally responded. She switched off the pan of water she was heating for the pasta she'd intended to serve and poured it down the sink.

'What's that supposed to mean?'

'Chips! Chips!' Bouncing on his toes, Marcus was rubbing his tummy and grinning broadly.

'Marcus,' Sally said sharply, 'I've told you before not to interrupt.'

'I want my chips! Chips, chips, *CHIPS*! Yum, yum, yum in my *TUM*!'

'Please, Marcus, I'm talking to Daddy right now.'

'Hey, big guy, why don't you go and wash your hands and then we'll have our chips? How does that sound?'

When they were alone, Sally was seething with frustration. 'You never back me up.'

'I do, you just don't realize it.'

'Maybe I need more of it from you.'

He looked at her steadily. 'Ever thought that Marcus and I might need more from you, that it would be a real novelty for us to have the best of you at the weekend and not the dregs?'

Marcus chose then to reappear, with copious amounts of water splashed down his front, and for the rest of the day they didn't have a moment to themselves. Yet when Marcus went to bed and it looked like they would have a chance to clear the air, Sally retreated to the study to work on her article. She knew hiding from Dan wasn't the answer, but she didn't trust herself not to retaliate and lose her temper over his absurd accusation.

It was nearly midnight when she finally switched off her laptop and went upstairs to bed. Dan was already asleep. She had no idea what time he'd come up here on his own. Having this unresolved ill-feeling between them didn't bode well for tomorrow.

Not when Dan's parents were arriving to stay for the next two days.

Chapter Nine

Normally Chloe wouldn't dream of driving the short distance to Corner Cottage, but in true Bank Holiday Monday fashion, the spell of warm dry weather had come to an abrupt, soggy end. A relentless downpour of rain had started in the night and it was showing no sign of letting up. She parked behind Dan's parents' Land Rover Discovery and, bottle of wine in hand, sprinted up the driveway to the front door where Sally was waiting for her.

'Your parents are already here,' Sally said, indicating the two dripping umbrellas in the porch, 'and they're doing sterling service. Graham's helping Dan in the kitchen and Jennifer's keeping the conversation going with Ronald and Glynis. She's a star.'

Chloe laughed. 'Don't, whatever you do, tell her that or it'll go completely to her head. Hello my best little boy in all the world, how are you?'

Marcus had materialized in the hall behind his mother. Smiling, he held out a small bowl of pickled gherkins to Chloe. 'Mm ... lovely,' she said, helping herself to one, at the same time kissing Marcus on the cheek.

'They're my favebit,' Marcus said, stuffing three into his mouth at once.

'*Favourite*,' Chloe corrected as he shot off down the hall in the direction of the kitchen. In his stockinged feet, he skidded on the oak flooring and a gherkin flew out of the bowl. He picked it up and put it in his already bulging mouth.

'Marcus! What have I told you about eating things from the floor?'

Giggling, he turned away and pushed open the kitchen door behind him.

'He seems on fine form,' Chloe said.

Sally sighed. 'He's mischief incarnate, ignoring everything I say and showing off horribly. He's been like it since yesterday when Dan's parents arrived. They gave him the biggest Easter egg imaginable and have been encouraging him to eat it behind my back at every opportunity. He's as high as a kite on sugar-overload. If there's any justice in the world he'll be sick on them before they leave.'

'How long are they staying?'

'Only until tomorrow morning, thank God. Come on, let's get you a drink. I'm two ahead of you already.'

'My compliments to the chef,' Chloe's mother said. 'This lamb is delicious, Dan. What have you done to it to achieve such perfection?'

'It couldn't be easier; I just marinated it overnight in red wine and juniper berries.'

Glynis turned to Sally. 'You're a very lucky girl having a husband who can cook so marvellously.'

'I am indeed,' Sally said quietly, exchanging a look with Chloe. 'I don't know what I'd do without him in the kitchen.'

It was a look Chloe knew of old. She had endured many such occasions with Dan's parents and knew the best way to get through them was to nod and smile and play dumb. It had to be said, though, as irritating as the Oliver seniors were, they were marginally less offensive than Sally's family. She had only met Kath Wilson once – at Dan and Sally's wedding – but in Chloe's opinion, she was an outstandingly poisonous piece of work. It made Chloe treasure her own parents all the more. Just as Sally had said, they were doing sterling service here. Without them, the conversation would have stalled many times over.

'Of course, you know what they say, don't you,' Jennifer said, passing the gravy boat to Glynis. 'That behind every successful man there's an astonished woman.'

Everyone laughed.

'But let's not forget that the kitchen is the safest place for a man.'

'Why's that, Dad?' Chloe asked Graham.

'Because no woman ever killed a man when he was doing the dishes!'

Again, everyone laughed.

'Time was when a chap knew to stay out of the kitchen,' Ronald said. 'I've made it my business to keep things that way. Couldn't boil an egg if my life depended on it. Proud of it too.'

There was another burst of laughter, but it was a token chortle, polite and short-lived. In the silence that followed, Marcus, who was sitting on Chloe's left, suddenly laughed loudly and for no apparent reason. His mouth wide open, he gave everyone a ringside view of the mushy remains of a half-chewed potato.

'That's enough, Marcus,' Sally said.

Marcus ignored her. Wobbling on his seat, his legs swinging under the table, he continued to laugh, now waving his small, chunky spoon and fork about, his head tipped back.

'I said that's enough, Marcus.' Sally's tone was sharp and raised. 'Dan, can't you make him stop? I might as well not be here the way he's carrying on. He won't do a single thing I ask of him.'

Picking up on the tension in her friend, Chloe put a hand on Marcus's shoulder. 'Basic rules of comedy, Marcus: perfect timing and always leave them wanting more. Eat up, or there might not be any pudding for you.'

He instantly fell silent and lowered his cutlery. He stared up at Chloe, his face adorably anxious. His eyes – Sally's soft, grey eyes – were wide and intense. 'Will be more choxy egg for me?' he asked.

'Later,' Dan said from the head of the table. 'For now, let's see if you can finish what's on your plate.'

'And then choxy?'

'Yes, but only if you've been very good. Can you do that?'

His eyes wider still, Marcus nodded and began shovelling peas into his mouth.

'Marcus—'

'Seconds for anyone?' Dan asked, cutting Sally off.

Disaster just about averted, Chloe waited for Dan to carve her some more lamb. An all-out battle of wills between Sally and Marcus would be the icing on the cake to what was turning into a dreadful way to spend the day. Only now did she realize that Dan and Sally had scarcely exchanged more than a few words throughout the meal. Had they argued earlier? Or was it just the strain of Glynis and Ronald staying with them? Whatever was going on, she hoped Marcus wouldn't get caught in any crossfire.

Since the day he'd been born, Marcus had been extremely dear to Chloe. Sometimes when she held him he soothed the dull, pulsing ache of the child she'd lost and other times he made the pain more acute, reminding her cruelly, and like nothing else could, that her own child would have been more or less the same age as he was. When the torment was at its worst, she could so easily sympathize with those poor women who steal a baby to satisfy their desperate need for one of their own.

'Still no man in your life, Chloe?'

Oh, God, not that old cookie. 'No, Glynis,' she said cheerfully, 'I'm afraid not. I'm a huge disappointment to everyone, I know. Spinsterhood beckons ever more surely.'

'Rubbish darling, and anyway, a spinster is an unclaimed treasure, that's all.'

Chloe raised her glass to her ever-supportive father. 'Thanks, Dad.'

Before coming here, she'd made her parents promise – Dan and Sally, too – that they wouldn't refer to her lunch date with Seth. The last thing she wanted was for Ronald and Glynis to interrogate her about him. Sadly, she and Seth hadn't been able to get together again since that day, due to him being busy in the run up to Easter, but he'd promised to call tonight to arrange something. She hoped he would call; she'd enjoyed his company. She certainly hoped he was better at using the telephone than Paul was. There'd been no response from him to her message on his voicemail and now she wished she'd never bothered. He'd thrown her a line, and fool that she was, she'd allowed him to reel her in.

'Better not to leave it too late, though,' Glynis prattled on. 'It would be a shame for you to miss out on a family, wouldn't it? Still, you'll always have your career.'

'Come on, Mum, give Chloe a break, will you?'

'A break,' Glynis repeated, looking at Dan as if he'd slapped her. 'I'm sure I don't know what you mean, Daniel.'

'If you want my opinion, you career girls bring it on yourselves. A shame that chap let you down so badly. What was his name again?'

'He was a bastard, Ronald,' said Jennifer, with feeling, 'and we don't mention him any more. Certainly not in polite company.'

'Bastard,' echoed Marcus, his head down as he scraped his plate with his fork. His pronunciation was as clear as Chloe had ever heard it. How did children do that? How did they home in on the one word in a sentence that was strictly out of bounds?

'Sorry,' Jennifer said, glancing apologetically from Dan to Sally.

Dan reached over and topped up her glass. 'No worries. He'll hear a lot worse before too long. Tell us about your next jaunt away. Is it Rome you're going to?'

'More wine this end of the table, Dan,' Sally said, bringing her empty glass down with a clumsy bang, 'we're running dry. And Marcus, will you please stop scraping your plate.'

'No, we're going to Florence. We hardly touched the surface when we went last year and Graham's found this charming little hotel on the internet. I can't think how we used to manage in the old days without the net. Do you use it much, Glynis?'

'Goodness me, no!' From the disgusted expression on Glynis's face anyone would think she'd just been asked if she used a vibrator.

The conversation rumbled on. As did Sally's wine consumption, Chloe noticed. When Sally had invited her to lunch today as a much-needed ally, Chloe had hesitated, saying that she had already arranged for her parents to spend the afternoon with her. 'Oh, please,' Sally had pleaded, 'say you'll come. I'll invite your parents as well; that way you'll get to see them without having to do any work.' Not having seen her friend in a while, Chloe had agreed, but now she regretted the decision. She was annoyed that she and her parents had been brought here to be emotional windbreakers for Sally. It wasn't the first time, of course, but usually the atmosphere wasn't as tense as this. Usually Sally was more fun. Today she was morose and self-absorbed and, to put it bluntly, well on the road to being drunk. If she wanted to give dear old Glynis and Ronald yet another reason to find fault with their son's choice of wife, she could not make a better job of it than she was doing right now. What had got into her?

Worried that it might not be Marcus who ended the day by being sick on his grandparents, Chloe decided to get Sally alone. With everyone now finished eating, Chloe pushed back her seat. 'Dan,' she said, 'since you did all the cooking, Sally and I will clear away.'

Sally drained her wine glass in one long swig, reminding Chloe of their first year at university when Sally could drink even the most hardened drinkers under the table. When drunk herself at that age, Chloe had been silly and giggling, but depending on the amount of alcohol she'd consumed, Sally could switch from being sullen to aggressive. Once, when they'd been staggering home in the early hours of the morning after a party, a teenage boy had leapt out of the shadows and tried to mug them. Sally had set about him with such unexpected ferociousness, he'd run off empty-handed.

'Good idea, Chloe,' Sally muttered, up on her feet and swaying slightly. 'I thought you'd never ask.'

Out in the kitchen, Chloe put the kettle on, then manoeuvred Sally into a chair. 'Right,' she said, 'what's going on?'

'Anything I can do to help?'

It was Glynis, presumably on the prowl for evidence to corroborate her suspicions that her daughter-in-law – shock, horror – was drunk.

'Absolutely not,' Chloe said breezily, going over to the door to keep her from coming any further into the room. 'You go back and join the party. Sally and I have it all under control.'

Peering over Chloe's shoulder, and in a ridiculously theatrical whisper, Glynis said, 'Is she all right? Only she doesn't seem herself.'

'She's got a headache, that's all.'

'Why are you both talking about me as if I'm not here?' Sally asked.

'Like I say,' Chloe said, 'go and join the others. We'll be through in a moment.'

With Glynis gone and the door closed, Chloe went over to the kettle that was now boiling. She made the strongest cup of coffee she could get away with, added cold water to cool it down and took it to the table where her friend was sitting with her head in her hands. 'Drink this,' she said. 'Doctor's orders.'

'You're cross with me, aren't you?' Sally said when several minutes had passed.

'No, I'm not.'

'Liar. You're having a miserable time here.'

'Not as miserable as the time you're obviously having. What's wrong? Have you and Dan had an argument?'

'Why do you ask that?'

'Because you've barely exchanged a civil word with each other, and that's really not like you two. Drink your coffee.'

'But it's revolting.'

'So is getting drunk at our age.'

Sally winced. 'You could try and dress it up to sound less sordid.'

'You would have seen through any attempt at that. Do you want to tell me what you and Dan have argued about?'

'We haven't argued. That's the problem. You know as well as I do that with Dan it's always a case of what he doesn't say. He wears that bloody stoic silence of his like a suit of armour. Nothing gets through it. In or out.'

'So what *isn't* he saying?'

'I think he resents the amount of time I devote to work.'

'You do put in quite long hours.'

58

'Don't you start as well. It's what I do. It's who I am. I can't change my basic make-up.'

'Is he worried that perhaps Marcus isn't seeing enough of you?' Chloe asked, treading warily. 'Is that the problem, do you think?'

'I spend as much time as I can with Marcus,' Sally said defensively.

'I know you do.'

'You're not suggesting that that's why Marcus has recently been difficult with me, are you?'

'Has he been difficult with you?'

Sally sighed heavily. 'You saw what he was like earlier. He ignores everything I say and does everything Dan asks him to do.' She slumped back into the chair. 'If you really want to know, I'm tired of being made to feel the bad cop to Dan's good cop.'

'Oh, Sally, it's just a phase. Children can be devious little monkeys, even the gorgeously cute ones like Marcus. They know instinctively how to play one parent off another to get what they want. Trust me, boys always grow up to be utterly devoted to their mothers. Before long it will be Dan complaining that he doesn't get a look-in with his son. Now finish that coffee, while I dig out the desserts. Dan said they were in the larder, didn't he?'

As she crossed the kitchen, it occurred to Chloe that the reason Sally had been drinking so much might have been because she wanted to embarrass Dan in front of his parents and provoke him into an argument. For both their sakes – and Marcus's – Chloe hoped things would come to a head and then quickly blow over.

Chapter Ten

With the volume pumped up, Seth was listening to Arcade Fire. Was there a finer band around at the moment? He didn't think so. When 'Intervention' came to an end, he pressed the replay button on the remote control for the CD player and closed his eyes. There it was again, that extraordinary slab of pure, awesome sound. It was amazing. Literally mind-blowing. Should death claim him now, this very minute, it wouldn't be a bad way to go. Some send off!

This time when the track came to an end, he removed his head-phones and switched off the music. He went downstairs, made himself a cup of coffee and when he came back up to the spare room that doubled as an office, he marshalled his thoughts firmly into line. 'Right,' he said out loud. 'Work.'

For Seth it was irrelevant that it was a bank holiday; for him it had been as busy as any other day and he'd spent most of it applying himself to the backlog of papers that had been accumulating on his desk for the last few weeks. The answerphone also required his attention; at the last count there were a dozen messages for him to deal with.

The trouble with his job was that it was almost impossible not to be on duty twenty-four seven. Only when he was away from Crantsford did he feel that he could properly relax. Even then he had to steel himself and switch off his mobile. He had been warned it would be like this and had imagined himself suitably prepared, yet the depth of his involvement and workload had come as a revelation.

He'd been here in Crantsford as Owen's assistant for six months now and the time had flown by. Regrettably Owen was not the most helpful of bosses and Seth had become resigned to having dumped on him anything Owen didn't want to do. Fair enough. Why wouldn't he want to take things easy? Widowed last year and only a few years off retirement, he was more than ready to wind down. Seth just wished he could do it with more grace. He also wished the man would greet some of the initiatives Seth wanted to put in place with a little more enthusiasm. Nonetheless, he did believe he was making a mark for himself. Slowly but surely.

Two hours passed and as a reward for his industry Seth went downstairs again, but instead of making another cup of coffee, he helped himself to a beer from the fridge.

He drank it straight from the bottle, leaning back against the worktop. Only then did he allow himself his real reward: to think of Chloe. He had to ration very strictly the amount of time he spent thinking about her because whenever he did he got completely distracted and ended up grinning like an idiot. He was doing it now. But what man wouldn't? She was lovely, every perfect, well-toned, streamlined inch of her. Being an expert on such things, he knew an eye-catching package when he saw it and with her long blonde hair, blue eyes and amazing legs Chloe was knockout hot.

But all it took to wipe the idiotic grin from his face was one thought. He hadn't actually lied to Chloe, yet nor had he been completely candid with her. He wanted her to get to know the real him before her opinion was tainted by prejudice. Prejudice was rife in all walks of life and he'd personally come up against sufficient forms of it to know that occasionally it was better to encourage some lateral thinking beforehand.

All he had to do was judge when it was the right moment to tell Chloe the truth, and hope that she'd take it well.

He checked the time: nine fifteen. Time to make that promised call.

Chapter Eleven

Sally woke up the next morning determined to be in a better mood. She had a fuggy head and a chafing reminder of how she had once felt as a young child. It was the day Terry had decided she was old enough to be initiated into what he called the Five Finger Discount. All she had to do was distract the man on the till while Terry helped himself to a camera and slipped it inside his jacket. She'd been ten at the time and petrified of being caught. She'd been wracked with guilt, too. But it didn't take her long to make the transition from being so scared she nearly wet herself to getting off on the adrenalin rush of what she and her brother were doing. The excitement was like nothing else she'd ever experienced. Running home with Terry afterwards, their pockets stuffed full, she would whoop and laugh at their cleverness and daring. Oh, how she loved the risk, and pitting her wits against another. After that first time, her conscience had not been troubled by guilt.

Unlike now.

She slid carefully out of bed, not wanting to disturb Dan. The rest of the house was perfectly quiet. But then it was only half past five. In the shower, she told herself she had nothing to feel guilty about. She had done nothing wrong. It had been a simple mistake of drinking more than was sensible. It could happen to anyone. There was nothing to feel bad about in claiming a headache and going to bed the minute Chloe and her parents had left.

It was probably as well that she'd fallen asleep the moment her head had hit the pillow because surely Dan's stoicism could only stretch so far. Had she been awake when he joined her in bed, he would have been bound to ask her what the hell she thought she'd been playing at. There wouldn't have been any danger of an ugly, dramatic scene erupting between them, not with his parents in the house, but she was glad he hadn't had the opportunity to confront her.

With everyone still sleeping, she quietly left the house and drove to work. As she passed Chloe's cottage, she made a mental note to call her friend and apologize for yesterday.

With hardly any traffic on the roads, she was in Manchester and at her desk by seven o'clock. It had seemed the best thing to do, to leave before everyone was up. She couldn't stand the thought of facing Dan's parents over breakfast. Which made her that most despised of creatures: a coward. When she got home tonight – and she would make a really big effort not to be late – Glynis and Ronald would be long gone and then she and Dan would be able to sit down and talk. She would try and explain to him just how he made her feel at times, how he couldn't go on repeatedly undermining her in front of Marcus. Really, was it any wonder she spent so much time at work when she was treated with so little respect at home?

With everything now neatly sorted in her mind, she switched on her computer. She read through her diary to see what appointments she had lined up and eagerly embraced the day head on. Suddenly life didn't seem such an uphill struggle. She was back in control.

By nine twenty, the office was buzzing with activity and Sally was drinking her fourth cup of coffee, brought to her by her wonderfully efficient assistant, Chandra. She was flicking through a client's file on the table behind her desk when there was a knock at her partially open door. She heard Tom McKenzie's voice. 'Morning, Sally. Okay if we come in?'

'Sure,' she said absently. 'You're only interrupting me in my latest bid to make legal history, but I can put that on hold for you.' She marked the page in the file, swivelled her chair round and looked up to see Tom the other side of her desk. At his side was a man Sally didn't recognize. He was tall, slim and suited and booted to kill. His suit bore all the hallmarks of many hours of expert tailoring having been applied to its creation. His white shirt, complete with cufflinks, showed off a boyishly handsome tanned face and hair recently lightened by the sun. He looked young. Much too young to be wearing such an expensive, grown-up suit.

'Sally,' Tom said, 'I'd like to introduce Harry Fox. Harry, beware, this is Sally Oliver. She's a human dynamo and takes no hostages when it comes to keeping the rest of us in line. A word to the wise: be very afraid of her.'

Sally got to her feet, smoothed down her skirt and stepped around her desk. She'd forgotten all about the New Boy arriving today. 'Hello,' she said, offering her hand, 'good to meet you. And don't believe a word of what Tom says; he's delusional most of the time.'

Harry smiled and shook hands with her. 'But just to be safe, I'll take him at his word and do my best to behave myself. I'd hate to get on your wrong side. Especially on my first day.' His dark, glinting eyes dropped momentarily to her legs then back to her face. Cheeky boy, she thought. We'll have to cure you of that.

'Well, then,' Tom said, rubbing his hands together, 'I'll leave you two to it. Glad to have you on board, Harry. Any problems, you know where to find me. Although I'm pretty sure you're in capable hands here. Sally will be sure to have everything arranged for you.'

Sally did a double take. 'Sorry, Tom?' she said. 'I'm not with you. What will I have arranged?'

Tom looked around her office, then back at her. 'Oh, good Lord, Sally. There's been an oversight, hasn't there? How embarrassing. My fault entirely. I forgot to tell you that Colin's away on holiday for the next fortnight and while his office is being decorated, I thought Harry could share your office instead.'

It was a while since Sally had shared an office with anyone and she was quick to lay down the ground rules. There would be no bags of sweaty gym clothes brought in. No radios or portable television sets either, no matter how important the cricket, rugby or football match. There would be no eating of anything particularly aromatic, such as pies, pasties and slices of pizza. And there would most certainly be no producing of any bodily odours either. She'd rubbed shoulders with enough male colleagues over the years to know these were the most frequently committed crimes in a shared working environment.

'Any rules on the wearing of perfume and aftershave?' Harry asked as he shifted a filing cabinet into position.

Oh, so he wasn't taking her seriously, eh? 'Depends what it is,' she said, returning to her side of the office.

'Only I have to warn you, the perfume you're wearing is having rather a powerful effect on me.'

Mmm ... a joker, was he?

'Versace Crystal Noir, isn't it?' he said when she didn't respond. 'I have a connoisseur's nose for these things. It suits you.'

The impudent boy's self-importance was breathtaking. 'You've known me for no more than a couple of hours. How would you know what suits me?'

He grinned. 'It's a gift. I can size a person up within seconds of meeting them. I'm never wrong.'

She began sorting through the papers that had become dislodged during the process of moving her desk to make space for him. She had been out of the office when interviews had been held to find somebody to add to the expanding tax department. If she remembered correctly, Harry Fox had been considered a dynamic 'bright young thing' when it came to Inland Revenue and VAT fraud. 'Exactly how old are you?' she asked.

'How old do you think I am?'

Young enough for a good clip round the ear, sonny! She probably had shoes at the back of the wardrobe that were older than him. 'Twenty-five, twenty-six?' she said.

He stopped what he was doing and sat down, staring at her across the room. 'You think I'm a gauche, wet-behind-the-ears office boy, don't you?'

Seeing that he was genuinely offended, and had perhaps learned his first lesson of the day, she offered him a conciliatory smile. 'I'll leave that for you and your unfailing *gift* to decide.'

Ten minutes later she was on her way to meet a client for a barrister's conference. Darren T. Child was one of her high-profile clients, a premier league footballer who was rarely off the front pages of the newspapers. His last outing in the tabloids was for yet another drunken brawl in a Manchester nightclub.

The conference was over before it had started. Her client hadn't bothered to turn up. None of the numbers she had for him, including his agent, had been answered and all she could do was leave several messages to call her as soon as possible. She headed back to the office, stopping en route at her favourite sandwich bar to pick up lunch.

'Someone's in luck today,' Chandra said when Sally stopped to check for any messages while she'd been out.

'Any particular reason why?'

'You'll see.'

And Sally did see. On her desk was a beautiful bouquet of red roses. Attached to the ribbon that held the stems together was a small envelope. She put down her case and sandwich bag. Dan, she thought with a happy smile. The perfect peace offering. She opened the envelope and pulled out the card. '*Sorry for getting off on the wrong foot with you. Can we start again, please?*'

The sound of tapping on her door had her turning round. Harry Fox was standing in the doorway. Staring earnestly at her, he said, 'Can we pretend that was my cocky brother you met this morning?'

Chapter Twelve

Rosie had been intriguingly mysterious on the phone earlier that morning, saying she'd met someone recently whom she wanted Dan to meet.

Marcus had been delighted at the news that he would be seeing Charlie and had rushed pell-mell to the back door for his shoes. Dan had had to explain that they wouldn't be going until the afternoon. They'd had an early lunch and then Dan had put Marcus to bed for a nap. Still hyped up from his grandparents' visit and the colossal amount of chocolate he'd consumed, Dan knew he would never make it through the afternoon unless he had some down time. It also gave Dan a chance to catch up on tidying the house.

His parents had left shortly after nine thirty with a look on their faces that came nauseatingly close to sympathy. His mother had almost forgotten herself and put a hand on his arm when she'd said, 'You would say if there was anything we could do, wouldn't you?'

'Just get the hell out, that's what you can do!' is what he should have said, instead of the polite non-committal, thank-you-but-I-don't-really-know-what-you're-implying shake of his head that his family was so good at. With Marcus at his side, he'd waved them off, furious that they would be leaving with the case closed on his marriage. As far as they were concerned, he must be ruing the day he ever met Sally. He didn't think he was exaggerating when he thought they would love nothing more than to drive a wedge between them. But they were making a big mistake if they thought for one minute he'd ever let that happen.

Time to get ready to go to Rosie's. Dan pushed open the door to Marcus's bedroom. He was still asleep and Dan took a moment to absorb his son and to think, as he often did, how similar he was to his mother, not just in appearance with the colour of his eyes or his fine dark hair, but in his temperament. He was as sharp as a tack and Dan didn't doubt he'd grow up to be as ferociously intelligent as his mother. He already had her iron will. Yet Dan wouldn't have him any other way.

Question was, in view of the disastrous weekend they'd just staggered through, would he have Sally any other way? Yes, if he was honest. He did think she had her priorities wrong at times, not so much for his benefit, but for Marcus's. Yet what if the boot was on the other foot and it was he who was going out to work? Who was to say that he wouldn't be doing the same as Sally? Didn't he used to stay late at the office to get just one more thing sorted, to make one last amendment to a report, or meet with one more important client?

He sighed. Perhaps he had been unfair to Sally. He'd certainly been unfair forcing her to spend two days in the presence of his awful parents. Was it any wonder she'd sought refuge in a few too many glasses of Chablis? Who the hell could blame her? It was a miracle they hadn't all ended up drunk! He'd try to make it up to her this evening.

But as he knelt down to wake his son, he acknowledged that there was something else bothering him. He had a horrible suspicion that his criticism of Sally might actually be rooted in jealousy. Was there, on a profoundly subconscious level, a part of him that felt lost in the long shadow cast by Sally's career as it went from strength to strength? He really hoped it wasn't the case. He hadn't opted out of his career only to succumb to petty jealousy. He'd be a liar if he didn't admit to occasionally missing the cut and thrust of his old life, but it was nothing like enough to make him regret the sacrifice he'd made. He knew he was doing the right thing, giving Marcus the best possible start in life by being at home with him.

In her typically efficient way, Rosie had everything organized in the garden to keep Marcus and Charlie occupied while they sat on the patio waiting for her friend to arrive. 'I've often thought that a lot of the world's problems could be solved by putting the opposing parties in a sandpit each with a spade and a plastic tea set,' observed Rosie.

'But how soon before they started to squabble over whose turn it was to play with the teapot?' asked Dan.

'Well, thankfully Marcus and Charlie are happy to take turns.'

Dan smiled at Rosie's diplomacy. They both knew that Marcus was the more dominant of the two boys and that Charlie was always happy to go along with his friend's inexhaustible instructions.

Currently, at Marcus's decree, the two of them appeared to be digging with sufficient vigour to get them to the earth's centre by teatime.

'Ah, that'll be Tatiana,' Rosie said in response to the distant sound of a car door shutting. While Rosie went to meet her friend, Dan got to his feet, ready to meet the person who apparently had an interesting proposition for him.

When Rosie reappeared, Dan assumed someone other than her expected guest had turned up. Dressed in jeans and a T-shirt, her hair in two long plaits and carrying a small red canvas rucksack over her shoulder, she looked like a teenage babysitter from the village. Except she moved with far more grace than any teenage girl Dan had ever encountered. She was slight of build, and he found himself wondering if she'd trained as a ballet dancer as she seemed to glide or even float over to the sandpit. Once there, she knelt beside the two boys and tipping back Charlie's sunhat, she planted a loud raspberry of a kiss on his cheek. He squealed with delight. 'And you must be Marcus,' she said, turning her head. 'I've heard a lot about you. You're Charlie's best friend, aren't you?'

'We're digging,' Marcus said importantly. He pointed to the large hole he and Charlie had created. 'For treasure. We're pirates.'

'Well, avast there, me hearties! Buried treasure! Count me in. Can I do some digging with you handsome pirates? I absolutely love digging.'

Both boys beamed and Marcus promptly offered her his spade. Smiling to himself, Dan thought how children could always discern genuine interest. Anyone faking it was treated accordingly. In this instance, Marcus was obviously utterly charmed by this girlish stranger.

'Later,' she said. 'I need to talk to your daddy first, Marcus. But make sure you save some buried treasure for me to discover. I shall be desperately upset if you find it all before I get a chance to have a go.'

She straightened up in one fluid movement and came over to where Dan and Rosie were waiting for her on the patio. 'Hello,' she said to Dan, 'I'm Tatiana. What a lovely son you have. He has such a thoughtful and intuitive face.'

Dan felt himself blush with fatherly pride. 'I'm no expert, but from the look on that thoughtful and intuitive face of his, I'd say you've just acquired yourself a fan for life.'

She shrugged off the compliment and sat down at the shaded end of the table. 'Rosie, the garden is looking beautiful. I wish I had your green fingers.' She held out her pale, delicate hands for them to inspect as evidence. 'See, not a hint of green to them. Perfectly useless.' She laughed lightly. 'Ooh, is that a goldfinch at the bird feeder?'

She's like a butterfly, Dan thought, flitting charmingly from one thing to another. He couldn't begin to think what kind of proposition she had in mind for him.

Five minutes later, when Rosie went inside the house to make drinks for everyone, Dan began to think that there might be more to Tatiana Haines than he'd originally thought.

'Has Rosie told you anything at all about me?' she asked, her vibrant green eyes suddenly focusing entirely on him across the table. It was like being zapped with two bright laser beams. The change in her was quite startling.

'Nothing other than that she met you recently at a charity fundraising event,' he said.

'Good. I asked her not to say anything; I wanted to make the pitch myself. Have you heard of the Kyle Morgan Trust?'

He shook his head. 'Sorry, no I haven't.'

'It's a charity for terminally sick children and I'm their fundraising manager. We provide respite and specialist nursing care in the home for families who are desperate for a break. And by a break, I'm talking about a couple of hours to go to the shops or time to snatch some much-needed sleep. Or even play with their other children.'

'How did you get involved?'

'Kyle Morgan was my nephew; my sister's son. I won't go into the details now, but he was born with a genetic disorder and died before his second birthday. After his death we heard of a charity down in the south-west that provided just the kind of care and support that would have helped my sister and her husband through the most difficult times of Kyle's short life. We then decided to try and get something similar started here in Cheshire.'

'How long ago was that?'

'Five years ago. Since then we've supported more than a hundred families, which is great, but we know there are many more in the region that we can't help yet because we don't have the funding. We're aiming to launch a major appeal in December to get a massive leap in donations. We don't receive any government funding; every penny is through events and rattling collection tins.'

'So where do I come in?' Dan had a sudden uncomfortable vision of himself as a charity mugger standing outside the supermarket in Crantsford.

'From what Rosie's told me about you and your line of work before you took time out to be at home with Marcus, I think you'd be a real asset to the trust. I'm hoping to twist your arm and convince you to join us.'

Chapter Thirteen

True to her resolution, Sally wasn't working late that evening.

She switched off her computer, tidied her desk and pulled on her suit jacket. As she did so, she glanced at the roses Harry had given her. They were as absurdly showy as the boy himself. Should she take them home with her? No. Dan might wonder why she'd been on the receiving end of such an ostentatious gift. The flowers were fine here in the glass vase Chandra had found for her.

Out in the corridor, her mind on making peace with Dan, she bumped into Harry. Literally. He'd been walking towards her carrying a tower of box files, his view all but obscured. At the collision, the files teetered and then the one on the top slid to the floor, banging sharply against her ankle. Gritting her teeth, Sally retrieved the file from the floor and added it to his load. 'Sorry,' he said. 'Is your foot OK?'

'It'll survive,' she said, noticing with irritation that her tights now had a hole in them.

'I seem to have done nothing but annoy you today,' he said, putting the files down. 'Aren't you taking my roses home with you?'

'I'm leaving them here to brighten the office. Goodnight.' She took a step to get past him.

'Look, could I extend my apology by buying you a drink?' he said. 'I'm just about finished here.'

It was far from unheard of at McKenzie Stuart to go for a drink after work with a colleague or even a group of them – in some department it was more or less *de rigueur* – but rarely did Sally do so. She could always think of something she would rather be doing than sitting in a noisy bar bitching about those not present. 'I'm sorry,' she said, 'I can't.'

'Can't or won't?' he said. His eyes were bright with what she could only describe as challenging mischief.

'My husband's waiting for me at home,' she said curtly. 'And if you carry on with this line of talk, I'll have you bounced out of here faster than you can say sexual harassment. Got it?'

Unabashed, he smiled. 'You have the most amazing eyes. They were what I noticed about you first. Then I spotted your legs.'

Her back straightened with stiffening rage. 'Are you hearing me?'

'Oh, yes. Question is, are you hearing me? I think you're beautiful. Possibly the most beautiful woman I've ever met. I could stare at you all day.'

'Have you got something of a Class A nature streaming through your blood?'

He laughed. 'You know, I think I might have. But it's not what you're thinking. Something this good couldn't be illegal.' He bent down and picked up the files. 'Have a nice evening. I'll see you tomorrow.'

Sally turned on her heel and marched off. Furious, she took the stairs, practically running down the three flights. She would have to talk to Tom. The fool of a boy would have to go. He was intolerable. Not to say unspeakably arrogant. How dare he treat her as some kind of sex object! *Possibly the most beautiful woman I've ever met.* What rubbish! *They were what I noticed about you first.* Well, I'll tell you what I noticed first about you, sonny. It was your bloody great ego!

She drove home faster than she should have, seething with anger, and just as she was passing Chloe's house, she noticed her friend's car on the drive. She slammed on the brakes and reversed hard.

'I don't believe it!' Chloe laughed. 'He came on to you on his first day? You've got to admire his nerve. Hey, talk about when Harry met Sally.'

'Admire his nerve? He's a menace! A pest!'

'Don't tell me you weren't just an itzy-bit flattered.'

'Certainly not!'

Chloe smiled, which only added to Sally's exasperation and made her pace all the more. She had come here expecting sympathy and understanding from her friend, as well as the opportunity to offload her fury before arriving home, but instead she was being made to feel unaccountably worse.

'And to compound it all, he's so young.'

'Is he good-looking?'

'Yes,' she said, 'but implausibly so. And he damn well knows it.

God only knows how much his suit must have set him back. Oh, and he's got one of those sticking-out-a-mile public school voices.'

'Like Dan's, you mean?'

'No! Nothing like Dan's.'

'So let me get this right. You have a fresh-out-of-the-box newbie in the office who's young and handsome and thinks you're beautiful. And your problem would be?'

'Oh, Chloe, don't be stupid. You can't have men behaving in such an insulting way in the workplace. It's intrinsically wrong.'

'You genuinely feel insulted?'

'Of course! He treated me like he was picking me up in a bar. He's undermining my position.'

'Mm … and that would be senior to him?'

Sally stopped pacing. She considered Chloe's words carefully. Yes, there it was. That was the truth of the matter. Harry Fox hadn't respected her. He hadn't taken her seriously. By treating her as an inconsequential bit of fluff, she had felt disparaged and emasculated, her every instinct affronted. No greater crime could the foolish boy have committed.

Now that she had put her finger on exactly what had enraged her so much, Sally turned slowly round to face her friend. Calm now, she registered that Chloe was dressed for going to the gym. 'I'm sorry,' she said. 'I'm keeping you, aren't I?'

'No worries. I'm glad you stopped by. I wanted to know how things progressed after Mum and Dad and I left yesterday. You were quite tense, weren't you?'

'Don't remind me. It was one of the worst weekends I've endured in a long while.'

'Did you and Dan get a chance to talk?'

Sally shook her head. 'That's what I'm hoping to do tonight.' She picked up her bag. 'I'd better go. Wish me luck.'

Marcus was already in bed, fast asleep when she got home. She crept into his bedroom and skimmed his forehead with a kiss. How peaceful he looks, she thought enviously. Not a care in the world.

She went to change, and after carefully hanging up her suit, she went back down to the kitchen. Dan greeted her with a glass of white wine. He raised his own glass and touched it against hers. 'Supper will be ready in ten minutes. How was your day?'

She thought of Harry Fox and said, 'I've had better. How about you? Your parents get away all right?'

73

'I'll tell you about it later. First I want to apologize for the weekend.'

'You can't help the parents you're born with,' she said with a tight smile.

'It's not them I'm apologizing for; it's … it's me. I was out of order when I criticized you for the amount of time you devote to work. Call it an error of judgement on my part. I'm sorry, really I am. Do you forgive me?'

Sally didn't know what to say. This wasn't the conversation she had imagined them having. Everything she'd planned to say now went out of her head. 'You've never asked me that before,' she murmured.

'Let's hope I never have to again,' he said, his expression grave. He put down his glass, then took hers, too. He held her face in his hands and kissed her on the mouth.

'No,' she said, pushing him away. 'It wasn't only you who made a mistake. I did as well. I behaved no better than a sulky teenager. I'm sorry. Am *I* forgiven?'

He kissed her again. 'Forgiven entirely,' he said as his hands began moving over her body. She kissed him back and pressed herself against him, her desire for him roused in an instant. She suddenly needed to be connected to the strong, hard warmth of Dan, knowing that it would blank out how frustrated and isolated she'd felt these last few days. 'Fancy an addition to the menu tonight?' she whispered in his ear.

He smiled and unzipped her trousers, then lifted her deftly up onto the worktop. Kissing him, she worked at the buttons on his jeans. 'I hate these button flies,' she said breathlessly. 'Don't ever wear them again.'

'Allow me.' He'd just undone the last of the offending buttons when they both turned towards the kitchen door. Marcus was calling from upstairs. 'Daddy. Can I have a dink? Daddy.'

'Don't move,' Dan said. 'Close your eyes and stay exactly as you are. I'll be right back.'

But left alone, Sally did move. How could she not when she felt so stupid perched on the chilly granite worktop with her trousers hanging round her ankles. Sex always seemed such a good idea when you were doing it, but seen in the cold light of day – or in this case, in the harsh glare of a halogen spotlight – it seemed a very strange thing to do.

By the time Dan returned, she had her trousers back on and the timer on the cooker was announcing that supper was ready. 'No chance of hitting the rewind button, then?' he said with a rueful sigh.

'We'll save it for later.'

He smiled and briefly rested a hand on her shoulder as he passed her to get to the oven. 'I'll hold you to that. Now sit down while I serve. It's fish pie,' he added.

From her chair at the table, which was already set with mats and cutlery, she watched him take the hot dish out of the oven. The pie looked and smelled delicious. 'Oh, something I forgot to tell you over the weekend,' she said, 'I'm making a duty visit to Hull to see my mother this coming weekend. That OK with you?'

'But it's Derek Lockley's memorial service this Saturday. It's on the calendar.' He inclined his head towards the calendar on the wall above the telephone.

'Damn,' she muttered. 'I forgot all about that.'

'Can you change your visit to another weekend?'

'I'd rather not.'

'Then you'll have to take Marcus with you.'

The swift decisiveness of his tone made her say, 'You could always take him with you.'

'To a memorial service?'

She tutted, forced to admit that it was hardly appropriate. But then neither was taking Marcus to see her ghastly mother. Her son might be connected genetically to Kath and Terry Wilson but no way on earth was she going to have him sullied by exposing him to them. 'I could ask Chloe to have him for the day,' she said at length. 'I'm sure she wouldn't mind.'

Chloe had decided she liked Seth a lot. He was warm and kind and made her laugh. He was also intelligent and articulate, and displayed just the right amount of interest in her without being overly pushy. His manners were impeccable – which would please her mother – and what's more, he didn't appear to be dragging any baggage around with him. There was no ex-wife lurking in the shadows; nor was there a brood of dependent children.

Having showered and changed after their workout, they were now sitting side by side at a small table in the bar of Cartwright Hall and tackling a super-sized platter of barbecued chicken wings. Keen to prove to him that she had more to her conversational repertoire than near-death experiences, she was telling him about one of her patients, who had given birth that day to a baby boy and had named him Dyson. 'Can you imagine when the poor boy goes to school? He'll be stuck with some awful nicknames, like Sucker, or Dusty.'

'I came across a child called Juniper the other day,' Seth said.

Chloe groaned. 'Please don't tell me her surname was Berry?'

'Thankfully not. But how about this for a corker of a name for a little girl: Clarity Shine. I'm not kidding, that was really her name. Brilliant, isn't it? Is having children something you want?'

Taken aback by the swerve of his question, and not caring if her answer would be committing dating suicide, she said, 'Yes. How about you?'

'Oh, yes, definitely.'

The speed of his reply surprised her again. She mentally added a tick in yet another box for him: he was scoring quite highly. Then it occurred to her that maybe he was compiling a similar list in his head about her. If so, she wondered if she had been awarded as many ticks as she'd given him.

'I have two brothers and one sister,' he went on, 'all married with six children between them.'

'Which leaves them wondering what on earth's wrong with you?'

'Something like that. I'm going to see my sister tomorrow, over in Whitchurch. It's the last day of the Easter school holidays so I'll get to see my two nieces. Which will be great. Not so great will be that I'll have to submit myself to my sister's usual interrogation.'

Remembering that, like her, it was his day off tomorrow, Chloe tried not to feel disappointed. It would have been nice to get together again. Whilst jogging on the treadmill earlier, she had indulged herself in a mild daydream of the two of them going for a walk in the Peak District. But now she warned herself to go steady. Too much too soon was a recipe for disaster.

'If I hadn't been anxious about kick-starting World War Three, I might have been tempted to say no to my sister,' he said.

When she didn't say anything, he asked, 'Don't you want to know why?'

Chloe glanced up, aware that she'd been caught out – her mind had wandered from the rosy picture of them out at the White Peak, to thinking how he'd fit in with the people who mattered most to her. 'I'm sorry?'

'I said, don't you want to know why I nearly dared to say no to my sister? Because trust me, seldom is anyone brave enough to say no to Rebecca.'

'Go on.'

'I was going to ask you if you wanted to spend the day with me. But then I lost my nerve and thought you might think I was pushing my luck.'

She smiled, experiencing a genuine rush of pleasure and fondness for him. 'I wouldn't have thought that at all.'

'Really?'

'In fact, I was going to ask you if you wanted to go for a walk in the Peak District. There's this great tea shop in Castleton where they serve the best cream teas in the world.'

'Stop!' He groaned. 'Now you're just torturing me. There I'll be tomorrow, thinking of what could have been and regretting being such a no-good coward when it comes to my sister.' He turned to face her head-on and put a hand on her forearm. 'Can we do it another time? Go to Castleton?'

'I don't see why not,' she said, trying not to read too much into the gesture – a friendly hand on her arm, that's all it was – 'but if I remember rightly, you do owe me dinner.'

He feigned a look of shock at the platter of chicken bones in front of them. 'I thought *this* was dinner. You mean you want more?'

'A cheapskate as well as a coward! Now I'm getting to know the real you.'

Outside in the car park, he walked her to her car. They'd gone through the procedure of 'there's no need, I can remember where I parked it' and 'call me old-fashioned, but a man always sees a woman safely to her carriage,' and they'd now reached the tricky stage of bringing the evening to a close.

Would he kiss her? That was the burning issue. As she played for time and pretended to hunt through her bag for her keys, Chloe knew she would feel cheated if he didn't. When she thought she'd given him enough time to come to a decision, she looked up to see him staring at her with an amused expression on his face.

'Finished?' he asked. He then swooped in for a kiss. A polite little kiss at first and then a long, long kiss.

Mm ... she thought; that was definitely worth waiting for. He knew all the right moves. No doubt about it.

Chapter Fourteen

'You have told her, haven't you?'

Seth gave the small crosshead screw one last turn then pushed the plug into the socket. He flicked the switch, pushed down the lever and within seconds he could feel heat rising from the toaster. 'As I thought,' he said, 'it was the fuse. You really should learn to change one, you know. It's not rocket science.'

Rebecca fixed him with a steely gaze. 'That's what husbands and brothers are for,' she said. 'And I repeat my question: you have told her, haven't you?'

Ignoring her again, Seth went to put the screwdriver back in his brother-in-law's toolbox in the under-stairs cupboard. Working away in Zambia, Peter was helping local farmers to market their produce more effectively, and for a split second Seth wished he was there with him. He'd been here less than an hour, doing the odd jobs around the house that needed doing in Peter's absence, and already his sister had got more out of him than he'd intended to divulge. She claimed his overly inscrutable face had given him away when she'd asked if he'd met anyone recently.

He swore her mission in life was to marry him off and have him settled down before his fortieth birthday. With less than a year to go, she appeared to be upping the ante. In the past six months, she'd brought a number of girls to his attention whenever he visited. The last one had been pleasant enough company during dinner, if a touch flaky – she'd referred just a little too often to her astral chart and her inner child for his liking – and he couldn't have imagined wanting to spend more than an evening with her, never mind the rest of his life. How Rebecca had thought they would be compatible, he'd never know. Anyway, Chloe had entered his consciousness by then.

The second he'd set eyes on Chloe at the gym, he'd wanted to get to know her better. But he'd deliberately not rushed straight in; he'd kept his distance, watching to see if she ever turned up with a partner. Happily for him she was always alone, and as the days passed and their sessions seemed to coincide more and more, he decided to ask her out. Time was when he would have been in there like a shot. He would have sauntered over, first opportunity he got, and clinched the deal.

He smiled at the thought, and of the memory of kissing Chloe last night. He'd sensed her waiting for him to make a move in the car park and he'd had a heck of a job holding himself back while she messed about with her bag. When their lips touched for the first time, he'd kept it brief, telling himself to go slowly. But there she was, so close, so gorgeous, and so wholly irresistible. So he'd kissed her again, one hand in the small of her back, holding her firmly to him, the other at the nape of her neck. He'd driven home afterwards with a smile on his face a mile wide.

Back in the kitchen, Rebecca was waiting for him. He'd stand more of a chance withholding information from a crack team of Mugabe's secret police than wriggling out of his older sister's questions. 'No,' he said, 'I haven't told Chloe.'

'And why would that be?'

'You know perfectly well why.'

'You don't think it would be better to be honest with her before you get too seriously involved?'

'I'm waiting for the right moment. I want her to get to know the real me before her view is coloured by prejudice. It's happened too many times in the past, as you well know.'

'Only because you picked the wrong girls to go out with.'

'I picked girls I was attracted to. That's usually how dating works. Maybe you've forgotten, having been married, ooh, for ever so many years.'

She wagged a finger at him. 'Little bro, play dirty and I'll call the children in from the garden and set them on you.'

He laughed. 'Rather that than put up with you when you're in such a doggedly bossy frame of mind. No wonder Peter took that job so far away in Zambia; it was his only chance of getting any peace.'

'Don't think you can distract me with an attack on my character. You're lying to Chloe, aren't you?'

'I can honestly say I haven't once lied to her.'

'Hmmm ... you mean you've glossed over what makes you the person you are?'

There was no arguing with this uncomfortable truth and Seth was relieved when the kitchen door flew open with a dramatic crash and a human tornado burst in and wrapped itself around him. 'Uncle Seth, come and play! Come and play! We've built a den!' Willingly Seth let his clamouring ten-year-old and eight-year-old nieces drag him out to the garden.

'Nice flowers. Is it your birthday?'

Sally was beginning to wish she had taken Harry's wretched roses home with her last night. Murray Adamson was the fourth client of the day to refer to them. 'No,' she said flatly as he settled himself in the chair opposite her desk and she closed the door.

'An anniversary, then?'

She took her seat behind her desk. 'Just a gift.'

Murray Adamson ran a hand through his distinctive silvery grey hair. 'From a particularly grateful client?'

'Yes,' she said, deciding the lie would shut the man up. She wanted to get down to business.

'In that case, if you do a good job for me, I'll buy you roses *and* champagne. What the hell, I'll throw in chocolates as well!'

'Thank you, but my fee will be sufficient.' She opened the file in front of her, *Adamson v. Adamson*. 'I've had a letter from the other side requesting information about your offshore accounts.' She passed the letter across the desk to him. He didn't so much as glance at it.

'The other side can go whistle,' he said. 'Julia's not getting her grasping hands on those.'

'You know as well as I do, there's no point in withholding financial information, not when there's always a paper trail.'

He leaned back in his seat with a slow smile. 'I got away with stuff last time. Stuff even you didn't know about. I don't see why I can't do the same again.'

It's just a game to him, Sally thought. 'As your legal representative I must caution you to—'

'Caution me baloney! It's *my* hard-earned money and I'll safeguard it the way I see fit. Now then' – he lifted his briefcase up onto the desk, opened it and pulled out a buff A4 envelope – 'this is what I'm prepared to reveal to the other side. And before you waste your breath on any objections, that's my final word on the subject.'

'Very well,' Sally said. 'But you'd better be sure your bases are all covered.'

'Trust me, they are.'

An hour later and she was alone. But not for long.

'Is it safe to come in?' Harry was peering round the door. When she gave him the go-ahead, he came in carrying a large tray of the best office china – teapot, jug, cups and saucers and a plate of mini chocolate éclairs.

'What's all this?' she asked as he took the tray over to his desk.

'A peace offering,' he replied. 'I made a prat of myself yesterday and I want to make it up to you.'

She hesitated. She'd come into work this morning all set to do battle with him, only to find a note on her desk saying he wouldn't be in until later and could they talk? With the wind taken out of her sails, she'd put her carefully prepared lecture on hold. Was now the time to let him have it? Or should she give him a chance to redeem himself?

'How do you like your tea? With or without milk?'

'With,' she said, deciding on the latter course of action. 'Just a splash.'

'Sugar?'

'No thank you.'

He handed her the cup and saucer. 'There,' he said, 'a conversation without me annoying you. You see, it is possible.'

Warily she asked, 'Where have you been all day?'

'Hiding from you.'

'I don't believe you.'

He smiled. 'I had an on-site meeting with a client that went on. And on. It was stupendously tedious.'

'I guarantee it couldn't have been more tedious or vexing than my last client.' She took a sip of her tea. 'Earl Grey,' she said, surprised. 'My favourite.'

'I know,' he said, 'I asked Chandra. I also know you love chocolate éclairs.' He offered her the plate. 'Bite size, so no messy cream squirting all over you. Tell me about your vexatious client.'

'Oh, he's the usual kind of maggot wriggling on the end of a fishing line.'

'And presumably not the reason why you became a lawyer in the first place?'

She looked at him closely, realizing that somehow he'd thoroughly disarmed her. 'How old *are* you?' she asked him.

'Ah, we're back to that again, are we? I'd have thought you'd have nipped along to HR and checked out my details by now.'

'I haven't had time.'

'I'm thirty.'

'You look younger.'

'So I'm told. I'm hoping one day it will work to my advantage. For now it's a pain in the butt. I occasionally have trouble with people not taking me seriously.'

She suppressed a snort of derision. Surely he couldn't be so guileless? 'I'm not surprised if yesterday was anything to go by.'

He met her gaze. 'I meant what I said. You are beautiful and I really could look at you all day. I just went about saying it entirely the wrong way. From now on I shall do my best to behave myself. More tea?'

Heavens, whatever was she going to do with him?

Chapter Fifteen

The service had already started when Dan slipped into a pew at the back of the church. The assembled gathering was mid-hymn, and after checking the Order of Service, he found where they were in the proceedings. He didn't recognize anyone around him, but up at the front there were some familiar faces – Jeremy Williams, David Taylor, Hilary Parr, Howard Bailey, Huw Alsop, Diane Fallows, Sue Halloran, oh, and there was Andy Hope. In many ways they seemed not to have changed at all, but of course they had. Just as he had.

He'd very nearly opted out of coming, not because of the distance involved – it had taken him three hours to get to Taunton and then another three-quarters of an hour to locate the village of Odcombe where Derek had grown up – but because for the first time ever he'd experienced a loss of confidence. Stupidly, he'd been bothered how his fellow Durham alumni would react to him being a house-husband, a stay-at-home father. In the end, it was what had propelled him out of the house and into his car. No way would he allow himself to start feeling he was achieving less than anyone else.

During the drive down, he'd made up his mind to find out more about Tatiana Haines's proposition. When he'd stopped for petrol at Taunton, he'd phoned the number she'd given him and agreed to meet her again at the trust's offices in Crantsford; he'd stressed that he wasn't interested in a full-time job, not while Marcus was so young. She'd sounded pleased that he'd got in touch.

Rosie had already offered to have Marcus as often as was necessary, so childcare didn't look like it would pose too much of a problem, but he still needed convincing that it was something he wanted to get involved with. While Sally was clearly surprised that he was even considering the job, she had no problem with him pursuing it further. Was it his imagination, or had Sally agreed to him working again, even part-time, just a little too readily? Had she secretly been harbouring the thought that it was high time he pulled his finger out and got back to doing something worthwhile? Did a part-time job working for a charity consititute something worthwhile in her mind?

One of the things that Dan had liked about Sally when he first met her was her elusiveness. He had loved the challenge of always wondering what she really thought about something. A safe and predictable partner who shared with him her every waking thought would have bored him within weeks. Now though, he'd like a bit more openness from Sally. But was that only because he was feeling less sure about himself?

It was those bloody nightmares causing all the trouble. If only he could find a way to stop them permanently. Bizarrely, he'd got so used to the regular dreams that when he did get through a night without one, he woke with the oddest feeling, as if something was missing or was in the wrong place. Maybe his brain now had a level of expectation built into it, rather like Marcus when he'd gone through a phase of always waking up at exactly three in the morning wanting a drink of milk.

Thinking of Marcus made Dan feel suddenly anxious. Unbelievably, this was the first time since giving up work to look after his son full-time that he had left him for a whole day. He'd promised himself that he wouldn't worry; Marcus couldn't be in better hands. Chloe adored him and wouldn't let him come to harm. Still, a quick text to Chloe to put his mind at rest would only take a few seconds. He'd got as far as putting his hand in his suit jacket pocket for his mobile when he realized two things: a) he was in church and using a mobile was hardly the done thing, and b) up at the front, Andy Hope was climbing the steps of the pulpit. He belatedly switched his mobile onto silent mode and watched Andy adjust the microphone in front of him, then unfold a piece of paper, presumably his speech. A quick glance at the Order of Service revealed that there would be three speeches in all. Dan braced himself. What could any of them say to put a positive spin on a man who'd taken his own life?

Sally drew up outside the house. The pocket handkerchief-sized garden was home to knee-high grass, a knocked-over dustbin and a street's worth of litter. A net curtain at an upstairs window was rucked up and resembled a bride's dress caught in her knickers.

Reluctantly relinquishing the clean safety of her car, Sally went and rang the front door bell. Her brother opened the door and, looking over her shoulder, he sneered. 'Latest five series BMW, I see. Not stinting yourself, are you?'

'Good to see you, too, Terry,' she muttered, stepping inside and thinking he would never change. He would always be a prime example of an unreconstructed man from the dark ages. With the door shut behind her, the smell of a fifty-a-day habit hit Sally, as did years of accumulated filth and grime. She could barely make it along the narrow hallway for piles of old newspapers and carrier bags of what appeared to be rotting rubbish. The stench made her want to cover her mouth with her hand, run back to her car and drive all the way home to her beautiful, spotless house. She had once seen part of an episode of *How Clean is Your House?* and had had to switch channels; it was too painful a reminder of what she'd grown up with.

Kath Wilson was where she always was: sprawled on the sofa in front of the television. On the coffee table, a half-eaten custard tart looked as if it had been used as an auxiliary ashtray – there were two either side of it spilling over with stub ends and ash. The woman looked her usual, miserable, disgustingly corpulent self.

'You've come, then,' Kath said, tearing her eyes briefly away from the television screen where a glamorous woman with unfeasibly white teeth was handling a sapphire pendant necklace. It was truly ghastly and could be Kath Wilson's for sixty-nine pounds and fifty pence. 'Terry,' she said, 'fetch us a drink, will you? I'm parched.'

Terry, who had been standing behind her, didn't offer Sally a drink. Even if he had, she would have said she wasn't thirsty. She only ate and drank anything in this house if she had made it herself.

'How are you, Mum?' she asked, sitting in the least offensively stained of the two armchairs. 'What has the doctor actually said about your hip?'

The woman shifted her massive bulk and faced Sally. 'He said it's shot. I need it replacing. And it was a top specialist who told me that. A consultant.'

'Are you in a lot of pain?'

'Would it please you if I was?'

Yes! Sally wanted to shout back. I hate you for reminding me of the person I once was. 'Of course it wouldn't,' she lied. 'Exactly how long have you been told you'll have to wait before you can have the operation?'

'Too long. That's how bloody long. It's them cutbacks. It's all right for the likes of you going private, the rest of us have to get in line and wait. And what's worse, we have to watch them bloody immigrants get in the queue before us. Hull's awash with them. You can't move for Poles round here these days.'

'Migrant workers don't get preferential treatment, Mum.'

'All thieving scroungers, the lot of 'em.'

'No they're not.'

'How would you know? You don't live here. You should talk to Joan down the road. She had her purse nicked by a Pole last week.'

'How did she know the thief was Polish?'

'Stands to reason he was. They come here with nothing, to rob us blind.'

Sally sighed. There was no point in arguing with such entrenched ignorant and bigoted views. During a previous visit home her mother had ranted about the gay couple who'd moved in next door, going on about how the whole street would die in their beds contaminated with AIDS. She'd probably imagined it seeping through the brick-work.

The door opened and in walked Terry with three mugs. Sally silently groaned. Now she'd be expected to drink from a cup she hadn't personally washed. An unbidden image of drinking Earl Grey tea from a bone china teacup with Harry Fox popped into her head. She shuddered. What would Harry make of this cosy little scene? She took the mug of indeterminate liquid from Terry just as he slopped some of it onto the carpet. She had to fight the urge to fetch a cloth.

She also had to fight the rising sense of regret and futility in com-ing all this way. Why had she done it? Why didn't she just cut the tie and have done with it? Let it be the last time, she told herself firmly. The very last time. With that in mind, she reminded herself why she was here: to discover how badly her mother needed this operation, or if in fact she needed it at all. But how to rule out a possible scam, other than make her mother get off her fat backside and see how well she could move? Yet even that wasn't failsafe. Her mother could fake it. She could give an Oscar-winning performance of a woman in pain and Sally would be none the wiser. The only way to know the truth would be to accompany her mother to the doctor, or better still the specialist she had allegedly visited. If she was going to pay for her mother to have the operation done privately, it would be perfectly reasonable for Sally to insist on going with her for her next hospital appointment. Another few minutes and she'd suggest exactly that. For now, she needed to excuse herself.

There was only one toilet and it was upstairs. It made a Moroccan hole in the ground seem like the last word in luxury and she was in and out as fast as was humanly possible, drying her hands on the back of her jeans rather than risk the grubby hand towel. On the landing she paused outside her old bedroom; the grimy door was ajar. She pushed it fully open and went inside. It was in a worse state than when she'd last seen it. The faded wallpaper was hanging off in places and the curtain track was falling away from the wall. The bed was submerged beneath bin bags of God knew what and there was a rolled-up carpet leaning against the wardrobe. The white chipboard dressing table, which she had used as a desk for the many hours of study she'd put in, had two handles missing and the mirror was cracked.

She'd been sixteen when she'd decided to go to university and study law. Harry had been right the other day when he'd said that acting for men like Murray Adamson had not been the reason she'd chosen this particular career path. At that young age, law had seemed the ultimate way to prove herself.

It had been a teacher at school who'd changed the course of Sally's life, a teacher who had seen something in her that could be put to better use than it then was. For years, Sally had been getting away with murder – her wildness was legendary and skiving off school came as naturally to her as did stealing, joy-riding, drinking and having sex. She never once got caught; she was too smart for that. Unlike Terry. Running wild kept her enemy – boredom – at bay. That was the one thing she couldn't hack. There was nothing worse. But gradually boredom began to win out and she derived no pleasure in any of her usual pastimes. Even sex palled for her. She was fifteen years old and could see no point in anything. Nothing gave her a thrill any more. She might just as well be dead. Others would have turned to drugs in her situation, but the control freak in her wouldn't allow that. Alcohol she could handle, but drugs were an unknown she'd never wanted to try.

But then Mr Atlee showed up as a new member of staff at school. He was charismatic and dynamic and announced on his first day that he was here to kick arses into touch and anyone who had a problem with that would be first in line for a good kicking. His approach was borderline psychotic but he got results and something in Sally responded to him. She knew she wasn't stupid – it was all a matter of choice as far as she was concerned – but she'd always supposed it was the challenge Mr Atlee threw at her. 'You've got a brain, Sally Wilson,' he shouted at her one day, when yet again she hadn't bothered to do her homework, 'you're just too scared to use it for fear of losing your credibility and the approval of your peers.' So she set out to prove to him she could do both: use her brain and keep her credibility. Some weeks later, after a classroom debate about animal testing, he congratulated her on winning the argument for her team – they'd been pro – and he'd said she was dangerously analytical. The description appealed to her like nothing else had in a long time. He'd also said that he didn't for one minute see her ever making a career out of losing. 'You're not genetically programmed to come second,' he'd added.

That day was the turning point in her life. From then on she turned her back on what had gone before and in spite of her mother's disbelief and her brother's taunts, she devoted herself to a future she'd previously never dreamt of. By the time she made it to university, the process of her reinvention was well under way. Chloe became an important part of it and then, with her career rapidly taking off, Dan added the crucial finishing touch of refinement and class, and *voila*, she was entirely reborn. She was inordinately proud of what she'd achieved. She'd done it all herself. She was beholden to no one.

She closed the bedroom door after her and went back downstairs to her mother and Terry.

Chloe was having a brilliant day. Seth had phoned earlier to ask if she was free to take him on that walk in the Peaks that he'd missed out on and when she'd explained about having Marcus with her, she'd invited him to join them for lunch instead. 'What's on the menu?' he'd asked.

'It's a Marcus's choice; bangers and mash with baked beans,' she'd said.

'If there's enough for me, I'll be there in half an hour!'

She'd been surprised to see him arrive in a bright red, two-seater sports car. The rumble of its engine had both her and Marcus rushing to the window. She'd wondered how comfortable it was for him, being so tall. 'Style above content,' he'd said when she aired the thought. 'A man has to suffer for his style.' She'd remembered seeing it in the car park the night he'd kissed her, but she'd had no idea then that it was his. It looked expensive.

Now as she cleared away the lunch things, she watched Seth with Marcus. The pair of them created a bittersweet tableau of the happy family scenario she so badly wanted for herself: Seth was lying on the sofa with a bandage comically tied around his head and Marcus was listening intently to his heartbeat with a stethoscope. When Sally had dropped Marcus off that morning, she had brought with her a box of games and toys to keep him amused. Most of it lay untouched as Marcus always liked to play with the stash of toys Chloe kept here for him, including her old stethoscope from her training days, along with a selection of bandages. Willing herself not to think the obvious – that Seth would make the most fantastic father – Chloe could see that Marcus liked him a lot.

He wasn't the only one. Chloe's feelings for Seth were definitely growing, but she was determined not to lose her head and throw herself into a relationship too fast. There would be no cutting corners this time. It wasn't easy, though, not when he seemed to fit so perfectly into her life. How many men would want to spend the afternoon with a toddler they'd never met before? There was little doubt in Chloe's mind that the more time they spent together, the more compatible they appeared to be.

A knock at the back door had Marcus jumping off the sofa. 'Daddy!'

'Sorry, Marcus,' Chloe said, going to answer the door, 'I doubt very much that will be Daddy for you yet.'

She was right. It was her mother, wicker shopping basket in hand and nosiness radiating off her like steam. 'Hello! Only me! I was just passing.' Craning her neck round the archway to the sitting room, she added in a surprised voice that wasn't fooling Chloe, 'Oh, you've got company. Now I feel awful for barging in.'

Chloe smiled. 'The car on the drive wasn't a big enough clue?'

Jennifer feigned vagueness. 'A car? Is there one on the drive? Silly old me.'

'Start displaying too many dotty-old-lady traits and I'll have to take steps with you,' Chloe said quietly. 'But since you're here, come and meet my visitor. Be nice to him,' she warned. 'Or else.'

'I don't know what you mean, I'm sure.'

Seth was now on his feet. 'This is my mother, Seth. Mum, this is Seth. Drink, anyone?'

'Yes! Dinky juicy for me.'

'Right then, Marcus, you can come and help me. Seth, try not to let my mother embarrass you too much.'

'Now that's what I call a man worth coming home for,' Jennifer said when she was gathering up her basket, having eventually got the hint that it was time she was on her way. 'He'll do very nicely.'

Chloe shot an anxious glance back to the sitting room where Seth was engrossed in a major Duplo building project with Marcus. 'A little louder, Mum, I don't think he heard you.'

'Nonsense. I'm being the model of discretion. Seriously, though, he's gorgeous. Bring him for dinner some time soon. Now give my love to Dan and Sally, won't you? By the way, is everything all right with those two?'

'Yes, of course. It was just having Dan's parents around. You know how tense that makes them both. Say hi to Dad from me.'

'Will do.'

'And Mum?'

'Yes?'

'Thanks for liking Seth.'

'Hard not to.'

Despite beginning to show signs that he was overtired, Marcus had no intention of missing out on any fun by having an afternoon nap and so Chloe suggested that they have some quiet together on the sofa. 'I'll read to you,' she said.

'Mind if I join you?' Seth asked. 'I can never resist a good story.'

At which point Marcus took the book from Chloe and insisted that Seth read to him. 'That OK with you?' Seth said.

She nodded happily and lifted Marcus onto her lap. Seth proved an excellent reader – was there no end to his talents? – and he held Marcus spellbound with the range of amusing voices he adopted for the various characters. Before long, Marcus's eyelids were drooping, and then his body went limp and he fell asleep, his head resting heavily against Chloe's shoulder.

'You've done this before,' she whispered to Seth with a smile. She carefully laid Marcus on the sofa. 'Peace,' she said. 'Come on, let's leave him to his forty winks.'

They hadn't got as far as the kitchen when Chloe felt a hand round her waist. She turned and found herself neatly wrapped in Seth's arms. He gazed at her for a moment, then lowered his head and kissed her. 'I've wanted to do that ever since I got here.'

'You should have said.'

He kissed her again. When he looked up, his expression was serious. 'Chloe, there's something I want to tell you. Something important. You'll say I should have told you before, but I had my reasons, which I hope you'll understand.'

She smiled. 'That sounds ominous.'

He held her hands in his. 'The thing is—'

The sound of the telephone ringing made them both start. Chloe rushed to answer it before it woke Marcus. 'Hi, Dan,' she said, her voice low. 'No, everything's fine. We've had lunch and he's having a nap now. He's been no trouble at all. No, really. How was the service?'

She turned round to mouth that she'd only be a few minutes and was shocked to see Seth pulling on his jacket. He pointed to the back door.

'Hang on a minute, Dan,' she said, confused. She covered the receiver with a hand. 'You're not going, are you, Seth?'

'I better had. I'll give you a ring. Thanks for lunch. It was great. Don't worry, I'll let myself out.' He didn't look like he could get away fast enough.

But why? What had happened? One minute they were kissing and he was about to tell her something important and the next … From outside she heard the sound of his car door shutting and then the engine starting up.

What on earth had got into him? What had he been about to tell her? She swallowed. Oh, dear God, no. Not that. Oh, please not *that*.

But even as she tried not to think it, she knew that it was the obvious explanation. Seth had been about to admit that he'd been lying to her all this time. He was married, wasn't he? That was what he was about to confess. He probably had a wife and children of his own; that's why he was so good with Marcus.

So why was he running away? Had his conscience suddenly got the better of him? Was that it?

She thought of his lips on hers just moments ago. She dragged the back of her hand across her mouth. The lying cheat! Good riddance to him. She hoped she never set eyes on him again.

A voice coming from the forgotten receiver in her hand reminded her that Dan was at the other end of the line. 'Yes, Dan,' she said, 'I'm still here.'

Chapter Sixteen

It was Monday morning, Sally had long since left for work and Dan was intent on his customary SAS mission of depositing Marcus at nursery without being spotted by enemy forces.

He was losing his touch. With her twin boys already charging ahead to terrorize the rest of the children, Lardy McFierce had him in her sights. Pen and clipboard in hand, she advanced towards him. 'Daniel! Just the person I was looking for.'

'With you in a moment,' Dan said, tugging off Marcus's anorak and hanging it on the low-level peg for him. Free of his jacket, Marcus shot off to find Charlie. 'Right,' Dan said, sensing that Lardy McFierce was bristling with super-charged efficiency, 'what can I do for you?'

'I'm sure you're aware it's the village fete at the end of May and we've decided that seeing as the bottle tombola was such a success last year, we're going to do it again. As well as people to drum up the necessary bottles, I'm looking for volunteers to run the stall. If enough people pull their weight and put their names to the rota, there'll be no need for anyone to spend more than fifteen minutes running the stall.'

What the heck? 'No problem,' Dan said. 'I'll do a turn on the stall.' He hurried away to his car before she could rope him in for anything else. He believed one hundred per cent in supporting the village and any activities it laid on, but getting involved with petty officialdom as pedalled by the Lardy McFierces of this world was something he was keen to avoid at all costs. Yet he knew it was a sad truth that if it weren't for those bossy finger-in-every-pie types, very little would actually get done.

As he drove through the village, this thought prompted him to wonder what Tatiana's colleagues would be like. After emailing her a copy of his CV on Saturday evening, he was now visiting the trust's office to meet the rest of the team, as well as the chief executive. It would be an informal interview, Tatiana had said, nothing to worry about. There was no such thing as an informal interview, of course. Often the more informal it was dubbed as being, the trickier it could be. Choosing what to wear had presented him with a challenge – one of his old Paul Smith work suits would be too smart and he'd look like a cocky jackass who was trying too hard; too casual and they'd think he didn't care or wasn't taking them seriously. His CV would leave them in no doubt that he was more than qualified to take on the role of trusts and major donations manager, but if he wanted the job he'd have to convince them he would fit in. One of his concerns was that the rest of the team might be a bunch of bustling do-gooders in hand-woven twinsets. In which case, there wouldn't be a chance in hell of him fitting in.

Point of fact, he wasn't entirely sure where he did fit in nowadays. Derek's memorial service could not have flagged up more how out of step he was with everyone else now. When the service had finished and they'd gathered in the local pub for a drink and a bite to eat, the inevitable round of What Are You Doing Now? ensued. Jeremy and David – both married with young children – had said he was a better man than they were as ten minutes in the company of their own kids was enough to drive them mad. *Guffaw! Guffaw! Only joking!* Huw – a financial analyst for a big city bank with a house in Pimlico, unmarried and still wielding his strong Geordie accent as a badge of honour – had given Dan a look of pity and disgust and scooted off first chance he got to talk to someone else. Diane and Sue had oohed and aahed over him, saying they'd give anything to swap their workaholic husbands for him. No patronizing there, then. And Andy – divorced, no children and based in Hong Kong – had punched Dan matily on the shoulder and said, 'Lucky old you, a kept man! You always were a jammy sod.'

Not one of them had given the slightest indication that they thought he was doing something as worthwhile as they were. They might just as well have patted him on the head and said, 'There, there, it's just a phase.' How different it might have been had he told them that he'd recently been released from prison. It wouldn't have mattered what crime he'd committed; he would have been the centre of attention. They would have been shocked, but at the same time they would have been hanging on his every word. He would have been of interest, someone to gossip about over future dinner parties. Whereas merely being the father of a two-and-a-half-year-old boy, he was a nonentity. A nobody. Was this how all mothers who stayed at home to look after their children were made to feel?

The car in front of him was going as fast as a blind snail on crutches and after checking his mirror, Dan put his foot down and overtook it. Sally often remarked that the only time he ever displayed impatience was when he was behind the wheel of a car.

Sally had arrived home after her day in Hull in the usual black mood her mother induced in her. Home before Sally, he'd poured her a glass of wine, taken her upstairs and run her a bath. 'You need a period of decompression,' he'd said. 'Have you eaten?'

She'd shaken her head.

'Scrambled eggs on toast?'

'You're a saint.'

'I know.'

Remembering how drawn Sally had looked that night, Dan felt angry towards her mother and brother. He suspected that her visit meant that they had asked her for yet another handout. He'd never said anything, but he knew that over the years Sally had regularly given in to their requests. Was it wrong of him to wish she'd tell them where to go?

The Kyle Morgan Trust was housed in an attractive converted barn on the road to Crantsford. He'd passed it many times before but had never given it a moment's thought. There was a turning circle at the front of the horseshoe-shaped building and a sign with four other businesses listed and an arrow directing him to a car park at the rear.

He'd been waiting in the small reception area for no more than two minutes when Tatiana appeared. She was dressed a little more formally than when he'd met her at Rosie's, but she still wore her hair in two long plaits and there was that same effervescent joyful air about her as she shook his hand warmly and led him through a pair of double doors. 'Everyone's so looking forward to meeting you. I think you can safely assume that it's a foregone conclusion that we want you on board with us. All we're worried about is that with your expertise and experience you'll think us very small potatoes. How's Marcus?' Whatever it was that made her fizz so abundantly, Dan could feel her enthusiasm rubbing off on him. I want this job, he suddenly decided.

Her patient off the examining couch now and sitting next to her mother, Chloe said, 'Exactly how long have you been feeling tired and nauseous, Chelsea?'

'She started complaining about a fortnight ago.'

'Mrs Savage, please, I need your daughter to answer my questions. Chelsea?'

Chelsea gave Chloe a shifty glance. 'Like Mum said, about two weeks ago.'

'Is there a specific time in the day when you feel particularly nauseous or tired?'

The girl wriggled under Chloe's direct gaze. 'Sort of,' she mumbled.

'I'm afraid my next question is going to be rather blunt and personal. Before I ask it, would you prefer your mother stayed or left us alone?'

'Hey? What the hell's going on?' Mrs Savage was almost out of her seat. 'I'm not going anywhere. Chelsea's my daughter. What you say to her, you say to me. End of!'

'Chelsea?' Chloe persisted, cringing at Mrs Savage's trash telly talk. 'Are you happy with that?'

'Of course she is! Now get on and tell us what's wrong with her. It's probably some bug. Whatever it is, we need it dealt with. We don't want anything to hold up her getting her boob job done. She's booked for next week.'

Ah, yes, the boob job that somehow Mrs Savage had found the money for in the face of the NHS telling her to come back when her daughter was older. 'Are your breasts particularly tender right now, Chelsea?'

Chelsea nodded.

'In that case, I have to ask you, are you sexually active?'

'Sexually active?' spluttered Mrs Savage. 'Course she isn't. What do you take her for? One of those cheap girls who fool around?'

'Chelsea, can you answer my question, please?'

'What if I was?' Her reply was hardly more than a whisper.

'You're displaying many of the classic symptoms of early pregnancy. When was your last period?'

'Pregnant! But she can't be! No way. She's got more sense than that. She's going to be a model.'

A tense silence fell on the room. Chelsea's face collapsed and she started to cry.

Mrs Savage looked like she could thump something or someone very hard. 'She can't keep it,' she said grimly. 'It'll have to be sorted. And soon.' Her eyes were narrowed and her mouth was set firm.

Ignoring her, Chloe reached for the box of tissues on her desk and came round to where Chelsea was sitting. She knelt beside the distraught girl, plucked a handful of tissues out of the box and gave them to her. 'You don't need to make any decision right away,' she said. 'It's important that you make a reasoned and informed choice. There's more than one option available to you and I can put you in touch with people who can help you. Meanwhile, I want you to do a urine test for me so that we can confirm the pregnancy.'

Chelsea raised her head. 'You mean ... you mean I might not be pregnant?' The hope in her voice was pitiful.

'We need to make sure, either way. When that's been done, you can start the process of deciding what to do.'

'The decision's made,' Mrs Savage said flatly, getting to her feet. 'Chelsea, come on, you stupid little bitch, we're going home. You and I need a talk. First off you can tell me who the bloody hell the father is.' She pointed a finger at Chloe. 'And you, you keep your mouth shut. If this gets out in the village, I'll know whose big gob spread it about. Got it?'

'I assure you, Mrs Savage, everything discussed in this room is considered private and confidential.'

'Yeah, well, it better had be.'

Snivelling noisily, the girl allowed herself to be led away by her bully of a mother. Chloe closed the door after them and went and sat behind her desk. Tired, she closed her eyes, recalling as if it were yesterday the symptoms she'd experienced with her own brief pregnancy. She hadn't had any nausea, but she'd been bone-weary and tearful. Even with a missed period, she'd put the change in her down to post-traumatic stress disorder. As with so many doctors when self-diagnosing, she had been woefully blind to what was really going on with her own body.

She opened her eyes and rubbed them. Thank goodness Chelsea had been her last patient of the day. And what a day it had been. Ron Tuttle had been admitted to hospital that morning with dehydration as a result of a urinary infection, a hysterical mother had brought her son in with a crayon stuck up his nose, the window cleaner had fallen off his ladder and broken his leg, and during her lunch break her father had called to say that Margaret Parr had died.

Years ago Margaret had lived in the village and she'd regularly babysat Chloe and Nick when they'd been little. With no children of her own, she had spoiled them at every opportunity and they always looked forward to her coming to the house. The funeral was to be held on Friday at St Michael's in Crantsford, where Margaret had moved five years ago. There was no question of Chloe not going. She had already arranged for cover for her patients.

She sighed, wishing she could go home. Unfortunately she had a practice meeting to get through yet. She turned to her computer, scrolled down through Chelsea's medical history and added today's notes. While she was convinced the girl was pregnant, she was less certain what the outcome would be. It wasn't too big a step to imagine Chelsea wanting to have the baby and keep it. It would be someone to love. Someone to love her back. But for Chelsea to keep the baby, she would have to stand up to her mother in a way she probably never had before. Of course, in the long term, going against her mother's wishes would be the easy part. The difficult part would be trying to cope with being a parent.

Chloe closed Chelsea's notes on the computer screen and experienced the by now familiar ache of envy. Perhaps she should just go out and have unprotected sex with the first available man and wind up pregnant. Would it be so bad? The stigma of being an unmarried mother was minimal these days. Oh, yes, there was the initial flare of gossip, but these things always settled down in the end.

Yet as much as Chloe craved a child, she also wanted the whole deal. She wanted the 'Honey, I'm home!' dream to come true for her. Since Saturday afternoon, she had ruled out that dream of ever getting off the starting blocks with Seth. She'd been stupid to hope for anything permanent from him. She cringed at the thought of how gullible she had been, how very quick to turn him into something he clearly wasn't.

If she'd needed any confirmation that he'd been lying to her, he'd given it by not getting in touch since Saturday. For all she knew his name might not even be Seth Hawthorne. Perhaps he was a con artist with a smooth line in befriending vulnerable single women and exploiting them. Where better to do that than at a gym? Wasn't it supposed to be one of the best places for meeting a member of the opposite sex, where all the single saddos hung out?

Annoyed that she'd just labelled herself as vulnerable and a saddo, Chloe pulled herself together. Get a grip, girl! Onwards and upwards.

Two days after her visit to Hull, Sally was still trying to get her mother out of her system. She was driving home from work and each time she thought of Saturday she had to ease her foot off the accelerator. Getting done for speeding would really be the final straw. Would she never learn to disregard anything that came out of Kath Wilson's poisonous mouth?

She had just suggested that she speak to Mum's doctor when Terry had waded in with an attack. 'Why do you want to do that?' he'd demanded. 'Why can't you give us the money? I mean, it's no skin off your nose, is it?'

Patiently, she'd tried to explain that to pay for her mother to have the operation privately would cost a small fortune in one lump sum.

'You're saying Mum's not worth it? You'd rather see her in agony?'

'That's not what I'm saying at all. If you'd listen to me, Terry, I'm offering to pay for a policy that would cover all the medical bills, and any future treatment Mum might need.'

'But that'll take for ever to organize,' their mother chipped in. 'I want it now.' She then gave Sally one of her famously vicious looks. 'I always did say you had a heart of stone. Now I know I was right.'

'How can you say that when I'm offering to help you?'

'Oh, don't give me one of your, Who me? faces. You've got no intention of helping me, have you? So why don't you just push off out of here. Go back to that useless wimp of a husband of yours. You're not welcome here.'

Sally had leapt to her feet at that. 'Dan is not a useless wimp of a husband!'

'Oh, no? Does he stand up to you? Or do you walk all over him? Got him right under your thumb, I'll bet.'

'I think you're confusing Dan with the man you were married to.'

'Just goes to show that it must be in the genes, then. I landed myself with a useless loser, and you've done the same. Yeah, I thought that would wipe the look of superiority off your smug face.'

Sally had grabbed her bag then. 'We've clearly said all we're ever going to say to one another. Please don't bother to get in touch with me again. You'll get no more money from me.'

She was out on the street and opening her car door with a trembling hand when a voice called out, 'Coo-ee. I thought it was you. Not often we get a fancy car like this parked round here. Just home for a visit, are you?'

It was her mother's neighbour, Joan – the victim of the alleged Polish mugging. She was clutching a selection of holiday brochures.

Battling with the lump of anger in her throat, Sally managed to say, 'Going somewhere nice?'

'I hope so. Your mum and I are planning a little holiday. We're thinking of going to Furta … Oh, the name's gone. Must be my age. Furtasomething or other. Your mum's dead excited about it. Terry and Janice are coming with us.'

'Fuerteventura?'

'Yes! That's it. Clever you.'

Yes, clever me, thought Sally bleakly as once again she realized her speed had crept up. Clever me for having such a delightful mother. The kind of mother who'd make out she was in dire need of an operation so she could con money out of her daughter. Well, those days were gone. The Bank of Sally Oliver was officially closed.

As furious as she was for her mother's deception, what had angered and upset Sally most was the way the hideous woman had spoken about Dan. How dare the bitch compare Dan to her father! A man who'd buggered off to Spain with some slapper when Sally was ten years old. A man who never bothered to get in touch with his family again, other than to send them a postcard saying he wanted to remarry and was instigating divorce proceedings. 'Coward!' Sally's mother had thundered, ripping the postcard into a shower of brightly coloured squares of blue sky and white sand. 'He hasn't even got the guts to come and tell me to my face that he wants a divorce.'

In the beginning Sally had been tempted to tell people at school that her father had died rather than admit that he had left them. But then her anger kicked in and she blamed her mother. If she hadn't been such a lazy, complaining, bitter old bag he wouldn't have gone.

Just as she'd been ashamed to tell her friends at school the truth about her father, Sally couldn't bring herself to confide in Dan about the way her mother had described him or the scam she and Terry had tried to pull. Admitting that Mum and Terry despised her to that extent was just too humiliating.

She loosened her clenched grip on the steering wheel and reminded herself that the one positive thing to come out of her visit was that she would never have to make that journey again. She'd been a fool all these years, paying them off to keep them tidily out of her life. Pretending they didn't exist would have been a far better option. It was what she was going to do from now on.

Chapter Seventeen

Chloe often came across death in her line of work, but she'd attended very few funerals – only those of her grandparents – and as she entered the church of St Michael and All Angels with her mother and father, she thought of the memorial service Dan had gone down to in Somerset last Saturday. Was it a sign of their advancing years that their attendance at such occasions was starting to catch up with the number of wedding invitations they received?

The church was almost full and an elderly couple had to shuffle along the pew to make room for Chloe and her parents. With sombre organ music playing in the background, people were chatting quietly amongst themselves. Her parents had struck up conversation with the couple on their left and were discussing, of all things, bindweed. With nothing else to do, Chloe picked up a Bible and flicked through it. It reminded her of when she and Nick used to be dragged along to church by her mother and they would read the smutty bits from the Song of Songs, all that *browsing among the lilies ... your two breasts are like two fawns ... My lover thrust his hand through the latch-opening* would have them sniggering so hard their eyes would water.

Their father never accompanied them to church and when they were of a suitably rebellious age, Chloe and her brother claimed that if their father was allowed to stay at home tinkering in his workshop, they should be allowed to do the same. It was getting up early on a Sunday morning that Nick bucked against; for Chloe it was the total tedium of the exercise that rankled. She could think of so many other things she would rather be doing, like swimming, horseriding, gymnastics, tennis, hockey, even doing her homework. Anything but sit through a mind-numbingly boring sermon. The Sunday School sessions had been worse, though. All that cutting and pasting and acting out biblical scenes. The only time she could remember enjoying it was when she got to play the part of a lion and bit Daniel on the bum. She wasn't supposed to, of course, but

Martin Jones who was playing the part of Daniel could be such a pain. He didn't speak to her for weeks afterwards.

For a brief moment the organ player paused, alerting everyone to stop talking, and then took up with a louder more strident piece of music. Chloe closed the Bible and placed it on the narrow shelf in front of her. Time to get down to business. She then felt guilty because she should have been thinking of Margaret. If nothing else, that was what funerals were for. To remember that person fondly and celebrate the life they'd led. Passing her now were the pallbearers with Margaret's coffin on their shoulders. A great sadness swept over her. Margaret had been such a part of her childhood. She had spent numerous Christmases with them at Laurel House, Chloe's parents refusing to allow her to spend the time alone. One year she had got quite tiddly on Dad's special egg nog; Nick had teased her horribly about it afterwards. It was a shame Nick couldn't be here today, but he was stuck in Boston on business. He'd promised to send flowers.

The coffin had been set down now and the pallbearers had found their places in the pews. The minister stepped forward and announced the first hymn.

Chloe reached for her hymn book, but then did a double take. Her senses reeled. *No!* It couldn't be! Surely not? She stared hard, incredulous. If it wasn't him, then he had a twin brother. An identical twin brother. Next to her, her mother whispered, 'Isn't that your handsome young man? You never told me he was a vicar.' She snickered. 'I hope you haven't been leading a man of the cloth astray.'

Chapter Eighteen

As he de-robed in the vestry, Seth could scarcely believe he'd managed to conduct the service without making a comprehensive cock-up of it.

He'd had many a distraction to deal with in his time – a bunch of Christmas revellers heckling him from the back row, a pregnant woman fainting, and any amount of bored children running amok – but this had thoroughly tested his mettle. Avoiding Chloe's eye hadn't been the problem as such – she was looking anywhere but in his direction – it was knowing that there was going to be some hefty fallout to follow. His sister had warned him that something like this was bound to happen, but stupidly he'd refused to listen. He really had only himself to blame. But thank goodness he'd known Margaret Parr, if only for a short while, and had been able to focus his thoughts on her. Had it been a funeral service for someone he'd never met before he may not have been able to apply himself so well. As it was, Margaret had been not just a regular attendee of St Michael's but a stalwart of its everyday running – the fastest polisher in the country, she used to joke about herself. Owen had originally been pencilled in to take the service, but he'd called Seth late last night to say he'd come down with a particularly virulent stomach bug and would Seth mind stepping in. If he had known how today was going to pan out Seth might have feigned a stomach bug himself.

He hung his robe and stole on the hook on the back of the vestry door and wondered what Chloe's connection had been to Margaret. Possibly a close and long-standing one if Jennifer Hennessey's presence was anything to go by. Presumably that had been Chloe's father in the pew alongside them. Whilst Chloe had avoided any eye contact with him, her mother had made no such effort. Jennifer Hennessey had clocked him the exact same moment as her daughter had and when he'd seen her whispering in Chloe's ear, it was clear that he was the subject of the exchange. Clearly amused, Jennifer had smiled at him several times during the service.

There had been a worrying moment during the burial in the churchyard – 'We therefore commit Margaret's body to the ground: earth to earth; ashes to ashes; dust to dust; in sure and certain hope of the resurrection to eternal life' – when he'd caught Chloe's eye and had feared she would make a lunge for him and shove him head first into the hole. He'd had to work hard not to break out with a burst of near-hysterical laughter. Twice he'd had to pause and compose himself. He hoped the mourners, most of them regulars of St Michael's, assumed he was suddenly overcome.

When it was over, and while everyone was indulging in the ritual of inspecting the flowers, he'd shot back inside the church. Several large swigs of communion wine might have helped to steady his nerves, but the thought of anyone catching a whiff of it on his breath knocked that idea on the head.

With his jacket on now, completing his clerical black suit, he checked his appearance in the mirror – hair OK, white collar straight, expression calm – he opened the door and went in search of forgiveness.

He found Chloe sitting on a bench in the dappled shade of the chestnut tree. When she heard his footsteps on the gravel and turned towards him, she didn't give the impression of having murder on her mind. She did look annoyed, though.

'May I?' he said.

She moved to one end of the wooden bench to accommodate him. 'Am I supposed to say something like, "That was a very nice service, vicar?"'

'You could if you wanted. Except, strictly speaking, I'm not a vicar.'

Her face flickered with scorn. 'What? You're an impostor? You dress up in black frocks and bury people for kicks?'

He smiled. 'I'm an assistant vicar, still in my curacy.'

'Oh. Well, it amounts to the same thing. Why didn't you just tell me what you did for a living? Why the pretence?'

'Would you have gone out with me if I had told you at the outset? And be honest.'

She looked at him with contempt. 'That's rich coming from you.'

He took a deep breath. 'I never lied to you, Chloe. That wouldn't be compatible with what I believe in.'

'But you weren't entirely straight with me.'

'With good reason. I knew that you'd treat me differently, that you wouldn't regard me as normal. I'd suddenly become this untouchable, unapproachable being. It's what you're doing to me right now. And I know what I'm talking about; it's happened to me before.'

'You mean you've conned girls like me before?'

'Absolutely not. But the minute they know I'm a minister, they're off faster than you can say *amen*. So hand on heart, now that you know, does it change things?' He watched her face intently, could see her choosing her words with care. Her foot was jiggling.

'Why did you leave so suddenly last Saturday and then not ring me during the week?'

Noting that she hadn't answered his question, he said, 'I was about to tell you the truth that afternoon and then I bottled it. I wanted to get in touch afterwards but I knew that if I did, I'd have to come clean with you and then that would be the last I'd see of you. I was sunk either way I turned. You don't need to tell me that I screwed up in a major way, and with only myself to blame. I'm sorry.'

She kicked at the gravel beneath their feet. 'I'd decided you were either married or a con artist.'

'Is being an ordained minister as bad, or worse in your eyes?'

'I don't know. It's weird. I mean ... well, you know, we kissed and—'

'I'm not a monk, Chloe,' he interrupted her gently. 'And I certainly haven't taken a vow of celibacy.'

Across the churchyard, Seth could see that the mourners had decided it was time to move on; groups of them were drifting away. 'There's a sandwich and drinks affair on at the church hall,' he said. 'Are you going?'

'My parents and I had planned to.'

'But now you're not so sure?'

'Are you going?'

'I'm invited, but if it would make it easier for you, I'll keep my presence to a minimum. How did you know Margaret?'

'She was an old friend of the family. She used to babysit my brother and me.'

'Aha! There you are!'

They both looked up to see Chloe's mother advancing towards them. As one, they rose from the bench.

'Lovely service, Reverend,' Jennifer said, holding out her hand. 'I must say, you'd increase the number of bums on pews at our church no end if you were our vicar. I expect you have more than your fair share of congregational groupies here, don't you? That's the price you pay for being such a dashing vicar.'

'Mum!'

'Good to see you again, Mrs Hennessey. How are you?'

'Please, call me Jennifer. Are you coming for the bun-fight? Chloe, what's that look for?'

Chloe felt like a sulky teenager at a boring grown-ups' party. She probably was the youngest present but that wasn't the reason she felt so prickly and on edge.

She only had to watch Seth for a few minutes to realize that her mother had been right about the groupies. Dressed in his black suit and with his dark, curly hair, he looked impossibly glamorous in this setting. She'd never seen him in a suit before and she had to admit, it did nothing to detract from his physical attributes. If anything, it added to them, made him appear taller and more powerful. And it was clear the good women of St Michael's loved him. They buzzed around him like bees round a honey pot. If his plate showed any sign of emptying, an eager-faced woman materialized at his side with another offering of dainty sandwiches. They clucked and fussed as though he wasn't capable of tying his own shoelaces. Chloe pitied the poor girl who ended up marrying him; she would be the most hated girl in Christendom.

An ordained minister. Oh God, she'd kissed a Church of England priest! Well, actually, she'd *snogged* a Church of England priest. Worse still, she'd entertained the occasional fantasy of making love with him. It was what you did when you started going out with someone. And they had been 'going out' together. It hadn't just been friendship. It had been a tentative relationship leading somewhere. Admittedly, she hadn't been sure just where they'd been heading, but you couldn't get involved with someone and not think about the 'next step'. Otherwise, what was the point? So, yes, she had fleetingly wondered what it might be like to be completely intimate with him. Only now to discover that she hadn't known the first thing about him. And while she was on the subject, what kind of a clergyman picked up girls in gyms, took them out, kissed them and deliberately led them up the garden path? No wonder the Church of England was in such a mess!

'All right, Chloe?'

It was her father.

'Me? Oh, I'm fine.'

'Your mother mentioned something about you and the curate chap being friends. He seems nice. Was he the one you were meeting for lunch that day I telephoned? Or have I got that wrong?'

'No Dad, it's me who got it wrong.'

Chapter Nineteen

The days stretched out longer and longer. The air was full of the sweet smell of freshly mown grass; roses scrambled over cottage walls; lilac trees drooped with exquisitely scented flowers and at Corner Cottage, Dan, with Marcus's help, was loading bottles into a wheelbarrow – Tabasco sauce, gin, peri-peri marinade, walnut oil, ketchup, cider, Tango, Grouse, Taylor's Port, Stone's ginger wine, Radox bubble bath, cheap sparkling wine and hair shampoo, the sort that brought a woman to a lathering climax if the advert on the television was to be believed.

It was the end of May and Eastbury was preparing for the May Bank Holiday fete. It was all hands to the pump, as Lardy McFierce kept saying. She'd got herself in a real headless chicken state yesterday when her tombola stall rota fell apart – Tracey Carter called to say her mother had been taken ill and she wouldn't be able to make the fete. In an attempt to re-jig the rota, Lardy McFierce had then rubbed Linda Hughes and Catherine Miller up the wrong way by bossily insisting they change their shifts to cover for Tracey, resulting in a walk-out. Dan had taken pity on the woman and her clumsy attempts to get the job done and had offered to run the stall himself, single-handedly, for the whole afternoon if necessary. It was no big deal, no real sacrifice.

Compare an afternoon's commitment to a village fete to the sacrifices he'd seen in the last month since he'd started working for the Kyle Morgan Trust, and it didn't register. As part of getting an in-depth understanding of the job, he'd now met a number of the families the trust assisted. As harrowing as the lives were that these people were living, their unfailing love and dedication to their children – who were unlikely to live beyond the age of eighteen – was awe-inspiring. Dan had asked Tatiana where they got the strength from to be so positive and upbeat and she said that for the parents it was simply a way of life that they got on with as best they could.

Most of the children had been born with a degenerative disease of some sort and required constant care. This meant the parents were physically and mentally drained, and with other children in the family to look after, it was a wonder to Dan they could face each day. The most important part of the trust's work was letting these parents know that they were no longer alone in coping with the demands of caring for a child twenty-four hours a day. One of the things that had struck Dan was that while understandably the focus was on the parents and the sick child, maybe more could be done for the siblings of these families. He had kept his counsel on the matter, not wanting to appear as though he were telling anyone their job, especially as what he was being paid to do was to manage the financial side of things. Any worries he'd had about working with a bunch of intense worthies had been dispelled the day he'd gone to meet everyone. He'd been impressed by their enthusiastic drive and sheer hard work. It was a predominantly female workforce and most of them were in their late twenties or early thirties and, like Tatiana, unmarried. When Dan had commented on this, Tatiana had laughed and said no husband would put up with the long hours she and the others worked. He had been about to dispute this when he'd remembered his own feelings of resentment over Sally working the hours she did.

With Marcus at his side, and pushing the heavy wheelbarrow of rattling cargo along the road in the direction of the village green, Dan had to agree that there was some truth in what Andy Hope had said when he'd called him a jammy sod. If it wasn't for Sally's ambition and hard work, he would not be able to take on a satisfying, worthwhile but relatively poorly paid job for the trust as well as spend time with Marcus. So far he'd been able to do a fair amount of the work from home and he hoped this would continue. The times he had to be at the office, Rosie had Marcus. It was a perfect arrangement and the whole thing hung together so neatly, it was as if it was meant to be. He'd never been an advocate of predestination, but he couldn't help but wonder about the concept now. Certainly, had he and Sally not got caught up in the Boxing Day tsunami, they wouldn't have the life they now had, for the simple fact that they wouldn't have Marcus. Prior to Marcus's conception, Sally had never concealed her conviction that she wasn't the maternal type. It had been a joke between them initially, but then as time went by it became a more serious issue and when unexpectedly Dan began to warm to the idea of fatherhood, he knew he had to tread warily. He surreptitiously waited for Sally's body clock to kick in, but it showed no sign of doing so. Ironically, it took a massive disaster to get Sally to change course. Dan could truthfully say that the day Marcus was born was the happiest day of his life.

If he was equally truthful, he'd have to admit that he'd just emerged from what, with the benefit of hindsight, he'd call a low point in his life. It had been triggered, he now believed, by Marcus being the same age as the boy he'd failed to save. But since he'd started work at the trust, the nightmares had stopped; it was as if a great weight had been lifted off his shoulders. He just wished he and Sally spent more time together. But what married couple didn't say that? Having made the mistake of criticizing her for putting work first, he now found himself biting his tongue on a regular basis. He was growing increasingly perturbed by just how little time Sally seemed to want to spend with him and Marcus.

From Chloe's kitchen window, Sally observed her husband setting up the tombola stall on the green immediately opposite. He was wearing a pair of blue knee-length shorts, a cream polo shirt, his favourite old brown leather deck shoes and a Panama hat. He looked so at home here in the village. More so than Sally did. It had been her dream to live somewhere like this, but now, if she were honest, she wasn't so sure it was right for her.

'Can you chop these mushrooms for me, Sally?'

Chloe's request had Sally turning from the window. 'When are your parents joining us?' she asked, taking a knife from the drawer.

'Any minute, I hope. As usual Dad's made the tomato sauce and pizza bases and without any of that we can't put the pizzas together.'

Running a take-away pizza stall from the kitchen window of Chloe's cottage had gone down so well two years ago, it was now an expected feature of the fete. It was also the biggest money-earner.

'Dan's really enjoying his new job, isn't he?' Chloe said, looking up from the chopping board where she was slicing peppers. 'I've never seen him so animated about work before.'

'Yes, I'm really pleased for him.' Sally tried to sound as if she meant it, that she shared her husband's happiness and everyone else's opinion about his new job. In short, they thought he was wonderful, a real hero of a man for giving his time to such a worthy cause when, with his qualifications and experience, he could walk into any high-flying job he wanted.

It wasn't the first time Dan had been awarded this status. When he'd risked his life in the tsunami to save that little girl and her brother, he'd been hailed a hero by everyone there. Back at home, here in the village and in the local newspaper, his efforts had also been applauded. His work colleagues had been full of praise and his firm, as did her own, made a not inconsiderable donation towards the fund that was growing at an unprecedented rate nationally. *BBC Look North West* had wanted to do a feature on him, but Dan had declined. They had both been relieved when the hoo-ha eventually died down and people stopped asking them about their experiences. Sally had hated talking about it, and even now she felt edgy if the subject came up. She'd deliberately never watched any of the subsequent programmes on the television. Dan was the same. Rarely did they talk about what they had gone through. Sometimes she felt as if it had never really happened to her, that she had acquired her experience of the disaster vicariously through the lens of a camera. If it weren't for one particular fear that the ordeal had left her with, she could very nearly convince herself that this was the case. Better that than relive the terrifying moment when the water had engulfed the room and she'd been sure she was going to drown.

When the first anniversary of the disaster had begun to loom and survivors around the world were planning an emotional return, she had felt guilty that she had undergone no such pull. She had felt marginally better when Dan had admitted that he had no desire to return to Phuket either, that he would find it too harrowing. To mark the occasion in a more personal and low-key way, Chloe invited them for Boxing Day brunch – they had Marcus by then – and they planted a commemorative holly bush in her garden. It was around that time, with everyone reminded of the catastrophe, that people started raking it over again. How does it feel a year on? they kept asking Sally and Dan. Sally had begun to wonder if they would for ever be defined as being tsunami survivors. Or more precisely, in her case, defined as the wife of a tsunami hero.

And here they were once more, she thought as she heard the sound of Chloe's parents arriving. Dan was being hailed a hero because he was doing something so worthwhile. Was it wrong of her to feel rankled by this? Wasn't it worthwhile what she was doing? Wasn't it a good cause that she was working for, keeping a roof over her family's head and food on the table? Did that count for nothing? Yet with whom could she possibly voice such a disloyal opinion and not be condemned for it?

*

For two solid hours, the queue for pizzas at one pound fifty a slice didn't let up. Now, though, trade had dwindled and Chloe, her parents and Sally were able to take stock. The kitchen looked as though it had been trashed during the course of a food fight, and they themselves looked like they'd been thoroughly roughed up. 'It must be about time to reward ourselves with a glass of wine,' Chloe said as she opened the oven door for the last of the pizzas.

'Already ahead of you,' her mother said, taking a bottle of white wine from the fridge.

Chloe put the pizzas on wooden mats on the table, where Sally was counting the money they'd made so far.

'How have we done, Sally?' Chloe's father asked, loading the dishwasher with as much precision as if it were a NASA rocket being prepared for launch.

'At this point, we're forty-five pounds up on last year.'

'I think we can safely call that a result,' Chloe said, flinging aside her oven gloves. She took a welcome glass of wine from her mother. 'Well done, team!'

Thirty minutes later, with the kitchen beginning to resemble its former self, Chloe's parents offered to go and mingle with the crowds on the green to sell the remaining slices of pizza. That left Chloe and Sally with nothing to do other than take two chairs outside to soak up the warm afternoon sun. With their glasses refilled, they sank back with a contented sigh. A fairground organ was playing and over the crackling address system, Dave Peach was announcing that following the Best Mongrel in Show competition, they could look forward to the arrival of the newly crowned May Queen, Chelsea Savage's reign having come to an end. Any plans Chelsea might have had for becoming a model were currently on hold. Very much against her mother's wishes, she was going ahead with having the baby.

Over at the bottle tombola Chloe could see Dan talking to Rosie; Marcus and Charlie were close by, playing happily with a couple of sausage-shaped balloons. She was about to switch her glance to locate her parents in the crowds, when she noticed a girl walking towards Dan and Rosie. She was wearing a striking red-flowered, halter-neck dress cinched in at the waist with a matching belt and her hair was long and dark and cascaded prettily down her back in a mass of ringlets. She had an arresting look about her. Chloe didn't recognize her from the village but whoever she was, she seemed to know both Dan and Rosie, judging from the way they greeted her. Perhaps she was someone from the Kyle Morgan Trust. Chloe had heard of the trust through the practice, but she had never had to refer a family to it.

Chloe sipped her wine, and taking her cue from Sally, she too tilted her head back and closed here eyes. Quite apart from preparing for the fete, it had been a busy week. She had been called out in the early hours for two nights running and she was looking forward to tonight, when she wouldn't be on call and could sleep uninterrupted.

'Still not heard anything from your sexy Rev?' Sally asked.

'Nope,' Chloe replied. 'Not a peep.' Since Margaret's funeral nearly five weeks before she had neither seen Seth nor heard from him. To her shame she had stopped going to the gym so that she wouldn't have to face him there. 'And I wish you wouldn't refer to him as my sexy Rev,' she said. 'Especially as you never even laid eyes on him.'

Sally laughed. 'I'm going by your mother's description. She said he was a particularly fine specimen of manhood. I also recall you being rather impressed by him.'

'I'm never going to live it down, am I?' Chloe said crossly.

'What, that you fancied a Church of England priest? I think it's hysterically funny. Just think; you could have ended up a vicar's wife!'

'All right, Sally, no need to make my disastrous love life sound any worse than it already is.'

'But honestly, you, a vicar's wife! Hey, do you remember that list we compiled at university, the list we swore we'd live by?'

'I knew you'd trot that out sooner or later.'

Sally laughed. 'Well, at least one of us has stuck by it.'

Chloe recalled the list with unease. Back then, when they'd been students, it had seemed clever of them to be so discriminatory, but now it was an unwanted reminder of when she'd first had lunch with Seth and she'd wondered if he'd been testing her for any hidden prejudices. The list had been a rule book of men they would never date. Car salesmen were out, as were financial advisers, politicians and journalists, all on the basis that they told lies for a living. But top of the list, because they pedalled the biggest lies of all, were pompous, sanctimonious, sexless, po-faced clergymen.

Opening her eyes, Chloe took a long sip of her wine. Whatever else she thought about Seth, she couldn't accuse him of being sexless or po-faced. There hadn't been anything pompous or sanctimonious about him either. As for lying, that was debatable. He'd misled her, that much she did know, which according to Sally was as good as a lie. But for all that, she occasionally caught herself thinking fondly about him. She missed his cheerfulness and kind demeanour, but most of all, she missed the way he'd made her feel. He'd brought a ray of sunshine into her life. Or was it simply that he'd given her hope – hope that maybe she had found the man of her dreams? Wasn't that what any relationship did?

None of this would she admit to Sally. As she'd said just moments ago, Sally thought the whole thing hysterically funny. And that annoyed Chloe. It irked her that her friend was deriving so much pleasure from something that had mattered to her. It seemed unnecessarily cruel. Cruel to Chloe and cruel to Seth who wasn't here to defend himself.

Surprised that she could suddenly feel sorry for him, Chloe thought hard about Seth and the reasons why she had refused to see him again. One, she could never countenance being romantically involved with a man who had such a strong religious bias; a bias she simply couldn't respect. It totally ruled out any chance of long-term compatibility. And two, to all intents and purposes, Seth was already married: he was married to the Church. As Sally had astutely pointed out, that meant Chloe could only ever be second best.

Sadly, Seth's world could never be her world. They were poles apart. But while it was true that these key points justifiably precluded a romantic relationship with him, Chloe wondered now if there was any reason why they couldn't be friends. The thought so instantly cheered her, she took the decision to ring Seth. Would it be too much to hope that he might understand and accept that they could only ever be friends? She hoped he could, if only so that she could go back to working out at the gym without worrying about bumping into him.

Having reached what felt like a satisfactory conclusion on the subject – even going so far as to picture herself speaking to Seth tonight – she decided to turn the tables on Sally. 'How's your newbie in the office?' she asked. 'Is he still making a pest of himself?'

She never got to hear Sally's answer, for she heard another voice. A voice she would know anywhere, any time. 'Hello, Chloe, am I too late for a slice of pizza?'

Chapter Twenty

Chloe sprang from her seat, spilling wine down her front. 'Paul!'

'I seem to remember wine being spilt the first time we met,' he said. He flipped his sunglasses up onto his head. 'Hello, Chloe, how are you? You look great. You too, Sally.'

On her feet beside Chloe, Sally stared coolly at him. 'What brings you here?' she asked. 'Presumably not the lure of a good pizza?' Her tone was as ice-cool as her gaze and her expression as aloof as the tough legal adversary Chloe knew her to be.

He smiled and addressed Chloe, face on. 'I came on the off chance that we could talk. Did you get any of my messages?'

'I did, but you didn't reply to mine. Why not?' Compared to Sally's controlled tone, Chloe's sounded tetchy and loaded with childish reproach.

'I'm sorry, but I didn't know that you had. My car was broken into and I'd stupidly left my mobile in it. It was taken, along with my laptop.'

'How did you have Chloe's number in the first place? And her address?' More cross-examining from Sally.

'I'd heard on the grapevine in Nottingham that Chloe had moved here permanently and all I did was check the phone book. So here I am.'

Here you are, indeed, thought Chloe. How easy and assured he was. Not a flicker of remorse in his manner. He appeared to be as confident as ever. Maybe even more so. Dressed in black jeans with a black and white short-sleeved shirt, he looked every inch the handsome, well-groomed man she remembered of old. He looked well. 'Seeing as you've come all this way, why don't you sit down?' she said, reminding herself that to be hostile towards him after all this time would only show herself in a bad light. Anyway, by responding to his messages, hadn't she wanted to show him how magnanimous and generous she could be? If only to prove she was a better person than he could ever be!

'Thank you,' he said.

'In that case,' Sally said, draining her glass and putting it on the window sill behind them, 'I'll leave you both to it.'

'Sally's never going to forgive me, is she?' Paul said when they were alone and he was sitting in the chair Sally had vacated, his long legs stretched out in front of him. He'd accepted a glass of wine and was looking dangerously at home.

Over the public address system – in what felt like another time and another place – Dave Peach was announcing that the Best Mongrel in Show competition was about to get under way. 'Do you really expect my best friend, of all people, to forgive you?' Chloe asked.

'I'd like to think that one day she might.'

'And what about me? Do you expect me to forget what you did?'

He frowned. 'That's my girl, straight to the heart of the matter. No bull. No hostages.'

'Well? Do you?' *That's my girl!* The nerve of him!

'I've changed, Chloe. No, I mean it, I really have. When I left you, I was a self-centred, arrogant bastard. I thought I had life all figured out. Now I know different.'

'So if you're no longer a self-centred, arrogant bastard,' she said, deliberately echoing his words for the sheer pleasure of saying them out loud, 'what are you? A paragon of goodness and honest virtue?'

'Far from it. I still make plenty of mistakes, but at least now I'm more aware of them and try to do something about it.' He turned and faced her. 'I've become a life coach.'

Chloe nearly choked on her wine. 'A life coach? Are you serious?' She'd have been less shocked if he'd announced he'd been made manager of the England football team.

'Very serious. And I've never been happier.' He laughed. 'But then who wouldn't be, after escaping the tedium of working in IT?'

'From IT manager to life coach; that's one hell of a leap. What brought that on?'

'I lost my way, you could say. I thought that being with Christine would make everything suddenly feel right.'

So her name was Christine, was it? Funny how he could say the name so effortlessly now, but at the time he'd refused to utter it when he'd at last come clean about his affair. 'And did everything feel right for you with *Christine*?'

He shook his head. 'Before long everything started to feel a whole lot worse.'

Oh, poor little diddums! Chloe wanted to snipe.

'We lasted five months together,' he carried on blithely. 'We were driving each other crazy. In short, we weren't the people we thought we were. And never could be.'

Five months, seethed Chloe. If he hadn't left her for those five wasted months, who knows what may have been? Her stomach lurched at the sickening reality of the situation; Paul, the father of the child she'd carried so fleetingly, was here beside her. Suddenly it all seemed more real and more painful than it had in a long while. How would he feel, she wondered, if she told him the truth? Oh, to shock him out of his appalling complacency, it was almost worth doing.

He'd started talking again. 'It wasn't until I met Liz that I began to understand where I'd gone wrong. Liz taught me so much. She opened my eyes not only to what I'd been running away from, but to what I really wanted to achieve with my life.'

Liz? Who the hell was Liz? 'And what exactly had you been running away from?' Chloe asked with strained patience.

'Myself, of course. Uh-oh, I think your mother's just spotted me.'

Chloe followed his glance and sure enough, striding across the grass was her mother, an empty pizza tray in her hand. If she could only get the right angle on it, Chloe thought, her mother would be able to throw the tray like a Frisbee and take Paul's head clean off with it.

'So it really is you! Well, well, well! Who'd have thought you'd have the cheek to show your dirty rotten face round here?'

'Hello, Jennifer,' Paul said politely, rising from his chair, his hand extended.

'Oh, don't give me any of your smarmy patter! You. Snake. In. The. Grass!'

Yess! Chloe silently cheered. Finally, after all this time, her mother had got to say the words face to face with the man she so thoroughly despised.

'You broke my daughter's heart,' Jennifer continued angrily. 'Don't think for one moment I'm going to welcome you back with open arms.' And with that she raised the empty pizza tray in her hands and clouted Paul's head with a satisfying crash.

Chapter Twenty-One

Very early in their relationship, Chloe had realized that one of the things Paul enjoyed about being her boyfriend was the strong bond she had with her family. It was a bond that initially he didn't understand or trust, but once he did, he allowed himself to become a part of it. His parents had divorced when he'd been eleven and from the little he had shared with her, it was clear the split had been hard on him. Reading between the lines, Chloe guessed that his parents had probably used him as a pawn in their battle with each other, and being kicked from pillar to post in the hope of point-scoring had left Paul confused and wary of committing to a relationship. How true that proved to be! The first time Chloe had taken him home to meet her parents they had welcomed him warmly. In the car afterwards he had asked her if they were always like that. 'Like what?' she had asked, worried that he was about to criticize them.

'They were so down-to-earth and friendly,' he'd said. 'They treated me like they'd always known me. It was nice. Or,' he'd added with a suspicious frown, 'was that a special show for my benefit?'

Relieved, she'd said, 'Oh, what you see is what you get with my parents. There's no side to them.'

No side at all. If Mum wanted to show her contempt for someone, she had no problem doing exactly that. With or without the aid of a pizza tray.

Other than an embarrassing blow to Paul's pride and ego, Chloe could detect no signs of any real damage to his head, and she declared him fit to fight another day.

'I've got some bridges to rebuild, haven't I? he said ruefully as they watched Jennifer marching away.

Chloe said, 'Surely you didn't think it could be otherwise?' She had no intention of apologizing for her mother's behaviour.

'I had hoped that sufficient time had passed for everyone's feelings to have calmed down.'

'You thought wrong.'

'Does that mean you're about to hit me, too?'

'I haven't made up my mind yet.'

His expression softened. 'Would a quiet dinner, just the two of us, help you to decide?'

'Dinner?'

'I came here to clear the air between us. I can't think of a nicer way to go about it than to take you out for dinner.'

'And what would Liz have to say about that?'

Without missing a beat, he said, 'She'd say it was exactly the right thing to do.'

Sally was quite used to seeing Dan with other women. It was a standing joke between them that one day he would run off with one of the mothers from nursery. Women always felt comfortable around him, and, likewise, Dan was quite at home in their company. Not once had Sally ever concerned herself with the thought that their marriage could come under threat from an outside source, namely a woman making a play for Dan. Even the close friendship Dan had with Rosie had never given her cause for concern. But now, observing this diminutive creature to whom Dan had just introduced her, with her bright, cheerfully animated face, her outrageously tiny waist, her stunning hair and eye-catching dress, Sally experienced a frisson of unease. This perky little thing looked like trouble. She had a way about her that managed to convey inner strength, yet at the same time an air of vulnerability. She was the kind of girl men instinctively want to protect but also want to take to bed.

Not listening to what Dan, Tatiana and Rosie were talking about, Sally backtracked through various conversations she and Dan had had about the trust. She couldn't recall him making more than a passing reference to Tatiana – merely something about her enthusiasm being infectious. Was that a typical male understatement, or something more insidious? A calculated step on his part to hide something from her?

Oh, come on! she told herself, moving out of the way as Charlie and Marcus began squealing and running round in pointless circles. Dan was hardly likely to sit her down and give her a blow by blow account of someone he worked with – 'Oh, and by the way, she's totally knockout gorgeous, but there's nothing for you to worry about.'

But the lawyer in her asserted that the devil was in the detail. So often it wasn't what people said, as what they didn't. And in this instance, Dan had barely opened his mouth about Tatiana Queen of the Bloody Fairies. Compare that to his frequent running commentaries on the females he regularly came in contact with in the village and suddenly there was a glaring admission of ... of what precisely? Guilt?

Trying to tune back into the conversation, Sally surreptitiously watched the way her husband interacted with Tatiana. Certainly he was smiling and maintaining eye contact with her and his general demeanour was that of someone having a good time – his laughter was louder than usual, his body language more exaggerated – but did that make him guilty of anything more dangerous than being a red-blooded male captivated by a pretty girl?

For her part, Tatiana was doing nothing remotely flirtatious or coquettish to attract Dan's attention – no flicking of her hair, no simpering, no fluttering of her eyelashes or leaning into him – but then she didn't need to. She'd probably still manage to be cute and alluring with her hair unwashed and wearing a shabby old candlewick dressing gown with a Marmite stain down the front.

Years ago Sally could remember a radio phone-in when male listeners were asked whom they would want to go on a date with: Madonna, Victoria Beckham or Kylie. Every single one of the men who called in said it would be Kylie. It was the classic girl-next-door attraction, that wholesome mixture of fresh-faced innocence and will-she-or-won't-she sex appeal. Some girls had it and some didn't. Tatiana had it in spades. Perhaps whatever 'it' was, it was something to do with being so petite. Which ruled Sally out; at five feet seven, she could never be described as petite.

But whatever height she was, Dan loved her. Right?

Thoroughly out of sorts now, Sally felt further disconnected from the conversation going on around her – Dan was now serving a customer and Rosie and Tatiana were talking about the disco being held in the village hall later that evening. She stifled a yawn, and, thinking of the work she could be doing at home, wondered if anyone would notice if she disappeared. Village fetes were hardly her thing. She always felt awkwardly out of place; it was why she opted to help Chloe run the pizza stall. Chloe's kitchen was somewhere she could hide but still be seen to be taking part. Playing one's part in the village was vital. Reveal yourself to be a slacker and heaven help you.

Over the public address system, Rosie's husband was announcing the arrival of the newly crowned May Queen. As if sensing something exciting was about to happen, Charlie came to a sudden stop and Marcus careered straight into the back of him. The collision made both boys fall over and land in a heap; Marcus let go of his balloon and when he saw it drifting skywards he began crying. Sally went to him, but he was inconsolable. All he cared about was his balloon sailing off into the distance. He pushed her away, struggled to his feet and wailed loudly, his arms stretched above him, his head tilted back so far he was in danger of toppling over again.

Then magically, he was quiet.

Tatiana was kneeling on the grass in front of him. In her hands, and pressed to her lips as she blew into it, was another balloon. As it took shape, puff by puff, a slow smile appeared on Marcus's face. By the time the balloon was its full size and Tatiana had it securely tied – she even produced a ribbon from her bag – Marcus was beaming happily and bouncing excitedly on the balls of his feet. He could not have looked more adoringly at her.

A shot of hatred mainlined straight to Sally's heart. First her husband, now her son?

'What the hell happened to you?' Dan asked.

The fete had finished more than an hour ago and after staying behind to clear up and then trundle an exhausted Marcus home in the wheelbarrow, he was dumbfounded to find Sally working at her laptop in her study.

When she didn't answer him but continued to type, he said, 'One minute you were there and the next you'd disappeared. I thought you'd gone back to Chloe's.'

She raised her gaze from her laptop and stared at him. 'I'm surprised you noticed I wasn't there.'

'What's that supposed to mean?'

She shrugged. 'You tell me. At what point did you actually miss me?'

He frowned and shook his head. 'I don't know what this is about, Sally, but for the record, it would have been nice to have your support for once. You could have helped me on the tombola stall for a few minutes after you'd run out of pizzas to sell. Would it have killed you to show your face with me?'

'Let me get this straight. You want my support? Oh, that's rich. Here I am working all hours to support you and Marcus and somehow that isn't enough.'

'Hey, I'm working too! And Marcus doesn't take care of himself you know.'

'No, you've got your charming coterie of women to help you on that score, haven't you?'

He laughed at this. 'Since when has Rosie become a one-woman charming coterie?'

'Don't laugh at me, Dan. Whatever else you do, don't you dare make fun of me.'

'But it's nonsense. And it sounds suspiciously like jealousy. What the hell's brought that on?'

'I'm not talking about Rosie, as you well know.'

'Who then? Chloe?'

'Don't be absurd. You know exactly who I'm talking about. Tatiana Haines.'

'Tatiana? You're mad. I barely know her.'

'You work with her; of course you know her.'

'She's a work colleague. Nothing more.'

'So why was she here at the fete?'

'She's a friend of Rosie's.'

'She didn't come to the fete last year. What was the big attraction this time round?'

Exasperated, his voice raised, he said, 'Rosie's only recently met her!' Then, truly stunned at what Sally was accusing him of, Dan took a moment to consider what he said next. 'You're serious about this, aren't you? You really think I'm capable of being unfaithful to you?'

'I see it every day in my work, Dan. No one's beyond reproach.'

'Funny that, because from the outside looking in at our marriage some people might think *you* would be the one most likely to have an affair. Certainly you have more opportunity than me, yet I've never once thought you would. I trust you, Sally. And I believe in our marriage.' He wanted to shore his words up by action, by going over to his wife and embracing her to show that he loved her, but he couldn't. He felt leaden with disbelief. And disappointment. She'd as good as kicked him in the teeth. 'I'll leave you to get back to your work,' he said. 'It's time for Marcus to have his tea. Can I get you anything?'

She shook her head.

What the hell happened to you? Dan had asked her and now Sally asked herself the same question. What had she just done? Could she not have found a more subtle way to voice her concern with Dan? Why had she gone at him so vociferously?

I believe in our marriage, he'd said. But what did that really mean? She couldn't remember the last time they'd made love or exchanged anything more passionate than a hurried kiss on the cheek. Things had definitely got worse since he'd started working for the trust. Dan's time was more divided than it had been and whereas before when she used to come home from work, he'd greet her with a glass of wine and something delicious to eat, now he would often be sitting at the kitchen table with a mass of papers spread out in front of him and apologizing that supper wasn't ready.

She was bleating pathetically, she knew, sounding like a fifties husband who, on his return from a hard day at the office, wanted to be presented with an immaculate house, his children tucked up in bed and his pipe and slippers brought to him. The image amused her momentarily and she felt some of the tension she'd been feeling flow out of her.

But then she thought of Tatiana and how effortlessly she had cured Marcus of his tears. At the time, a savage hatred for the girl had made Sally want to snatch the balloon out of her hands and burst it, but with a forced smile on her face, she had politely thanked her, saying, 'How fortuitous that you had a spare one with you.'

Laughing, Tatiana had pulled a bag of balloons out of her handbag, saying, 'I can't tell you how many times these little fellas have saved the day in my line of work. There's nothing better for stemming the flow of tears.'

A regular Mary Poppins, Sally had thought nastily.

Shortly afterwards, when everyone had gone to cheer the crowning of the new May Queen, including Dan with Marcus riding on his shoulders, Sally had quietly slipped away. She wasn't needed there.

Question was: was she really needed here at Corner Cottage? Dan and Marcus had such a close relationship there were times when she felt she had to crow-bar her way into it.

Chapter Twenty-Two

'So basically you're saying you messed up? Didn't I tell you that was exactly what would happen?'

'Cheers, I knew I could rely upon you to lighten my day.'

'Good God, don't tell me you phoned me for sympathy?'

'I believe in many things, Becks, but not the chance of extracting a single word of sympathy or understanding from you.'

'That's my boy. Now tell me what actually went down. Did she stumble across your cassock and assume you liked to dress up in women's clothes?'

Seth shifted his position in the creaky old wicker chair and stared up at the darkening sky. Somewhere in the neighbourhood of terraced houses, a dog was barking. To the left of him, he could hear the ten o'clock news on his eighty-two-year-old neighbour's television. From the other side of the fence, he could hear music; he didn't recognize who or what it was, but the bass line seemed to be making a bid for escape by burrowing under the fence into Seth's garden. 'Maybe I would have stood more chance with her if I was into cross-dressing,' he said, reaching for the beer on the table in front of him.

'Hang on a moment, that sounds worryingly like self-pity. Which you have absolutely no right to feel. You know full well you got what you deserved because your game plan was flawed from the get-go.'

Seth smiled. 'Go on,' he said, 'I dare you to tell me to practise what I preach, or that I'm reaping what I've sown.'

'I wouldn't stoop so low. Now tell me what happened.'

Seth told his sister about the funeral service and how he hadn't seen or heard from Chloe in the intervening weeks, that he'd even stopped going to the gym for fear of bumping into her and causing her any embarrassment.

'You don't think you've given her the wrong message, do you?' Rebecca said when he'd finished. 'If you'd rung her, just once, if only to apologize, maybe she might have given you another chance. By not getting in touch you haven't exactly given her a reason to think better of you.'

'But there's no point. She made her views very clear. Only a miracle would get her to change her mind.'

'How strange. I could have sworn it was written into your contract that you had to believe in miracles. But then as a card-carrying agnostic, what do I know?'

'I could go off you, Becks.'

'Yeah, and who would you turn to for advice then? And for what it's worth, seeing as I think you were genuinely more than just interested in this Chloe, I reckon you should get in touch with her again. Do it soon. First thing tomorrow morning. After all, what have you got to lose?'

Tuesday morning and Sally was alone in her office. Harry had moved into an office of his own some weeks ago, but today she found herself missing his presence.

Despite their getting off on the wrong foot she had come to appreciate his company. Now that he was behaving himself – he'd stopped all that absurd infatuation nonsense – she had come to respect his keen intellect and his shamelessly ambitious work ethic. He teased her now and then, mimicking the way she said, 'Oh, don't be absurd!' Until he'd pointed this out to her, she'd had no idea that she said it so often. He had a deceptively charming knack for cheering her up, of making her laugh when she least expected to.

She could do with a good laugh now.

What was happening to her and Dan? Yesterday had been an unmitigated disaster. After Dan had put Marcus to bed, they had eaten their evening meal in near silence and afterwards watched a programme on the television that she had no recollection of. It was a relief to go to bed and not worry that she would say something she would later regret.

She had woken up this morning knowing that all it would have taken from her was one word – sorry – and she and Dan would not have slept with their backs to each other. Sorry ... and everything would have been all right. Sorry ... and she wouldn't have woken feeling everything was slipping away from her. Or more precisely, that she was pushing it away from her, just as Marcus had thrust her hands away from him at the fete yesterday.

But was she sorry?

Truth was, she wasn't. A woman knows when another woman is a threat and Sally knew in her bones that Tatiana had the capability to cause trouble. Hadn't she already?

Putting her own marriage out of her mind, she reached for the client file from the top of the pile on her desk and opened it. It was a messy case with both sides fighting tooth and nail for more than their fair share of the assets that were up for grabs. Twenty minutes later she realized she had lost count how many times she had reread the same page and that its meaning still hadn't penetrated her brain. She couldn't concentrate. And that wasn't like her. Normally nothing distracted her. Caffeine. That's what she needed. Lots of it.

She could have asked Chandra to make her a cup of coffee, but since she was on the phone, Sally went to the kitchen to make it herself. There was no one there and she was glad not to have to make small talk with anyone. Or worse, listen to the work experience lackeys bragging about how wasted they'd got the night before. While she waited for the kettle to boil, she flicked through a discarded copy of *Heat* magazine. And people paid good money to read this kind of rubbish?

She was on her way back to her office, when the doors of the lift opened and Harry stepped out. 'Aha!' he proclaimed eagerly. 'Just the person I was looking for.' His hand on the lift door button, he said, 'Have you got a minute?'

'A quick one, yes.'

'Excellent. there's something in my office I want to show you.' And before she knew what he was doing, he'd taken her by the arm and manoeuvred her into the lift, and the doors were closing.

'No!' she cried out. Spilling her coffee, she jabbed at the panel of buttons. But it was too late; the lift was moving.

OK, she told herself, stay calm.

No need to panic.

It was two floors up to Harry's office. That was all. It was no big deal.

Harry was staring at her oddly. It slowly registered that he was talking to her, that he'd asked her something. To her relief the lift juddered to a stop. There. She'd made it.

She faced the doors, waiting for them to open, poised like a racing greyhound about to be released from the trap.

But the doors didn't open. She pressed the button.

And again. Panic began to rise in her.

'I don't believe it,' Harry said. 'It looks like we're stuck.'

'We can't be,' she said. Her voice sounded small and far away. The knot of panic in her stomach was tightening and she could feel the air being sucked out of her chest. She frantically tried the button once more. The lights began to flicker.

'I don't think that will help,' Harry said, as though it was the most reasonable thing in the world for this to be happening to them. The lights flickered again, then went out.

Darkness.

'This is all your fault!' she cried desperately. 'If you hadn't man-handled me the way you did, I wouldn't be stuck here with you. How could you do this to me?'

'Sally,' he said. Except it didn't sound like Harry. He sounded serious. Authoritative. In the darkness, she felt the forgotten cup of coffee being taken from her hands. 'Listen to me,' he said. He now had her hands in his and was holding them tightly. 'We'll be out of here in no time at all. OK?'

She struggled to speak but couldn't. A low wattage light above their heads came on and in the dim light, she watched Harry press the red emergency button. The lift juddered and she let out a star-tled cry. 'What did you do that for?' She backed away from him. 'Please,' she gasped, 'I have to get out of here!' She covered her head with her hands and slid down the mirrored wall of the lift until she was crouched on the floor. She squeezed her eyes shut and tried to concentrate on her breathing.

In.

Out.

In.

Out.

It wasn't working. She was going to suffocate. She knew it. A long way off, almost drowned out by the sound of crashing in her ears, she could hear Harry talking to someone. But it didn't make sense. There were only the two of them here. A hand on her arm made her start. She opened her eyes. It was Harry. He had removed his jacket and was pulling her into his arms. 'Help's on its way,' he said. 'Hang in there, Sally. Five minutes, ten, tops.'

'I can't … I can't breathe,' she rasped. A sob caught in her throat. She was beyond caring. She wanted to curl up and die. Just let it be over.

He turned her face towards him and held it so firmly she had no choice but to look at him. 'Do exactly as I do,' he said. 'Imagine each breath as a step out of here.' He inhaled deeply, then exhaled slowly. 'Come on, Sally, try it. Do it for me. Look into my eyes. Show me you can do it.'

His words began to cut through her panic and the deafening crashing in her ears, but light-headed now, she had no way of connecting with her lungs. She felt clammy all over and was shaking hard. She could scarcely feel her hands; they were numb with pins and needles.

'Sally, what colour are my eyes?'

Eyes? She was suffocating! Who cared what colour his eyes were?

'My eyes, Sally. Tell me what colour they are.'

His voice was so insistent, she wondered whether it was important. She focused her own eyes on his and choking back trembling fear, she said, 'Brown. They're brown.'

'What kind of brown are they? Look closely. Tell me, are they light brown or dark brown? Or some other kind of brown? What do you see?'

'Dark ... brown,' she said falteringly. 'Dark, like ... like chocolate.'

He smiled. 'Good girl.' He released his hold on her and brushed her hair away from her face. 'Now take a small breath and think how like chocolate they are and how wonderful it would be to eat some when we get out of here. That's it, breathe in slowly. Now out. And again. You're doing brilliantly, Sally, I'm so proud of you.' He stroked her cheek. Feeling dazed but calmer, she allowed him to lay her head on his shoulder. He put an arm around her and she could feel his warm, firm body through his shirt. It felt good. Reassuring. He made her feel safe. She'd stopped shaking now. 'I'm sorry,' she mumbled with a deep, shuddering breath.

'What for?' he asked.

'For this. For you having to see me this way.'

'It's my fault. I had no idea you suffered from claustrophobia. I feel such an idiot for putting you through this. I'll make it up to you, I promise. Are you still breathing?'

She nodded tiredly. 'It's like we're in a film, isn't it?'

'Don't say that, or I'll have to change into my Bruce Willis vest and start battling our way out of here. Hang on, I can hear voices. Sounds like the cavalry's arrived.'

He made to stand up, but when the lights flickered, she clung to him, grabbing hold of his hand. 'Please,' she said, 'don't leave me.'

He stayed with her on the floor.

A disembodied voice shouted to them from somewhere in the lift shaft. It declared itself to be part of the emergency services and asked if they were all right.

'We're doing fine,' Harry shouted back. 'What seems to be the problem?'

'A power failure. The light you've got on there is hooked up to the emergency generator. It's got a limited supply of juice, but don't worry, we'll have you out of there before it runs out. How many of you are there?'

'Just the two of us.'

'Any injuries?'

'No.'

'That's good. Now stay nice and calm and I'll be right back with you.'

Harry turned to Sally. 'We should do something to celebrate getting out of here, you know. What do you fancy doing?'

Ignoring his question, she said, 'You won't tell anyone about this, will you? I couldn't take the shame of everyone knowing what a fool I've been.'

He squeezed her hand. 'Of course I won't.'

'I never used to ... to suffer from claustrophobia.'

'When did it start?'

'Remember the Boxing Day tsunami?'

'Who could forget it? God, you weren't there, were you?'

She nodded. 'I got trapped and ... and ever since, I can't stand to be in a confined space.' Tears filled her eyes and her chest tightened. She hated this debilitating weakness she'd been left with since that dreadful day. It was like a curse. And she despised herself for letting it get the better of her, allowing it to make her so pathetically helpless and vulnerable.

'I feel such a fraud compared to you,' Harry said. 'The scariest situation I've ever been in was the day I met you. I took one look at you and knew my life was never going to be the same again. You completely took my breath away. You still do.'

Slowly, she turned to face him. Their eyes met and held. And held. 'Your eyes really are as dark as chocolate,' she murmured. He moved closer to her. Then closer still. Until finally the gap closed, his lips touched hers and they kissed. After all these years, it was a revelation to feel lips other than Dan's against hers. 'That was probably a mistake,' she said when she pulled away.

'Don't say that.' He kissed her again and she didn't resist him.

It was only when the lights flickered and then came back on with full brightness and a cheer went up the other side of the lift doors that they stopped. By the time the doors had slid open, they were on their feet, perfectly composed and standing a chaste twelve inches apart.

Chapter Twenty-Three

Chloe was nervous about meeting Paul for dinner. She couldn't decide what worried her most. Would all her hurt and anger finally bubble up and cause her to disgrace herself thoroughly in public? Or would something far worse occur? Would she fall for him all over again?

Paul hadn't stuck around for long at the fete yesterday – just long enough to get her to agree to have dinner with him – and since then she had alternated between wanting to snatch up the phone and cancel or willing the time away so she could have her moment and tell Paul exactly what she thought of him.

She was fifteen minutes late when she stepped into the restaurant. The old Paul would have glanced pointedly at his watch – he'd been a stickler for punctuality – but the new Paul merely rose from his chair and leaned in to kiss her.

'You look great,' he said. The kiss – as perfunctory as it was on both cheeks – jarred with her. It smacked of assumption. Assumption that she'd forgiven him and they were all set to be lifelong best mates.

'Busy day?' he asked as she settled herself at the table.

'Frantic. It's always the same after a Bank Holiday weekend; there's a stampede to the surgery. I also had two new medical reps booked into the diary.'

'A full-on day, then. What would you like to drink?'

His relaxed and ultra-controlled manner further annoyed her. Where were his nerves? Where was the contrition? By the time they'd got the business of ordering their drinks and meal out of the way, Chloe was bristling with the need to hold Paul to account. It was that kiss that had done it; he had touched her with such a sense of entitlement.

One of the things she liked about being an adult was that she was free to make her own decisions. But try telling her mother that! Mum had been horrified when Chloe had told her she was meeting Paul for dinner. Her advice was to slip something deadly into his food when he wasn't looking. 'And don't, whatever you do, make the mistake of compromising with him,' she'd instructed. 'That's lowering your standards so that he can climb up to be on your level.' Her parting words of advice were that physical violence never solved anything, but heavens it felt good, so why not try it? To which Chloe had replied, 'Mum, I'm not going to follow your example and whack Paul.'

'Oh, darling,' her mother had said, 'do take off your crown of self-righteousness, it really doesn't suit you. Now remember what I said about slipping him something deadly.'

'What's so funny?' Paul asked her when the waiter had brought them their drinks.

Unaware that she'd been smiling, Chloe said, 'I was thinking of something my mother said to me earlier.'

'Ah. Did it involve me?'

'Not everything revolves around you, Paul.' Although, gallingly, it looked like it did.

The waiter was back with a basket of bread. He shuffled the flower vase and salt and pepper grinders to make room for the basket and left them alone again.

'That was said with feeling,' Paul remarked, offering her a bread roll. 'But I do understand how you feel. I know that deep down you must have harboured a real need to extract some form of revenge on me.'

'You flatter yourself that I gave you that much thought.'

'Didn't you? Don't you?'

His conceit was breathtaking. Worse, though, was that he was right. One way or another she did think of him more than was healthy. 'Revenge is about gaining control after we've been make to feel powerless,' she said, determined not to let him have the conversation all his way. 'It's a need to create order and balance in our lives. If someone has wronged us, we have a basic desire to get even. It's the human condition.'

'That's very true,' he said. 'In which case, what did you want to do to get even with me?'

'I wanted you dead,' she said matter-of-factly.

He stared at her. 'Metaphorically or for real?'

'Very much for real.'

'That's quite an act of revenge,' he said with a frown.

'It was quite a stunt you pulled on me. One minute I thought you were planning to propose and the next you were leaving me for someone else. Something like that can upset a girl, you know.'

'But to want me dead, that's serious revenge.'

'As break-ups go, it was brutal. I was hurt. And very angry. What's more, your timing could have been better.'

'And you're still angry?'

'Wouldn't you be?'

'I never once spoke about us getting married. How did you possibly think I was about to propose to you?'

Chloe knew that the honest answer was that it had been a chronic case of wishful thinking on her part. But she couldn't bring herself to admit it. 'It seemed the natural order of things,' she said. 'Seeing as we'd been together so long. But evidently the natural order of things for you was to have two women on the go at the same time.'

'That was an inexcusable mistake on my part. I mentioned yesterday that it was all part of me running away from myself. I confused my unhappiness with myself with our relationship. As a consequence, I acted very badly towards you.'

'When did your conscience kick in?' Chloe was intrigued.

'When I met Liz.'

Aha, Liz. 'And is she your latest girlfriend?'

He raised his eyebrows and laughed. 'Definitely not. Liz is my business partner. We run Forward Thinking, a life coaching business. It was Liz who turned my life around.'

Chloe was tempted to laugh, too. The concept of anyone being allowed to turn Paul's life around was a leap of imagination too far.

'It's thanks to Liz that I can see things so clearly now.' He smiled. 'I'm a much nicer man to know these days.'

And so humble and modest, she thought when their first course was brought to their table. She asked him if he was still living in Nottingham.

He shook his head. 'I left Nottingham earlier this year. I'm living in Cheshire now, in a village called Lymm.'

She looked up sharply.

'Do you know it?'

'I'm Cheshire born and bred; of course I know it. What made you move to Lymm?'

He shrugged. 'Liz and I decided to set up our business in Alderley Edge and when I was looking for somewhere to live, I found a great little cottage in Lymm. You should come and see it. I'd value your opinion on what I've done to it so far. How's your avocado?'

'Rock hard and tasteless if you want the truth.'

He reached across and speared a cube with his fork. It was another overly familiar gesture that jarred with her. What was wrong with saying, 'May I?' She immediately recalled Seth saying these very words to her. He'd always been so polite and self-effacing. Thinking of him made her remember that she hadn't called him as she'd said she would. But then Paul's sudden appearance in the village yesterday had put most things out of her mind.

'You're right,' Paul said. 'It's awful. Much too bitter.' He turned around in his seat and instantly attracted the attention of their waiter. He reached over, took the plate from Chloe's place setting and handed it to the waiter. 'Could you ask the chef if he could rustle up an avocado that's actually fit to eat, please? Thank you so much.'

'You might have asked if I wanted it changing,' Chloe said, nettled.

'But it was inedible,' he said. 'You wouldn't be valuing yourself if you didn't complain about it. Know what you want in life, Chloe. Set out your goals and never be afraid to say no. Those are the fundamental life choices you have to make if you really want to be the confident person you're meant to be.'

'Right,' she said, unsure what else to say.

'Being a life coach has taught me never to put up with anything I don't want to. Self-awareness comes through self-assurance and leads to being truly positive. It's when we start carrying around with us a positive aura that we become magnetic and attract like-minded people.'

Chloe supposed this kind of talk went down well among the champagne-swilling crowd in the wine bars of Alderley Edge.

'Suddenly the sky's the limit,' Paul continued happily. 'Anything and everything is possible. Positive energy, that's what it's all about.'

There was nothing inherently wrong with what he was saying, but it definitely had a whiff of the newly converted about it. When their waiter reappeared with a tight smile on his face and placed a new starter in front of her, Chloe couldn't help but fear that he and the chef had probably added something unspeakable to it. She wanted to go after the waiter and say that it hadn't been her who'd wanted to make a fuss and that if anyone's meal needed tampering with it was Paul's.

'How is it?' Paul asked after she'd taken a mouthful.

'It's perfect,' she said quickly. Anything less than perfect and he'd be off again, flexing his self-assurance muscles.

'You're sure?' Once again his fork was across the table and he was helping himself to a piece of avocado. He chewed on the mouthful thoughtfully. 'You're right. Now wasn't it worth complaining about? You mustn't make yourself a doormat, Chloe. Behave like a victim and you'll be taken advantage of. It's all about making others respect your boundaries. You should come on one of the workshops Liz and I are doing in Greece during the summer. You'd get so much out of it.'

She stared at him with undisguised disbelief. Did he have any idea how offensive he was being? She put down her knife and fork. 'Paul, I'd really appreciate it if you didn't insult my intelligence a moment longer by expecting me to sit here and listen to any more of your "winning strategies" claptrap. And since you raised the matter, the only person who has ever taken advantage of me was you!'

He paused before speaking. 'I can see why you'd think that I took advantage of you, but I didn't. The bottom line is that I took the coward's way out of our relationship because I wasn't thinking straight. I'd begun to worry we were pulling in different directions and that scared me.'

'What kind of different directions?' she asked.

'It was your need to have children.'

'But I never made a big thing of it. I really didn't. God, I used to tiptoe round the subject, terrified that you'd think I was trying to trap you into parenthood.'

'I know, but I was an idiot back then.'

'And you're not now?'

He smiled and his eyes met hers. 'I've changed, Chloe. And I'd really like to prove to you that's true.'

'How do you propose to do that?'

'By spending more time with you.' He intensified his gaze on her. 'I know it's asking a lot, but do you think you could forgive me so that we can work on making it right between us? I screwed up badly and I want to make amends. I can't stop thinking how great we used to be together.' He shook his head. 'It's one of life's terrible ironies that it's only when we lose something that we realize how precious it was. And you *were* precious to me, Chloe. You really were. I was a jerk for not appreciating you when I had the chance. I suppose it might sound odd, but in the last six months I've just had this burning need to confess everything to you.'

Chloe swallowed. Here then was the contrition she'd wanted, the apology she had wanted all this time. So why did she feel so cheated? Why did it feel such an anticlimax? What exactly had she expected to feel? Victorious? Was that it? Punching the air and turning cartwheels? If so, she had been seriously deluded. This was nothing but a hollow victory. Perhaps worse than that, it was a Pyrrhic victory. The words 'I'm sorry' were never going to bring back what she'd lost.

Looking at Paul now, she experienced a painful stab of sadness. Almost overcome with the need to share her own confession with him, she felt her eyes pooling with tears. She looked away and blinked hard, hoping he hadn't noticed.

But he had. 'I'm sorry it still hurts after all this time, Chloe,' he said. 'You've no idea how bad that makes me feel.'

His choice of words rankled sufficiently for her to pull herself together. Why was it always about him and his feelings? She took a long, fortifying sip of wine and said, 'Oh, please, don't whatever you do feel bad on my account.'

He caught her tone and looked hurt by it. 'Tell me about you. What have you been up to? Is there a new man in your life?'

'Yes,' she lied. Her pride would have her say nothing else.

'And?'

'And what?'

'Is it serious?'

'Is that any of your business?'

'Point taken,' he said. 'But just so that you know, I'm not seeing anyone right now.'

Chapter Twenty-Four

Sally had once watched an episode of *Footballers' Wives* with Chloe. It had been one of their rare girls' only nights together – a bottle of wine, a take-away curry and something daft to watch on the telly. The glossy lifestyle portrayed in the programme had been about as bizarrely unreal as it could possibly be, and yet here was Sally, chez Darren T. Child, and able to testify that what she'd seen on the television had not been a far-fetched aberration of a screenwriter's mind.

Darren T. Child's prowess on the pitch had afforded him a pile of considerable proportions in sought-after Prestbury, where his neighbours included a stellar cast list of footballing celebrities. The seven-bedroom, five-bathroom house was a monstrosity of vulgarity, equipped with an indoor pool, a snooker room, a gym, a cinema and garaging for five cars. On her arrival, Sally had seen three of Darren's cars – two Humvees and a Ferrari – all of which were in the process of being washed by a man in grey trousers and shirtsleeves. Everything about the house screamed of a twenty-five-year-old man having more money than he knew what to do with.

The interior was not entirely unknown to Sally; she had seen it in an issue of *OK!* at the hairdresser's. The magazine had run a piece depicting the blissful life of Darren T. Child. There had been numerous shots of him and his wife sprawled across a four-poster bed, shots of them amorously knee-deep in shag pile, shots of them guzzling champagne in the jacuzzi, shots of them canoodling in the back row of the home-cinema, and shots of them in the pool performing the kind of heavy petting that would get them thrown out of the public baths in nearby Macclesfield.

Sally had been shown through to an enormous sitting room decorated with inexorably bad taste. It was the epitome of teenage-girl chic: pink leather sofas, pink carpets, fluffy pink cushions, pink wallpaper. All that was missing was a layer of clothes littering the floor and pop star posters on the walls. Clearly the decorating had been left to Mrs Child. Either her or Lady Penelope. On the grounds of this room alone, Darren had every right to file for divorce.

The woman who had answered the door to Sally, a housekeeper perhaps, had informed her that Darren was in the swimming pool and wouldn't be long. That had been twenty minutes ago.

Meeting Darren in his own home had been the only way Sally had been sure of nailing her client. He'd refused to come to Manchester to the office, claiming that he'd get mobbed. Sally had no idea if this was true or whether he just suffered from an inflated opinion of his celebrity status, but surely a pair of sunglasses and a baseball cap would provide sufficient disguise? Or what about wearing one of those jackets with a hood? She'd have thought that, given his background, he'd be right at home dressed as a hoodie.

She immediately checked herself, shocked at her snobbery. Her background and Darren's weren't that dissimilar, so why was she allowed to rise up from the bottom of the barrel, but resented Darren for doing the same? So what if his wealth was hugely conspicuous? It was *his* money; he could do with it exactly as he wanted. As his lawyer, it was her job to defend him, to have his best interests at the core of her dealings. It was none of her business – unless it directly affected his divorce settlement – to question his private life. If he wanted to spend every night at some club or other abusing his body with alcohol and drugs and getting off with half-dressed girls who were only after associated celebrity, that was entirely his affair. 'I'm not paid to judge you, Darren,' she'd once told him. 'You're paying me to protect your assets and that's what I intend to do.' He'd grinned at this and said, 'I'd pay you top whack, like, to do that, and make no mistake.' She'd suspected he'd been referring to something other than his financial assets. She'd been tempted to bring David Swann from the office with her for the meeting – he was a member of the team handling Darren's case – but knowing how star-struck he would have been at meeting one of the country's current best players, she'd come alone. Besides, she could handle the likes of Darren with one hand tied behind her back.

The sound of girlish giggling alerted Sally that her wait might nearly be over. Whatever exercise Darren had been up to, it probably hadn't involved the swimming of any lengths. The sound of a slap – a hand on a pert buttock? – followed by, 'Now get lost, like, I got business to do.'

You most certainly have, thought Sally. She stood up and straightened her suit skirt.

Dressed in a snow-white towelling robe and a towel slung around his neck, Darren slowly swaggered in. All that was absent from his entrance was the 'Eye of the Tiger' soundtrack. 'Hello, Sally, mate. How you doin'?'

'I'm very well, Darren. How are you?'

'I'm good, mate. Bleedin' 'ell! What've you done to that table?' He was staring in horror at the papers she'd spread over a large glass coffee table.

'It's important paperwork, which we need to go through,' she said.

'You what? But that's what I pay you to do. I don't do paper-work.'

'We need to go through it together, Darren. That's how this works. It's a team thing. In the same way a footballer can't win a match single-handedly,' she added with a smile, hoping to find an analogy he could grasp, 'I need your help. I can't do this alone.'

Darren was not the sharpest knife in the box – he had been pilloried in the press recently for asking who Tony Blair was during an interview with Jonathan Ross – and Sally knew to tread carefully. It was easy for people to make fun of him, but she always tried to bear in mind the sad truth that the education system had completely failed him.

'You taking the piss, or what?' Darren had squared his jaw and was shoving his hands deep into the pockets of his towelling robe. The robe pulled open at the top revealing a smooth, hairless chest. Sally's gaze lowered to his legs; they were tanned and smooth and as hairless as his chest. Had it been David Beckham or Frank Lampard who'd started them all off on shaving their bodies? His feet were knobbly with calluses and looked seriously unattractive. He was twenty-five now, and at the top of his game, but how soon before arthritis slowed him down? Or whatever other ailments footballers suffered from in later years. Although that Gary Linekar wasn't exactly hobbling around on sticks, was he?

'I said, are you taking the piss out of me?'

Sally started. Then snapped her concentration back into line. 'No, Darren,' she said, 'I was simply trying to impress upon you that I need your help. Shall we sit down and take a look at what I've brought for you to see?'

He took the big pink leather armchair next to the sofa where she'd been sitting. He flicked the armrest up on the chair and a panel of buttons appeared, reminding Sally of the chair Jimmy Savile used to sit in for *Jim'll Fix It*. Darren pressed a button and the chair reclined at the same time as a foot rest popped up. 'Now then,' she said, when he seemed to be comfortable. 'The first document I want to go through with you is—'

'Can I say something, mate?'

'Of course, Darren.' Why did he have to keep calling her *mate*? She knew it was a linguistic tick on his part, but really, did he have no idea how irritating it was? He'd called her *mate* the first time they'd met. 'How's it going, mate?' he'd said. It was as bad as all those other words and phrases that drove her mad. You couldn't ask anyone how they were without them saying, 'I'm good.' *No!* she wanted to scream. Your health was being enquired after, not your behaviour. 'Like' was another pest, jammed into a sentence almost every other word, along with 'sort of'. And since when had 'yes' been replaced with the word 'absolutely'? What was wrong with people these days? Couldn't they speak properly? Marcus's favourite penguin, Pingu, had a more extensive vocabulary than half the dimwits on the radio or television these days. Mm ... she thought, picking up on her own repetition, *these days* ... better make that *nowadays*. Better still, *currently*. OK, so she too was guilty of repetition occasionally. The admission made her thoughts wander to that strictly out-of-bounds danger zone: Harry. She thought of him teasing her for always using the word 'absurd'. He'd told her he loved it when she said, 'Oh, don't be absurd, Harry.' He said it made him smile because she sounded so prim. He said her primness made him want to smother her in kisses.

She snatched her thoughts back from venturing any further into that particular minefield and, remembering where she was and what she was supposed to be doing, she said, 'Right, Darren, shall we get on?'

He frowned. 'You wozn't listening to a word I was saying, woz you?'

He'd been speaking? Oh, God, what was happening to her? Why wasn't she concentrating? 'I'm sorry,' she apologized, 'it's been a busy week and I have a lot on my mind.'

He looked at her hard. 'Just as well you ain't a footballer; you wouldn't last two minutes on the pitch.' He pressed a stubby finger to his temple and tapped it. 'First thing you learn: keep the focus, never take your eye off the ball. Do that and you're history.'

Sally couldn't believe it. She was being lectured to by – of all people – Darren T. Child!

'And I was trying to tell you, like, you look like you could do with a bit of R and R.'

'R and R,' she repeated, confused. What was he suggesting? An illicit drug to relax her?

'Rest and relaxation,' he said. 'Don't you know nuffink?'

'*Anything*,' she corrected him without thinking.

Once again he looked at her hard, drumming his stubby fingers on the arm of the leather chair. 'You fink I'm trash, don't you?'

'Of course not. Don't be absurd.' She winced. Thanks, Harry! 'But you're right, it was wrong of me; I shouldn't have corrected you. The trouble is I'm so used to doing it with my son it just slipped out.' She picked up a wad of papers from the table, doing her best to regain control of the meeting.

'Ow old's your kid?'

'He's two and a half. Just over, in fact.'

Darren snorted. 'Two and a half, bleeding 'ell, and you're correcting him? He must love that.'

Sally bristled. She was not about to discuss how she raised Marcus. Even so, she couldn't resist saying, 'How else will he learn if I don't teach him the right words?'

Darren shrugged. 'Right words, wrong words. Don't mean nuffink. The kid'll speak 'ow he wants to speak and there won't be a fing you can do about it.' He smiled. 'But I know this much, mate. I didn't get all this' – he waved a hand around him – 'by speaking like you do. How much wedge do you take home?'

'Really, Darren, I hardly think—'

'A hundred K a year, like? Two hundred?'

'What I earn is entirely my own business.'

'Whatever it is, I bet I earn that much just gettin' up in the morning. So next time you take a pop at your kid, just think of me.'

'Not everyone is blessed with your particular talent.'

'Yeah, but, like, who's to know what special talent your kid 'as if you keep chipping away at his confidence? Best fing me mum and dad did was to split up and dump me on me nan. She was a diamond of a woman. Still is. She let me do exactly as I wanted. Which, as you know from all the tabloids, was bunking off school and kicking a ball about all day. 'Ow would it have been, like, if she'd forced me to go to school? Eh? I wouldn't be here and nor would you, mate. You certainly wouldn't be earning a nice big fat fee off me. Am I your richest client?'

Sally had had quite enough of Darren's overblown ego and

self-importance. Time to crush it down to size. 'No,' she said, quite truthfully. She saw the blatant disappointment in his face. Don't play those games with me, *mate!* 'And unless you fully co-operate with me' – she indicated the table of papers – 'your wife will walk all over you and you'll end up as one of my poorest clients. Now, please, can we get on?'

They were an exhausting and frustrating hour into the meeting when the strange sound of a crowd cheering came from the pocket of Darren's towelling robe. He took out a mobile and snapped to his feet. He started to pace about the room. 'No way, mate! ... No way! ... Wicked! ... Yeah, like really wicked! ... Yeah, you too, mate ... Nice one ... Crackin'.' He rang off and grinned at Sally. 'Guess who that was?'

'I couldn't begin to guess.'

'It was my agent with some hot news.'

'You're not being transferred, are you?' Sally's mind was fast considering how a huge transfer payment would put her settlement plans back to square one.

'Nah. I'm writing a book. A real book. My auto ... my auto-whatsit.'

'Your autobiography. Congratulations.'

'Yeah, I'm pretty chuffed. Me nan will be dead proud.'

'Will you have a ghost writer?'

'Yeah, whatever. And the best bit is they're paying me a cool one million big ones. Life just gets better and better, don't it?'

'There's no chance this literary triumph can be held off until after your divorce settlement has been finalized, is there?'

'This what triumph?'

'The writing of your autobiography.'

He pointed a finger at her. 'That, mate, depends how long it's going to take you to pull your finger out and get that blood-sucking bitch off my back. All I know is they want me to sign a contract in the next week or so.'

Which meant the settlement for *Child v. Child* would definitely have to be rejigged. Mrs Child would doubtless want a slice of the literary action, especially so since she would probably feature in it. Who knows, the girl might even try to get the book stopped. Either way, like any good soap opera, *Child v. Child* looked set to run and run.

Later, when Sally was rounding up the now redundant papers

and preparing to leave, Darren said, 'You know, mate, and I don't wanna stress you out or nuffink, but you really do look like you could do with a holiday. I could lend you my villa in Marbella if you fancy it. Your kid would love the pool.'

She drove back to the office feeling immensely dissatisfied with herself. She'd as good as insulted a client – a high-profile client who was likely to be a repeat offender and therefore important to keep sweet. Not only that, she'd let her mind wander to the point of professional suicide. And on top of all that, Darren had offered her the use of his holiday home. Whilst she would never take him up on his offer, his generosity made her feel small and petty. It compounded the host of negative feelings she was already experiencing. No matter how hard she tried to shake herself out of it, she kept finding fault with everything around her, and at times, that included herself. She couldn't understand why Darren, of all people, had been nice to her.

Or why Harry should profess to be falling in love with her. 'Oh, don't be absurd,' she'd said in the face of his declaration. It had come directly after their getting stuck in the lift together. She had literally run to her office to hide there until the worst of the clamouring guilt shrieking inside her head had subsided. She still couldn't believe that she had kissed Harry. A kiss that could in no way be described as a light, tentative peck on the cheek, an innocent, meaningless exchange. Oh no, it had been a kiss loaded with sexual significance, a kiss that would have left no one in any doubt that she had been a willing participant. Harry hadn't forced her into it. He hadn't tricked her. It had happened as naturally as them both taking a breath of air.

All she could say in her defence was that as natural as the desire to kiss him had been, it had happened only because the situation had been so wholly unnatural. It had been an extreme situation, which in turn had caused her to act out of character. But for all her rationalizing, she knew the kiss she had shared with Harry had touched her so profoundly there was a very real risk of it happening again.

When they'd finally been freed from the lift and after everyone had had their fill of asking them if they were OK, Harry had followed her to her office. He'd sent Chandra off to make some coffee, sat her down in her chair and asked her how she was really feeling. 'You still look very pale,' he'd said.

'It's shock. Shock at what we did.'

'I could apologize, but it won't make it any less true.'

'I know, but for peace of mind we have to go on as if it had never happened.'

'What if I have no intention of doing that? What if I told you there's a very serious chance that I'm falling in love with you?'

'Oh, don't be absurd, Harry.'

He'd smiled and that was when he'd told her how seductive he found her when she admonished him so primly.

'Please don't tease me,' she'd said. 'Or joke about what we did. I have a husband to think about.'

'Were you thinking of him when I had my arms around you?'

God help her, but she hadn't. 'You won't make things difficult, will you?' she'd said, more of a statement than a question.

'Difficult?' he'd repeated. 'Are you worried that I'm now going to start chasing you round the office or bombard you with sexually explicit emails?' He stepped towards her. 'I care about you, Sally. Why would I want to do anything to you that would cause you a moment's pain?'

He'd been dangerously close to her. Close enough for her to reach up, slip a hand around his neck and pull him to her so she could kiss him again. But she hadn't. 'Thank you,' she'd murmured, praying fiercely that he wouldn't come any closer. That they – that *she* – wouldn't do anything stupid.

'What for?' he'd asked.

'For being so understanding.'

He'd smiled at that. It hadn't been a happy smile, though.

'I'm sorry,' she'd said, 'that didn't come out the way I wanted it to.'

He'd put a hand on hers. Don't, she'd thought. Please don't. But she hadn't slid her hand out from under his. 'I don't deserve you,' he'd said, 'but for now it's enough for me to be near you. Don't take that away from me, will you?'

Remembering his words and the expression on his face made Sally's heart lurch. How had she got herself into this mess and allowed Harry to do this to her? How had he got under her skin, to the extent that he made her feel panicky and wildly out of control whenever she thought of him? Because of him, her concentration was all over the place, and that was something she couldn't afford to give in to. Any more unprofessional behaviour like she'd just displayed with Darren and she'd lose all credibility.

It was a stroke of luck that Harry was now away in London

working on a big tax fraud case. With him out of the office, she might stand a chance of putting this madness behind her. It was three days since they'd kissed, and surely after another few days she'd be over the worst and back on an even keel.

To banish Harry from her thoughts, she called home on her mobile in its cradle on the dashboard. She suddenly needed to hear Dan's voice.

When the answerphone kicked in, she remembered that Dan wasn't at home today; it was an office day for him at the trust. She fleetingly considered ringing his mobile but decided against it. He would probably be busy.

She knew she had no right to think badly of Dan when it came to his work relationship with the impossibly perfect Tatiana Haines, but her heart always hardened a little when she thought of the two of them together.

From that one brief meeting with her at the fete, Sally had discerned that Tatiana was everything she wasn't. She was carefree, open and natural, and zinging with exuberance and enthusiasm. Sally's accusation that Dan might be attracted to Tatiana had predictably never been referred to again and Sally cringed whenever she thought of that ugly scene in her study. She also cringed when she recalled Dan's words about her being more likely to stray from their marriage vows than him.

She gripped the steering wheel tightly. What if Dan knew her better than she knew herself?

Chapter Twenty-Five

It was some day off Seth was having.

All in all it was proving to be the kind of week Theology College warns you about but in no way prepares you for. Sod's law meant that the minute Owen had left for his fortnight's walking holiday in Austria, all hell had broken out in the parish.

It had started with two members of the church youth group – Ricky Young and Jez Lucas – being caught red-handed removing car number plates when they'd been on their way home after a party. Needless to say they'd been drinking. The police had decided to take a tough line and had invited the two fifteen-year-old lads to explain themselves at Crantsford police station. The parents were called and Jez's mother – who was bringing up Jez and his brother on her own – had phoned Seth at one o'clock in the morning to ask him to give the two boys a character testimony. Seth had willingly played his part; they weren't bad lads, they'd just made an error of judgement whilst wearing their lager goggles. At their age he'd got up to far worse pranks. He and a friend had set fire to an abandoned caravan once. They hadn't meant to; they'd been mucking about inside it, setting light to a can of hairspray and watching it explode. It had exploded all right and they'd been lucky to get out of the caravan with nothing worse than singed hair.

Suitably shamefaced, Ricky and Jez had eventually been allowed home with a metaphorical cuff about the ears. Seth also made them promise they would personally apologize to the owners of the vehicles and offer to wash their cars for two consecutive weekends.

The following day he'd had three funerals to prepare for. It was the home visits he found so difficult. The tears he could cope with. It was the anger – the need for the griever's shock to be vented – that was more of a challenge. That and the endless cups of tea.

The phone had been ringing non-stop in Owen's absence, most of the calls about petty parish squabbles that Seth was expected to resolve. More worrying was the call yesterday from the local paper, which had got hold of a story about Own refusing to marry a young couple in the church. The reporter wanted to know if this was now standard practice for the Church of England, to pick and choose whom it would marry. While Seth knew that Owen had stricter views on this particularly thorny issue than he did, Seth had done his best to smooth the waters and explain that what Owen had actually told the couple concerned – or what he hoped Owen had said to them – was that they were more than welcome to be married at St Michael's, just as they were welcome to attend the services on offer. He'd then very politely and firmly ended the call, knowing all too well that the less said to a reporter, the better. Personally Seth believed that it was better to be totally inclusive and have a church full of people celebrating the marriage of two people in love than play into the hands of those who claimed the church was too elitist and blinkered, preferring to slam its doors on unbelievers.

Annoyingly the telephone call had made him late for his visit to Meadow Hill old people's home, which in turn made him late for a diocese meeting in Chester. He'd reached home just in time to be confronted by Arnold Gosling on his doorstep, demanding to know why he hadn't returned his call, and what he was going to do about the youngsters congregating in the churchyard late at night?

This morning he'd been woken by the phone ringing again. It was bad news: Kenneth Garside, a long-standing member of St Michael's, had been admitted to hospital and wasn't expected to see the day through. He'd hurriedly thrown on his clerical suit, but by the time Seth made it to the hospital, the dying man was beyond recognizing who was praying for him. He died ten minutes later.

'He's gone, then?' said a voice when Seth pulled aside the curtain and stepped away to let Margery, Kenneth's widow, be alone with the man she'd been married to for more than fifty years.

'Yes,' Seth had murmured to the man in the bed opposite, wanting to add, if it's any of your business.

'Well, don't hang about here any longer or the rest of us will get twitchy. You lot are worse than the Grim Reaper.'

And a good day to you, thought Seth as he went to find a vending machine for some coffee. Plenty of his fellow ordinands from college would have smiled benignly at the miserable old bugger, pulled up a chair and eagerly set about the task of sharing the gospel with him. But right then, Seth hadn't had the stomach for it. The big mistake people made about the clergy was to assume that they didn't experience the same strengths, weaknesses and emotions as everyone else.

Many a time Seth had felt the urge to ram his fist into the smug face of someone who had crossed him, if only to disabuse them of the notion that he was some meek, mealy-mouthed do-gooder with no backbone.

He was driving home from the hospital when he saw blue flashing lights in his mirror and knew his day had just got a lot worse.

Inevitably, the two police officers found the whole thing highly amusing. 'On your way to a tarts and vicars party?' the taller of the two asked him. He looked about nineteen and was built like a telegraph pole.

Oh, oh, very funny, I've not heard that one before.

'So what's a vicar doing driving a fancy car like this, then? It's a TVR, isn't it?'

Seth let the technical inaccuracy of his job title go and said, 'That's right.'

Lanky Boy whistled. 'You vicars must earn more than I thought you did. Or did you dip your hand in the collection plate to buy it?'

The two men both laughed. Seth politely joined in with them, wishing they'd just get on with the necessary paperwork so he could go home. It was his day off, after all. He knew there was no way they'd let him off; booking a clergyman for speeding was too much of a trophy. He could picture them back at the station later, sharing the joke with their colleagues. He wouldn't be surprised if it was leaked to the local press. Just what St Michael's needed on top of the story about the young couple being turned away by Owen. Not forgetting Ricky and Jez's late-night prank that might also find its way into the public domain. Seth could see the headlines now: *Prejudiced and law-breaking ministers ... no wonder younger members of their flock are out of control!*

The temptation to find a way out of his predicament was so great, Seth considered doing something he always swore he'd never do – use his previous life to get out of a tricky situation. Just a few words and he'd have these two officers waving him on his way.

'All right, pal,' Lanky said, 'this is your lucky day – we're going to let you off. But a word to the wise: no more fancying yourself as Lewis Hamilton, OK?'

'Thank you. Thank you very much.'

Astonished and relieved, Seth drove the rest of the journey home at a steady two miles an hour under the speed limit. His car was one of the few possessions he still had from what he referred to as his previous life, and so long as he could afford to run it, he had no intention of parting with it. Besides, the older ladies in the parish loved it when he gave them a lift. The expression on their faces when he drove them home after a service was priceless, especially if he had the top down. 'Ooh,' they'd coo, 'it's so much nicer than Owen's rusty old banger.'

At home he found his answerphone full of messages – almost all of them asking if he'd heard about Kenneth dying that morning. He played through every message, hoping, as he did every day, that there might be something from Chloe. There wasn't. His sister's voice echoed in his ears: call her, give her the opportunity to change her opinion of you.

Why not? If his day was to be made worse by her refusing to speak to him, then so be it.

Sitting at his desk, he leaned forward for the phone and hunted through his address book for Chloe's number. What was the worst she could do? Slam the receiver down? Call the police and have him arrested for stalking her?

He tapped in her landline number – since it was her day off too, she might actually be at home. He almost dropped the phone when he heard her voice after only one ring. It wasn't her recorded answerphone voice, either.

'Hello,' she repeated when he hadn't said anything.

'Chloe, it's me, Seth.'

'Oh,' she said.

'Please don't hang up.'

'I wasn't going to.' He could hear indignation in her voice, as though he'd accused her of lacking courage.

'You weren't?'

'Don't sound so surprised. How are you?'

This was good. She was prepared to talk. To ask how he was. 'I'm well,' he said. 'Well, actually, I'm not. I've had a shit week and today's been no better.'

There was a silence down the line and then: 'Are you allowed to swear?'

'Did I swear?'

'You said shit.'

'Now who's swearing?'

She laughed.

This was definitely good. She sounded more relaxed now. 'So how are you?' he asked.

'I've had a weird week. Paul, my ex-boyfriend, showed up unexpectedly.'

Oh, great! Perfect. Exactly what he needed to hear. 'What did he want?' Seth managed to ask, keeping his tone level.

'Funnily enough, he wanted me to forgive him.'

'And did you?'

'Not really. Although I suppose you would tell me I should or I'll go to hell or something.'

'You know, Chloe, I'm going to have to rid you of these stereotypical images you have of my profession.'

'I've never heard it called a profession before. I thought it was a calling. Or a vocation.'

'You think my job's a holiday?'

'I said *vo*cation.'

'I know, I was teasing you.' He paused. Took a breath. Plunged in with both feet. 'Would I be pushing my luck if I were to ask if you'd like to meet for a drink? I promise I won't embarrass you and show up in my collar or vestments.'

The silence in his ear was so intense Seth could hear his own pulse ticking. Don't say anything, he warned himself. Don't push her.

'Just a drink?' she asked eventually.

He was sensitive to her testing his suggestion. Testing it for any strings that might be attached. 'There might be some talking involved,' he added.

'A drink and some talking. Anything else?'

'Don't worry, Chloe, we'll just be two friends meeting for a drink and catching up.' To reassure her, he laid all his cards on the table. 'I promise I won't try to kiss you again. I totally accept where I stand with you. Do you think you can be friends with a curate?'

Dan was in a particularly good mood. His idea to add a new dimension to the work the trust did had gone down surprisingly well. 'I don't want to come across as the new boy getting above himself,' he'd tactfully explained to Tatiana before outlining his thoughts. 'I know I'm here for my financial acumen, not my big ideas.'

'You should have more faith in your input,' she'd told him after she'd listened to what he had to say. 'I think what you're proposing is spot on. Only trouble is, funds are limited so we have to prioritize and sibling care tends to get overlooked. Find us the money, Dan, and we'll do it.'

Now as he weighed out the Arborio rice for the leek risotto he was going to cook for supper, Dan knew exactly where he was going to start looking for the cash that the trust would need. First he'd approach his old firm in Manchester, then he'd tap his old university mates with their big corporate connections. What was more, and because he so believed in the cause, he would be brazen about it. He'd shake them all till the money tumbled out of them. And kept on tumbling.

He was slicing a leek when he heard Sally letting herself in at the front door. He glanced at the clock – it was eight forty-five. He called out to her, but she didn't respond. At once he felt his good mood evaporate. For too long now he and Sally had been chafing at each other. He had no idea how she could have come up with that extraordinary accusation about him and Tatiana having anything more than a strictly working relationship, but he'd decided to let it go, putting her behaviour down to problems at work. She had seemed oddly jumpy and on edge this week and if it was work that was causing the change in her, the last thing she needed was any further antagonism at home.

It was also the last thing Marcus needed to be around. Children picked up on negative vibes as easily as they caught a cold. They had antennae that picked up anything that wasn't right. Parents were supposed to be the buffer zone in a child's life and Dan was adamant that Marcus's buffer zone would not be breached. To this end, he cranked up his mood and plastered a cheerful smile on his face. 'Hi,' he said brightly when Sally came into the kitchen. 'Good day?'

'Not bad,' she said.

Sally's heart sank. Why did he always have to look so damned happy? She watched Dan return his attention to slicing the leek on the chopping board in front of him. She'd bought him the knife as part of a criminally expensive set last Christmas. 'Just what I wanted,' he'd said when he'd opened the present. She'd teased him that he was so easily pleased.

Before they were married they used to play a game called If This Were The Last Day Of Your Life, What Would You Do? To begin with, their answers invariably revolved around spending all day in bed together making love. They then created a rule that forced them to be more inventive. Under this new rule Dan revealed a side of his nature previously unknown to Sally. He said he'd want to carry out an armed robbery on a bank just to know what the adrenalin rush felt like. Another time he said he'd like to see if he could out-ski an avalanche.

Looking at her husband now as he ladled stock into a frying pan of rice, Sally wondered what his answer would be this very minute if she were to ask him the question. Would his wish be to make the perfect risotto?

He suddenly turned and faced her. She willed him to put down the ladle. Hug me, she thought. Just one hug to make me believe everything's all right between us.

'I'm afraid I'm running late tonight,' he said. 'Supper won't be ready for a while yet. Why don't you treat yourself to a soak in the bath?'

Feeling as if she'd been dismissed, Sally went upstairs. There seemed no room in Dan's life for her; he had his hands full with Marcus, the house and now the trust.

He was so deeply entrenched in his own world, he had no idea of the danger they were in.

Chapter Twenty-Six

Gemma Cawston was seventeen. Back in January, while giving the mandatory safe sex talk, Chloe had prescribed Gemma the mini pill. Going by the girl's embarrassed demeanour, Chloe had taken it as read that it was a matter she would rather her mother and father didn't know about.

Chloe knew Gemma's parents – they were both on her patient list – and she knew they were exactly the kind of people who would be shocked and hugely disapproving to learn that their teenage daughter was sexually active. Gemma was their only child and had come to her parents late in their lives – the baby they thought they'd never have – and they were extremely protective of her. They were also, in Chloe's opinion, much too pushy. It was impossible to have a conversation with either of them without some reference being made to how well Gemma was doing at school, whether it was an exam she'd come top in, or a perfectly executed piano or flute recital she'd given. Parental pride was all very well, but too much of it could be counterproductive.

From the look of her, Chloe strongly suspected that Gemma was sinking beneath the weight of her parents' expectations. There was something about her manner that caused Chloe to treat Gemma's visit to the surgery as more than just a routine check-up for another supply of the mini pill. It was the tired, pale face, the downcast eyes, the fingers fiddling distractedly with her sleeves that dangled almost to the ends of her hands that concerned Chloe.

'Have you experienced any problems with taking the pill?' Chloe asked her.

Gemma shook her head.

'No irregular bleeding? No nausea or headaches?'

Gemma shook her head again.

'In that case, let's see how your blood pressure's doing, shall we?' Chloe moved her chair round the desk to sit alongside her patient. Gemma pushed back her right sleeve. 'How's school?' Chloe asked as she fixed the nylon cuff tightly round the girl's arm.

'It's OK.'

Chloe began pumping up the cuff. She then deflated it a little and listened to the beat of Gemma's pulsing blood. She completed the test and smiled. 'That's fine. So nothing special going on at school, then?'

Gemma pushed her sleeve back into place and shrugged. 'Just the usual stuff.'

'You'll be applying to university in the autumn, won't you? Any idea what you'll do?'

'English. History. I don't know. I can't make up my mind. Maybe I'll take a gap year. If I can get Mum and Dad to agree.'

'Oh, well, there's plenty of time yet to decide. Roll up your sleeve and I'll do your left arm as well.'

Gemma looked at Chloe, startled. It was the first time she'd met her eye. 'Why? You said my blood pressure was OK.'

Chloe smiled. 'No harm in double-checking. You'd be amazed how often I've come across a difference between the left and the right arm.'

'What if I don't want you to double-check?'

Keeping her voice light, Chloe said, 'Then I'd have to ask you why.'

Gemma swallowed and chewed anxiously on her lip. Her nervous hesitation was all Chloe needed to know that she'd been right to follow her instinct. She continued to smile and held out the nylon cuff, ready to wrap it around the girl's arm. Very slowly, her gaze now avoiding Chloe's, Gemma pushed back her sleeve. Her arm was a mass of disfiguring criss-crosses. Most of the marks were pale or softly pink, but there were fresh, more livid slashes scorching Gemma's skin. The ugliness of the marks was horribly at odds with the girl's natural prettiness.

Chloe put down the blood pressure testing kit. 'How long have you being doing this, Gemma?' She took the girl's arm and gently eased the sleeve back further still. What looked like a recently applied plaster partially covered the girl's bicep.

'Since February,' Gemma murmured.

'And do you know why you do it?'

'It's … it's how I escape.'

'What are you escaping from?'

'Everything.'

'And what usually triggers this need to escape?'

'When I feel it's the only way I can control my life.'

Chloe nodded. Self-harming was rife among high-achieving girls like Gemma. 'And presumably your parents have no idea about this?'

Gemma rolled her eyes. 'What do you think? All they care about are my grades and getting into Cambridge. They've even started telling people which college I'm going to apply to. It hasn't crossed their minds that I might not want to go.'

'Have you tried discussing it with them?'

'Whenever I try to hint that maybe I might not be clever enough to be offered a place at Cambridge they just laugh and tell me not to be so silly, that of course I'm clever enough.'

'It's never about how clever you are, but that's not the point.' Chloe slid Gemma's sleeve down her arm. 'I'm going to give you a supply of sterile dressings and antiseptic. It's important that you keep the risk of infection to a minimum.'

Gemma's eyes widened. 'You're not going to lecture me about not doing it?'

'Would you stop cutting yourself if I did?'

'Probably not.'

'Then I shan't waste my breath. I'd like to put you in touch with someone you could talk to, though.'

'A psychologist? A counsellor?'

'Something like that, yes.'

Gemma seemed to consider the suggestion. 'Mum and Dad would find out, wouldn't they?'

'Not necessarily. On the other hand, you can always come and see me any time you want.'

Again Gemma went quiet as she thought about Chloe's suggestion. 'Thanks,' she said. 'But I'm fine.'

When she was up on her feet and at the door ready to leave with the prescription Chloe had printed off for her, she said, 'You didn't take my blood pressure a second time. Was that because you didn't really need to?'

'Correct. Although I have done it in certain cases before now. The readings can vary; I wasn't lying to you.'

'So you suspected I was cutting myself and wanted to make sure?'

Chloe nodded.

'What gave me away?'

Everything, Chloe wanted to say, just as Gemma had said earlier.

'I'm a doctor,' she said simply. 'Now take care, and I know it's easier said than done, but try not to let things get on top of you. And remember what I said: come and see me whenever you want. Even if it's just to mouth off about something that's happened at school.'

A shadow of a smile passed across the girl's pretty face. 'You'd make a great mum, you know.'

Chloe swallowed back the compliment. 'That remains to be seen.'

A practice meeting kept Chloe at the surgery until late and by the time she was on her way home – after remembering to call in at Laurel House to check the tomato plants in the greenhouse while her parents were away in Florence – she was starving hungry. Lunch had somehow passed her by and as she followed the path round to the back of her house, she tried to remember what she had in the fridge.

The sight of a large bouquet of flowers on the back doorstep stopped her in her tracks. She let herself into the house, dumped her medical bag and jacket on a chair and went back out for the flowers. Who on earth had sent her such an extravagant bouquet?

She put the flowers on the table in the conservatory and retrieved the small card that was attached to a stick poking out from behind a lily – a flower she had to admit she hated; its sickly sweet scent was too pungent for her liking. It made the back of her throat tickle.

Dear Chloe,

Thank you for giving me a second chance. With love and deepest regret,

Paul.

Chloe stared at the card in her hand. *Deepest regret.* What did he mean by that? It sounded more like the kind of sentiment you'd express to the recently bereaved. And the word *love*, was that just a straightforward salutation, or did he mean something more by it? Or was she being ridiculous and over-analysing his message? His last words to her the other night when they'd left the restaurant were that he'd very much like to see her again. She'd said she'd think about it.

But why not see him again? He'd apologized for what he'd done to her and admitted he had behaved badly; why not forgive him and give him a second chance? After all, as he'd said himself, he was not the man he was. He'd changed. What if they could not only rekindle what they'd once had, but could develop it into something

155

even better? Something truly lasting that might lead to marriage and them having children together.

She gasped. What was she thinking? How could she even entertain such an idea? Was she really so desperate to satisfy her intense craving for a child that she would risk getting involved with Paul again?

As shaming as it was, she really was that desperate. *You'd make a great mum*, poor Gemma had said, little knowing that those innocent words could make Chloe feel so empty and desolate.

Furious with herself, she tossed the card angrily onto the table next to the flowers and went upstairs to change. Within minutes she was dressed in jeans and a T-shirt and was back down in the kitchen. She opened a bottle of wine, put on a CD – 'Sam's Town' by The Killers – turned up the volume and make a start on peeling some potatoes for her supper. With every flick of the peeler she reminded herself what a prat Paul had sounded the other night, all that garbage about positive thinking and self-awareness. Well, she'd show him what positive thinking was!

How dare he assume she was giving him a second chance?

How dare he think he could just walk straight back into her life?

How dare he send her flowers and think that those rotten stinking lilies would make everything right between them?

So worked up was she, she stormed over to the conservatory, grabbed the bouquet and took it out to the garden. She threw it on the ground and stamped on the flowers hard. She stamped and stamped and then stamped some more.

How was that for valuing herself?

Chapter Twenty-Seven

It was mid-June and the sun was hot and high in a cloudless blue sky.

Dan was playing super-heroes in the garden with Marcus and Charlie when Rosie returned from her visit to the doctors' surgery. He broke off from the game – removing his cape made out of an old beach towel – and offered to make lunch for everyone. The city of cardboard boxes they'd been saving from imminent disaster instantly forgotten, the boys chased after Dan, clamouring noisily for a drink. Dan ignored them. 'Rosie,' he said, cocking his ear, 'is it my imagination, or can I hear a strange sort of squeaking?' He looked exaggeratedly around him. 'It seems to be coming from somewhere down there.' He looked directly at the two boys, who immediately threw themselves at his legs. 'Aha!' he said. 'It's you two. Well, unless you take off your masks and invisibility cloaks I won't be able to see you to give you a drink.' The boys shrieked with laughter and pulled off the masks Dan had made earlier from an empty cereal packet.

Charlie and Marcus ate their lunch on a blanket under the apple tree and Dan and Rosie sat at the wrought iron table. As Dan sliced the last of the French stick and offered it to Rosie, he noticed she didn't seem to be very hungry. She hadn't touched any of the pate or brie and had only nibbled on a few pieces of bread. Without wanting to pry, but at the same time not wanting to appear as though he didn't care, Dan asked Rosie how she'd got on at the doctor's. She smiled. 'Chloe confirmed what Dave and I already knew: I'm pregnant.'

'Hey, that's brilliant! Congratulations! When's it due?'

'January. And before you ask, we're not going to find out what sex the baby is. We didn't with Charlie and we don't see any reason to do things differently this time round. It might sound silly, but we don't want to tempt fate. We've had one perfectly healthy child, and part of me is worried that second time around we might not be so lucky.'

Dan understood exactly what Rosie was saying. He'd thought it himself whenever he'd entertained the idea of he and Sally having another child. Could they really hit the jackpot twice in a row? But having grown up as an only child Dan would prefer Marcus to have a brother or sister as a playmate; someone he could fight with in the early years but then feel close to when he was older. He'd been thinking for a while now that it was something he and Sally ought to discuss. 'Have you said anything to Charlie?' he asked Rosie.

'We've decided to wait until things are more definite. You know, when he notices I look different.'

Dan laughed. 'Bear in mind that he's a bloke; he might not notice a change in you until you're coming home from the hospital with the baby in your arms.'

That night, Dan and Sally were in bed early. But they weren't sleeping; they were both working. Sally was making notes for another article for the Law Society's *Gazette* – her first had been so well received she had been asked to write a follow-up piece – and Dan was putting a report together for the trust. The figures made impressive reading. In just two weeks his efforts to raise money for his pet project were gathering a pleasing momentum. Tatiana had said that in her view he now had sufficient pledges of financial support to present to the board to make something happen. His big hurdle was to convince the board that what he'd instigated was sustainable. But then that was true of any funds raised for the trust's benefit, as far as Dan could see. It was all on a wing and a prayer.

When he was satisfied that the spreadsheet contained all the information he needed for the presentation he was going to give tomorrow, he closed down his laptop, put it on the floor beside the bed and turned to Sally. She appeared to be lost in thought, staring across the bedroom at the wall. 'How's it going?' he asked.

She took a moment to reply, seeming to have difficulty tearing her eyes from the spot on the wall. 'Slowly,' she said. 'I know what I want to say, but I can't seem to find the right words.'

'Would a drink help? Shall I go down and put the kettle on?'

She clicked her biro, closed her legal pad, and yawned. 'No thanks,' she said. 'Let's call it a night.'

The turned out the lights. Sally lay on her side. Dan did the same. They had their backs to each other. It was a warm, sultry night and through the open bedroom window, Dan listened to the sound of a car driving by. 'I forgot to tell you,' he said. 'Rosie and Dave are expecting another baby.'

'Really? Was it planned?'

Dan rolled over onto his back. He kicked away his side of the duvet. 'Rosie didn't say otherwise, so I assume so. The age gap between Charlie and the baby will be a good one.'

'What makes you think that?'

'Stands to reason; Charlie will be less demanding by then and more able to understand what's going on.'

'You don't think he'll be of an age to be thoroughly put out and jealous? He'll have had all this time to be the centre of attention and suddenly he won't be *numero uno* any more.'

'Most kids go through that and survive it pretty well.'

Sally also now turned onto her back. 'Are you saying you'd risk that with Marcus?'

'Yes,' Dan said, deciding to be honest. 'Although in the big scheme of things, it's hardly that huge a deal, is it? A few months of jealousy can soon be overcome.' He turned his head to look at Sally. 'I know it would complicate things, but would it be so out of the question for us to consider having another child?'

In the half-light, Sally stared at him, her eyes wide. 'You're not serious, are you?'

Until now, this very moment, Dan hadn't realized just how serious he was. It had taken Rosie's news to bring to the fore of his mind what had been vaguely there at the back of it for some time. 'I've never wanted Marcus to be an only child,' he said. 'If we're going to have another baby, we should think about it before—'

'Before what?' she interrupted him. 'Before I'm too decrepit? Was that what you were going to say?' She sat up. 'And is that all I am to you now? A baby-making machine? When did that happen? When did I change from being the woman you wanted to make love with, to being a human incubator?' Out of the bed now, she was pulling on her silk dressing gown.

'Maybe it was when you started being so unapproachable,' Dan said quietly. 'The day you became so touchy about everything that I had to watch my every word or action for fear of being accused of something.'

'I am not touchy!'

'No? Well then, how come we're having this argument? All I did was suggest we might try for another baby.'

'Oh, that's it; make it sound like I'm the one being unreasonable!

You don't touch me in God knows how long and suddenly you want sex to get me pregnant. You're unbelievable!'

'If we haven't had sex recently it's because we've both been so busy. You especially.'

'There you go again, making out that it's my fault.'

'Sally, this isn't about fault. It's about adding to our family.'

'But why? We have Marcus. Isn't that enough for you? Why do you want to risk us having another baby that might ... that might turn out like the ones your precious trust looks after?' She tied the belt on her dressing gown with a vicious yank. 'Or would that suit you just fine because it would feed into your hero complex? Good old selfless Dan! No matter what you throw at him he can cope with it. He saves the life of a child, stays at home to bring up his own and at the same time devotes himself to the needs of the less fortunate. You'll be walking on water next!'

Dan stared at her, staggered. 'Is that how you see me?'

Her rock-steady gaze didn't waver from his. 'Yes. Do you have any idea how hard it is to live with a hero?'

Shocked, Dan got out of bed. He didn't trust himself to say another word. Take this any further and they'd both say things they'd really regret. In silence, he left the room and went downstairs.

He'd been in the kitchen for nearly half an hour, just sitting at the table, when he concluded that Sally was not going to come down after him. Perhaps, wisely, she had decided they both needed time to cool off. He rubbed his face. How had this happened? How had they reached this appalling point when they could say such things to each other?

What worried him most was how on earth they would find their way back to how it used to be between them.

And what the hell did she mean by a hero complex?

Chapter Twenty-Eight

'Uncle Seth, Uncle Seth, are you going to marry Chloe?'

Seth scooped up the two squealing girls, one in each arm, and dangling them over the edge of the pool, threatened to throw them in. After a good deal of thrashing and hysterical laughter from the pair of them, he set the two girls down. Immediately they started dragging him towards the pool. 'Tell us or we'll push you in,' they shrieked. 'Tell us! Tell us! Are you going to marry Chloe?'

'Mind your own beeswax,' Seth said, and in one deft moment, he grabbed his squawking nieces by their hands and jumped into the pool with them.

Amused, Chloe watched their antics from her sun lounger. She was glad that she had accepted Seth's invitation to spend the day with him in Shropshire at his sister's house – a converted mill complete with stream, pool and amazing views of softly undulating countryside. Rebecca was spending the day down in Leamington Spa at a friend's wedding and wasn't expected back until late that night. Her parting words as she'd hurried out of the house shortly after Seth and Chloe had arrived were to warn Chloe to take no nonsense from either her brother or her daughters, Phoebe and Isabella.

Since they'd redefined the nature of their relationship, Chloe really appreciated Seth's presence in her life. He was fun to be around and she always looked forward to spending time with him, whether it was at the gym or having a meal together while watching a DVD. Initially, if she were honest, she'd been anxious that he might view their friendship as a way to win her round into pursuing an altogether different relationship. But he'd been as good as his word and never once hinted that he wanted anything more from her. If indeed he did. And whilst she knew she'd upset him by dropping him the way she had, he seemed to have forgiven her and accepted the way things were. He'd probably come to terms with the undeniable truth, that there was no point in pursuing her as a long-term girlfriend because it would leave him wide open to criticism. People would say that if he couldn't convert her, who could he convert?

All that aside, it was an enjoyable novelty having such a good male friend to hang out with. Dan and Sally were great, but they had their own busy lives to get on with and didn't need her butting in all the time.

It was funny, but being with Seth made her feel independent and strangely liberated. She could be herself. There was no need to go out of her way to impress him or pretend she was something that she wasn't. She had done that too often when she'd been throwing herself into relationship after relationship, on the rebound and desperately trying to find a replacement for Paul. The thought of the person she'd allowed herself to become was a mortifyingly painful memory. As was the thought of how she'd reacted when Paul had sent her those flowers. How could she have allowed herself, albeit momentarily, to wonder if she and Paul could make it work again? How desperate could a girl be?

He had telephoned the following evening, minutes before she had been on her way out to meet Seth for their first let's-be-friends drink. 'Did you receive my flowers?' he'd asked.

She had thought of them outside in the garden, still lying crushed and decimated, and replied, 'I did, thank you.'

'I meant what I said on the card,' he'd gone on. 'I genuinely hope—'

She'd cut him off mid-sentence. 'Paul, I don't know exactly what it is you want from me, but please don't think a bunch of flowers and dinner is going to make me forget what you did. I wish you well, but really, I'd rather not have any more contact with you.'

'I understand,' he'd said. 'My resurfacing is still too raw and painful for you. Perhaps when I get back from running the summer school in Greece with Liz we could meet again. I'd really like to help you move on and—'

'Stop! That's the whole problem, Paul: you really don't understand. Now please, you're making me late. Goodbye.' She'd put the phone down, not with a dramatic bang, but very slowly, very surely. There. That was Paul dealt with.

There had been no further communication from him and she hoped that by the time he returned from Greece, he'd have lost interest in pestering her.

'Fancy a swim, Doctor Hennessey?' Seth was at the side of the pool, his elbows planted in front of him as he raised himself partially out of the water. His curly black hair was slick and wet and swept back from his forehead. He looked more like a glamorous male model posing for the camera than an uncle babysitting a couple of nieces.

Chloe surveyed the pool – Phoebe and Isabella were down at the shallow end playing a complicated game that involved one of them being a princess and the other pretending to be a suitor and diving for her crown. 'You know, Reverend Hawthorne, I think I just might.'

He smiled and offered his hand.

'No way,' she said. 'I've seen what you do to poor defenceless girls.' Instead, she dived in just a few feet away from him. When she rose to the surface on the other side of the pool and looked back to where he'd been, he'd disappeared. He then bobbed up behind her.

'This isn't too boring for you, is it?' he asked, wiping the water from his face.

'I can't think of a better way to spend a hot summer's day.'

'Really? You don't mind entertaining the girls with me?' He inclined his head towards the shallow end of the pool – the princess was becoming shrill and shirty now and demanding a necklace to be found as well.

Chloe laughed. 'I'm pretty much redundant in the entertainment department. You're doing a great job all on your own. They adore you, don't they?'

'I wouldn't go as far as to say that. And I'm sorry what they said earlier, you know, about me marrying you. It's nothing more than high spirits. They're always like it.'

The temptation to tease him was too great. 'You mean they say it to every friend you introduce them to?'

'Oh, yeah, without fail. They're worse than certain members of my parish who are constantly asking me when I'm going to find a nice girl and settle down.'

This was the first time Chloe had heard Seth refer directly to his parish and it was a reminder to her that despite the number of evenings they'd spent together, the one topic that Seth had assiduously avoided was his work. The few times she'd asked him anything about it, he'd given no more than a one-word answer and immediately changed the subject. Perhaps he'd been wary of saying more in case it gave her the opening to launch an attack on his beliefs. However, now that she felt their friendship was on surer ground she felt the need to start probing. 'Seth,' she said, swimming closer to him, 'can I ask you something?'

'Of course.'

'What made you go into the Church?'

'Ah, a long story. I used to be a policeman.'

'A policeman? You're kidding?'

He shielded his eyes from the glare of the sun and looked at her. 'People are always surprised by that. But it's in the family. My dad recently retired from the Met and his father before him also worked for the force.'

'So you've turned out to be the black sheep of the family. What made you leave?'

He tipped backwards so that his head was submerged up to his forehead in water. He then righted himself and ran his hand through his hair. 'I was working for the vice squad,' he said. 'Day in, day out I was dealing with the kind of stuff that made me despair of the world we live in. It was the video evidence I had to watch that really did it. Especially when children were involved.' His eyes flickered to where Phoebe and Isabella were still playing noisily. 'Call me a wimp, but I didn't have the stomach for it. Several of my older colleagues had become inured to the horrors of the job and I knew I didn't ever want to reach that point. I never wanted to watch a video of a two-year-old boy being tortured and not be shocked by it.'

'So you decided you'd try and save these monsters' souls rather than send them to prison?'

He frowned. 'Would that be so very wrong?'

'Sorry, I could have put that better.'

'Whichever way you want to put it, you think I'm misguided and idealistic, don't you?'

'I don't, actually. As a GP I've seen a number of child abuse cases and know as well as you do that there's always a reason why it goes on, that often the abuser was once abused themselves. But back to my original question; why the Church? Why not social work, for instance? Or why not make a transfer to another department or division in the police force?'

'The simple answer is that I genuinely felt called.'

'How? In what way?'

'It's ... it's a long story—' he broke off. 'Do you really want to know?'

She nodded.

'OK, but tell me when the cringe factor has reached a level that you can't take it any longer.'

She nodded again.

'Well, I can honestly say, hand on heart, that it was the thought of all that Shloer that attracted me.'

'Shloer?'

'Sorry, it's a theology college joke.' He adopted a falsetto tone. 'Can I tempt you into another glass of non-alcoholic grape juice, vicar?'

Chloe smiled.

'That's better,' he said, 'you were looking much too serious.'

'Does that mean I'm not going to get an answer to my question?'

'For now, all I'll say is that I came to the understanding that a life without faith would mean that the hokey-cokey really was what it's all about. Come on, let's swim before the girls start bossing me about to get the barbecue going for lunch. The first to do four lengths doesn't have to do the washing-up.'

'You're on!'

'Uncle Seth, did you deliberately let Chloe win?'

'Of course I did, Phoebe. It's what a gentleman should always do.'

'Don't you believe him, Phoebe,' Chloe said, joining the girls at the wooden bench table. 'He couldn't have beaten me if I'd had both arms tied behind my back.'

Amused, Seth watched Phoebe looking at Chloe thoughtfully. 'I don't think it's possible to swim with your arms tied behind your back, is it?' she asked.

'Fish don't have arms,' Isabella said, adding her voice to the debate, 'and they swim perfectly well.'

'They have fins, silly. I'm right, aren't I, Uncle Seth? Fins are like arms, aren't they? Mummy says we were fish once and that means we used to have fins. Mummy's right, isn't she, Uncle Seth?'

'Only a fool would disagree with your mother, Phoebe. Now then, who's for a burger, a chicken drumstick or a lamb chop?'

'Everything for me!'

'Eight burgers for me!'

Seth laughed and placed the enormous platter of barbecued meat on the table. 'Manners!' he roared at his nieces as they began stabbing at the meat with their forks. 'Guests get first pick. Chloe?'

Once they'd filled their plates – Seth enforcing a strict 'one portion of meat equals a portion of salad' rule to the girls – and Phoebe had poured their drinks out and Isabella had handed round napkins, he gave the go-ahead to eat.

'But, Uncle Seth, aren't you going to say grace?' Isabella turned to Chloe. 'Uncle Seth always says grace when Mummy's not here. But not the proper one. He says a rude one. My favourite one is when he says rubber-dub-dub, thanks for the grub.'

'Maybe we'll pass on that today,' Seth said, catching Chloe's eye.

Both girls looked at Chloe. 'You'd like to hear Uncle Seth say one of his rude graces, wouldn't you?'

Chloe smiled at Seth. 'I can't think of anything I'd like more.'

'OK,' he said. He bowed his head. 'For what these two young savages are about to receive,' he intoned in his most ludicrously sanctimonious voice, 'may the Lord keep them from being sick all over the carpet, the sofa, the telly, and themselves. At least until Chloe and I are long gone. Amen.'

It was almost eleven o'clock when Rebecca returned home, and gone midnight by the time Seth was driving Chloe back to Eastbury. Rebecca had invited them to stay the night, but since he had Morning Service at eight o'clock the next day followed by a Family Service at ten thirty, which he was leading, Seth declined.

'Are you exhausted?' he asked Chloe. 'Five games of Twister on the trot is a record, I might add. As a result Phoebe and Isabella will have elevated you to the very highest level of approval and admiration.'

'I've had a great day,' she said. 'Thanks for inviting me. And if ever you need to improve your swimming speed, give me a call.'

He smiled. 'You know my views on that. A gentleman knows how to behave.'

'Yes, but a true gentleman would never admit it.'

'Ah, got me there.'

As he kept his eyes on the road, Seth tried not to feel so pleased that everything about the day had gone so well. The only downside had been that he'd continually had to check himself when he was around Chloe. Countless times he'd instinctively wanted to reach out and put his arm around her. He'd promised himself that he'd be able to cope with being just a friend to Chloe, but he'd misjudged how much strength it would take to keep his distance from her, both physically and mentally.

They'd been driving for several miles when Chloe said, 'Seth, does it bother you that I don't go to church or believe in God?'

'Are you asking me that because you're paranoid I'm going to try and convert you?'

'I don't think so.'

'Or is it because my belief makes you feel defensive of your lack of belief, something that until now you've never had to question?'

In the silence that followed, Seth wondered if he'd gone too far. What was he trying to do? Spoil a perfectly good day?

'No,' she said at last. 'I'm a scientist at heart and so approach things quite differently from you. You appear to have all the answers to something that can't be proved. It naturally makes the scientist in me react with suspicion and distrust.'

'Chloe, if there's one thing I really want you to understand about me, I work consistently within the parameters of my inadequacies; I don't have all the answers. I can't, for instance, explain away the nature of suffering. What I do know is that we're better off with the power of redemptive love than without it.' He paused and glanced sideways at her. 'And that's me sounding one hundred per cent defensive.'

'I'm sorry, I didn't mean to make you feel you had to defend yourself.'

He smiled. 'Don't worry. I'm used to it. As you no doubt gathered, my sister doesn't share my views. That goes for the rest of my family too.'

'Did your family treat you differently when you left the police force to become a vicar?'

'You bet they did! My parents did everything they could to make me change my mind. They thought I was having some kind of breakdown.'

'Are they OK with it now?'

'They're still coming to terms with it. They think I'm some kind of weird Holy Joe and do crazy things when I go to see them, like hide the bottle of wine they've just opened, or apologize if my father swears in front of me. I end up telling them to stop buggering about and to pass the wine before I die of thirst.'

'Can I ask you something else?'

'Fire away.'

'Do you believe every word of the Bible?'

'I most assuredly do not. Check out Exodus thirty-five, verse two, when it says that anyone who works on the Sabbath should be put to death. A command like that shoots down the zealots with one easy zap, don't you think? The Bible, or any book of faith for that matter, should not be used as a weapon. I believe in challenging and provoking, not mindless rhetoric.'

A few minutes passed and then Seth said, 'I'm not made of stone, Chloe. Cut me and I'll bleed just like you. Just because I get to wear a bit of white plastic round my neck, it doesn't mean I'm protected from my basic instincts. My humanness is as fallible as your or anyone else's.' He smiled. 'Which means you'd better watch yourself the next time you challenge me to any kind of a race.'

She laughed. 'In your dreams, Reverend Hawthorne.'

Oh, frequently, he thought to himself. And some.

Chapter Twenty-Nine

It was August and to celebrate her birthday, Chloe's parents had invited her to lunch, along with Dan and Marcus. Seth had also been invited. 'Don't go getting any ideas,' Chloe had warned her mother. 'He's just a friend.'

'Of course he is, darling,' her mother had said. 'I understood that the first time you told me. And the second. And all the times that have followed since.'

But Chloe didn't trust her mother and she'd begged her father to keep her on a tight leash today. 'I'll do my best,' he'd said, 'but once Jennifer gets something into her head there's not a power on this earth that can shift it.'

It was a shame that Sally hadn't been able to join them for lunch. She'd had to go haring over to Hull to deal with some kind of emergency her mother was at the centre of. It was one of life's great mysteries to Chloe why her friend – one of the most assertive people she knew – never told Kath Wilson just where to get off. 'Tell her to go to hell,' Chloe had said to Sally on the phone last night. 'Tell her it's your best friend's birthday.' All Sally had said was, 'One of these days I will. Meanwhile, enjoy your day and say hi to your parents from me.'

'So, Seth,' Jennifer said when they were all seated and Chloe's father was urging them to tuck into what was on the table – poached salmon, Mediterranean roasted peppers and aubergines with couscous, and new potatoes glossy with garlic butter – 'What do you think of that bishop who keeps attributing the recent crop of natural disasters to God's wrath for same-sex marriages?'

'The man's two shades of stupid,' Seth replied. 'And probably certifiable into the bargain.'

'Well said!' cheered Jennifer delightedly. 'My sentiments exactly. The fewer men like him in charge of the Church the better in my opinion. Now then, where do you stand on the question of women priests?'

'Mum, I'm sure Seth doesn't want to talk shop.'

'If that's the case, Chloe, I'm sure Seth is perfectly capable of telling me that for himself.'

'He's much too polite to do that.'

Jennifer looked at Seth across the table. 'Good gracious! Is that true? Are you too polite to tell me to shut up?'

Seth smiled. 'Not at all. But with Marcus sitting next to me I'm holding back in the hope of setting him a good example.'

As if several paces behind in the conversation, Marcus dabbed the air with his fork and said, 'What does two shades of stupid mean?'

Lately, with his third birthday coming up next month, Marcus's speech had come on in leaps and bounds. He talked so much that sometimes Chloe had a job getting a word in edgeways with him. 'It's a way of saying someone is incredibly stupid,' she explained to him.

'How stupid? As stupid as a baby?'

'What makes you think babies are stupid?'

Marcus looked back at her sagely. 'Charlie says they are. His mummy's going to have one soon. It will cry and cry and then be sick everywhere.' He turned to look at Dan. 'Daddy? Will we have to have a baby like Charlie?'

'It's not a matter of *having* to have one,' Dan said. 'Do you think you would like a baby brother or sister?'

Marcus thought about this. 'I'd prefer a dog,' he said slowly.

Everyone laughed. All except for Dan, Chloe noticed. She had a pretty good idea why. Sally had confided in her that Dan was pressurizing her into having another child. Lucky you! Chloe had wanted to say. All around her there were women falling pregnant or giving birth and it was as much as she could do some days not to cry out with envy and frustration. I want a baby of my own! She wanted to yell at the top of her voice when yet another heavily pregnant woman waddled into her surgery. Was she for ever destined to be denied the one thing that would make her feel there was some point to her life?

Just as a good friend should, she'd listened to Sally grumbling that Dan was currently obsessed with providing Marcus with a brother or sister, but she hadn't been able to summon up any sympathy for her. Didn't Sally know how lucky she was? She had a fantastic husband, a gorgeous son, the career she always wanted and the chance to make her family complete. What on earth did she have to grumble about?

Once or twice over the years Chloe had known occasional moments of envy regarding Sally and her marriage, and never more so than now. She wasn't jealous of Sally being married to Dan, but she was jealous that she was married to someone who cared so deeply about her. Thinking that she would give anything to be in Sally's shoes, Chloe suddenly felt the pain of her longing so acutely she was overwhelmed by it. Frightened that she might actually cry, she took a gulp of her wine. It was a mistake. Her throat had tightened and she couldn't swallow. She forced her throat to relax but all that happened was that she made an embarrassing choking noise. With everyone occupied in helping Marcus to something to eat, it was only Seth who noticed. Sitting next to her, he leaned in closely. 'You OK?' he asked quietly. She covered her mouth with her napkin and nodded vaguely. He put a hand on her back. 'Are you sure?' At his touch, and as if by magic, the tightness from her throat relaxed and she was able to swallow.

'Nothing worse than a mouthful of wine about to go down the wrong way,' he said, his hand still on her back.

'Especially in such polite company,' she managed to quip.

'More salmon, Seth? What's that about polite company, Chloe?'

'Nothing, Mum.'

Watching her mother filling Seth's plate, joking predictably that a big lad like him needed feeding up, Chloe tried to restore her good mood. It was her birthday, after all. And never mind that she was now a year nearer the dreaded big four-o. Never mind that yet another year had passed and she was no nearer to being a mother. On the positive side, she had a satisfying job, a lovely home, parents who'd do anything for her, and great friends. Including Seth. As she'd done in the past, she mentally slapped herself out of her self-pity by reminding herself that compared to many people, she had it all. She had only to think of those who had lost everything in the tsunami and she was instantly ashamed of her pathetic self-absorption.

Appropriately reproved, she listened in to Dan and Seth's conversation. From the sounds of things it looked like Dan had found himself a fellow *Simpsons* fan. Chloe felt her mood lift. It was good to see how well Seth got on with her parents and Dan. She unexpectedly found herself thinking the unthinkable: Seth would make the perfect father for the child she craved. He was intelligent, amusing, compassionate and not to say extremely easy on the eye. No doubt about it, any child of his, girl or boy, would be beautiful.

Shocked at what she'd allowed herself to think, she slammed the thought from her mind. Hadn't she promised herself that she would never again size up a potential husband purely on the grounds of the suitability of his genes?

What was wrong with her that she could be so flaky and desperate? Couldn't she be with a man without considering the possibility of robbing him of his sperm to solve all her problems?

Taking a sideways glance at Seth – he was making Marcus laugh by doing a brilliant Ned Flanders voice to Dan's Mr Burns – Chloe warned herself that she would have to be extra careful with him. He could so easily tick all the right boxes. But for all the wrong reasons.

It was a shocking truth, but in her current state – a state that was likely to get worse with each birthday that passed – she couldn't trust herself when it came to men. Her brain might be telling her to go steady, but her body clock was screaming at her to grab the first available man and drag him home to bed. She was a danger to herself. And quite probably to Seth as well. If she started giving out the wrong signals, who knew what would happen? The last thing she wanted to do was spoil their friendship. It was a friendship that had become quite precious to her, and she guarded it protectively.

Never before had she felt the need to protect someone. But that was how she felt with Seth. Particularly when Sally said things like, 'Committed any original sin yet with Friar Tuck?' or 'Have you experienced any divine intervention yet?' Ever since Chloe had told Sally that she'd forgiven Seth for not being straight with her from the outset, Sally hadn't had a good word to say about him. Her comments rankled with Chloe, and not just because they were exactly the kind of remarks she would have made if the boot was on the other foot. No, what really upset Chloe was that Sally's pithy remarks were a constant reminder as to just how shallow and unworthy Chloe really was. Every one of Sally's teasing jibes showed Chloe for the hypocrite she was. Oh, yes, she was prepared to have Seth as a friend, but to have him as a boyfriend was out of the question. As reprehensible as it was to admit, even to herself, and as fond of Seth as she was, she was embarrassed by his choice of career. No matter how hard she tried, she simply couldn't view his work in the way she knew Seth would want her to. And it was acknowledging this embarrassment that made her feel guilty and in turn made her protective of him. She hated the thought of anyone finding fault with him. After all, she was doing a great job of that all on her own. None of this made her feel good about herself.

If only Seth did a normal job, or had stayed in the police force, then maybe everything would be different between them.

Yet as she looked at everyone sitting around the dining table – Dan, Marcus, Seth and her parents, all chatting quite happily together – who but her seemed bothered by how Seth chose to earn his living?

Why did she have to make such a big thing of it? Why couldn't she be as accepting as everyone else?

Chapter Thirty

'I know exactly what will happen when we leave here.'

Curled under Harry's arm, her head resting on his shoulder, Sally said, 'You do?'

He stroked her hair. 'You'll feel guilty and regret what we've done. You won't even be home before you'll be planning to tell me it's over. You'll say it was a moment of madness and it must never happen again. You'll remind me that you're married with a young son and that you have to do the right thing.'

She uncurled herself and gazed at him thoughtfully, losing herself in the depths of his sultry dark eyes. She remembered vividly how he'd calmed her that day when they'd been stuck in the lift, forcing her to focus on the colour of his eyes. That was the day when it all started, when she'd first been tempted into the thrill of an affair. 'Is that what you want me to do?' she asked. 'To end it now?' Hearing herself say the words, she felt a tug on her heart, as if feeling the loss of him already.

He held her tightly. 'I never want it to end. I love you. I love you in way I've never loved anyone before.' His voice was low and impassioned. 'I don't know what I'd do if you did say it was over.'

'Then stop thinking about it. Let's enjoy the time we have left here.' They both turned and glanced at the clock on the bedside table.

'Six hours and fifteen minutes before we have to go,' Harry murmured. 'Mmm ... can you think of anything we could do to pass the time?' He was smiling now, dazzling her with what she called his killer smile. He moved one hand slowly down her spine and with the other, he pulled her mouth towards his.

She kissed him and he kissed her back with a fierceness that made her breathless. Her body ached from the many times they'd already made love but once more he aroused her effortlessly and she welcomed his touch, responding to the strong sureness of his hands on her skin. The way he touched her, it was as if he'd never needed to acquaint himself with what pleased her. He was either a very experienced lover or knew instinctively how to please a woman.

'Close your eyes,' he said. She did as he said and felt his hands circling her waist. Slowly they moved up towards her breasts. Her eyes flickered open. 'Close them,' he said. 'Or I won't play any more.' She obeyed without hesitation, knowing how the rest of the game would play out.

Afterwards, they ran a bath and got in together. Harry had added so much bubble bath, only their heads showed above the bubbles. Massaging one of her feet, he was making her laugh. 'You look beautiful when you laugh,' he said.

'Don't be absurd,' she replied.

He tweaked her big toe. '*Don't be absurd,*' he mimicked.

She threw a handful of foam at him but it fell well short of its target. 'You're always making fun of me.'

'And how you love it! Next foot.'

She offered him her right foot and not for the first time thought how young he looked. When they'd booked into the hotel last night she had been convinced the receptionist had clocked the age gap and would hurry off to have a good snigger about it with a colleague the minute their backs were turned. 'Harry,' she said, 'do you ever think of the age difference between us?'

'Never. Why? Do you?'

'Now and then.'

'Eight years is nothing. Besides, you should look in the mirror more often. You look no more than thirty.'

'But you look about twenty, which puts us back to square one.'

'You worry too much.'

'That's patently untrue. If I was the sort of person to worry too much I certainly wouldn't be here with you.'

He smiled. 'I stand corrected.' He stopped washing her foot and closed his eyes.

When Harry had first asked her to spend a night with him, Sally had made it very clear she was never going to have an affair with him. 'But you're having an affair with me already,' he'd argued. 'In your head you've already gone to bed with me. Mentally you've already climaxed in my arms.'

'Don't be absurd,' she'd admonished him. Which, of course, had just made him laugh. They'd been in her office at the time – the door firmly closed – and he'd come up behind her, kissed the back of her neck and whispered in her ear how he longed to make love to her.

'It's going to happen, Sally,' he'd said, his hands sliding round her ribcage to her breasts. 'I won't give up. But I won't rush you. Come to me when you're sure. When you're ready.'

For a while she convinced herself that she could contain her feelings for Harry by allowing herself the occasional daydream about making love with him. Surely that was all that lay at the bottom of this: a basic animal urge to have sex with someone attractive, who appeared to find her attractive? Give it a week or two and it would pass, she reasoned with herself.

It didn't pass. Instead, the intensity of the attraction grew and grew until it was almost all she could think of. She began to live in daily fear of grabbing Harry in his office and satisfying herself right there and then; exorcizing herself once and for all of the crippling desire she felt for him.

She didn't actually say the words, 'Harry, I'm ready,' but just as he always seemed to know what was in her mind or what she was about to say, he knew when she was ready to take the next step with him. Monday of this week, he'd knocked on her office door, stepped inside and told her he'd booked them a room at a hotel for Friday night.

'Where?' was all she said.

'Somewhere miles from here. But don't worry about anyone seeing us,' he'd added with one of his killer smiles, 'your clothes will be confiscated on arrival. I don't have any intention of letting you stray beyond the four walls of our room.'

At home that evening she'd explained to Dan that she had to go to Hull at the weekend to sort out a problem her mother had with an insurance claim over a ruined carpet. He'd raised an eyebrow when she'd further explained that she would drive over Friday evening after work, stay the night in a hotel and deal with whatever it was she had to do the next day. 'I thought you said you'd had enough of your mother and wouldn't be at her beck and call any more,' he'd said.

'She's my mother, Dan. I can't pretend she doesn't exist. No matter how much I wish she didn't.'

After they'd checked in at the hotel and had been shown to their room, Harry had opened the bottle of champagne that was waiting for them in an ice bucket. For a few awkward moments they'd behaved like strangers, sipping the champagne and remarking on its quality and dryness and inspecting the room. Just when she didn't think she could keep up the act any longer, he took her glass from her and put it on the dressing table. Standing in front of her, he was suddenly very still. Very quiet. He seemed almost to be holding his breath. 'I'm going to kiss you now,' he said, finally. 'And then I'm going to undress you and make love to you.'

He kissed her long and hard, as though it might be the last chance he got, then, as he slowly and methodically removed every piece of her clothing, he never once lost eye contact with her. It was like an intensely erotic game that he was playing with her; she sensed his enjoyment, how he took pleasure in controlling her. She sensed, too, the air of reckless excitement that sparked between them.

Looking at Harry at the other end of the bath now – his head tipped back and his eyes closed – she thought how alike they were. Or rather, she thought how alike her old self was to Harry. Harry was passionate, impulsive and reckless and being with him allowed her to rediscover the wild Sally of old, the Sally Wilson who had been hard-wired to crave risk and excitement, the Sally Wilson who had been locked away for her own good. But thanks to Harry, that Sally was back. And life was all the better for it! Never had she felt so free or euphoric. All she cared about was when she and Harry would be able to snatch another twenty-four hours like these. No matter how difficult it proved to be, she would find a way. She needed more of this. More of Harry. So much more of him. She didn't kid herself that she loved him, but she did love the way he made her feel: fantastically alive and energized.

In comparison, Dan depressed her and drained the life out of her. He made her feel as though she was always in the wrong, as though she was permanently failing in some way. She simply could not live up to the unrealistic expectations he had of her. Harry, on the other hand, never found fault with her. He never questioned what she did or said. He repeatedly said that he needed her. When had Dan last said that to her?

'What are you thinking of?'

Harry had his eyes open now and was looking straight at her.

'You,' she answered him.

'Really? You weren't thinking of Dan?'

'Why do you ask that?'

'I wouldn't blame you if you were.' He scooped up a handful of water and let it trickle through his fingers. 'Can I ask you something? It's about your relationship with your husband.'

She nodded warily.

'Does it suit you, having a husband who stays at home to look after your son, leaving you to be the breadwinner?'

'Suit me?' she repeated. 'In what way?'

'You like to be in control, don't you? And as things stand at home, there's no danger of you being subjugated, of being controlled by your husband. You're the decision maker. The one who calls the shots.'

When she didn't reply, he leaned forward and lifted her so that she was sitting astride him. 'But now and then, I think you quite like someone else to take the lead for a change. Am I right?'

Sally opened her mouth to respond, but Harry put a finger to her lips. 'Turn round and I'll wash your back.'

She did as he said and as his soapy hands moved in slow, deliberate circles on her shoulders, Sally sighed and closed her eyes. The moment she did, she had a sudden replay in her mind of the way Harry made love to her, how he instigated it, how he dictated the pace, and how much that fuelled her desire and intensified her pleasure. How odd, she thought, that she had allowed Harry to take the lead in almost everything they did when it was something she now realized she rarely allowed Dan to do. In or out of the bedroom.

Was that one of the reasons why there was now such an unbridgeable gap between them? Through her determination always to be in control of her life, had she turned Dan into the kind of man to whom she would never feel sexually attracted? And if that was true, was that why she had lost all respect for him?

Chapter Thirty-One

With Chloe's parents booked to go to a local outdoor production of *Midsummer Night's Dream* the party, at Dan's invitation, had moved seamlessly from Laurel House to Corner Cottage.

It was gone nine o'clock now. Seth had just left to go home and put the finishing touches to his sermon for tomorrow morning and Marcus was upstairs asleep in bed. Alone with Chloe, Dan fetched another bottle of wine from the kitchen and joined her back out in the garden. He took the space on the wooden bench that Seth had vacated. It wasn't yet fully dark and above their heads swallows swooped and dived through the still warm air. It was a perfect evening to round off what had been a perfect day.

In his happily, slightly drunken state, Dan decided it was such an exceptionally enjoyable day it went a long way to make up for the recent run of bad days. If not bad weeks. Marcus may have drawn the short straw when it came to grandparents, but Chloe's parents made excellent stand-ins, fussing kindly over him but never spoiling him. Seth had also made his mark on Marcus when he'd surprised everyone, not least of all Chloe, by enthralling him with a routine of magic tricks. 'Again! Again!' Marcus had squealed, bouncing up and down on his chair when Seth had made a ten-pence piece vanish from Marcus's hand then reappear behind Chloe's ear. Today was the first time Dan had met Seth and whilst he knew how Chloe felt about him – that it was a strictly how-many-times-do-I-have-to-tell-you platonic friendship – he was pretty sure there was nothing platonic about the way Seth regarded Chloe. It was obvious to Dan that Seth clearly viewed her as more than a friend.

He turned and looked at Chloe. She was one of the most attractive women he knew; a classic blue-eyed blonde with a body most women would give their back teeth for. Lost in her own thoughts as she stared up at the darkening night sky, she seemed to be on the verge of smiling. She looked happier than he'd seen her in a long while. Was that down to Seth? He noticed that she was absently stroking the silver bangle Seth had surprised her with after lunch. 'Chloe?' he said.

'Mmm?'

'Can I ask you something?'

'No you can't.' She still had her eyes on the sky.

'Why not?'

'Because I know what you're going to ask.'

'You do?'

She turned to look at him. 'You're going to ask me something about Seth, aren't you?'

'Actually, I was going to ask you if you'd had a good birthday.'

She smiled. 'Liar.'

He smiled, too, and put his arm round her. 'You know me so well.'

'So go on, then, get it out of your system. Ask away.'

'OK. And no interrupting and leaping down my throat, but the way I see it, Seth's a great bloke and you could—'

'You're only saying that because he's a fellow *Simpsons* aficionado.'

'I thought I said no interrupting. But seriously, what would you do if Seth said he wanted more than friendship from you?'

She shook her head. 'That's not going to happen.'

'But if it did?' Dan pressed. 'What if he did hit on you?'

'Don't be silly, Dan, that would be like you hitting on me.'

'You really believe that? You think Seth and I both feel the same way about you?'

'Yes.'

'But you told me that in the beginning, when you first got to know each other, things were quite different between the two of you. You said he kissed you.'

'That was then,' she said with a shrug, 'this is now. We've recalibrated things.'

Dan snorted. 'Well, I've got news for you. Seth and I view you through very different eyes. Don't get me wrong, you're eminently fanciable, but after all these years, you're like a sister to me. In Seth's eyes, you're no such thing. No, no, hear me out. I'm a man; I know about these things. Trust me, when he looks at you, he sees a real hottie.'

'Dan! You've had too much to drink. Now be quiet before I get cross with you.'

'Get as cross with me as you like, but it won't change a thing. I suspect that if Seth wasn't so concerned about losing you altogether, he'd be making his feelings very clear to you.'

She frowned and hesitated fractionally before saying, 'He's given me absolutely no indication that that's the case.'

'Can I say something else?'

'Would it make any difference if I said no?'

'None whatsoever. Look, I think I know where you're coming from, but just because Seth doesn't appear to fit the ideal profile, it doesn't mean he's not worth a punt. I really like him, and I'd hate to think that you couldn't give him a chance purely because he's a man of principle and strong belief.'

Chloe turned fully in his arm to face him. 'This is the last time I'm going to say this, so listen up. I'm inordinately fond of Seth, but a full-on relationship with him is out of the question. Apart from the obvious differences between us, it would be too weird. I mean, well, given his principles and strong beliefs as you put it, we wouldn't even be able to have sex unless we were married. What kind of a sensible, grown-up relationship would that be?'

Dan sighed. 'It sounds exactly like marriage to Sally!' He immediately regretted his words. 'Forget I said that,' he muttered, sinking the last of his wine in one long swallow. He could feel Chloe's eyes on him. 'I said forget it.'

She continued to stare at him. Oh, what the hell, he thought, taking his arm away from her shoulder to pour himself some more wine. She might know something. Sally might have said something to her. He offered Chloe the bottle. She shook her head. 'I expect it's just a phase,' he said. 'You know, working too hard, crashing out in bed exhausted and falling asleep immediately. It's what happens, isn't it?'

'It can happen, certainly. But who are you talking about? You or Sally? Or the pair of you?'

'Sally. Has she said anything to you? You know, something in confidence?'

Chloe smiled. 'If it was in confidence I could hardly tell you, now could I?'

'Unless it was something serious. You'd tell me then, wouldn't you? You wouldn't hide something important from me? I know the two of you are best friends and all that, but you and I have a history, too. That must count for something.'

The smile slipped from Chloe's face. 'What's really worrying you, Dan?'

He blinked. 'I ... I think Sally's having an affair.'

'You're kidding?'

'Shit, Chloe! Why would I joke about something like that?'

'But why? Why would you think that of her?'

He put his glass down on the wooden table and covered his face with his hands. When he looked up, he said, 'She's been acting so strangely lately. She works ridiculous hours and when she is home she's here in body but not in mind. It's as if there's an invisible wall between us. I can't get close to her. Sometimes she seems closed off to me, in a world of her own. I can't remember the last time we made love. If I so much as attempt to touch her she tells me she's got an early start the next day. At the weekend it's always a headache she's got. Do you think there could be someone at work she's secretly seeing?'

Chloe put a hand on his arm. 'I think I know what the problem is,' she said. 'And don't be angry that Sally shared this with me, but she told me that you're keen to have another child.'

He nodded. 'That's true.'

'Well, a pound to a penny, that's what's troubling her. She's not sure about taking that step and thinks you only want sex with her to get her pregnant. Hardly a turn-on, is it? It's a classic way to kill a girl's libido. And a man's for that matter. I've seen many a patient with the same problem.'

'Has she actually told you this?'

'No, but it doesn't take a genius to put the two things together.'

'Is that your professional opinion?'

She smiled. 'It's my professional and best friend opinion. Why not try talking to her about it?'

'About having another child?'

'About everything that's bothering you. Make some time to be alone together and really talk. Go away for a weekend. So long as I'm not on call, I could look after Marcus for you.'

He smiled ruefully. 'I sound paranoid and pathetic, don't I? I'd totally convinced myself that Sally didn't love me any more. Back in May, when we had the fete in the village, she actually accused me of having something going with Tatiana from the trust. Which, for the record, I wasn't.'

'What made her think you were?'

'I have no idea. But not long after that she asked me if I knew how hard it was to live with a hero.'

'She said that? But why?'

'I don't really know. I'd just told her about Rosie expecting another baby and it all got out of hand and suddenly she was accusing me of having a hero complex ever since we came back from Phuket. Do you think I do?'

'Oh, Dan, not for a single second. What you did back on Phuket was heroic, but it's not as if you ever mention it. In fact, I can't recall the last time you did refer to it. I know you don't like to.'

It was dark now, the only light spilling out from the French windows behind them. They both stared up at the star-studded sky. Dan said, 'Earlier this year, I went through a period of having the most awful nightmares about the tsunami. Do you ever dream of what happened?'

'Not about the tsunami, specifically.'

'About something else connected to it?'

'Something that happened afterwards.'

'Paul?'

'Sort of.'

Dan was about to ask Chloe what she meant by this when he heard the sound of a car pulling onto the drive at the front of the house. 'Sally,' he said. 'She's back. She'll probably be in a terrible mood after spending so long with her mother.'

Chloe didn't stick around for much longer. With everything she and Dan had discussed, she felt uncomfortable being with her friends. She would inevitably end up watching their every move and exchange to gauge the situation between them and she didn't want to do that.

She walked home reflecting on what Dan had shared with her. No way would Sally have an affair. How could she when she dealt with the consequences of adultery on a daily basis? Why would she make the same mistake, knowing more than anyone what was at stake? No, it was crazy. Dan had jumped to an irrational conclusion.

But what was all that nonsense about accusing Dan of having a hero complex? Caustic and razor-sharp ripostes were hardly new territory for Sally, but what she'd accused Dan of was out of order. What had led her to make such a nasty comment?

She'd reached home and was just putting her key in the lock of the back door when a thought occurred to Chloe. It was a thought that hit her with a force so powerful it made her stop what she was doing. *Do you think there could be somebody at work she's secretly seeing?* Dan had asked Chloe. What if Sally's newbie admirer had persisted and she had fallen for him? What if—

The sound of the telephone ringing from inside the house had Chloe rushing to let herself in to answer it.

It was Seth. 'I thought I'd wish you a happy birthday one last time, Doctor Hennessey,' he said.

Instantly cheered by his voice and the formal way he addressed her when no one else was around to hear, she laughed. 'Reverend Hawthorne, I thought you had a sermon to polish.'

'All done.'

'And the subject matter?'

'Patience. I've decided to test the congregation's patience by delivering an extra-long sermon, so if you read in the newspaper next week that a curate in Crantsford came to an untimely death, you'll know they failed the test.'

'In that case, I shall make a point of checking the newspapers.'

'And make sure they give me a good send-off. I want Arcade Fire's "Intervention" played at my funeral. Oh, and everyone's to be in fancy dress.'

'Do you have a theme in mind?'

'Daft question. Gotta be *The Simpsons*.'

Chloe groaned. 'I learned two very disturbing things about you today. One: you're obsessed with a cartoon, and two: you make things disappear.'

'I'll take that as my cue to get off the line and leave you in peace. Goodnight, Chloe. Sleep well.'

'You too. Oh, and thank you for my present. It's lovely. I really like it.'

'I enjoyed choosing it for you. Goodnight.'

'Goodnight.' Chloe hung up and touched the silver bangle on her wrist. It was beautifully made and probably quite expensive. She thought of what Dan had said about Seth earlier and wondered if he could be right. Did Seth view her as more than a friend? Was this a gift from a man who was holding back his true feelings for her?

The telephone rang again.

'If in the unlikely event I survive tomorrow's sermon, is there any chance I might see you at the gym in the afternoon?'

She smiled. 'I think there's every chance of that.'

'Excellent. Sleep well.'

'And you. And good luck for tomorrow morning.'

'Thank you.'

Oh, Seth, she thought with a mixture of happiness and sadness when she rang off. Why did you come into my life to complicate it so? I'm not the right girl for you at all. I wish I was. But I'm not.

Chapter Thirty-Two

'Seth?'

'Yes?'

'Are you gay, or what?'

A cacophony of sniggering broke out in the minibus, along with several ear-splitting whistles and raunchy cheers. In the passenger seat next to Seth, Patricia O'Connor – mother of fourteen-year-old Abigail who had predictably opted to travel back from the bowling alley in the other minibus, driven by Owen – glanced at him. The silly woman was pink with embarrassment. But Seth's amusement far outweighed any embarrassment he felt. He was more than used to the youth group's antics, especially on their monthly night out.

When the noise had finally died down, he looked at Jez Lucas in the rear-view mirror and said, 'What's the context of your question, Jez? Are you referring to my sexuality or asking if I'm a sad loser?'

Jez's face coloured. His mate Ricky thwacked him on the head. 'He wants to know if you're a bender, Seth.'

'And why do you want to know that?'

'Cos he's one and wants to know if you'll go out with him,' someone shouted from the back row of seats.

Everybody laughed. Patricia whipped round in her seat. 'That's enough, you lot!' she ordered. 'Of course Seth's not gay. He wouldn't be a curate if he was, would he? The Bible's very explicit on the subject.'

Known for her hard-line views – homosexuality was an abomination in the eyes of the Lord, blah, blah – Seth let her comment go and addressed Jez in the rear-view mirror again. 'Why would you think I'm gay, Jez?'

The boy shrugged. 'You're not married and we've never seen you with a woman, so I just thought maybe you were playing for the other side.'

Ricky laughed. 'You haven't got a girlfriend either, Jez. Does that make you a queer?'

'Take no notice of them, Seth,' Patricia said as once more Jez became the butt of noisy, derisive taunts. 'They've consumed too much junk food. No one believes for a moment that you could be a homosexual. The very idea is preposterous.' Her tone, though hushed so only he could hear, was annoyingly bracing.

'Really?' he said. 'I don't think the idea is that preposterous. In fact, I'd go so far as to say I'd be a perfect candidate. I'm single, I work out, I like to cook, I even like musicals.' This latter admission was an all-out lie, and despite knowing he was playing with fire, Seth couldn't help himself. He hated prejudice and there was far too much of it within the parish in his opinion. He personally knew several high-flying clergymen and women who were gay and would challenge anyone who dared to accuse them of being in the wrong job. They were men and women of irrefutable faith, just as he was.

As he stopped at the traffic lights, he caught Patricia looking at him doubtfully. He immediately regretted what he'd said. Oh hell, how soon before the parish was a bubbling pot of gossip about his sexuality?

Two days later and his prophecy was fulfilled. He was alone at St Michael's, having just been up to the bell tower to nail down a couple of loose floorboards that the bell ringers had brought to his attention at the PCC meeting last night, and was enjoying himself by playing 'Intervention' on the organ. He was no music scholar, but he played well enough to amuse himself. He was almost at the end of the song and really letting rip, the notes soaring, in danger of rattling the stained glass windows out of their frames, and giving full voice to the lyrics – '*Working for the Church while your life falls apart*' – when he noticed Owen making his way up the nave of the church. He had a seriously agitated expression on his face and Seth stopped playing at once. He swung himself off the organ stool and approached the other man.

'Could I talk with you, Seth?' Owen asked.

'Of course.'

'Perhaps the vestry would be best.'

Owen led the way. He insisted that Seth take the seat behind the desk they shared, while he paced the worn carpet from one glass bookcase to the other. 'There's no easy way of saying this, Seth,' he said, 'but I feel it's my duty to bring it to your attention before you hear it from some other source.'

Seth placed his elbows on the armrests of the chair and said, 'Right, I think I know what this is about.'

From beneath his straggly eyebrows Owen looked at him sharply. 'You do? Does that mean there's some substance to the rumour?'

'Substance,' Seth repeated with a hollow smile. 'That's an odd choice of word, isn't it? Are you asking me if there's any truth to my being gay?'

'You mean you are?'

'I didn't say that.'

Owen came to a stop in front of the desk. 'Seth, as my curate, your welfare is my responsibility. I also have the parish's welfare to consider.'

'But presumably my private life is not up for consideration. It's no one's concern but my own.'

'I'm afraid that's too simplistic an approach. If your private life is at odds with that of ... of the parish's best interests, not to mention the Church's teaching, then it's very much my concern.'

'You're saying there's a danger that my sexuality could affect my work here in Crantsford? You have evidence of this?'

'Insomuch as people are talking about you, Seth. Yes.'

Seth leaned back in the creaking leather chair. He was working hard at keeping his temper. 'And you didn't think it your duty, your *Christian* duty,' he said slowly and with emphasis, 'to discourage the gossipmongers?'

For the first time in the conversation, Owen looked like a man on less sure ground. 'Of course I did,' he blustered.

'Good, so you told them there was categorically, unequivocally no truth to the rumours. You explained in no uncertain terms that I'm as heterosexual as you are.' Seth didn't mean to, but he suddenly laughed. He snapped forward in the chair and got to his feet. 'Excellent,' he said, 'I'm glad we've got that all sorted out.'

Frowning, Owen didn't give the impression of having got anything sorted out.

Seth almost felt sorry for him. Perhaps he'd been unfair with the man. Instead of trying to prove a point, wouldn't it have been better to have given an outright denial and have done with it? The way things were now, the poor man would forever be wondering in which direction Seth's interest lay. In a split second of remorse, he decided that whilst Owen could be a bit of an old woman, irritatingly traditional and stubbornly stuck in his ways, not to mention a real pain in the arse, he bore him no malice and the least he could do was put him out of his misery. He put a hand on Owen's shoulder. 'Look, if it puts your mind at rest, and the parish's, I'll bring my girlfriend to the barn dance.'

Owen's shaggy eyebrows rose. 'You have a girlfriend? Why didn't you say?'

'As I said before, my private life is my own. The last thing I want is people gossiping about me. For whatever reason.'

Leaving a visibly relieved Owen in the vestry, Seth walked back out into the interior of the church. He knelt at the wooden altar rail and prayed. He prayed that God would forgive him for the lie he'd just told Owen.

Girlfriend? What girlfriend?

And what on earth had made him say such a thing?

Wishful thinking?

Chapter Thirty-Three

Two weeks had passed since their night away and they were taking more and more risks, grabbing each other in their offices, stealing frantic pleasures when and how they could behind closed doors. Sally couldn't help herself. Never had she felt so alive or exhilarated, or so greedy for sex. Harry made her feel stronger and more empowered than she had ever known. He was her drug of choice and she lived in daily need of him. She loved knowing that when they were apart he fantasized obsessively over what he would do to her when they next went away together.

Harry's concern that she would immediately regret their night away had been way off course. She'd had only one thought in her head as she'd driven home that day and that was how she was going to stop herself from blurting out how wildly changed she felt inside.

She pitied anyone who had never experienced even a fraction of what she was feeling. At the oddest times she would catch herself looking at people around her – in a meeting, in a shop – and wonder how they could bear their safe, dull little lives.

A knock at her office door had her turning round from the window that looked down onto Deansgate. 'Yes,' she said, trying to keep the eager hope out of her voice that it was Harry.

It wasn't Harry. It was Marion Brooke, one of the more efficient and capable members of her team. 'Have you seen this?' Marion asked. She laid out a tabloid newspaper on Sally's desk. Sally sat down to look at it. A grinning Darren T. Child stared back at her. With a swimming pool in the background, he had his arms around a blonde girl wearing only the bottom half of a bikini. For the sake of propriety, the girl's Spacehopper breasts were partially hidden by one of Darren's chunky tattooed arms. The photograph in itself was of no surprise to Sally – Darren with a blonde lovely on his arm was a regular occurrence – but the headline was a different matter: *'DARREN AND TASTY TINA BACK IN SACK!'* Sally read on, and after wading through all the footballing puns – *Darren scores again with his missus! – Darren and Tina go for extra time! ... Darren raises his game! ... Darren's back in the premier league with Tina!* – the gist was clear: the divorce between Mr and Mrs Child was off. Oh, well; you win some, you lose some.

'Do you want me to make a call to his agent or manager for official confirmation that we're to terminate proceedings?' Marion asked.

'Yes, go ahead.'

Marion's gaze lingered on the photograph. 'They look surprisingly happy, don't they?'

Sally snorted. 'I give them four months tops before they'll be at each other's throats.'

'That sounds very cynical.'

Sally folded the newspaper and pushed it away from her. 'When we've received confirmation we'll swing into gear with our bill.'

Left on her own, Sally dismissed Darren from her mind and wondered what Harry was doing, or what he was thinking. How easy it would be to email or text him to find out. But she wouldn't. Harry was desperate for her to communicate this way in secret, but she'd flatly refused. Emails in the workplace were too dangerous. Who knew who could access them? The same for text messages. Having such a forbidden fruit was all part of the game for Sally: it kept Harry keen. She smiled to herself. Sex and power – was there ever a more powerful combination?

'She's here!' Marcus shouted loudly. 'Tatty's here!' Standing on the middle bar of the wooden gate where he'd been patiently waiting for the last ten minutes while Dan trimmed the hedge, he waved madly at the charcoal-grey Honda that drew up on the pavement. 'Hello, Tatty,' he called excitedly to Tatiana when she got out of her car.

'OK, buddy,' Dan said, 'off the gate so I can let our guest in.'

Marcus did as he said but his attention was caught by the tell-tale sound of rustling as Tatiana put her hand inside her bag. Bending down so that she was eye to eye with him, she gave him a packet of chocolate buttons.

'Thank you,' he said solemnly. He then put his arms around her neck and hugged her. 'You smell very nice. Do you want to come and see my bedroom? Daddy helped me tidy it specially.' Having let go of her neck, he was now holding one of her hands.

'What a tempting offer and from such a perfect little charmer.'

She smiled up at Dan. 'I'm going to refrain from saying that he obviously takes after his father.'

'Oh, shame, I could do with a compliment or two. Come round to the back and I'll sort us out a drink. What would you like?'

'Tea would be lovely, thank you.'

From inside the house as he waited for the kettle to boil, Dan watched his son. Outside in the garden, Marcus was sitting on Tatiana's lap chatting nineteen to the dozen with her. First love, Dan thought. Marcus had got it bad. And who could blame him?

Tatty, as Marcus had started calling her after meeting her again last week at Rosie's, definitely had something special about her. You couldn't help but feel good around her. She had a way of making you feel uplifted just by being in the same room. The children the trust took care of adored her; their eyes would light up when they saw her. The parents loved her too, and not just the fathers. Dan had teased her at work the other day and called her Saint Tatiana. She'd responded by saying that given his own contribution at the trust – Brothers and Sisters Have Fun, which was to be launched next month – he wasn't doing so badly in the saintly stakes either.

He took the tray of drinks out to the garden. Marcus was now playing with Tatiana's long dark hair, which today she wore loose. It looked smooth and glossy in the bright afternoon sunshine. 'He's not taking liberties and annoying you, is he?' Dan asked, passing her a mug of tea.

'Not at all.'

When Dan was seated and he'd given Marcus permission to open his bag of chocolate buttons, Tatiana raised her mug. 'Here's to you, Dan. With all the funding you've personally brought in, you're everybody's hero right now.'

He winced. 'Hardly that, I'm sure.'

'Don't underestimate what you've done. It's a fantastic achievement. You should be extremely proud of yourself. But I can see I'm embarrassing you so I won't say another word about how delighted everyone is that you joined us. To save your blushes, I'll just give you the papers I mentioned on the phone this morning. Marcus,' she added, returning her attention to him, 'could you let your daddy and I have a little chat together? And when we've finished, why don't you show me your bedroom?'

He climbed down from her lap and, smiling happily, went to play with his sit and ride tractor, hooking a trailer of plastic flowerpots to it.

'That's some chat-up line of my son's,' Dan said. 'Come up and see my bedroom, indeed.'

Tatiana laughed. 'As I said earlier, he's a real charmer. His speech has come on, hasn't it? He must be such great company. Any plans to follow Rosie and Dave's example and have another child?'

Dan gave as casual a shrug as he could. 'Not immediately,' he said. *Not ever* was the truthful answer. Not unless Sally underwent some kind of Immaculate Conception. Sex had never been more off the menu than it was now. Perhaps he was partly to blame. He'd got so exasperated with being rejected he hadn't pursued the matter. He'd tried talking to Sally just as Chloe had suggested, making it clear that his desire to touch her was nothing to do with wanting to impregnate her, but the way she looked at him with her pale, questioning, ironic eyes, he'd been left in no doubt that she didn't believe him. Despite Chloe's claim that it was crazy to imagine Sally having an affair, he genuinely feared the worst. The thought of another man's hands touching Sally, of another man kissing her, sickened him. It filled him with the sort of rage he didn't know he could feel. It made him scared to confront Sally. What if he tackled her and she confirmed his suspicions? What then? How would he react?

Was it wrong of him to do nothing, to stick his head in the sand in the hope that if she was being unfaithful, the safest thing he could do was to let her get it out of her system and wait for her to come back to him? Wasn't that the truest and ultimate mark of his love for Sally, that he would be prepared to forgive her?

Or was it the ultimate mark of a coward? Would a real man take this kind of crap? Wouldn't a real man take action and say, 'OK, Sally, let's cut to the chase; are you or are you not having an affair?' A real man wouldn't allow himself to be dragged down into this inner circle of hell, would he?

What frightened Dan most was that he didn't know how much longer he could keep up the exhausting act of pretending that everything was all right. Only two things kept him from caving in – the thought of how gleeful his bloody parents would be if they knew Sally was being unfaithful to him, and, of course, more importantly, his instinctive need to protect his son.

He looked over to where Marcus was playing. Deep in concentration, his lips *brmm*ing, he was steering his tractor through an obstacle course of toys on the lawn. The purity of his son's happy innocence pained Dan. How could he do anything that might destroy that happiness?

'Dan? What is it? What's wrong?'

Tatiana's voice was so gentle and tender, Dan almost didn't hear it. But then he realized that his eyes had filled. Furious with himself, he swallowed hard. 'Sorry,' he muttered, getting up from the seat. 'Hay fever. Back in a minute.'

Moments later, making a play of stuffing a handful of tissues into his pocket as if to ward off any further threat of pollen, he said, 'Those papers, shall we take a look at them?'

Tatiana stared at him steadily. He could see the concern in her face. For a terrifying moment he thought she was going to say something. He knew it would be his undoing if she did. But she didn't. Instead, she smiled brightly and passed a file across the table towards him.

It was such a little thing for her to do, but it meant so much. He wished he could thank her, but he couldn't. He probably wouldn't ever be able to thank her.

Chapter Thirty-Four

Even wearing an old T-shirt and scruffy knee-length cut-off jeans, Chloe had to admit that Seth still managed to look great.

She'd mentioned last weekend that she was going to spend her day off this week redecorating her bedroom and he'd immediately offered to help her. Late last night he'd called in to help move the larger items of furniture that would be in the way – the bed they'd moved to the middle of the room – and to sand down where necessary. At eight thirty this morning he'd arrived all raring to go. They'd been painting for three hours now. Seth had been in charge of the ceiling and walls and she'd taken responsibility for glossing the window frames and sills and skirting boards. 'How about an early lunch?' she suggested.

'Excellent idea,' he said, reloading the roller with white paint from the tray on the top rung of the stepladder. 'Just this bit in the corner to do and then I'll be finished up here.'

She watched him approvingly. He worked methodically and with careful attention to detail. Just as she did. She'd dreaded him being one of those careless, sloppy decorators, splattering everything in sight with flecks of paint. It was on the tip of her tongue to say, 'We make a great team, don't we?' but she held back. What if he thought she wasn't talking about their DIY compatibility? What if there was the merest hint of truth in what Dan had said to her about Seth the night of her birthday? Would a comment like that give him reason to think things had changed between them?

But if she was honest, hadn't things changed?

She couldn't speak for Seth's feelings, but hers had certainly undergone a vast change. She could think of no one she would rather spend time with. Since her birthday she had caught herself thinking about Seth a lot, wondering where he was, what he was doing, who he was with. If he were suddenly to disappear from her life she would miss him enormously. What she couldn't bring herself to dwell on, was how she'd feel if he were to meet someone else. A 'someone else' who held the same beliefs as him. A 'someone else' who wasn't riddled with petty prejudice like she was. Everyone else liked Seth – well, Mum and Dad, Dan and Marcus; Sally had yet to meet him – so really, what was the problem? Why did she continue to hold back, to make a big deal out of something that was nothing of the kind? He was a curate. A clergyman. A priest. A man of the proverbial cloth. Get over it! Did it make him any less of a man?

Not from where she was standing right now – with a fine view of his legs and their perfect muscle tone – that was for sure!

Chloe had always thought of herself as being her own boss, as being intelligent enough to form her own opinions. Never had she knowingly allowed herself to be influenced by another, but with regard to Seth, she was doing exactly that. She wished it wasn't so, but Sally's approval of Seth mattered to her. It went all the way back to when they were students, when no matter what silly disagreements they had, it was carved in stone that having a best friend's approval over a boyfriend, or even a potential boyfriend, was crucial.

Once or twice Chloe had thought of ringing Sally to arrange an evening together so that she could meet Seth properly, but she'd never got further than just thinking about it. She hated the idea that Sally might meet Seth and still think negatively about him.

There was also a more worrying concern: Dan's suspicions that Sally might be having an affair. Since Dan had shared his fear with her, Chloe had shied away from talking to Sally. She badly wanted to believe that her friend would never do such a thing, but what if she was wrong? The seed of doubt having been planted, Chloe had been unable not to give it room to grow and she knew that if she were to be alone with Sally she would end up asking her outright if she was seeing anyone. And what if the consequence of that was for Sally to admit that she was having an affair and swore Chloe to secrecy? Would she really be able to do that? Could she keep a secret like that from Dan? The answer was no. She cared about him too much to betray him so cruelly.

Seth was climbing down the stepladder now. When he was at the bottom of it, looking back up at his handiwork, Chloe said, 'You've done a brilliant job. You're quite a perfectionist.'

'Thanks,' he said.

'We work well together, don't we?' There, she'd said it. Let him make of it what he wanted.

'Good enough to set up a decorating business?' he replied, turning round to face her with a smile.

'I think that would be pushing things. A beer and a bacon sand-wich suit you for lunch?'

They ate in the garden, sitting on the lawn on an old bedspread that Chloe's mother had thrown in her direction last summer.

It was such a beautiful day; a shame to be wasting it stuck inside the house decorating. When Chloe voiced this regret, and that she felt guilty about depriving Seth of a more enjoyable day, he said, 'You didn't exactly force me, Chloe. I offered to help you. Besides, I am enjoying myself. I like creating order out of chaos.'

'Watch it, pal. That sounds worryingly like you're saying my bedroom was a chaotic mess before you got your mitts on it.'

He laughed and lay back on the bedspread, his hands clasped behind his head. 'Trust me, I wouldn't be so stupid.'

'Well, any time you need a favour from me, just say the word.'

He looked up at her, his eyes soft and beguiling. 'Do you really mean that?'

Seeing him lying stretched out before her, Chloe was startlingly more aware of his physical presence, his inherent masculinity. She was used to running alongside him at the gym, sitting close to him, swimming with him, but like this – him lying beside her, his body seemed infinitely more intimate. And inviting. It really wouldn't take much on her part to kiss him. No effort at all. 'Of course I mean it,' she murmured, remembering the one time they had kissed and how it had made her feel. 'Why wouldn't I?'

'If you really are serious,' he said, raising himself up onto his elbows, 'there is something you could do for me. Are you doing anything this coming Saturday evening?'

Chapter Thirty-Five

Once again, Seth found himself at the top of a stepladder.

The St Michael's Barn Dance was a legendary affair. So Seth kept being told. It was the culmination of months of preparation by a committee of hard-working enthusiasts. After ten years of putting on the event, they had the procedure down to a fine art. The band and caller had been booked last year, the marquee had been erected, the hog roast and drinks had been organized, the tickets had been sold, the raffle prizes rounded up, and now there was just the marquee to decorate.

This was where Seth came in. He'd been given very specific instructions on where and how to hang the tons of greenery that had been delivered that morning. The instructions had come, and were continuing to come from Barbara Hicks, a retired head teacher who had an infuriating habit of treating everyone as a five-year-old who still needed to be accompanied to the toilet by a responsible adult. If she'd told Seth once how to festoon the stage for the band and caller, she'd told him a hundred times. Yet still she didn't trust him to do the job unaided. Hovering at the bottom of the stepladder and fending off any offers of assistance from the legion of helpers, she was keeping a keen eye on his every movement, at the same time maintaining a running commentary – 'A little to the right, Seth, no, no, not that far! That's right, there. Mm ... perhaps a little higher. There. Perfect.'

Whatever the level of scrutiny he was currently under, Seth knew that this evening the level would be greatly increased. He'd be lucky if there was a single pair of eyes not observing his every move. He just hoped Chloe was prepared for the degree of interest her presence would create when they walked in together.

When he'd explained to her what his favour would entail, and the reasons behind it, she'd laughed out loud. 'You're joking?' she'd said. 'How could anyone seriously consider you were anything but heterosexual?' Then the laughter had slipped from her face. 'This is

198

exactly what I can't stand about organized religion,' she'd said hotly. 'Churches are stuffed full of hypocritical, judgemental idiots.'

'I couldn't agree more,' he'd said.

'So how can you be one of them?'

He'd very nearly pointed out to her that she had judged him at Margaret's funeral, but instead said, 'One way or another we're all hypocritical and judgemental. We're all idiots when push comes to shove.'

'But aren't you tempted to ignore Owen and the tongue-waggers? Just let them get on with wondering whether you're gay or not. It's none of their business which way your interest swings. Hang on, you're not homophobic, are you?'

'Certainly not. But if people think I am gay and the knock-on effect does affect my work in the parish, then I need to set the record straight.'

'So a twirl around the dance floor with me on your arm will put an end to the gossip? That's essentially what this is about?'

He'd nodded. 'I quite understand if you don't want to do it. It was just a thought. Maybe a barn dance is the last way you'd want to spend an evening. I can't say that it rates too high on my wish list.'

The smile had slowly reappeared on her face. 'I'll have you know, thanks to Mum and Dad, both my brother and I are champion barn dancers. I could dosi-do for England if it were ever made an Olympic event.'

'I don't know whether that's a good thing or not, seeing as I'm officially a dosi-do virgin. Now you're going to draw attention to my incredible two left feet.'

'I thought it was your sexuality you were worried about, not your feet. But don't fret; by the end of the evening, there'll be no doubt in anyone's mind about your hetero credentials. We'll Gay Gordon those malicious gossipers to kingdom come!'

He'd groaned at that. 'Any chance I could end the evening with at least some of my fine, upstanding reputation in place?'

'Depends how well you dance!'

He would have liked to have asked Chloe if she had only agreed to come tonight out of a sense of duty – as in one good turn deserves another – or whether she would have accepted an invitation without him wording it as a favour.

They were spending so much time together these days he was almost tempted to think that his sister might be right; that Chloe's attitude towards him was changing. Dare he imagine she might view him as more than a friend? It was such a fragile hope, he rarely allowed himself to pursue it, happy just to be in Chloe's company. Some days he could convince himself that close friendship would always be enough for him, but in his heart he knew it wasn't true. He had only to picture her with another man – the threat of the ex-boyfriend surfacing again was never far from his mind – to be acutely aware that if he couldn't have her he certainly didn't want her in the arms of another. Real love was supposed to be selfless, yet what he felt for Chloe was a long way from this ideal. He wanted her with all his being. He wanted her all to himself. So far he seemed to have done a good job of covering up the extent of his feelings for her, but one day soon he would give himself away. What if his guard slipped tonight? What then?

He sighed heavily. Why worry about that when in all probability after tonight there was every chance that Chloe might have her worst fears about him and his work confirmed – that the two were inextricably bound and she wouldn't see where she would fit in. It was quite likely that in the last month or so she had grown used to him as ordinary old Seth. Seth the friend to whom she referred ironically as Reverend Hawthorne. But after tonight there would be no dodging the fact that he was married to the Church and nothing would change that.

'Good heavens, Seth! Whatever are you doing with that viburnum?' Barbara Hicks' voice roused him out of his thoughts with a start. He had a sudden uncharitable thought of the woman dying, pitching up at the Pearly Gates and demanding to rearrange the whole show. Seth had no real idea what heaven might be like – he viewed any clergyman who claimed he did as suspect at best and a charlatan at worst – but he had a pretty good idea what hell felt like. Hell was standing at the top of a stepladder with Barbara Hicks bossing him about.

Chloe was nervous.

What was it she had thought when she'd seen Seth surrounded by his parish groupies at Margaret's funeral? She'd pitied the poor girl who ended up marrying him, since she'd be the most hated girl in Christendom. Not that Seth was taking her to this barn dance as his wife, or even as a prospective wife – just a friend masquerading as a girlfriend – but all the same, it would make her a target of sorts. She just hoped she could fulfil her part of the bargain. It seemed so unfair that Seth had been put in the position he had by a certain element of his flock. Narrow-minded bigots! She'd show them! How could they have turned on Seth like that? One minute fussing around him like bees round a honeypot, the next turning on him. Hypocrites!

She was almost at Seth's house – they'd agreed to meet there and then walk on to where the event was being held – when her mobile went off on the dashboard. Caller ID showed that it was Sally. 'Hi stranger,' Chloe said. 'Long time no speak.'

'I was thinking that myself,' Sally said, 'hence this call.'

Trying not to think of the last conversation she'd had with Dan, Chloe said, 'What have you been up to? What's kept you so busy you can't pick up the phone?'

'Oh, the usual: work.'

'I've warned you about that before. All work makes Sal a very dull gal. She's never around to go out to play any more.'

'Yeah, yeah, I know. But if it makes you feel any better, I've just left the office and I'm heading for home.'

'You've been at the office today? But it's Saturday.'

'Spare me the lecture. What are you doing at the moment?'

'I'm on my way to spend the evening with Seth.'

'Really? He's not still chasing after you, is he?'

Hackles immediately up, Chloe said, 'He's not chasing me at all.'

'If you say so. Where's he taking you tonight? To a fun-packed pray-in?'

'We're going to a barn dance, actually.'

'A barn dance! How quaint. Next you'll be saying you've taken up knitting or doing jigsaws.'

Chloe waited for her friend's laughter to subside. 'Sally?' she said tightly.

'Yes?'

'Why do you hate Seth so much?'

'I don't hate him. I just don't think you're cut out to be the girl-friend of a man like him.'

'I'm not his girlfriend. I'm his *friend*. And anyway, how would you know what kind of a man he is? You haven't even met him. Dan on the other hand has and he likes him. As do my parents.'

'Wow. I've clearly rattled you. You sound cross and defensive.'

'I am. Ever since Seth came into my life you've done nothing but disparage him.'

'That's rich. I seem to recall you falling over yourself to disparage him when you realized he'd been lying to you.'

'He didn't lie. And I regret my behaviour now. I was wrong and acting like the worst kind of idiot.' All at once, Chloe heard Seth's voice in her head saying everyone was an idiot, that everyone was hypocritical and judgemental. She felt her cheeks flush. How easy it would have been for him to point out that she was guilty of the same crime she was prepared to condemn others for. But he hadn't. He'd let it go. 'So what's keeping you so busy at work, then?' she asked Sally, wanting to change the subject.

'Oh you know how it is. These things just build and build.'

Don't do it, Chloe cautioned herself. Don't say anything. But she couldn't stop herself. Right now she wanted to get back at her friend, and petty or not, this was the only way she knew how to do it. 'How's that young admirer of yours?'

'Which young admirer?'

'The one you said was sexually harassing you.'

'Oh, him. I'd forgotten all about that. I'm pleased to say he's behaving himself impeccably. All he needed was a good dressing-down and he soon jumped into line.'

Was it Chloe's imagination or had Sally sounded just a bit too nonchalant in her reply? 'And how's that mother of yours?' Chloe segued. 'I still haven't forgiven you for missing my birthday in favour of visiting her.'

'Yeah, I'm sorry about that. But it looks like I'll have to go and see her again soon.'

'What for?'

'She's got herself into debt. I'm trying to sort things out for her. Don't, whatever you do, let on to Dan. You know how he thinks I'm chucking good money after bad with her.'

There was a lot more Chloe could say on this particular subject, but there wasn't time. 'I'm going to have to go now, Sally,' she said. 'I'm at Seth's. Why don't we get together tomorrow?' she added, wanting things to be right between them.

'I'd love to, but Dan's gone and got us invited to Dave and Rosie's for a barbecue. I'm dreading it. Rosie will probably be showing off her pregnancy and that'll have Dan banging on again about us having another child.'

Once more there was much Chloe could say in response to this, but she let it pass. 'I expect it won't be as bad as all that. Give my love to Dan and Marcus. Bye.'

She put her mobile in her bag and locked her car. It was the first time she'd visited Seth at home and she was curious to see what his house was like inside. Externally it was a classic Victorian mid-terraced house with a bay window, a tiled entrance porch, and a stained-glass front door.

She received no response to her first ring, so she tried the bell again. There was no sign of Seth's TVR on the road and she guessed he had it tucked safely away somewhere round the back of the row of houses. It didn't look too bad an area, but a car like that would attract an above average amount of attention.

The door opened and there was Seth. Dressed only in a towel wrapped around his waist, his hair wet and dripping down his neck and shoulders, he was clearly running late. 'Sorry,' he said, 'I was in the shower. Come on in. Let me make you a drink and then I'll get dressed. What would you like? There's a bottle of white already open in the fridge. Or there's some red in the rack. Or what about a gin and tonic?' He led her through to the kitchen and opened a cupboard for a glass. His words and movements were fast and jerky and Chloe could see that he wasn't himself.

'Why don't I see to my own drink,' she said, 'while you go and get dressed.'

He sighed and ran a hand through his wet hair. 'I'm really sorry about this,' he said. 'I was all set to jump in the shower an hour ago when the phone rang. It was one half of a couple I've been preparing for their wedding in two weeks' time. She was in tears; the groom's got cold feet. You look lovely, by the way. You've done your hair differently. It suits you. Makes you look— Oh, hell! I'm rambling, aren't I? It must be nerves. Sorry. Really sorry.'

She smiled. 'I don't mind a rambled compliment in the least. You don't look so bad yourself.' She cast her gaze over his sexy, glistening chest. *No! Where had that come from? Sexy, glistening chest?* Embarrassed, she tore her gaze away from him and looked awkwardly out of the window onto the small garden. Inappropriate behaviour! she warned herself. Two strikes and you're out!

'I bet you say that to all the half-naked men you come across, Doctor Hennessey,' he said lightly. 'Give me ten minutes and I'll be back down for a glass of Dutch courage myself.'

On her own, she poured herself a glass of wine. She stared unseeingly out of the kitchen window, her thoughts wandering and then finally settling on the lasting image of Seth, fresh from the shower. Unsettled at her reaction – an unmistakable rush of undiluted lust – she took a large, steadying gulp of wine, but immediately reprimanded herself: easy girl, no drinking too much. The curate's pretend girlfriend can't let the side down by showing up plastered.

OK, Seth told himself. Nice and cool. No need to make a big drama out of this. It's just a simple church hoedown. A few dances to get through. A plate of roast pork and baked potato to eat. A beer or two to enjoy. And a stunning faux girlfriend to show off. Nothing to it. A piece of cake.

But was it fair of him to put Chloe through this charade? Why couldn't he just have been straight with Owen? Look, he should have said, I'm not gay and it's not for the lack of trying that I don't have a real girlfriend.

Vanity had been his downfall, of course. He'd been too vain and stubbornly proud to be honest with Owen.

He took a deep breath and guided Chloe round to the back of Max and Stella Wainbridge's beautiful black and white half-timbered house. For years Max and Stella had offered their house and garden as the venue for the church barn dance. They were both retired and as members of the PCC they were key figures in the running of St Michael's. They were that rare thing in the Church of England: traditionalist at heart but open to the possibility of change. Seth had liked them from his very first meeting with them, when they had welcomed him warmly to the parish.

Stella was first to spot Seth. Dressed in jeans, checked and tasselled shirt and a cowboy hat, she waved enthusiastically and came towards him. 'Brace yourself, Chloe,' Seth said, 'it's show time; we're on parade.'

To his complete surprise, he felt Chloe's hand slip into his.

Chapter Thirty-Six

The light was fading when the band took to the stage. There was a guitarist, an accordion player, a girl in dungarees with a fiddle under her chin and a bearded old boy sitting on a bale of hay with a banjo. The caller didn't have any trouble corralling participants for the first dance; a sudden surge of people rushing to form a circle left Seth and Chloe momentarily shipwrecked at their table. 'Nothing else for it,' Chloe said, putting down her drink and taking Seth's from him. 'Time to initiate you.'

'I'm warning you now, if you crack one joke about me losing my virginity, I won't be responsible for my actions.'

She laughed and dragged him to his feet. People smiled when they joined the circle and Chloe could see the looks of endorsement on their faces. As far as she was aware she'd thus far not put a foot wrong in her role as The Curate's Girlfriend and had answered everyone's questions without hesitation or resorting to lying. They'd met in the spring ... at the gym ... she lived in nearby Eastbury ... she was a GP ... like her father ... yes, Seth was wonderful ... yes, he was excellent company ... yes, very generous, very caring.

The questions she hadn't been asked, and the ones she dreaded, were anything to do with the church-going habits. Seth had insisted that he didn't want her to feel obliged to lie on his behalf. 'Just tell them the truth,' he'd said. The nearest she'd got to resorting to a lie was when someone said, 'Your church in Eastbury has a splendid vaulted roof. It was replaced in the mid-nineteenth century after a fire, wasn't it?' Despite frequenting St Andrew's as a child and maintaining the family tradition of going there for the midnight carols service at Christmas, Chloe couldn't for the life of her recall what the roof looked like – it could be wood-chipped or artexed in marshmallow pink for all she knew – and so she had simply smiled and agreed that it was indeed a splendid roof.

The caller was walking them through a dance called the Lucky Seven, a relatively easy one to get things started. Seth looked at her anxiously and she squeezed his hand. 'You'll be fine; just follow everyone else.'

'I'll only be fine if I can stick to you like glue.'

'Sorry, after I've danced the first sequence with you I'll have to move on to someone new and dance the next sequence with him.'

'That doesn't sound much fun for me.'

'Don't you believe it,' she whispered in his ear. 'The women here are champing at the bit to get their hands on you.'

'I'm more worried about the men and you.'

'You think they'd risk touching the curate's girlfriend? Hey ho, we're off.'

The first sequence completed, Chloe waved Seth goodbye and moved around the circle. Her next partner was Max Wainbridge, a spry, white-haired gentleman sporting a multi-coloured waistcoat. He was stronger than he looked and grasped her firmly. 'If I'm not mistaken, you've done this before, haven't you?' he said.

'A misspent youth,' she admitted.

'Is there any other kind?' He laughed loudly. 'Seriously though, Stella and I are delighted that Seth has such a charming companion in his life. And not just because there were a few simpletons making scurrilous, not to say malicious, aspersions about him. If I had my way I'd name and shame them and run them out of town.' He laughed again. 'But don't quote me on that. Not exactly the done thing to say. No, Seth's a lucky lad to have you to turn to. Being a minister can be a tough and lonely job. It's not the cushy number people think it is.'

When she moved on to her next partner, Chloe encountered a similar conversation. And the same again with the next partner, the next and the next. Only Max had referred directly to the rumours about Seth, but the general consensus was that Seth had been a dark horse keeping her slyly under wraps the way he had. When she had very nearly completed the circle, she found herself dancing with Seth's boss, Owen. Seth had introduced her earlier and Chloe hadn't liked him on sight. But there again, she was biased; she despised him for not taking a firmer line with his gossiping flock. He seemed a tired, weak, distant and ineffectual man; a man who could be easily coerced. Even the way he held her was limp and half-hearted. She also didn't like the way he was dressed – in formal work clothes, dull grey suit and dog collar. Was he pulling rank on Seth by not wearing civvies?

She looked over to Seth and thought how vibrant and dynamic he looked in comparison. Wearing nothing fancier than a pair of faded jeans and a blue and white shirt, he was easily the most attractive man here. He stood out from the crowd effortlessly. He was also looking her way, she realized. Their eyes met and she thought how proud and happy she was to be here with him tonight. He gave her a dazzling smile, and smiling back at him, she experienced a curious sensation of peace, of letting go. Why had she battled against her feelings for Seth for as long as she had? Why had she been so stupid? She had no answer, but filled with a joyful sense of discovery, she didn't care.

As if floating on air, she felt Owen propelling her away from him to complete the circle and then she was moving slowly but irrevocably towards Seth. He took her in his arms. 'I think I've got the hang of this,' he said with a cheerful smile.

'Me too,' she murmured.

It was gone midnight and they were walking through the quiet streets of Crantsford back to Seth's house. Something extraordinary had happened to Chloe this evening. There had been a seismic shift in her emotions and it scared and thrilled her in equal parts.

He invited her in with the offer of a drink. She was glad he did; she wasn't ready yet to end the night. Nor was he, it seemed.

Laughing and joking, they performed a neat dosi-do round the kitchen as they made coffee. 'You enjoyed tonight more than you expected to, didn't you?' she said when they were in the sitting room. She took the sofa and he, after a moment's hesitation, took the armchair furthest away from her.

'What can I say?' he said. 'I'm a Strip the Willow convert. How about you? Was it very awful for you?'

'Not in the slightest. Do you think we fooled everyone?'

'In what way?'

'Me being your girlfriend.'

Suddenly his expression was grave. Gone was all trace of the carefree laughter and joking of only minutes ago. 'There was no doubt in anyone's mind,' he said flatly. 'You put on a very convincing performance. Thanks.'

Troubled at the dramatic transformation in him, she said, 'Seth, what's wrong?'

'Nothing,' he said. His gaze was disturbingly shuttered.

Even more troubled, Chloe tried again. 'I don't believe you. Please tell me what's wrong.' She longed to put her arms around him, to remove the awful expression of misery on his face.

The silence lengthened.

'OK,' he said finally. 'There is something wrong. I thought I could do this. But I can't.'

'What can't you do?' she asked softly.

He looked straight at her. 'I thought I could settle for being your friend. *Just* your friend.' He flung himself forward, rested his elbows on his knees, covered his face. 'But I can't go on pretending any more. I really can't.'

She put down her untouched mug of coffee and rose silently from the sofa.

'I understand completely,' he said morosely, his head still down. 'You made it very clear to me that we could never be more than friends. You never once gave me reason to hope for more, so I'm not blaming you in any way. It's my fault. I deluded myself. I arrogantly believed that quiet persistence on my part could win you round. I was wrong.'

Chloe knelt down in front of him. She touched one of his hands that was covering his face. He looked up, startled. She kissed him lightly on the mouth, was about to kiss him again when he pushed her away from him. 'Please don't,' he said hoarsely. 'Don't kiss me out of pity. That's more than I can take.'

Her heart ached for him. 'I'm not. Honestly. I—' She saw the raw pain burning in his eyes and her voice broke. She hated knowing that she had done this to him. That all this time he'd been suffering. 'I discovered something very important tonight,' she said. 'I woke up to how I really feel about you. If you'll have me, I'd like to be promoted from your pretend girlfriend to your real girlfriend.'

He stared at her and swallowed. He opened his mouth, but he didn't speak.

'Say something,' she said anxiously.

'I can't,' he said thickly.

For the longest time, they gazed at each other in silence. Slowly the pain faded from his expression and she saw the depth of his feelings for her in the intense blue of his eyes. He put a hand to her face and when he kissed her, it was with great tenderness and passion. His arms closed around her, and still kissing her, he lifted her onto his lap. Wrapped in his embrace, bending to the shape of him, she felt the perfect fit of their bodies.

Chapter Thirty-Seven

Chloe woke with a warm, glowing feeling inside her.

She turned onto her side and looked at the alarm clock: eight forty-five. Dare she risk having a shower? No, she didn't want to risk missing Seth. He had promised to ring her when he was between services – right now he would be conducting early Morning Service and at ten thirty he had Family Service. She had invited him for lunch, but disappointingly he was going to be busy with the cleaning-up operation after last night. It was a shame because she was overcome with the bizarre need to break out with the pots and pans and cook for him.

She stared up at the ceiling, the ceiling that Seth had done such a perfect job of painting. She smiled. Did he do anything badly? 'I'm not perfect, Chloe,' he'd once said to her, 'don't for one minute think a dog collar protects me from being selfish, hot-tempered, or foul-mouthed.' She'd yet to see any evidence of these traits, but one thing she did know: he made her feel happy. Oh, and he kissed like a dream.

Last night, when she had reluctantly suggested it was time she drove home, he'd kissed her again, making her melt against him. 'Don't go yet,' he'd said.

'But you've got to be up early.'

'Who says I'm going to go to bed?'

'I do,' she'd said firmly. 'I don't want to hear that you dozed off during your early Morning Service.'

When he eventually agreed to let her leave, they'd then spent an age in the hallway, spinning out their goodbye kiss like a couple of teenagers. 'Text me when you get home,' he'd said. She had and she'd received a message back saying she should have stayed because there was no way he could sleep now.

The telephone rang by the side of her bed. Chloe practically jumped on it. 'Hello,' she said in her best M&S this-is-not-just-food voice.

A silence followed by an embarrassed but very recognizable cough at the other end of the line had her sitting up straight. 'Dad!'

'Oh, so it *is* you, Chloe. I thought perhaps I'd misdialled. Dare I ask who you thought was ringing you?'

'No!'

In the background Chloe could hear her mother saying something to her father and then her father fumbling – unsuccessfully – to cover the mouthpiece of the phone and replying, 'She thought I was someone else ... I don't know who ... that's what I've just asked her.'

Glancing anxiously at the clock – what if Seth was trying to get through? – Chloe shouted down the phone at her father. 'Dad, stop talking to Mum and get on with why you called me!'

'No need to shout, Chloe,' her father said. 'I'm not deaf. Not yet, anyway. Are you around next weekend?'

'Of course. Where do I ever go?'

'Oh, don't be like that.'

'So where are you and Mum off to?'

'Stratford. Any chance you could water the pots and tomato plants as usual?'

'Consider it done. How long are you away for?'

'Four days.'

'No problem. Oh, sorry, Dad, I can't chat, there's someone at the door.'

'At this time of day? It's not even nine o'clock. People have no manners these days. Bye, love. Speak to you soon.'

There wasn't anyone at the door, but it was the only way Chloe could think to get her father off the phone quickly. She was still feeling guilty about this when five minutes later the phone rang again. Once again she lay back and said breathily, 'Hello, Reverend Hawthorne.'

'Is that you, Chloe?'

'Mum? What are you ringing me for?'

'More to the point, what are you doing sounding as if you're operating one of those kinky sex lines?'

'And what would *you* know about them?'

Ignoring her question, her mother said, 'I take it things have progressed somewhat with the delectable curate? When did this all happen? And don't put the phone down on me, I'll only ring back straight away and hog the line so the poor man can't get through to you.'

Chloe and her brother had often joked of their mother that resistance was futile. 'OK,' she conceded. 'You're right, things have moved on between us. But only since last night. Satisfied?'

'Aha! I knew it! I knew it the moment I clapped eyes on him. Mark my words, Chloe, he's a good 'un.'

'And with that seal of approval, can I put the phone down? Or was there something else you were calling about?'

The moment she'd got her mother off the line, the phone rang again. 'Hello,' Chloe said, dispensing with any attempt to sound alluring.

'Hello, you. Is your phone always so busy on a Sunday morning?'

She smiled and relaxed back against the pillows. 'It was Mum and Dad making a nuisance of themselves. How are you?'

'Looking forward to seeing you again, with a bit of luck. I don't suppose that offer of lunch is still on, is it? I've been given a reprieve. After last night, your popularity is such that I've been told to sling my hook for the afternoon and spend it with you. Max and Stella were adamant that my help wouldn't be required in the clean-up operation.'

Had anyone ever actually died of boredom? Sally wondered. Fed up, she turned to go in search of another drink and bumped into Dave Peach. He held out a jug of Pimm's that contained an excessive amount of chopped fruit bobbing about in it – more than enough to satisfy the five-a-day police. 'You look like a girl in need of a top-up,' he said, indicating her empty glass.

'Thanks,' she said.

'Having fun?'

'Yes,' she lied. 'Perfect weather for a barbecue,' she said, grabbing the first banality that came to mind and hurriedly moving on before she was overcome with the urge to say something she meant.

Having thought that it was going to be a quiet barbecue with Dave and Rosie, plus children, her heart had sunk when they'd arrived and been confronted with a sizeable, not to say raucous crowd, all with children. But a crowd wasn't such a bad thing. A crowd meant she could lose herself in it and wouldn't have to suffer the tedium of Rosie going on about her wretched pregnancy or of being forced to look at any baby scan photos.

She shuddered at the thought and wandered down to the bottom of the garden, where, for the time being, there were no children. It had struck her as odd that Chloe hadn't been invited, but perhaps she'd been excluded because she didn't have any children.

Sally's thoughts then turned from now to last night, when Chloe had said that Seth was taking her to a barn dance. What was going on with Chloe? Was she that desperate for a man in her life she was prepared to set her sights so low? And why was she so defensive about him? She'd been distinctly touchy on the phone last night. Downright snappy at one point. She supposed it was probably all to do with Chloe's desire to have a baby. Seldom did Chloe discuss the subject, but Sally knew Chloe would give anything for a child of her own.

Laughter from the patio had her looking up. A noisy group had congregated around Dave and Rosie's newly purchased hot tub. Sally had no intention of stripping off and submerging herself in that bubbling cauldron of chemicals like so many already had. God knew how many kids had weed in it.

On the opposite side of the garden, Dave was now firing up the gas barbecue, watched over by a circle of men with cans of beer in their hands – Dan among them with Marcus hoisted on his hip. Nearby, Rosie and a gang of other women, mostly mothers from the village, were laying out plates of food on two large tables. Observing their interaction – their laughter and easy, inclusive chatter – and the children running around and getting in the way, Sally knew what it felt like to be an alien. This wasn't her world, the cosy world of Mummies and Daddies. It was all so trivial and mundane. Nothing bored her more than being in the company of people with whom she had no connection. She'd always felt this way, but the difference now was that it was getting harder to hide her true feelings.

Another surprising absence from the guest list was Tatiana, Queen of the Fairies. But maybe her childless state also precluded an invitation. Sally no longer suspected Dan of having an affair with Tatiana; she'd decided he wouldn't dare to for fear of the risk of tarnishing his immaculate image.

She picked out the fruit from her glass, tossed the bits over her shoulder and drank the Pimm's in one long swallow. God, she was bored. Bored out of her mind. Bored enough to do something silly. Like break her rule and text Harry. Except she wouldn't. Harry had given her his mobile number in the hope that she'd relent and surprise him with a text message. He hadn't yet learned just how strong-willed she really was.

He liked to tease her that he'd unleashed the bad girl within her and had enabled her to let go in a way she'd never done before. Little did he know that she was fully acquainted with the bad girl within her. Oh, but what wouldn't she give to be with Harry right now? Looking about her, at the assembled gathering playing at their tedious little lives, it amused her that she was living a double life. Didn't these people know they were slowly suffocating themselves with their boring layers of respectability and domesticity?

When she and Dan had flown home with Chloe and Paul from Bangkok after the tsunami, many on the flight had sworn that from then on they'd make the most of the time they had here on earth. Such a resolution begged the question of what the hell she was doing here at Dave and Rosie Peach's barbecue. Why wasn't she in bed having great sex with her lover?

Lover. She repeated the word with relish. Harry, her *lover*. How different next weekend would be compared to this one. Next week she was going to help her mother again. Which meant, this time next week, she would be in bed with Harry.

With a bowl of raspberries between them, Seth lay on his side next to Chloe. Her eyes were closed in the dappled sunlight but her lips were enticingly parted. 'You have a very erotic mouth,' he said.

She opened an eye lazily. 'Are you allowed to say such an outrageous thing on a Sunday?'

He placed a perfectly ripe raspberry between his own lips, bent his head and dropped the raspberry into her mouth with a kiss. 'I can say whatever I like,' he said. When she'd swallowed the raspberry, he moved the dish of fruit out of the way and kissed her again. Her soft, sweet-tasting mouth opened wide against his and he lost himself in kissing her. He'd never felt the way he did when he kissed Chloe. No one had ever made him feel the way she did.

All during the barn dance last night he'd had people telling him he was lucky to have such a lovely girlfriend. One or two had gone so far as to ask when they might expect to hear the sound of wedding bells to ring out for him. He'd hated his duplicity. Was this really what he'd reduced himself to? He'd known then that he couldn't carry on with the charade any longer. He had to tell Chloe the truth.

Remembering now how he'd risked everything with his confession and how she'd reacted, he pulled her closer to him and slipped a hand under her top. Her skin was silky smooth and he slowly inched his fingers upwards. When his hand settled on her breast, she let out a small but unmistakable breath of pleasure. Her response to his touch added to the flare of his own desire and he slid his hand round to her back and unhooked her bra. She arched against him and he kissed her neck, his teeth grazing her skin. He kissed the base of her throat and then lifting her top, he lowered his mouth to her breast. She moved against him, her hands on his shoulders. But then suddenly, the pressure of her hands on his shoulders increased and she was pushing him away.

He raised himself up and she rolled out from beneath him. 'What's wrong?' he said, concerned.

Pulling down her top, but not looking at him, she said, 'It ... it doesn't feel right.'

'You mean I'm not doing it right?'

She swallowed. 'Oh, God, no! You're doing it right. Much too right, in fact.'

'So what's the problem?' Although he had a fairly good idea what was going through her mind.

She looked at him now. 'I'm making you do something you shouldn't do, aren't I? I'm ... I'm compromising you.'

He'd known this was yet another bridge they had to cross. 'You're worried about my spiritual integrity, is that it?' he asked, trying to keep a straight face. 'You think what we were doing is a violation of my calling?'

'Well, isn't it?' She had her hands behind her back and was struggling to do up her bra.

'I wasn't about to have full-on sex with you, Chloe, if that's what you're worrying about. I know when to hit the stop button. Here, turn around and I'll do that for you.'

When he had put her back together again, he turned her to face him. She was frowning. 'Now I feel stupid,' she said. 'Talk about killing the mood.'

He took her hands in his. 'I think we need to be sure of a few ground rules. Basically you want to know where I stand on sex outside marriage, don't you?'

She nodded and he could see the awkward embarrassment in her face.

'Sex within the bounds of a loving and committed relationship is what's important to me. Anything else just won't feel as satisfying. It's got to be the real deal. Or nothing.'

'But how do you know for sure if the relationship is the real deal?'

He smiled and stroked her cheek. 'Human nature being what it is, I'd say that's half the fun, wouldn't you?'

She caught his hand in her own and pressed the palm of it to her lips. 'I'm sorry,' she murmured.

'What for?'

'For doubting you. I should have known better than to think this wasn't something you hadn't already worked through. I just don't want to wake up one morning feeling that I'm responsible for making you do something you'll regret. For leading you astray.'

He laughed out loud and pulled her into his arms. He lay her down next to him. 'When I joked the other day that I was a dosi-do virgin, you didn't think that I was implying anything else, did you?'

When she didn't answer him, he said, 'For the record, the old me would have had your knickers off on a second date. I would have chalked your name up with all the others and, what's more, I wouldn't have returned your call the next day.'

She turned in his arms. 'I don't believe you.'

'You think I'd lie to you about something like that?'

She stared into his face. 'How many? How many women have you slept with, Reverend Seth Hawthorne?'

'I'm not saying. I'm too much of a gentleman, as I've told you before.'

'More than twenty?'

'I'm not saying.'

'More than forty?'

'Still not saying.' He mimed the closing of a zip across his mouth.

'My God, Seth, what were you, some kind of sex addict?'

'Oh, yeah, me and Russell Brand, we were in rehab together. Look, I'm not proud of it, but back then I was a right bastard. How about you? How many partners have you had?'

'Me? I'm practically a chaste nun compared to you.'

'Quality over quantity?'

'Not exactly.'

'Were they all good? Just out of interest.'

She smiled and raised an eyebrow. 'Why, worried you might not come up to standard?'

'No chance.' He put a hand to the nape of her neck, brought her face close to his and kissed her.

When he let her go, she said, 'You dodged the bullet once before, but this time I want you to answer my question. What made you leave the police force for the Church?'

'You sure you wouldn't rather I distracted you with another kiss?'

She sat up and shook her head. 'The truth.'

'OK,' he said. He put his hands behind his head, got himself comfortable. 'Do you remember the Hill House rail crash back in January 2001?'

She nodded. 'That was the train that derailed in the snow. When more than twenty were killed. You weren't involved, were you?'

'I was one of the lucky ones to walk away with nothing more serious than cuts and bruises. I was knocked out for probably no more than a minute or so and when I came to there was chaos all around me. People were crawling on their hands and knees through the mangled wreckage in the snow, blood pouring from their injuries. In the distance I could hear a girl's cry coming from somewhere. I followed the sound of her cries. When I found her she was in a bad way. She was losing a lot of blood. One of her legs had been ripped off at the knee and her stomach was ...'

He paused, remembering the shocking scene of utter carnage. He'd nearly been sick at the sight of the poor girl. It was a scene he rarely revisited in his mind. In his work as a policeman, before he'd transferred to vice, he'd seen countless pictures of car accidents, and many times had been on the scene of the aftermath of the real thing, but he'd never come across anything as horrific as this.

'When she realized I was there,' he continued, 'that she wasn't alone, she asked me if she was dying. There seemed no point in lying to her. She asked me if I would hold her. "Right to the end," she whispered as I held her. "Right to the very end. I don't want to die alone." Her last words were to ask me to pray for her. Me, pray? I hadn't done that since I was eight years old and wanted a new bike for Christmas! But I did as she asked; God knows I didn't know what else to do. Yet once I started I didn't feel so powerless or so alone. She died in my arms. A complete stranger. I later found out that she was only twenty-one. Her family got in touch with me; they wanted to thank me for what I'd done. When I said I hadn't really done anything, they argued that the littlest things in life often created the greatest good. They said they would never forget the kindness I'd shown their daughter. I'd never felt so humbled or so in need of turning my own life around. As conversions go, it took me a while, but two years later I resigned from the police force and took up a place at theology college.'

He shifted his gaze from where he'd been staring up at the pale sky through the fluttering leaves of the tree above them and studied the thoughtful expression on Chloe's face. He could see that she was considering what he'd said. He was fairly sure he knew what she would say in response.

'But what convinced you that there was a god in any of that?' she asked quietly, proving him right. 'Surely it would make you think otherwise. Such needless destruction. Such pain and hurt. All that senseless fear and grief.'

He reached up to run his fingers through her hair. 'It was watching the innate goodness of virtual strangers rushing to the aid of fellow passengers who were dying or badly hurt than convinced me that whether we realize it or not, there's a force for good working through each and every one of us every minute of the day, and in the least likely situations.'

She lay down beside him, her head resting against his. 'Would it be very crass of me to say I'm glad you were one of the lucky ones that day?'

He kissed her lightly on the forehead. 'I'm glad I was lucky too.'

Chapter Thirty-Eight

It was September and two days after they'd returned from a week in Cornwall, Dan was in the kitchen blowing up balloons.

It was Marcus's birthday. Could three whole years really have passed since that day in the delivery room when Marcus had entered the world? The years may have passed in a blink of an eye, yet the counterbalance to this was to imagine a time when Marcus hadn't been around. Had the world really existed before his birth? It was difficult to reconnect with those days when they didn't have him, when holidays were spontaneously snapped-up last-minute bargains for a couple of sun-drenched weeks in Greece or the Caribbean.

This year's break – a traditional seaside family holiday down in Cornwall – was a throwback to Dan's own childhood when he and his parents used to go to Devon to stay in the same cottage, year in year out. Children liked continuity and Dan could foresee Marcus looking forward to the prospect of returning to St Ives next year. As for Sally, Dan wasn't so sure.

Before their holiday her behaviour had been markedly erratic, up one day, down the next. Yet whatever her mood, he had played his part. If she was quiet and withdrawn to the point of being closed down, he would leave her in peace. If she was amused by something that had gone on at work and wanted to share it with him, he would listen attentively. When she was tired and frustrated by an awkward client or annoyed over trivial office politics, he would smooth the roughened edges of her day. In short, he would play whatever role it took to bring her back to him. Countless times he had wanted to tell her that he missed her. He wanted his wife back. He was tired of living with this imposter.

He'd reached the point of almost dreading their week away. He'd been anxious that being thrown together for seven whole days and in such close confinement would be a strain too far and one of them, probably him, would be tipped over the edge. But the holiday had gone better than he'd hoped. Sally had seemed to be enjoying herself, playing with Marcus on the beach, building sandcastles and hunting in rock pools with him for crabs. They were midway through the holiday when, following the consumption of a bottle and a half of wine between them over supper one night, he risked touching her in bed. To his surprise, she didn't roll away from him. If he was honest, his performance hadn't been too brilliant – having gone without for too long ensured things were over before they'd really begun – but spurred on, he'd given it another shot the next night and to his relief found his stride fully reinstated. It was either the sea air or the quantity of wine they were drinking, but from then on they made love every night. He knew they were on surer ground when, on their last night in the cottage, it was Sally who made the first move. If she was having an affair, would she really do that? It was all the encouragement he needed to believe they were over the worst.

He'd also been encouraged by her decision to leave her mobile and laptop at home. 'I don't want my mother badgering me while we're away or anyone from work being able to get in touch,' she'd said when they were packing up the car. This was a first. She had never cut the tie with work so resolutely before. And if there was a lover on the scene, wouldn't she want the security of being able to stay in touch with him?

With shame, Dan now had to admit that he'd been wrong. He'd been paranoid to imagine Sally was seeing someone behind his back. He had put himself through hell for no real reason. He could now see that the problem had been nothing more sinister than Sally working too hard. And not just that; she had that foul mother of hers to deal with into the bargain. All she'd needed was time away. He'd been a fool not to realize it before.

Down to the last remaining balloon, Dan gave it a final puff, then cursed when it went bang in his face. Oh, well, not to worry; they had more than enough. After all, how many balloons did two small children need?

Although it was Marcus's birthday today, his proper party wouldn't be until the weekend. Today there would be just a small gathering of close friends to mark the occasion. It was both Chloe and Seth's day off, so they would be coming, along with Jennifer and Graham, and Tatiana and Rose with Charlie. On Saturday it was Charlie's birthday, and he and Marcus were having a combined party in the village hall, where an armed division of squealing toddlers dressed as pirates would be assembled and all hell would probably break loose. Hopefully this afternoon's celebrations would be a lot quieter and easier to manage.

Sally had promised to do her best to get back in time, but knowing that she had the inevitable mountain of work to catch up on from last week, Dan wasn't holding his breath in the hope that she would.

He opened the fridge door and poured a cup of apple juice ready for when he brought Marcus downstairs. With only an hour until the guests would start arriving, it was time to wake him from his nap. As he closed the fridge door, Dan's eye caught on the latest piece of scribbly artwork Marcus had produced at nursery. It was a picture of Marcus in the garden with Dan. Way off in the distance, in the top-right hand corner of the piece of paper, was Sally, isolated and imprisoned in a tall, bendy building. Mindful of how Sally might react to it, Dan had been in a quandary about displaying the drawing but Marcus had Blu-tacked it to the fridge door himself.

Marcus was already awake when Dan pushed open his bedroom door. His hair rumpled and sticking to his scalp, one of his cheeks flushed red, he was looking intently at one of his many books from the shelf above his bed. With his finger moving along the words he was giving a convincing impression of reading the book aloud to his cuddly toys. Had Dan not known that Marcus knew the book by heart he could have easily believed his son was a child prodigy. But like all parents, he'd made that assumption a long time ago. Of course Marcus was a genius. He was the smartest boy who had ever lived!

'Daddy!' Marcus flung the book away from him and scrabbled to his feet, and as if suddenly remembering that it was his birthday, he said, 'Is it time for my party?'

Dan went over to the bed. 'Very nearly. First, though, we need to get you changed.'

Marcus clapped his hands. 'Is Charlie here?'

'Not yet.'

'Is Tatty here?'

'She'll be here later.' Dan carried Marcus over to look at the clock on the wall above the chest of drawers. 'Everyone will start to arrive when the big hand is pointing to the number twelve and the little hand is on three. Which means we've got exactly fifty-five minutes to get you spruced up. Do you still want to wear the clothes you picked earlier?'

Nodding hard, Marcus wriggled out of his arms and slid to the floor. He started tugging at his sleep-crumpled shorts and T-shirt. 'Help me, Daddy. Help me.' Had there ever been a child more excited to get to his own birthday party? thought Dan with a smile.

'I've got to go,' Sally said.

Standing behind her, one of his hands inside her blouse, Harry said, 'Another five minutes won't hurt.'

'Harry, no,' she said.

He laughed. 'You don't mean that.'

God help her, but he was right. She would willingly stay here in his office for the rest of the day if she thought they could get away with it. He held her closely and she could feel the hardness of him pressing against her. Five minutes was probably all it would take. Certainly if Monday was anything to go by. Within minutes of being back in the office after her week away, Harry had locked her in his office with him and done what he'd threatened to do since they'd started their affair. 'I missed you,' he'd said as he slumped against her afterwards. 'Don't ever go away like that again.'

'But look how the denial has sharpened your appetite for me,' she'd replied, relishing the depth of his need for her.

On her last day at work before going on holiday he'd begged her to let him ring or text her whilst she was in Cornwall, but she'd stood firm. Concerned that he might try and email her whilst she was away she'd made it clear that she wouldn't be taking her laptop with her. Being completely deprived of Harry had increased her desire for him and she'd resorted to having sex with Dan just so she could close her eyes and pretend she was in bed with Harry. The first time she had done it she had experienced a vague sense of guilt, but by the following night she reckoned Dan was happy enough, so why worry?

Extricating herself from Harry's grasp, she said, 'I really have to go. I'm going to be late as it is.'

'One more kiss, then I'll let you go.'

Chloe was cross. What was Sally playing at? Sometimes she didn't think her friend deserved Dan and Marcus. Surely she could find the time to be with her son on his birthday? Twice now Dan had had to explain to Marcus that they couldn't light the candles on his cake yet, not until Mummy was here. Frankly, if it were down to Chloe, she'd light the candles, let Marcus blow them out and to hell with his mother being here to share the moment. It was high time that girl got her priorities sorted.

Quite apart from Sally letting her son down, Chloe also felt personally slighted. Today was to be the day when Sally finally met Seth. Glancing across the kitchen, she watched with proprietorial pride as Seth chatted with her father. As she continued to observe him, she experienced the by-now familiar strong physical pull of him. The time became suspended and something stirred in her; a warmth, an inner light. Love? She thought it might be. It both stilled and thrilled her. Yet the physical pull of him was now only a part of his attraction; it was the awareness he'd given her of his inner self that really had the power to move her.

She knew that he had an uncanny knack for sensing when she was staring at him and it didn't surprise her when he looked over her father's shoulder and caught her gaze. His eyes held hers and he curved his lips into one of his slow, melting smiles. He then returned his gaze to her father, giving him his total attention once again.

It was hard for her to equate the Seth she knew with the promiscuous man he had described to her and she couldn't resist teasing him about it. He handled her jibes with good grace and parried them by threatening to wear his full ecclesiastical robes when they went out next together. In a more serious mood, he'd asked her if his track record from his former life bothered her at all. The honest answer was no. In fact, she couldn't think of a single thing about him that bothered her. Well, apart from the obvious: that she was likely to die of sexual frustration any day soon. Being with Seth was a double-edged sword: the more time she spent with him, the more she wanted him.

'How many times did I tell you as a child that it was rude to stare, Chloe?'

Chloe took the glass of wine her mother had fetched for her.

'I can't say I blame you. He's absolutely gorgeous. An unearthly beauty. What helped to change your mind about him?'

'In what way?'

'From friendship to something more involved.'

'Mind your own business, Mum.'

'You will be careful, won't you?'

Chloe looked at her mother. 'Why do you say that?'

Jennifer took a sip of her wine. 'Be patient with him. He has to play by different rules from the rest of us.'

'I know that, Mum.'

'Good. Now tell me about the pretty girl Marcus and Charlie can't take their eyes off.'

'Her name's Tatiana and she works with Dan at the trust. It was Rosie who introduced them.'

'And?'

'And what?'

'Is she married? Is there a boyfriend?'

'I don't think so.'

'Mm ... things aren't right here at Corner Cottage, are they?'

'Stop it, Mum.'

'So where's Sally?'

Good question, thought Chloe.

Sally locked her car, fixed a harassed expression on her face and let herself in. 'Sorry everyone!' she cried, feigning breathlessness, as if she'd run all the way from Manchester. 'Honestly, those roads just get worse and worse. Forty-five minutes I was stuck on the M56. Hello, Marcus, are you having a lovely time? Any chance of a gin and tonic, Dan? I'm absolutely dying for one.'

Congratulating herself on such a perfect entrance, Sally shrugged out of her suit jacket and began working the room. She spun the usual old baloney to Rosie – pregnancy going well, blah di bloody blah – kissed Graham Hennessey – Yes, excellent holiday in Cornwall, thanks ... yes, fantastic weather ... we were very lucky – and fast disconnected herself from her surroundings. Boring. Boring. *Boring!* When would it ever end? How she longed to shock them all out of their smug small-mindedness. But why was Chloe looking at her that way? And what the hell was Tatiana Queen of the Bloody Fairies doing here? But check out the angelic curly-haired sex god standing next to Chloe! Holy Moses! It wasn't her curate, was it? Well, who'd have thought it?

A large and welcome gin and tonic in her hand now, and her game face on, Sally strolled over. Oh, oh, time to light the touchpaper, stand back and have some fun!

She kissed Chloe's cheek. 'And you must be Chloe's sexy unobtainable priest, Seth Hawthorne,' she said, offering him her hand. 'I've heard so much about you.'

'I've heard a lot about you, too. It's good to meet you at last.'

'I'm disappointed in you, though. You don't seem to have done a very good job on Chloe. If you ask me, she's still as big a sinner as ever. Or is she beyond redemption?'

'Thanks a bunch, Sally!'

'Don't look so grouchy, Chloe, I'm only joking. Seth knows that, don't you, Seth?'

'Sally,' Dan called to her. 'Marcus wants to blow out the candles on his cake now. Do you want to come over?'

Chloe was furious. Could Sally have been any ruder or more patronizing? It seemed she could, because now, on her second large gin and tonic, she was telling Seth that he didn't look anything like she'd expected.

'How did you think I'd look?' Seth asked her, smiling.

'Well, you know; a bit wet and insipid.'

Chloe stifled an exclamation. But Seth said, 'Based on what? Chloe's previous taste in boyfriends?'

Sally laughed. 'God, no! The one thing you can rely on Chloe for is her impeccable taste in good-looking men.'

On the verge of telling Sally to shut up, Chloe felt Seth slip his hand in hers and squeeze it gently. She took it as a hint not to react. 'I'm intrigued,' he persisted smoothly. 'Just why did you think I'd look wet and insipid?'

Sally swirled the ice cubes round in her glass, making them rattle. 'Based on just about every religious fanatic I've ever come across.'

Chloe had had enough. 'Sally, I don't know what you're stoked up on, but take it down a notch, will you?'

'It's OK, Chloe,' Seth said, his hand squeezing hers again. 'Sally's entitled to her opinion.'

'You're damned right I am! Hey, has Chloe told you about the list we used to keep?'

'Not that I can recall,' Seth replied evenly.

Chloe shot her so-called friend a threatening look. 'He doesn't need to know about that.'

Sally laughed. 'I don't see why not. Not that it really means anything. After all, we were young and usually in the crazy zone when we were compiling it.'

'Sally please, just button it. OK?'

'The thing is,' Sally carried on, ignoring Chloe's plea, her eyes glittering with intent, 'a vicar would have been the last man either of us would have considered dating. Back then, you would have been so lame and so low in the food chain as to be worthy of nothing but our derision. Funny how things change, isn't it?'

Chloe let out a strangled cry of incensed disbelief. But his manner quite unruffled, Seth moved his hand to Chloe's shoulder and said with quiet dignity, 'Then I have to consider myself exceedingly fortunate.'

His politeness in the face of such a blatant insult was more than Chloe could bear. She leaned forward to whisper in Sally's ear, then tipped her glass of wine down her front.

Chapter Thirty-Nine

'If it makes you feel any better, I wasn't offended by what Sally said. I've been on the receiving end of far worse insults and have learned the hard way to ignore them. I was more concerned about her upsetting you. Which she clearly did. What did you whisper in her ear?'

'You don't want to know.'

Back at home now, Chloe was taking out her fury on making coffee. She was banging and crashing her way through the simple process to no avail. What she'd really like to do was get hold of Sally and tell her in no uncertain terms that she was a bitch on wheels. No, actually what she'd like to do was slap her very hard.

She and Seth had left the party while Sally was upstairs changing out of her wine-soaked top. Dan had been disappointed to see them leave so early – he'd been expecting them to stay on for supper to make an evening of it – but she'd lied and said she had a headache. She couldn't ever recall lying to Dan before. Walking home, Seth had asked if she'd rather be alone if she wasn't feeling well and she'd lied again and said she was suddenly feeling a lot better. She might not have a headache, but she was burning up with hatred for Sally.

'How about I do that?' Seth suggested, a look of puzzled amusement on his face as she battled with the cafetiere. 'In your current frame of mind, you're likely to send that coffee into orbit.' He took the cafetiere from her and she watched him gently press down the plunger.

'I'm sorry,' she said. 'Sorry that I have such a bitch of a friend. She was horrible to you. I don't think I'll ever forgive her.'

He stopped what he was doing. 'Don't say that. Nothing's ever that bad.'

'You're not going to go all preachy on me, are you?'

Smiling, he poured out their mugs of coffee. 'Do I look that dim-witted?' He added milk, knowing exactly how much she liked. 'But

I'd be interested to know what's really troubling your friend. She gave the impression of spoiling for a fight. People who do that are usually avoiding one with themselves.'

'Well, she'll get one from me if she doesn't get her act together.'

'Come on,' he said, 'let's go and sit outside. And when I think it's safe and I won't get my head bitten off, I'll risk kissing you to cheer you up.'

Despite the foul mood Sally had put her in, Chloe smiled. 'You can kiss me now, if you like.'

He put their drinks down and came round to her side of the breakfast bar. He placed his hands around her waist and bent to kiss her, lightly and lingeringly. 'Better?' he said when he pulled away.

'Almost,' she said.

He tutted. 'Almost isn't good enough.' He kissed her again, this time taking her face in his hands. Her heart soared and it wasn't long before her body ached for his touch. It was all she could do to stop herself from ripping his clothes off and satisfying herself. Never had she wanted a man as much as she wanted Seth. Abruptly, he stopped kissing her and suddenly hugged her with a fierce shudder. Pressed against him, she could feel his heart hammering in his chest. 'In your professional capacity as a doctor,' he said, 'do you think it's possible to die from abstinence?'

'The way I feel, I think it's highly likely.'

He tilted his head back and gazed down at her. His pupils were fully dilated, the blue of his irises intensely dark. He inhaled deeply, then let out his breath slowly. She could see he was suddenly nervous. That he was working up to say something. Something important. 'I hadn't wanted to say anything,' he said, his voice low, 'not this soon. But the way I see it, I'm damned if I do and damned if I don't. I love you, Chloe. I love you in a way I've never loved anyone before. I think about you all the time.' He smiled hesitantly. 'And not just about how much I want to make love to you, which I only do on average about twenty-three hours a day.'

'What do you think about in that other hour?' she asked.

The smile broadened. 'OK, I admit it, I lied. It's a full-time, twenty-four-hour job fantasizing about you naked in bed with me. Not that I'm complaining, you understand. There are worse things I could be obsessed with.'

Chloe rested the palms of her hands on his chest. Through the soft, warm fabric of his shirt, she could feel the tautness of his muscles and the beating of his heart, still thumping fast. Her own heartbeat had picked up speed. 'Can we rewind the conversation a bit, please?' she said.

'To which bit in particular?'

'The part when you said you loved me.'

'That sounds ominous.' An anxious frown instantly clouded his handsome face and eyes. 'I knew I shouldn't have said anything.'

She placed a finger on his lips. 'Ssh ... It's my turn to speak. When you said you loved me, you didn't give me a chance to respond. I just want you to know that I love you. Nobody's ever made me as happy as you do.' She removed her finger and kissed him. She felt him quiver in her arms and went on kissing him. And would have continued doing so had Seth's mobile not started to ring.

'Aren't you going to answer it?' she asked him when he didn't move.

'It'll keep.'

'It could be important.'

'Nothing's more important than kissing you right now.'

She smiled and slipped out of his arms. She passed him his phone from the counter.

It was soon obvious from Seth's body language that the call wasn't particularly important; a nuisance parishioner by the looks and sounds of things. He was doing a lot of nodding and rolling of his eyes. Chloe watched him with amusement. And love. Oh, yes, she loved Seth. She loved the littlest thing about him. She loved the way his curly hair flopped about on his head when he laughed or when he was on the running machine at the gym. She loved the way his blue eyes darkened with desire for her. She loved the soft, sensual way he kissed her. She loved the way he said she was beautiful. She loved his integrity. She even loved his obsession with Arcade Fire. But best of all, she loved the way he made her feel, so light of heart and cherished.

Would it be tempting fate to think that maybe, just maybe, she and Seth might be made for each other? That they had a real and lasting future together? Or was she, as ever, getting ahead of herself?

With Marcus finally settled in bed and clasping a newly recruited teddy to his platoon of cuddlies – a present from Chloe and Seth – Dan went to look for Sally. As he knew he would, he found her downstairs in the study. She looked up from her laptop. 'Just finishing,' she said absently.

'That's OK, no hurry. I'll make a start on supper.'

'Actually, I'm not very hungry. Just a sandwich would suit me. Will it keep for tomorrow what you've prepared?'

'Probably better if I freeze it. There's rather a lot of it, I was expecting Chloe and Seth to stay on for the evening. What did you think of Seth?'

'He's all right, I suppose. Although if I'm completely honest, I found him a bit hard to take seriously.'

Surprised, Dan said, 'In what way?'

'Come off it, Dan, the man believes in virgin births and the dead being raised. How can anyone with half a brain take him seriously?'

'Chloe seems to.'

'Yeah, well, right now she's getting off on the unobtainability of him.'

'You really think that's the extent of her attraction for him?'

'I'd put money on it. It's a novelty thing. Once that's lost its shine for her, she'll be giving him the elbow.'

'For what it's worth, I think you're wrong. I think she's very fond of him. And he of her. What's more, from what I've seen of them together, they make a great couple.'

She shrugged. 'If you say so.' She then returned her attention to her laptop.

Leaving her to get on, Dan turned to go. But he hesitated. 'Sally,' he said, 'is everything OK at work?'

She raised her head sharply. 'What do you mean?'

'You would say if things were getting too much for you, wouldn't you? You work so hard.'

She stared back at him wordlessly, her eyes chillingly pale and direct. He feared he might have gone too far and touched a nerve that she would prefer to be left well alone. 'I just want you to know that I appreciate everything you do,' he added.

He closed the door after him and tried to remember when exactly it was that he'd started walking on eggshells around Sally.

Chapter Forty

As partners' meetings went, it was the same old game of attack and defend. It was as predictable as night followed day and Sally could play the game in her sleep. Which was just as well, because her mind wasn't on what porkadellic Duncan Patterson was bleating on about for the gazillionth time. He could produce as many excuses as he could out of his sprawling, canyon-sized backside and still no one would be interested in listening to him. Get with the programme, Duncan: no one gives a damn! You're nothing more than an ego-maniac windbag who can't ever bill your clients on time!

As she doodled absent-mindedly on the notepad in front of her, Sally had something much more important preying on her mind than anything Duncan Patterson had to say. 'How's Harry?' Chloe had whispered in her ear yesterday. Every time she replayed those words in her head, she had to take a small, steadying breath. What did Chloe know? And whatever it was she did know – or thought she knew – how had she come by it? No way could Chloe have seen them together. Or even overheard a conversation. Yet her friend appeared to suspect something and had used it to strike back at Sally. She had even childishly tipped wine down her front. How petty and pathetic. And because of what. Because Sally had dared to speak the truth about Chloe's latest man?

OK, he was a looker – she'd give him that – but he certainly wasn't Chloe's type. Could Chloe honestly see herself as a vicar's wife? All those dreary sermons to sit through. All that po-faced hypocrisy and brain-numbing mumbo-jumbo to swallow. Really, the whole thing was absurd. Chloe was making a massive mistake, not to say an embarrassing fool of herself. The rate she was going she'd kid herself Pete Doherty was ideal husband material if it meant she could get a baby out of the arrangement.

But Chloe's wanton hormonal stupidity aside, how had she jumped to such a conclusion about Sally and Harry? And if Chloe had, was there a chance Dan had? Was it something the pair of them had discussed behind her back? But based on what, exactly? She and Harry had been so careful. No emails. No texts. No phone calls when she was at home. Nothing that could be inadvertently stumbled across. That had been the rule. Despite Harry's pleadings. And thank God Harry had never broken that rule and sent her something to provoke her into a response.

How's Harry?

Perhaps it had been nothing but a vicious shot in the dark to get back at Sally. A cowardly one at that. When Sally had come back downstairs after changing, both Chloe and Seth had left. A headache, so Dan had informed her. Yeah, right! But out of all the lines of attack Chloe could have pursued, why had she chosen Harry and implied that Sally had something going with him? In bed last night Sally had tried every permutation she could with those three small words, trying to shape them into something else. Something perfectly innocent that she had misheard and misinterpreted. But try as she might, she could come up with nothing truly convincing. The closest she could get was, *Why so snappy?* or *Why so crappy?* It sort of worked, given that Chloe was clearly cross with her. And maybe that slip of the wine glass had been a bona fide accident, even if Chloe's apology had been somewhat desultory.

As soon as she'd arrived at work this morning, Sally had rushed to speak to Harry, but annoyingly he was out of the office for the day, busy with some fraud case up in Burnley. For the first time she had been tempted to use the number he'd given her.

At last! Pens were being capped, notepads and files slapped shut – the meeting had finally drawn to a welcome close. Up on her feet, Sally hurriedly gathered her things together and headed impatiently for the door.

'Could I have a word, Sally?' Tom McKenzie, who had just chaired the meeting, had his hand on her arm.

'Of course,' she said brightly, trying to disguise her irritation at being delayed.

'Let's go to my office,' Tom said, already leading the way.

Stationed in a glass-partitioned cubicle outside Tom's office was Fern Elliot, Tom's PA. Back in the dark ages of manual typewriters and typing pools she'd graduated from the old school of secretaries, the school that churned out fire-breathing dragons who dressed in sensible court shoes and American tan tights. The Iron Lady was her unofficial office title and she guarded Tom with a possessiveness that Sally knew at times made him feel uncomfortable. Nonetheless, he wasn't averse to taking full advantage of her slavish devotion by getting her to collect his dry cleaning, or to shop for presents at Kendals for his elderly mother, and Harvey Nichols for his wife. Fern's main claim to fame – apart from worshipping the ground Tom walked on – was to consider the rest of the firm's lowly employees as beneath her. Sally included. Sally gave her a cheery, insincere smile as she followed behind Tom into his office.

Tom offered her a chair, but instead of taking up his seat behind his desk he wandered over to the window that looked down onto the street. He fiddled with the venetian blind, seeming to debate with himself whether the angle of the aluminium slats should be altered by two millimetres. He appeared to be on edge. Why?

'Everything all right, Tom?' she asked, deciding it had to be a personal matter he wanted to share with her. Or perhaps it was something of a sensitive nature that he hadn't felt able to risk airing during the meeting. Perhaps he wanted to sound her out about how to get rid of some dead wood in the firm. Duncan Patterson, for starters.

He turned round. 'That was exactly the question I was going to ask you, Sally. Is everything all right with *you*?'

Taken aback, she said, 'Of course. Why wouldn't it be?'

He cleared his throat and staightened his perfectly straight tie. He moved round to his side of the desk and sat down heavily. 'I want you to know that if you've got problems and you need time off, or someone to talk to, just tell me.'

Sally looked at him quizzically. 'Problems?' she repeated. 'What kind of problems do you think I have?'

Prising open a paperclip, Tom said, 'Look, quite apart from you being a key and valued member of the firm, I've always had the utmost respect for you. You know that, don't you?'

She nodded slowly. She didn't like the sound of where this was going. 'I sense a "but" coming,' she said stiffly.

'I want you to understand that I'm only saying what I'm about to say because I care about you. I'd rather you heard it from me than from anyone else.' Tom paused. 'The thing is.' He cleared his throat again. 'The thing is, certain people in the office seem to think that you ... that you and Harry are ... more than just work colleagues.'

Sally kept her gaze perfectly level. Then, assuming incredulity, she burst out laughing. 'What is this, Tom, a belated April Fool's Day prank?' She made a great play of looking round his office. 'Should I be looking for a hidden camera?'

Tom's face was a mixture of embarrassment and confusion. But he didn't say anything.

Sally stopped laughing. 'My God, you're serious, aren't you? This isn't a joke, is it?'

'It would be a strange sort of joke, Sally.'

'But you can't really think Harry and I ... I mean, come on, he's a boy. He's years younger than me. What the hell would I see in him? Or he in me? Oh, really, Tom, it's too absurd for words. I'm married. And very happily so. Besides which, when would I have time for a sordid office fling with Harry Fox?'

Relief began to show in Tom's face. 'I knew it couldn't possibly be true,' he said. 'But I thought you ought to know what was being said about you. It goes without saying that I'll do my best to quash any more rumours, but you know as well as I do that office life plays by its own rules.'

'Thanks. I appreciate that. And not that it really matters, but to satisfy my own curiosity, who brought this outlandish, not to say malicious, work of fiction to your attention?'

Once more Tom dropped his gaze. Which told Sally all she needed to know. The Iron Lady. It had to be. Tom wouldn't cover for anyone else so loyally.

'Whoever it is,' she said coolly, 'I'd be grateful if you dealt with him or her appropriately. Superficially it has its amusement value and I'm prepared to let it go, but if the rumour doesn't go away, then I'll take my own steps to deal with the matter. After all, quite apart from my reputation being on the line, there's Harry to consider. Now, if there isn't anything else, I need to put my thoughts in order for a two o'clock conference this afternoon.'

Back in her office, the door firmly shut, Sally leaned against it. That was close. That was bloody close. But what a performance! Adrenalin racing through her, she smiled and punched the air. Oh, yes, it was some performance she'd given. She went over to her desk and sat down. Still smiling, she swivelled round in the chair and it was all she could do to stop herself laughing out loud.

Chapter Forty-One

There was a very different atmosphere at work that morning. Normally there was a mood of cheerful industry about the place, a buzz around the photocopier, a joke over coffee, but today everyone was unnaturally quiet and downcast.

The trust had lost one of its most popular children. Jordan Kemp had died from kidney failure last night. Five years old, he had been one of the real stars of the trust, known for his enquiring eyes, his cheeky smile and infectious laughter. Everyone had known that his life expectancy was cruelly limited, but his death now, so sudden and out of the blue, had hit them all hard. Particularly Tatiana.

It was Tatiana who had received the news first and Dan knew that she had been especially attached to Jordan. Dan had met the family only a few weeks ago, yet he too was touched by the child's death. He suspected, though, that his feelings were mixed up in imagining the unthinkable: how he would cope with the loss of his own son. Whenever he watched those harrowing scenes on television when parents of a murdered child appealed for the killer to hand himself in, or when parents of missing children tearfully and politely begged whoever was responsible to return their child to safety, the same thought would pass through Dan's head: how can the parents be so calm? Why aren't they wild-eyed and screaming into the camera, 'Bring back my son you sick, crazy, psychotic bastard! Because if you don't I'm going to track you down and kill you!' No way would Dan be able to sit through such a coolly staged televised appeal. Not unless he'd been injected with sufficient sedative to stop a rampaging bull in its tracks.

He thought of the contrast of today with Saturday, when it had been Marcus and Charlie's combined birthday party. It had been an all-out sugar and shriek fest. And that was just the parents, as he'd joked with Tatiana first thing this morning – before they'd got the news about Jordan. Tatiana hadn't been able to make it to the boys' combined party, and Rosie, at Charlie and Marcus's insistence, had given Dan a piece of birthday cake to bring in to work for her, along with a party bag.

Leaving his printer to churn out the report he'd been working on, Dan went to make himself some coffee. The office kitchen, a glorified broom cupboard, was situated at the end of a carpet-lined corridor, the walls of which were covered with framed photographs of the families the trust had supported. He pushed open the kitchen door and found Tatiana there. With a start she glanced at him over her shoulder and he saw that she was crying. She looked unutterably sad. He shut the door after him and because it seemed the most natural thing in the world to do, he went to her and put his arms around her. She rested her head against his chest and sobbed helplessly, her tears falling wet and warm on his skin through his shirt. She was so small against him, but the pain of her sadness was colossal. He could feel it shuddering through her as she clung to him.

Finally she raised her head from his chest. 'I'm sorry,' she stammered, 'I promised myself I wouldn't lose it over Jordan. At least not until I got home.' She wiped first one eye with the back of her hand, then the other. Her mascara had not survived her tears, yet somehow the smudging emphasized the colour of her eyes, giving them a depth and intensity he'd never noticed before. But then he'd never been this close to her before. Still standing within the circle of his embrace, she looked up at him and their eyes met. And held. He suddenly felt like he was about to step over a cliff edge. He knew that he should let go of her. But he didn't. Instead, he bent his head and brushed his lips over her mouth. Scarcely making contact with her, it was barely a kiss, but it made him catch his breath. And made him want to kiss her again. He did and she kissed him back in a way that caused something deep inside him to burst free. He pulled away, shocked. 'I'm sorry,' he apologized. 'I shouldn't have done that.'

She stared at him, not saying anything.

He willed himself to let go of her but he couldn't. 'I'm sorry,' he repeated, even though he realized with dazed disbelief that he wasn't sorry at all.

'Don't be,' she said at length. 'You were being kind. It was just a kiss to comfort me. That was all.'

He shook his head slowly. 'I don't think it was. I think it's something I've wanted to do for some time, only I didn't know it until now.'

Her eyes widened. 'I've wanted you to do it for a long time, too,' she said quietly.

'Really? You never gave me any idea.'

'I was hardly going to advertise how I felt about you, was I? Given your circumstances.' She slipped out of his arms. 'And now that we've both reminded ourselves that you're married, I'm going to get back to work and pretend the last five minutes never happened.'

You might be able to, Dan thought when he was left alone and staring out of the window, just as he'd found Tatiana doing. He put a hand to his chest, where her tears had left a cool, damp patch on his shirt and kept it there, wondering. Just wondering.

That evening Sally was in a strange, jittery mood. She'd scarcely eaten any of her supper and she kept fidgeting in her chair and laughing exaggeratedly at things on the television that normally she would have tutted at dismissively. Right now, she was reading the local newspaper, turning the pages noisily and messily.

Or had Dan got it wrong? Was it him who was behaving oddly and being overly sensitive to Sally's manner? Certainly he had more on his mind than usual. Mostly guilt. He couldn't stop thinking of the amazing sense of release he'd experienced when he'd kissed Tatiana. For a split second everything had made perfect sense.

Now, of course, nothing made sense. His crime might not rate too highly when compared to what a lot of other people got up to, but for him it was a massive deal and gave him a chill of shame. He'd as good as cheated on his wife and he felt disgusted with himself. What was so disconcerting for him was not the physical betrayal he'd committed, but the knowledge that he'd emotionally betrayed his wife. As fleeting as the moment had been, he'd felt more of a connection with Tatiana when their lips had touched than he had with Sally in a long time. He'd left work while everyone was having lunch, without speaking again with Tatiana. Even before he'd arrived at Rosie's to pick up Marcus, he'd regretted his decision. He should have spoken to Tatiana before leaving. He should have apologized and assured her – and himself – that he had no intention of compromising her. He respected her too much to do that.

As he flicked through the TV channels hunting for something to distract him, he glanced over to Sally and wondered how she would rate his walking-on-water status now. Suddenly angered by the hurtful memory of her accusation, he was tempted to throw today in her face. *Think I'm perfect now, do you?*

'Oh, I forgot to say,' Sally said, tossing aside the messed-up newspaper. It slid off the sofa where she was sitting and landed on the floor in a crumpled heap. She made no effort to pick it up. 'I have to go and see my mother again. I've checked the calendar; this coming weekend's free, so I'll go then. That OK with you?'

'Are you asking me, or telling me?'

'Don't be silly.' She laughed.

What was with all the laughter? And why hadn't she picked up the newspaper from the floor? For someone who placed the apples in the fruit bowl in a perfect pyramid and who liked to have the corners of every towel in the airing cupboard in perfect alignment, this was real left-of-field behaviour, like Paris Hilton claiming she was staying in for the night to wash her hair.

'Not entirely free,' he corrected her, 'it's the Harvest Festival at church on Sunday and Marcus's class from nursery is taking part.'

'Oh, you don't need me there.'

'But Marcus might like you there,' he pressed. And because he knew that Tatiana had promised Charlie she wouldn't dream of missing his big moment when he carried his harvest box up to the front of the church, Dan had his own reason for wanting Sally by his side that day. He wanted her there to ensure he wouldn't do or say something else he would regret.

'I doubt Marcus will even notice my absence,' Sally said. She stood up abruptly. 'You know what, I think I'll go and see Chloe.'

'But it's almost ten o'clock. She could be in bed. Why don't you ring her?'

Sally laughed again. 'Who knows, I might just catch her in bed with her saintly Reverend. Wouldn't that be a blast?'

Dan listened to the front door shutting and shook his head. As before, he contemplated the imposter who was masquerading as his wife. The old Sally would never have said what she just had. A blast? Catching her best friend in bed with a man she was clearly more than just fond of. Where was the so-called blast in that?

With a bottle of wine in her hand, Sally walked purposefully through the dark, lamp-lit village. In her head she was rehearsing what she was going to say to Chloe. First she would hand over the wine as a peace offering and apologize for being out of order with her remarks about Seth, even though she still stood by them. She knew her friend of old and knew that Chloe wouldn't stay angry with her for long. An apology here, an apology there and they'd be the best of friends again. Then, when they'd kissed and made up and drunk a glass or two of wine she would wait to see if Chloe raised the subject of Harry. No way would Sally bring his name into the conversation. Do that and it would be an admission of guilt, an admission that Chloe was on to something. No, the trick was to pretend she hadn't heard what Chloe had whispered in her ear.

When Harry had returned from seeing his client in Burnley this afternoon, she'd asked Chandra to buzz his office upstairs to tell him to come and see her, that there was a tax matter she needed to discuss with him regarding Murray Adamson's divorce. Once they were alone – the door firmly shut and Chandra sent away on an errand – she'd dispensed with the subterfuge and told him what Tom had said about them having an affair. She told him about her no-holds-barred denial and how it had been an Oscar-winning performance. His face had dropped. 'You're going to suggest we end things, aren't you?' he'd said.

'End things?' She'd laughed, grabbing his tie and pulling him to her. 'You've got to be joking! Big kudos to me, I want us to celebrate my incomparable acting skills by going away together at the weekend!'

He'd laughed, too, and kissed her hard. 'Big kudos to you indeed,' he'd said. 'That's what I love about you; the greater the risk, the greater the thrill. You're incredible!'

Aren't I just, thought Sally.

There were lights on at Chloe's cottage, but no sign of an extra car on the drive. Which implied that Chloe was home alone. No act of intercession between the sheets tonight, then. Smiling to herself, she rang the doorbell.

'Oh, it's you,' Chloe said when she opened the door to her.

'You don't sound too happy to see me.'

'I can't think why that would be the case. Can you?'

A suitably repentant expression on her face, Sally said, 'That's why I'm here. I want to apologize for what I said. Can I come in?'

'It's a bit late. I was just going to have a shower and get ready for bed.'

Sally offered the bottle of wine. 'An olive branch. I was a total bitch yesterday and I really want to clear the air between us. Please.'

'All right,' Chloe said, rather ungraciously in Sally's opinion. 'But your apology had better be good.'

*

Chloe took the bottle from Sally and led her through to the kitchen. She had no intention of drinking any wine at this time of night and she plonked it on the work surface with an inhospitable bang. She'd had a bad day at the surgery and the last thing she needed was Sally expecting forgiveness over a late-night drinking session. Taking Paul out of the equation, she had never been the type to harbour a grudge, but she was prepared to make an exception in Sally's case. 'Right,' she said, not standing on ceremony, 'you were outstandingly vile to Seth yesterday.' She folded her arms across her chest. 'Care to explain why?'

'Call it a moment of madness.'

'I'd call it more than that. You knew exactly what you were doing. It was a carefully constructed attack on the man I love.'

'The man you love? You can't be serious.' The expression on Sally's face was unpleasantly sardonic.

Chloe bristled, annoyed that she'd wrong-footed herself by sharing something so intimate when she was so angry. 'I *am* serious, as a matter of fact,' she asserted. 'What's more, Seth loves me.' Damn! Why did she sound so defensive, as if she were trying to convince herself of Seth's love for her?

'Bloody hell! This is all a bit quick, isn't it? You'll be telling me next the two of you are planning to marry.'

'Would that be so very awful?'

'Have you been to bed with him?'

Chloe hesitated. 'That's none of your business.'

The scorn on Sally's face deepened. 'Well, if you have, what does that say about the saintly Reverend Hawthorne? And if you haven't, what does it say about you? What's he done to you, Chloe? Turned you into some pathetic, dried-up little nun?'

'It's called respect, Sally. Something you wouldn't know anything about, given your behaviour of late.'

'Rubbish! It's my respect for you that makes me want to open your eyes to what's really going on inside your head. The only reason you're so quick to convince yourself that you're in love with Seth is because you're desperate for some man to get you pregnant. Any man will do. Even a man who believes in holy gobbledegook and fairies at the end of the garden!'

'OK, that's enough. I'm not listening to any more of this. Out. Now.'

'Oh, come on. I'm just hitting the honesty button. Climb down from your bloody high horse and face facts. You're desperate to have a baby and the first bloke who claims to be in love with you, you grab the chance with both hands.'

'Honesty! You want to talk about honesty? Well, try this on for size: how about you telling Dan what a lying, cheating bitch you are?'

'And what's that supposed to mean?'

'It means I know about you and your affair.'

'Affair? What affair?'

'Get real, Sally. I heard your intake of breath when I whispered Harry's name in your ear yesterday afternoon.'

'Oh, so that's what you whispered. I was wondering what that was about.'

'You're not fooling me, Sally. Now get your sorry arse out of my house and go home to your husband and child. And when you've got a minute, try looking in the mirror and asking yourself whether you like the person looking back at you. Because right now, I don't much care for the person you've become. I doubt many other people do either.'

Chapter Forty-Two

After a sleepless night, Dan decided there was nothing else for it. He had to see Tatiana again, and before the Harvest Festival service. He hated to think that she might feel awkward around him and badly wanted to clear the air. He'd called Rosie after breakfast and asked if she could have Marcus for a couple of hours. She had an antenatal appointment with Chloe late in the afternoon, but so long as he was back in time, it would be fine.

He was nervous when he drove to Crantsford. Nervous because he hadn't really prepared what he was going to say. He'd lain in bed for most of last night, unable to stop his brain from replaying that moment when he'd held and kissed Tatiana. Each time he thought of it, his confusion grew.

He was a happily married man, right? Happily married men did not kiss their work colleagues. Happily married men did not have the kind of reaction he'd had when he'd kissed Tatiana. And happily married men did not deliberately pick a fight with their wives when they emerged from the shower at six o'clock in the morning. Which was exactly what he'd done this morning. All Sally had done was comment on the fact that she was running low on her favourite shower gel. Any other morning he would merely have said he'd add it to the shopping list on the chalk board in the kitchen.

But not today. 'Why don't you pick some up during your lunch break?' he'd said. She'd given him a look so cool, resentment had leapt from him. 'I work too, you know,' he'd said peevishly. 'Not that you'd ever give me credit for that.'

'What's got into you?' she'd asked.

'You,' he fired back. 'Everything has to revolve around you, doesn't it? Whether it's something as trivial as running low on shower gel or something important like Marcus. What you want, you get. If you want to go off to that witch of a mother of yours rather than show your support for your son, then that's fine. We just have to step into line with your wishes, don't we? Doesn't it ever concern you, the extent of your sidelining of Marcus and me?'

'At this precise moment,' she'd replied as she clipped the metal strap of her watch into place on her wrist, 'my only concern is you making me late for work.'

'And there we have it. For Sally Oliver, work comes before everything else.'

'Oh, save the sarcasm for someone who gives a damn! Honestly, Dan, what with Chloe turning on me last night and now you, is it any wonder I prefer being at work?'

'You argued with Chloe? What about?'

'She took offence over something I said. But if you ask me, that new boyfriend must be a bad influence on her. She hasn't been the same since she met him. Now if you don't mind, you might have time to pick an argument, but I haven't.'

Dan pulled into the car park at the back of the offices of the trust, switched off the engine and released his seat belt. He thought about Sally's attitude this morning. She was becoming increasingly cavalier. Breathtakingly so. Could he honestly say, hand on heart, that he still felt the same way about her as he used to? How many times had he made excuses for her behaviour in the past few months? Reluctantly he raked over all those occasions she'd been distant with him. And the time she'd criticized him for being difficult to live with, claiming he had a hero complex. Was it really his love for her that had forced him to make so many allowances?

But if he loved Sally, would he have kept a mental tally of all these negative thoughts about her? Would he be spending so much time analysing her every word and gesture? And what of his suspicion that she'd been having an affair? How had he so easily dismissed that from his mind?

Because he was a coward, that was why. The consequences of confronting her would be too awful to contemplate.

He pressed the palms of his hands to his closed eyes and breathed deeply. Where had it gone so badly wrong?

But he knew exactly when it had gone wrong. And he was to blame. It was that night in Thailand when he had got her pregnant. Less than a week after they'd flown home she'd shocked him by admitting that she was having second thoughts about having a baby. Six weeks later, an innocuous blue line on a pregnancy test kit heralded a whole new way of life. He supposed he had to be grateful that she hadn't gone behind his back and terminated the pregnancy.

He lowered his hands, opened his eyes and flinched at the thought. Now he was definitely overreacting and demonizing Sally. She would never have done that.

Staring through the windscreen at the building in front of him, as if seeing it for the first time, he wondered what he was doing here. Then he remembered: Tatiana. He suddenly doubted whether it had been wise of him to come here to talk to her. In his current frame of mind it would be dangerously easy to do entirely the wrong thing. But she deserves an apology, he reasoned. She needs to know that nothing has changed between us.

It was a persuasive argument and one that had him opening his car door.

It was still compellingly persuasive when he reached the reception desk and smiled at Emma, who was busy on the phone.

And he was still utterly, one hundred per cent persuaded, right up until he tapped lightly on Tatiana's door and pushed it open.

But then it all fell apart. He took one look at her sitting behind her desk and he knew he should have stayed at home.

She put down her pen and smiled uncertainly at him. 'I didn't think you were coming in today.'

'No,' he said.

'And yet here you are. Are you going to come right in, or just stand in the doorway?'

He took a step into her office, then another, and then closed the door behind him.

Another wrong decision. Keep the door open and he wouldn't do anything he'd later regret. Just how dangerously close did he need to sail to the wind? 'I wanted to speak to you,' he said.

'I rather thought you might. Do you want to sit down?'

He shook his head and went and stood next to the bank of filing cabinets, gluing his shoulder to the end one, as if it would anchor him and keep him from getting too close. Distance was vital. 'How are you feeling?' he asked.

'Slightly shy of you, if you want the truth.'

Realizing she'd misunderstood him, he said, 'No, I meant, how are you feeling about Jordan now?'

'Oh. I see. Much better. Thank you for asking. Are you sure you wouldn't like to sit down? How about some coffee?'

'I don't want you to be shy or awkward around me,' he blurted out, ignoring her questions.

She looked at him gravely. 'I don't think I can oblige you on that request. Not just yet.'

'But I want you to feel like you've always felt around me.'

Her cheeks flushed a delicate shade of pink and he saw his gaffe. 'I'm sorry,' he said, 'that was clumsy of me.'

Leaning back in her chair, she sighed. 'I'm sorry, too, Dan. I should never have said how I felt about you. I've ruined everything. Now nothing will ever be the same between us.'

'No!' he said, moving towards her desk and forgetting all about keeping his distance. 'You mustn't think that. It was me. *I* kissed *you.*'

'I could have stopped you. But I didn't.' She swallowed. 'And to my shame I probably wouldn't stop you if you did it again. See what a bad person I am? I'm a potential marriage wrecker, Dan. I can hardly believe it myself. In my defence all I can say is that I never intended to fall in love with you.'

He stared at her, profoundly shocked. 'You love me?'

'What's not to love?' She turned huge, sad eyes on him. 'So there it is; the genie is well and truly out of the bottle. I'm sorry.'

'Please don't keep apologizing. And don't ever describe yourself as bad. You're the least bad person I know.'

'Your wife might not share your view of me.'

'These days my wife shares very little with me.' The admission was out before he could stop it. Seconds passed while the bitter truth of his words hung between them. He steeled himself to say the right thing. 'Which is why it wasn't a good idea for me to come here. I wanted to apologize to you for yesterday, but deep down I was fooling myself. I wanted to see you again, to see ... well, let's just say that the way things are at home with Sally, it would be the easiest thing in the world for me to start an affair with you. But I won't do that. I care about you too much to make that mistake. You deserve to be treated better.'

Without knowing how he'd got there, he suddenly found himself on her side of the desk, standing next to her. He knelt down on one knee beside her so that he could look her in the eye. 'I wish things were different, Tatiana. Really I do.'

'I understand.' She touched his face with her hand. 'You're a good man, Dan. I knew that the minute I met you.' Her eyes were dark and devastatingly forlorn. The expression in them wrenched at his heart.

'I'd better go,' he said.

'Yes,' she murmured. 'You better had.'

But he didn't move. Just one kiss like yesterday, he thought. One kiss to lock away in his heart. He tilted his head fractionally closer to hers. If she resists, I'll stop, he told himself.

His lips had just made contact with hers when he jerked his head back. What was he thinking? How could he be so selfish? How could he take what he wanted just to satisfy his own needs? 'I'm sorry,' he mumbled, full of remorse. 'I want to but I can't. Forgive me, please.'

She nodded sadly.

'Will you be at the Harvest Festival service on Sunday?' he asked, getting to his feet.

'I promised Charlie I'd be there for him. I don't want to let him down.'

'And nor should you.'

'Will your wife be there?'

He shook his head. 'She's otherwise engaged.'

Chapter Forty-Three

The sky was bright and glittery and with a sharp nip in the air the weather was hinting unmistakably that autumn was just around the corner.

St Andrew's had been packed with fidgety children and adults unaccustomed to being in church. Now, everyone stood around in groups outside, children letting off steam by running in and out of tombstones. More than a few people were laughing over Lardy McFierce's two boys, who had started fighting when one of them had tripped the other up as they walked to the front of the church with their extravagantly filled boxes of harvest produce. Jars of pesto, tins of cannelloni and borlotti beans and perfectly scrubbed supermarket carrots had rolled comically in all directions.

The sight of Marcus carefully making his way up the aisle with his cargo of fruit and vegetables had brought a lump to Dan's throat.

With Marcus's help Dan had spent most of yesterday afternoon decorating a cardboard box with brown paper and straw and filling it with apples, damsons, runner beans and tomatoes, all kindly donated by Chloe's parents from their garden. Jennifer and Graham hadn't been able to come to the service, but Chloe had put in an appearance and joined him in the pew. While her presence had had the effect of magnifying Sally's absence, it had given Dan a vague sense of protection from doing or saying anything improper with Tatiana, who along with Rose and Dave had sat in the pew in front of him. He'd stared at the back of Tatiana's head and shoulders, trying not to think of the expression on her face the last time he'd seen her.

'OK, everyone? Ready to come back to ours for lunch? You're invited too, Chloe.'

Breaking off from her conversation with Tatiana, Chloe said, 'I'd love to, Dave, but I can't. Sorry.'

Dave grinned. 'Got a better invitation from that man of yours.'

'Something like that,' Chloe said with a happy smile.

'No worries. We'll catch you another time.'

Rosie had telephoned Dan last night to suggest they have lunch together after the service. 'It won't be anything special,' she'd explained, 'just a thrown together affair of whatever's in the fridge. Tatiana's already said she's coming.' His response should have been to apologize and say he and Marcus couldn't make it, but he hadn't. Instead he'd asked if there was anything he could bring.

The words, 'a thrown together affair' resonated in his ears as he said goodbye to Chloe and went to round up Marcus and Charlie. When he had them both in hand, he turned to find Tatiana waiting for him. Squealing loudly, both boys let go of Dan and rushed full tilt at her, nearly knocking her off her feet. 'You are all right with this, aren't you?' she asked when she had them under control.

'As long as you are,' he said.

She nodded.

'I'm not doing anything wrong, Dan told himself as they set off with Rosie and Dave. Lunch, that's all this is. Lunch with a beautiful girl who'd said she loved him. Lunch with a girl he'd kissed and might do so again if his resolve let him down. What could possibly be wrong with any of that?

Harry was in a serious mood. Which wasn't what Sally wanted at all. Sex, glorious sex, was what she wanted. If she'd wanted a tediously serious conversation, then she could have stayed at home and got that from Dan.

She reached for the bottle of champagne on the bedside table and emptied it into their glasses. 'Have this,' she said, 'it might sweeten your mood.'

'I don't need sweetening,' he said, refusing to take the glass from her.

'Oh, go on, don't be boring.'

'I mean it, Sally.'

'So do I. Now take this from me or I'll have to spill it over you and then lick you dry.' She tipped one of the glasses and allowed a small amount to splash onto his chest.

He shook his head and smiled. 'You're mad,' he said, taking the glass from her.

'No, I'm not,' she said, licking her lips and then him. 'This is the sanest I've felt in ages.'

'I still think we should be careful,' he said.

'What? Just because the Iron Lady has been stirring things?'

'From what you said of your chat with Tom it sounds like it's more than one person who's on to us. If that's the case, we should cool it for a while.'

'But I don't want to cool it. I want you, Harry. I want you every minute of the day. And that includes now.'

'And I want you, Sally. But I also want my career. All I'm suggesting is that we don't take any more risks at work. Is that so very bad?'

Yes, thought Sally. It's the risk that gives me the biggest kick of all.

How am I doing? Dan kept wanting to ask someone. Do I look like a total bastard? Do I look like the kind of husband who can't stop thinking about being unfaithful to his wife?

Another ten minutes and he'd somehow tear Marcus away and go home. He looked through the open doors of the conservatory where they were drinking coffee and out to the garden where Marcus and Charlie were playing on the new wooden climbing frame Charlie had been given for his birthday. It was a stupendous bit of kit; a large, complicated climbing frame that wouldn't be out of place in a public park. It dominated Dave and Rosie's garden and was clearly a lot of fun for two small boys. Dan didn't like the odds stacked against him of leaving here without Marcus kicking up a huge fuss.

'It really is a great climbing frame, Rosie,' Tatiana said, as if picking up on Dan's thoughts.

Rosie laughed. She turned to her husband. 'Shall I tell them how long it took you to put it together?'

Dave rolled his eyes. 'I'll save you the bother. It took me two whole days to put the bugger together. And I'm a builder; pity the poor devil with no real practical skills! More wine, anyone?'

Tatiana shook her head. 'I'm driving.'

'Dan?'

Wanting to be sure of keeping a clear head, Dan said, 'I'd better not, I've got some work to do later.' He was just about to start making noises about it very nearly being time he was going when he heard Marcus shouting to him. 'Look at me, Daddy!'

With his hair standing on end like a dark dandelion puff ball and his arms waving, Marcus was hanging upside down at the very highest point of the climbing frame, his legs hooked over a wooden bar. Holy shit! When had he learned to do that? Fighting the urge to rush over and snatch his son down, Dan called back to him, 'You be careful, Marcus.'

'I'm the king of the castle,' Marcus chorused gleefully. 'And you're the dirty rascal!'

What happened next had Dan's blood freezing in his veins. A late season wasp came into view and started to dive-bomb Marcus. Since he'd been stung by one very recently, he'd developed a fear of them. Not understanding the seriousness of what was going on. Charlie was jumping up and down and laughing at his friend, who was now waving his arms about his head.

It seemed to take Dan an age to get to his feet and to shout to Marcus to keep perfectly still. But Marcus wasn't listening. He was screaming wildly now, his arms windmilling frantically to get rid of the wasp. Then seemingly, as if the inevitable was happening in slow motion, Dan watched powerlessly as the tension went out of Marcus's body and his legs began to straighten, first one, then the other.

He landed with a sickening thud on the grass below.

Chapter Forty-Four

Dan knelt beside his son. His son who wasn't moving. His son who wasn't crying.

'Marcus,' he said. He turned him over as gently as he could. Was that the wrong thing to do? Dan didn't know. But he had to do something. He had to hold his son. He had to know that he was all right.

'Marcus,' he said again, conscious now that everyone else had caught up with him and was standing round.

His eyes closed, his face ashen, the only colour to Marcus was the blood around his mouth. There was so much of it, it was difficult to see just exactly where it was coming from.

'Marcus,' Dan tried again, holding him tenderly. The still, limp weight of his precious son reminded Dan of all the times he'd carried him sleeping from the car into the house. Of the times he'd carefully carried him upstairs and laid him peacefully in bed. But it also reminded him of another time. Of the boy who had been ripped from his arms and swept out to sea. The boy he hadn't been able to save.

Icy fear gripped at Dan's heart and he squeezed Marcus tightly. Amazingly his son's eyes then flickered open and his body sprang to life. He coughed and spluttered, spraying blood down the front of Dan's shirt. He started to cry. Never had Dan been more pleased to hear his son cry.

Marcus had very nearly bitten through his lower lip and it was obvious he needed stitches. Tatiana offered to drive them to the hospital and sitting next to Marcus in the back of her car – they'd moved Charlie's seat across from Rosie's – Dan phoned Chloe on his mobile. If there was one doctor's opinion in the world he trusted implicitly, it was Chloe's. She said she would meet them at A & E.

Next he tried ringing Sally, but there was no answer from her mobile. It was switched off.

*

Tatiana dropped them off at the entrance to the hospital and went to park the car. Miraculously it was a quiet afternoon at A & E and by the time Tatiana caught up with them, they were being ushered into a curtained cubicle. A man about the same age as Dan introduced himself as Doctor Flannigan and Dan did his best to answer his questions as clearly as he could while all the time trying not to sound like a negligent parent. The kind of negligent father who allowed his son to nearly kill himself.

The doctor was brisk and straightforward and listened impassively. He'd probably heard it all before. Father lets child play with matches. Father lets child wander off. Father lets child play in paddling pool.

Dan noticed that Marcus had turned grey. The doctor noticed too, and quickly reached for a bowl. Dan couldn't fault his reactions. He caught the lot. 'Concussion,' the doctor said matter-of-factly. 'We'd better do an X-ray, just to be on the safe side.'

When finally it was over and Dan went to look for Tatiana in the waiting area, he saw that she wasn't alone. Chloe and Seth were with her. It was Marcus who spotted them first. Sporting a collection of stick-on badges and a plaster covering most of his swollen, stitched-up chin, he waved at Chloe, pointing proudly to his badges.

'He's all right, then?' Chloe said. The relief in her voice matched Dan's.

'He'll mend,' Dan said. 'There's a danger he might be sick again or feel a bit dizzy, but he's certainly well enough to go home. Sorry to spoil your afternoon.' He said this more to Seth.

'It wasn't a problem. Really.'

'Which doctor did you see?'

'Doctor Flannigan.'

'Right, I'll just go and have a quick chat with him. Then we'll get going.'

Once more Dan sat in the back of Tatiana's car with Marcus. Once again he tried ringing Sally. 'Still no answer?' Tatiana asked, looking at him in the rear-view mirror.

Dan shook his head.

'Maybe she's out of range.'

That was one way of describing Sally, Dan thought as he watched Marcus quietly playing with one of the badges he'd been given, carefully sticking it on one finger, then another.

'You OK?'

Dan glanced up and met Tatiana's gaze in the mirror. 'Yes.'

'Are you sure?'

He blinked. 'I should have been out there in the garden with him. He's three. What the hell was I thinking?'

'Don't beat yourself up. We were all there keeping an eye on Marcus and Charlie. And even if we'd been in the garden with them, Marcus could still have slipped.'

'But he's my son. He's my responsibility. I let him down.'

'You didn't let him down. Don't ever think that. You're a great father to him. The best I know.'

He smiled at her gratefully. 'Thank you,' he said. 'And thanks, too, for offering to drive. I should have said something earlier.'

'You had far more important things on your mind.'

He turned to look out of the window. Recently harvested fields were dotted with neatly bundled bales waiting to be taken away. He watched a large broad-winged bird circling an area of the stubbly ground. Was it hoping to swoop down on some poor exposed fieldmouse?

Dan returned his gaze to the interior of Tatiana's car. In particular to the back of Tatiana's head. She had a graceful, slender neck. It was beautiful. Even when she was driving she looked poised. He remembered something from the first time he'd met her. 'Did you ever train to be a dancer, Tatiana?' he asked.

She gave him an odd look in the mirror, visibly surprised at his question. 'Yes,' she said, 'I spent five years at ballet school. Why do you ask?'

'I thought so,' he said with a small shrug.

They drove on in silence, following behind Seth's TVR.

Tatiana parked on the road in front of Corner Cottage and while Dan was lifting Marcus out of Charlie's seat, she said, 'I'll ring you tomorrow to see how he is.'

'Aren't you going to come inside?'

They were on the pavement now. 'I'd better not,' she said, stroking Marcus's cheek. He smiled sleepily at her.

'Not even for a cup of tea or coffee?'

'It wouldn't feel right,' she murmured. 'Not now. Take care little chap,' she said, kissing Marcus on the top of his head. 'No more scares for us all. Is that a deal?'

Dan didn't want her to leave. But he knew he had to let her go.

While Seth put the kettle on and made them a drink, Dan watched Chloe lift Marcus up onto the kitchen table and go through much the same procedure with him as Doctor Flannigan had earlier. Dan had always found it a weird experience observing Chloe with her professional hat on. Whilst she was in no way as brisk or impassive as Doctor Flannigan, her manner was quietly focused and thorough, and immensely reassuring. When she had finished she declared Marcus to be in good shape. 'You'll be amazed how fast the swelling will go down,' she said. 'Thankfully children heal incredibly quickly.' Addressing Marcus, she said, 'Another time, sweetheart, just let the wasp have a sniff around you to satisfy his curiosity and then he'll be on his way.'

'But he wath going to thing me.'

Chloe smiled at the sound of Marcus's newly acquired lisp and lifted him down from the table. 'A sting would have been better than frightening the life out of us all.'

He shook his head doubtfully and looked at Dan. 'Can I have a dink now, Daddy? With a thaw like the doctor thaid.'

'Of course. And then we must get you out of those dirty clothes. Maybe you'd like a bath?'

Marcus looked anxiously at the dried bloodstains on his sweat-shirt and jeans. 'Will Mummy be croth?'

'Of course she won't,' Dan said, registering that this was the first reference Marcus had made to his mother. 'Which reminds me, I must try ringing her again.' He took out his mobile and pressed redial. 'Still nothing,' he said seconds later, with irritation.

There was no real urgency to get in touch with Sally now, par-ticularly as she would be home later that evening, but it rankled with Dan that she had been unobtainable when who knew what the consequences of Marcus's fall might have been. He wasn't proud of it, but he wanted to shame Sally. He wanted to push home the point that when her son had been hurt, she hadn't been there for him.

Leaving Seth and Chloe to keep an eye on Marcus in the kitchen, he went to the study and opened the desk drawer where Sally kept her address book. He turned to the back of it, to the page for the letter W. It was a long time since he'd had any wish to speak to his mother-in-law, but if he was going to prove a point with Sally, what better way to do it than via Kath Wilson?

When the telephone was finally answered over in Hull, Dan could hear the loud blare of a television in the background. 'Mrs

Wilson?' he said. He'd never known her well enough to call her by her Christian name, or felt the need to do so for that matter.

'Yes. Who's that?'

'It's Dan.'

'Dan who? Terry, turn that telly down will yer? Who did you say you were?'

'Dan Oliver. Sally's husband.'

'Why didn't you say? *Terry!* I said turn that bleeding telly down! So what do you want, Dan?'

'I need to speak to Sally. Is she still there with you or has she already left? Only Marcus had an accident this afternoon and—'

'Why the hell do you think she's here? She's not been to see me for months. Chance would be a fine thing.'

The door opened and Dan looked up to see Chloe bringing in a mug of tea for him. It must have been the look on his face, but her expression dropped.

'I'm sorry,' he said into the phone, 'it's a bad line; I must have misheard you. What did you say?'

'I said we've not seen hair nor hide of her in months. She's too lah-di-da these days to bother with her own family. That's probably your doing anyway.'

'In that case I'm sorry to have bothered you, Mrs Wilson,' Dan said. 'Goodbye.' He rang off.

'What is it, Dan?' Chloe asked. 'What's happened?'

He swallowed back his shock. No. Not shock, exactly. Acceptance. He'd known the truth all along, hadn't he?

'Sally was supposed to be spending the weekend with her mother,' he said quietly. 'Sorting out her debts and loans, she told me. As she's done for several weekends now. Except Kath Wilson claims Sally hasn't been to see her for months. Certainly not this weekend.'

Chloe came and put the mug of tea on the desk.

'Tell me honestly,' he said, 'did you know?'

'Did I know what?'

'That she's been having an affair?'

'You don't know that. Not for sure. There might be some perfectly reasonable explanation for why she's—'

'Don't, Chloe,' he interrupted her. 'Don't keep trying to think well of her. It's gone beyond that. She's having an affair. I know she is.'

Once again he saw a change in Chloe's expression. He leapt on it. 'You know something, don't you?' he said.

'Not definitely,' she murmured uneasily. 'It was only after you'd put the idea in my head that I began to suspect. It was her behaviour. She just wasn't the same Sally any more. But I didn't know for sure. And let's face it, we still don't. There could be some other reason why she's pretended to be somewhere she wasn't.'

'Are you saying that because she's your oldest and closest friend?'

'She might well be my oldest friend, but right now she isn't my *closest* friend. She's behaved appallingly to me recently. Especially over Seth. If she is seeing somebody, I think it's someone from work.'

Dan slumped back in the chair. 'I've had enough, Chloe,' he sighed. 'I've tried everything with her. For Marcus's sake, I really tried. But not any more. She's pushed me as far as she's ever going to.'

'What will you do? Will you confront her when she gets back this evening?'

'Yes.'

'Do you want me to have Marcus for the night?'

He shook his head. 'After what he's gone through today, I'd rather he slept in his own bed. Don't worry; there won't be a big ugly scene. I wouldn't do that to Marcus. I'll make sure it's all very civilized. That's how we Olivers do things,' he added in a heavily mocking tone.

It was gone nine o'clock when Dan heard Sally's car on the drive. He'd been waiting for her in the kitchen ever since he'd put Marcus to bed. He hadn't eaten, not even to finish the tomato soup he'd heated for Marcus. Nor had he drunk any alcohol. He hadn't wanted anything to cloud his judgement or fuel his anger.

'How was your mother?' he asked casually when Sally came into the kitchen.

'Oh God, you *so* don't want to know. The woman gets worse. I honestly don't know why I'm putting so much effort into helping her. It's not as if she shows an ounce of gratitude either.'

'I know the feeling,' he said quietly. He folded the newspaper he'd been reading and pushed it away from him.

'How was your weekend?' she asked.

He got to his feet. 'Oh, you know, the usual. I got all choked up with fatherly pride at the sight of Marcus playing his part in the Harvest Festival service this morning. Daft, I know. But that's the kind of sentimental fool I am. Afterwards we had lunch at Dave and Rosie's and then the day took on an altogether different shape. Marcus had an accident. He fell from Charlie's new climbing frame. I had to take him to casualty. He needed nine stitches, but don't worry, he's absolutely fine. He's fast asleep upstairs.'

'Why didn't you ring me?'

'I did.' He looked her square in the eye. 'I tried several times. But you didn't have your mobile switched on.'

It gave him no pleasure, but Sally was definitely beginning to look unsettled. 'Oh, hell!' she said with a wave of her hand. 'You're right about my mobile. I only noticed what I'd done when I set off for home.'

'But because I really wanted to let you know what had happened,' he carried on, keeping his voice as neutral as he could, 'and knowing just how concerned you'd be, I did what anyone would have done in my position; I phoned your mother.'

Sally froze.

'After all, it stands to reason, that would be the obvious number to ring if I was trying to get hold of you in an emergency, wouldn't it? And guess what she told me. She said you weren't there. What's more, she said she hadn't seen you in months. Where were you, Sally? Or more to the point, who were you with?'

Chapter Forty-Five

Think, Sally! Think!

But she couldn't. For the first time in her life, she couldn't think what to say. Playing for time, she said, 'I'll go upstairs and look in on Marcus.' She turned to go.

'Don't,' he said. 'Don't you dare, not until you've told me the truth.' His tone was sharp.

'OK,' she said, facing him now. 'You want the truth, do you?'

'Yes,' he replied. 'If nothing else, you owe me that.'

'Oh, please,' she said with a weary shrug, 'let's not turn this into a cliché fest.'

'I'm not turning this into anything other than what it already is, Sally. You're having an affair and you've been caught out. I'd say that just about sums it up. Unless, of course, you have something more inventive to offer?'

'An affair? Are you mad? When would I have time for an affair?' Again, playing for time, she walked over to the kettle, filled it at the tap and plugged it in. Until now she hadn't thought of the consequences of being found out. She had been so sure she wouldn't. Even with Chloe's risible comments, she hadn't felt particularly worried. She'd been totally confident that Chloe had nothing more concrete to go on than a guess based on a conversation they'd once had. Chloe had no actual evidence and as a result Sally had been convinced she could bluff her way out of any accusation made, just as she had with Tom in the office.

But now, face to face with Dan's uncompromising certainty, the ground felt shakier beneath her feet. Could she get away with saying her mother's memory was going? Or that the woman had been deliberately vindictive? Or that she had sworn her mother to secrecy, knowing that Dan wouldn't approve of Sally helping to pay off her debts?

Her brain immediately jumped on this last possibility.

My God! she thought. She could get away with it. She really

could. She almost smiled at her cleverness.

Adopting a contrite expression and her most sincere and penitent tone, she turned to face Dan. 'You're not going to like this, Dan, but yes, you're right; I have been lying to you. The thing is, for some time now I've been paying off my mother's debts and the reason she claimed I hadn't been there with her this weekend was because I'd sworn her to secrecy. I told her that you'd hit the roof if you discovered what I was really doing, that you didn't mind me helping her to sort out the financial mess she'd got herself into, but actually giving her money would make you go ballistic. So you see, when you phoned her, she obviously took the whole secrecy thing too far.' Sally dropped her shoulders and sighed. 'I'm sorry. I shouldn't have hidden something as important as this from you.' *Oh, my God, she was good! She really was*.

Dan stared at her and she waited for him to apologize, to say he'd made a terrible mistake to doubt her the way he had. Could she ever forgive him? he'd ask. Yes, she'd say. Because, no matter what, she didn't want anything to change between them. She needed Dan.

Just as she needed Harry.

If Harry was her mind-blowing class A drug, Dan was her rock; he anchored her. He gave her stability and constancy and provided her with a sense of permanence that enable her to do the job she did.

'I'm sorry I lied to you, Dan,' she said when he still hadn't said anything. 'It was wrong of me.'

Next to her, the kettle started to boil. It clicked off. And then Dan did something that surprised her. He started to clap.

'Bravo,' he said. 'I knew I could rely upon you to be inventive, but that really was some kind of turnaround, Sally.' He stopped clapping. 'I'm almost impressed.'

'I don't understand,' she said. 'I tell you the truth and you throw sarcasm back in my face. Why?'

'OK,' he said, 'if that's the truth, show me your bank statements. Show me these payments you've made to pay off your mother's debts.'

Once more Sally felt the ground moving beneath her. 'What the hell's got into you, Dan? What kind of marriage do we have when you start asking me for proof?'

'You can't, can you?' he said, ignoring her question. 'You don't have any bank statements to show those payments, do you? You're lying. I know you are.'

Sally wasn't ready to give up yet. 'If you really loved me,' she tried. 'You wouldn't say something as hurtful as that. Don't you trust me?'

'No,' he said simply.

That shook her. She really hadn't seen that coming. 'Don't you love me?'

'Do *you* love *me*? Do you think how much you love me when you're in bed with your lover?'

Fast running out of questions to hide behind, Sally said, 'Don't be absurd, Dan. I don't have a lover.' Even to her ears her denial lacked conviction.

'You do,' he said. 'I know you do. I've humiliated myself for long enough pretending you weren't seeing someone else, but today I reached the point of no return. The game's up, Sally. It's time to accept that you can't have your cake and eat it. Your lover might be happy to share you, but I'm not.'

The equanimity of his tone riled her. He was talking to her as if she were a child. Who the hell did he think he was? 'You ought to try listening to yourself, Dan,' she tossed back at him angrily. The gloves were off now. 'You stand there full of pompous self-righteousness; is it any wonder I looked elsewhere for some excitement? Have you any idea how stultifying our marriage has become?'

'Well, some honesty from you at last. And thank you for your frankness. Presumably he's someone from work?'

'Does it make any difference to you who it is?'

'Is it serious?'

She laughed, still wanting to provoke a reaction from Dan. 'It's anything but serious.'

'What's that supposed to mean?'

'It's about fun, Dan. Excitement. Freedom. Of feeling alive. Really alive. What's the biggest thrill you get out of life these days? What leaves you feeling exhilarated? What would it take to make you lose control?'

'You're saying I'm boring?'

'Yes. You're safe and predictable. And I'm sorry, but that's not enough for me. I need more.'

'Then I hope you find it with this other man. Because it's over between us. I don't know how we're going to arrange things, but I don't want to stay married to you any more. It's selfish of me, I fully accept, but I'd appreciate it if you moved out. If only for a few days. I'd rather not see or talk to you for a while.'

'How very typical of you to be so rational.'

'Would you have preferred a blazing row? Voices raised? Plates thrown? Sorry, but I wouldn't do that to our son. He deserves better. He certainly deserves a better mother than you.'

Sally glared at him. 'I wondered how long it would take before you would play that card. I just didn't expect you to be so vicious with it.'

'I have no intention of retracting it. Or apologizing for it.'

'Good for you, Mr Oh So Bloody Perfect! And what a hero you'll be to everyone now. A fully fledged single father bringing up his son on his own because his wicked wife had a sordid affair.'

'I hope you find the man is worth it. You're throwing away a hell of a lot for him.'

'Oh, he's worth it all right! Don't you worry about that.'

Sally overslept the next morning and woke with a spectacular hangover. She lay very still, piecing together how she'd wound up in a strange bed. Alone.

She hadn't spent the night how she'd expected to. With a hastily packed case in the boot of her car, she'd left Corner Cottage and used the number Harry had given her for his mobile.

Except Harry hadn't answered. All she'd got was his voicemail. She'd left him a message to call her immediately and it was then that it had hit her that she didn't actually know his address. All she knew was that he was renting a new-build apartment somewhere in Altrincham. She'd ended up driving into the centre of Manchester and checking in at the Hilton. If nothing else she would be on the doorstep for work in the morning.

But now work couldn't be further from her mind. She'd launched a massive attack on the mini-bar last night and combined with a bottle of wine from room service, she was now paying the price. Bleary-eyed and smelling none too fragrant, she dragged herself to the shower and for a full ten minutes blasted herself beneath the powerful jets.

When she was dressed she made herself a cup of coffee and checked her mobile. Nothing. Zilch. Zippo. Harry hadn't tried ringing her back or texting her.

She checked out and drove the short distance to the office. Just a normal Monday morning, she told herself when she was passing briskly through the reception area and exchanging a nod with the two receptionists.

She managed an upbeat 'hi' with Chandra and then collapsed inside her office, the door firmly closed. She snatched up the phone and punched in Harry's extension number. He answered on the third ring. 'Where the hell have you been?' she demanded.

'Sorry, I've got a client with me just now. Could I call you back?'

'How long will you be busy for?'

'Erm ... an hour should do it. Goodbye.'

Right, she thought. An hour to pull herself together. She opened a desk drawer and rummaged around until she found the small mirror she kept there. Her reflection told her what she suspected. She looked awful. Exactly like a woman who'd consumed one too many mini-bar miniatures to knock herself out. There were dark shadows under her bloodshot eyes and her skin looked sickly. Her usual range of Clinque make-up just wasn't up to the job. She needed stage make-up. And lots of it.

She sighed. Things weren't supposed to have taken this direction. So long as she was always careful, she'd really believed she could keep things going with Dan and Harry on parallel tracks.

Maybe she still could.

A few days to let Dan stew in his own juices and he'd soon come round. Saying he wanted a divorce was merely a gesture on his part. She'd have to play the part of repentant wife, but given the performances she'd given of late, she didn't doubt she could pull it off.

But Dan would insist that she give up Harry. Could she really do that?

No. She couldn't. And wouldn't. She'd carry on seeing him, no matter what lies it took. Even now, just thinking of Harry – the way he looked at her, the way he touched her – she could feel her heartbeat quickening.

It wasn't his fault, but Dan had never had that effect on her.

Feeling marginally more optimistic, and knowing that she would be talking to Harry in less than an hour, she opened her diary and saw to her dismay that Murray Adamson was due in thirty-five minutes. Hell! She'd never be able to get rid of him in half an hour.

To further frustrate her, the wretched man turned up late. 'Sorry about that,' he said, sounding not the least bit sorry, 'I got caught in traffic. You OK? You look a bit green about the gills. Not got something catching, have you?'

'Thank you for your concern, but I'm fine,' she lied. She felt anything but fine. She felt ghastly; sick and clammy. 'Now then,' she said decisively, pushing a bulky document across the desk towards him. 'As I told you on the telephone last week, this is what I'm proposing—'

Whatever it was that Sally had been about to say went completely out of her head. 'Um ... I wonder if you would excuse me for a couple of minutes. I've suddenly remembered something.'

She made it to the toilet in the nick of time. Bent over the pan, her life passing before her, she heard the outer door open and shut. *Damn!* An audience. Just what she needed. It was impossible to vomit discreetly and after she'd yanked on the handle and flushed away the evidence of last night's excesses a voice called out to her. 'You all right in there?'

Oh great, it was the Iron Lady! No way was Sally going to reply; she didn't want to give the nosy old bitch the satisfaction of knowing who it was chundering up their insides. Her back against the door, she stood there in silence, her eyes closed.

'Sally? It is you in there, isn't it? Anything I can get you?'

'Err ... no thank you,' Sally was forced to answer.

'Something you ate?'

'More than likely,' Sally muttered weakly. Oh, God, here we go again. She lurched forward in the confined space and bent over the toilet. Please, whatever vindictive god is up there, she prayed, make that evil woman go away.

Another flush, another moment of recovery. It was over, surely? Remembering her abandoned client, she thought of a way to get rid of the Iron Lady. 'Fern,' she said as sweetly as her revoltingly sour mouth would allow, 'could you do me an enormous favour and ask Chandra to make my client a cup of coffee. Oh, and get her to tell him I'll be with him in five minutes.'

'Goodness! I didn't realize you had a client waiting. Why didn't you say? That's not at all professional.'

Oh, silly me, thought Sally when she heard the outer door closing. Perhaps you'd have preferred me to throw up all over my precious client!

The coast now clear, Sally emerged from the cubicle to wash her face and hands. She hardly dared look in the mirror above the basin, but it was hard to avoid. She groaned at the sight of her reflection. Rough didn't come close. She looked seven shades of shit. She ought to go home. It wasn't fair to inflict this face on anyone.

Home. The word jarred with her. Did she even have a home any more? Of course she did, the lawyer in her snapped. Corner Cottage was as much hers as Dan's.

But home. Somewhere she could rest her weary head and be sick in private. She didn't have one of those right now. Dan would hardly welcome her back and put her to bed like he might have done before.

Before last night.

A wave of longing for Dan's tender care surged through her. How good it would feel to be tucked up in bed with a soothing cup of tea, the curtains drawn and knowing that Dan would be there to rub her back or hold her hair away from her face if she was sick. Kind, dependable Dan.

No! No, no, *NO*!

She thumped the ceramic basin with her fist. Kind and dependable wasn't what she needed. She needed Harry. Wild, unpredictable Harry.

When she felt able to, she made her way back to her office. There was no sign of Chandra, but the Iron Lady was hovering maddeningly. 'I did my best to occupy him,' she said in a hushed voice. She pulled a face and pointed to Sally's lapel, where a piece of something unspeakable was masquerading as a brooch. 'You might like to dispose of that.'

'Sorry to keep you waiting so long,' Sally said when she closed the door after her.

'Feeling any better?' He looked at her sympathetically.

'Better?' she repeated.

'The woman who brought my coffee said you were otherwise detained being sick. Not very professional of her. If you ask me. She could have covered for you better.'

Sally smiled grimly. 'You're right, she could have.'

'Would you rather we took a rain check and did this tomorrow? Or some other time when you're feeling better?'

'Would that be very inconvenient for you?'

He put his finished cup of coffee down on the desk. 'Not at all.' He grinned. 'I'd much rather see you when you're looking your usual gorgeous self.'

She didn't have the strength to fire off an appropriate salvo. 'What time tomorrow?' she said, turning the page of her diary. 'Oh, sorry, I can't do tomorrow. The day's full up. The day after?'

He fished out a small black leather diary from his jacket pocket. 'Yes,' he said. 'That'll be perfect. How about just before lunch? Then when we've finished I can take you for a bite to eat.' He smiled at her. 'You do owe me, after all.'

'A very quick lunch,' she conceded, the thought of food turning her stomach again. 'I have a busy afternoon ahead of me.'

'As do I.'

They both stood up at the same time. 'I am sorry about today,' she said when they were standing at the door.

'I forgive you. Presumably it's morning sickness you're suffering from?'

She nearly choked on her answer. 'Good God no!'

Five minutes later and she was slowly taking the stairs up to Harry's office. Her head was pounding painfully now. She should never have drunk so much. But then if she couldn't get drunk when she'd totally screwed up, when could she?

Harry was too junior to have anyone guarding his door and so she knocked on it and waited for him to answer. She would feel infinitely better once she was wrapped in his arms. What's more, he would hand over the keys to his apartment and she would be able to sleep the rest of the day away. And when he came home from work, she'd be feeling miraculously better and they'd spend the night having mind-blowing sex.

With no response to her knock, she tried again and went in.

But Harry wasn't there. His office was empty.

She went over to his desk and checked his diary. According to the entry, written in his neat, sloping hand, he was out for the rest of the day.

She groaned.

No Harry.

No bed.

Could things get any worse?

Chapter Forty-Six

Not wanting to let Marcus out of his sight, Dan hadn't taken him to nursery as normal and he was working from home.

Work had so far consisted of watching a whole *Thomas the Tank Engine* DVD with his son and reading a selection of books – *Spot the Dog*, *Paddington Bear* and the endless stories about the supremely ordered lives of Topsy and Tim. Dan would put money on it that there wasn't a book in the series called *Topsy and Tim's Mother Has an Affair*.

He was now making lunch. For Marcus's benefit, soup was on the menu again. Just as last night, Dan had no appetite.

He may have appeared to Sally to be perfectly in control of himself at the time, but the reality had been quite different; inside he'd been close to breaking down. The strain of being so cool and detached had given way the minute Sally had driven off and he'd allowed himself to be angry. He gone out to the garden in the dark to vent his rage. He'd taken an axe from the shed and swung it at the trunk of a gnarled old plum tree that was so diseased it hadn't produced any fruit in years. With every thunk of metal on wood, he thought of the complacency in Sally's voice.

Rage had made him drive the blunt blade of the axe deep into the gnarled wood till his shoulders ached and the tree had creaked and groaned and crashed across the lawn, its branches crushing flat a flowerbed. He'd then attacked the prostrate trunk some more, until finally his anger had been snuffed out with exhaustion and sadness.

He'd never known such misery. He'd gone to bed a shattered, beaten mess. But despite his exhaustion, he had slept only intermittently. He lay there in the darkness trying to come to terms with what he'd done: he'd confronted Sally and the outcome had been to bring about an end to their marriage. Just as he'd feared.

Every time he'd come close to sliding into oblivion his brain had jerked him awake by picturing Sally with the unknown man who had destroyed their marriage. In his fractured mind's eye he visualized

Sally being undressed, her head tilted back in a moment of ecstasy, her crying out another man's name. It had been bearable suspecting the worst of her, but *knowing* it was far more painful. It was a pain that ripped through him. Again and again. There was no let up from it. He couldn't imagine there ever would be. It was as if Sally had bequeathed him an incurable disease. Perhaps it was a broken heart.

He switched off the gas. 'Soup's ready,' he called to Marcus.

The rules had been dispensed with and, like Dan, Marcus was still wearing his pyjamas and dressing gown. His hands full of a fluffy green frog, a colouring book and a small red plastic bucket of chubby crayons, Marcus dumped his hoard onto the table, adding to the debris of breakfast that Dan hadn't bothered to tidy away.

Paying no attention to the mess, Dan helped Marcus into his chair – the chair he'd long since claimed as his own, opposite the space Sally always occupied. Thinking of that empty seat, once again Dan wondered if he'd done the right thing last night. For Marcus's sake, should he have been a better man and told Sally he would forgive her if she promised him she would end the affair?

He poured the soup. Time to face facts, Danny Boy, he told himself. You are not that better man. You are as basic a man as ever walked the planet. If someone hurts you, you want to hurt them back. Instinct means you want to protect yourself any way you can from being hurt. And if that means banishing the woman you once loved with all your being, then so be it.

He swallowed at the thought of how in love with Sally he'd once been. She had been his world. He would have done anything for her. *Anything.*

Now he couldn't stand to look at her, never mind forgive her. How could he when she'd morphed into a human wrecking ball and seemed wholly unmoved by the consequences of her actions?

But a part of him couldn't shake off the thought that he might be partly to blame. Or even hugely to blame. She had described him as boring. Was he? Had being at home with Marcus changed him? And was there another reason why she'd had an affair? Was it because she'd suspected he'd been having one with Tatiana? Had her suspicions made her jealous and insecure, forcing her to seek affirmation elsewhere?

Yet what of his own suspicions? Wouldn't a better husband have forced the issue before it got out of hand? But then who in their right mind pokes a sleeping tiger?

He'd just sat down at the table when there was a knock at the back door. The use of the back door, rather than the front, signalled that it was someone who knew them well. A friend.

Hardly in the mood for socializing, Dan ignored it. But that was impossible with Marcus sitting next to him. 'Door, Daddy,' he said helpfully, his head tilted at an angle that always had the power to tug at Dan's heart. 'Thumone'th knocking.'

When whoever it was knocked again, this time more forcefully, Dan reluctantly went to see who it was.

Chloe took one look at Dan – dishevelled and unshaven – and wished she'd come sooner.

From her bedroom window late last night, she'd seen Sally driving out of the village. Twice she'd picked up the phone to speak to Dan, and twice she'd thought better of it, afraid he might think she was interfering. He knows where I am if he needs me, she'd told herself when she'd gone to bed. There had been no time during morning surgery for her to speak to him, but she had set aside her lunch break to call in. She was glad she had. From the look of Dan, their worst fears had been confirmed.

Without uttering a word, she stepped over the threshold and embraced him. He leaned against her and she staggered under the weight of him. Holding him tightly, she said, 'I'm so sorry, Dan. So very sorry. Tell me what happened. What did she say?'

Sally's day had passed in a nauseous daze.

It was now six o'clock and all she'd managed to get down, and keep down, was strong black coffee and paracetamol. Marion, Chandra and Tom had urged her to go home – word had gone round that she was suffering from food poisoning – but she'd flouted their advice and battled on. 'Sickness is for wimps,' she'd joked weakly.

Chandra had switched off her computer ten minutes ago and left, encouraging Sally to do the same. At the age of twenty-four, Chandra still lived at home with her parents and two younger sisters. Sally thought of her arriving home in Rusholme and being greeted by her family, of spending a happy, trouble-free evening watching the television. When Chandra had started working for Sally, she had told her that her name came from Sanskrit and meant 'the moon'. She was a cheerful, uncomplicated girl who never seemed to experience a moment's worry. Sally suddenly envied the happy simplicity of her life; still living at home, no real responsibility, no real cares to keep her awake at night.

On her desk, her mobile went off, making her jump. Harry! At last. Swivelling round in her chair, she checked her door was shut. 'Harry!' she cried. 'Where've you been all day?'

'Tied up with a client for hours on end.' He laughed. 'Not literally, of course. There's only one person I'd want to play those games with and it's not a balding, sixteen stone, fifty-five-year-old man with breath that may well be responsible for global warming.' He laughed again.

Sally tried to join in with his good mood but failed. 'Didn't you get my messages?' She'd left three in all. Every one of them asking him to ring her. But not a single one containing the reason why.

'Only now. What's up? You sound glum.'

'I've left Dan,' she said.

'You've done what?'

'I've left him,' she repeated. Was it a bad line or was Harry being particularly dense?

'But why? What made you do that?'

This was not the response she had expected. 'We slipped up,' she said. She told him about Marcus having to go to hospital and Dan not being able to get hold of her on her mobile.

'Shit!'

'A fair enough assessment in anyone's book.'

'And your boy, he's OK?'

'Apparently so. I didn't get to see him. He was asleep when I got back and when it all hit the fan Dan asked me to leave. When I couldn't get in touch with you, I ended up spending the night at the Hilton here in Manchester. Where were you, Harry? Why didn't you ring me back?'

'You tried ringing me last night? Sorry, I had no idea. I went for a drink with a friend when I got home.'

A drink? With a friend? Sally couldn't believe how blasé he was. 'Well, next time, check your bloody voicemail,' she snapped.

There was a pause. A long pause.

'Listen,' he said, 'I'm going to have to go. My balding, overweight client is insisting on taking me out for dinner tonight. An evening of halitosis; just what I need.'

'Harry, you can't just leave me like this! I need you. What time will you be home?'

'I'm not sure at the moment.'

'What do you mean by that?'

'I'm staying over. With a bit of luck I'll have the preliminaries of the case buttoned up by tomorrow afternoon.'

'But I need you here *now*. Where am I going to spend the night?' Another pause.

'I'm sorry, Sally, really I am, but surely the best thing all round would be for you to go home to Dan. You have your son to consider. I'll speak to you when I get back.'

The mobile went dead in her ear.

Sally stared at the small device in disbelief. Then she threw it hard across her office. It bounced off the wall, dropped to the floor with a crash and split neatly in two.

She checked back into the Hilton. Once again she ordered room service. This time she added a steak sandwich and fries to go with the order of a bottle of Merlot. She drank steadily and angrily. The more she drank, the clearer the situation became to her. Crystal clear, in fact.

Glum. He'd actually said she sounded glum. How the hell else was she supposed to sound?

How dare he tell her to go back to Dan! As if she was a silly teenager who'd run away from home in a fit of hormonal angst.

For God's sake, if it wasn't for Harry she wouldn't be in this mess.

It was all his fault.

If he hadn't come on to her the way he had she would never have got involved with him.

He'd had his fun with her and now he was bailing out when things started to get serious. She'd been nothing but a bit of fun for him.

Bastard!

He was *so* going to pay for this. By God, he'd pay.

She had a good mind to report him for sexual harassment.

Yes! That was exactly what she'd do. That would serve him right.

Let's see you wriggle out of that one, Harry Fox!

Chapter Forty-Seven

Sally woke for the second morning in a row with a thumping head-ache and a mouth that felt as if it had been coated with asphalt and stone chippings. Groggy and horribly nauseous, she groaned, recalling the red wine and vodka chasers. Oh, not again. Why had she done it? What had she been thinking?

She had been thinking too much; that had been the problem. She'd overreacted. Harry had only said the things he had because he wanted the best for her. He didn't want to be responsible for breaking up her marriage. It was understandable. All she had to do was convince him that her marriage was her responsibility, not his.

It was to his credit, she had concluded by the time she was showered, dressed and applying a mask of make-up, that he hadn't whooped and cheered that she was now a free woman. It was when she was slipping on her watch that she noticed the time. It was gone ten o'clock. She'd never been this late for work before. Furious with herself, she checked out, snapping angrily at the receptionist who didn't seem capable of grasping that she was in a hurry. It was ten forty-five by the time she was climbing the stairs to her office. Her head had resumed its earlier thumping and her stomach was churn-ing ominously.

'I didn't think you'd be coming in today,' Chandra said when she saw her, adding: 'Shouldn't you be at home in bed? You still don't look well.'

'Too much to do,' Sally said offhandedly, breezing past to get to the safety of her office. 'Any calls for me?' Now that she didn't have a functioning mobile, it was possible that Harry had tried calling her here.

'Nothing. Apart from a message from Tom. He said he urgently wanted to see you if you did make it in today. Shall I tell him you're in? Or would you like some coffee first?'

Sally smiled gratefully. 'Coffee would be wonderful. You're a star, Chandra.'

She had only managed a few sips of her coffee when there was a knock at her door and Tom came in. His expression was one of solemn concern. He couldn't have looked more sombre if he'd been attending a funeral. 'What is it?' she asked him.

He pulled out a chair and sat down. She noticed what appeared to be a piece of folded A4 paper in his hands. 'Tom?' she repeated.

'I'm afraid it's not good, Sally,' he said.

'I can see that. What's the problem?'

He swallowed. 'It's Harry Fox. He's formally accusing you of sexual harassment.' Tom waved the piece of paper in front of him. 'It's all here in an email he sent me first thing this morning. He's also sent a copy to the rest of the partners. He claims you actively pursued him from the day he started work with us. He says you abused your position by saying you would blight his chances of promotion if he didn't do as you wanted.'

Sally's head began to spin. 'But he … he can't have said all that,' she stammered. 'It's simply not true. Please tell me you don't believe a word of it, Tom.'

Tom shook his head grimly. 'I don't know what to believe, Sally.' He unfolded the piece of paper in his hands. 'He's been most explicit, giving dates when you insisted the two of you spend weekends together. He says it finally got too much for him this weekend, when you announced that you'd left your husband to be with him. He claims you've deluded yourself all along imagining him to have feelings for you. He hasn't stated in his email who he's instructed to act for him, but he's hinted it's a firm here in Manchester.'

Sally gasped. Then she rushed from her office to be sick.

By mid-afternoon the only topic of conversation of any interest to anyone was Sally. Sally and Harry. Emails were circulating at the speed of light, most of them titled *When Sally Met Harry*. Sally only knew this because Chandra had offered to keep her informed. Her loyalty touched Sally. 'I know you couldn't possibly have done those things you've been accused of,' the young girl said. 'You're not that kind of a woman.'

Sally could have wept. What did Chandra know of her? What did any of them know of the real Sally Oliver?

Tom had suggested that she should go home and stay there until he and the rest of the partners had decided what to do next. Apparently Harry was lying low. He'd taken a fortnight's holiday as of today.

But home was the last place Sally wanted to go. She sat in her office in a state of shock. In one fell swoop, her reputation would be shot. Not just here at McKenzie Stuart, but in the whole of Manchester's legal system. She would be a joke. A laughing stock.

How could she fight back? How could she retain any semblance of respect?

And how could Harry have done this to her? More to the point, why? Why had he turned on her this way?

On the brink of wasting vital energy on crying, she pulled herself together. Self-pity wouldn't get her anywhere. She needed a plan. She also needed some clean clothes; she'd worn the same suit for two days running. Nothing else for it, she would have to go home.

She would tough it out with Dan, she told herself after she'd informed Chandra she was going home after all. What's more, there was no reason on earth why she shouldn't move back in properly. It was her house as much as Dan's. Hell, she was the one paying the mortgage; she could damned well call the tune!

By the time she was driving into the village, she wasn't feeling quite so sure of herself. Moving back in was an admission that Harry didn't want her. It was a double whammy: first Dan had rejected her, now Harry.

Dan's car was in its usual place on the drive and she parked behind it. She looked up at the house, remembering the day she and Dan came to view it for the first time. Corner Cottage had represented so much to them. It had symbolized the next all-important step in their lives; it confirmed that they were doing everything right. They were moving in the right direction; they were getting on. Nothing could stop them.

She put her key in the lock of the front door and for a split second it crossed her mind that the key might not turn, that Dan might have changed the locks. But the key turned just as it usually did and she let herself in. She closed the door and stood very still on the mat, listening out for signs of Dan and Marcus.

Nothing. The house was as still as the grave. She hadn't anticipated that. She didn't know whether to be relieved or disappointed. Out of habit, she put her briefcase at the bottom of the stairs and went through to the kitchen. It looked like a bomb had hit it. There were plates, bowls, mugs, plastic cups and pans strewn across the work surfaces. The table was also a chaotic mess of clutter – books, newspapers and toys lay amongst sweet and cake wrappers and a tipped-over packet of breakfast cereal. Cheerios had spilled out, some ending up on the floor.

She went upstairs, following a trail of toys and discarded clothes. Marcus's bedroom carpet had disappeared beneath a multi-coloured sea of Duplo, cars, trains, track, jigsaws and cuddly toys. His bed was unmade and the small wooden table and chair he liked to sit at were tipped over.

She had never seen the house look like this before. She bent down to pick up Marcus's pyjamas from the floor. The cotton fabric was soft and smooth after countless times of being worn and put through the washing machine. She could smell her son on the patterned fabric. His warm, tucked-up-in-bed little boy smell.

She crossed the landing to her and Dan's bedroom. Here again the bed was unmade and whilst the room was nowhere near as untidy as Marcus's, it was a far cry from its customary neat order. Her gaze came to rest on the dressing table, the silver-framed photograph of her and Dan on their wedding day was gone. Curiosity made her open the top drawer. Sure enough, there was the photograph, face down. She closed the drawer and went and sat on the bed. She suddenly felt overwhelmingly tired. How tempting it was to lie back and pull the duvet up over her.

But what would that solve?

What might solve everything was apologizing to Dan. *I'm sorry, Dan.* Would that be so very difficult? Not if it meant everything could go back to how it had been. She hadn't fully comprehended until the other night, when Dan had found her out, just how much she had subconsciously relied upon his calm, dependable nature to contain that dangerously wild streak within her. Yet perhaps it had been inevitable that one day the Sally Wilson of old would break free of the constraint of his steadfast love.

But what if she begged Dan to forgive her? Would he? And if her marriage looked to be rock solid, would Tom and the rest of the partners somehow make Harry's accusations go away? Could he be made to retract his allegations?

Even if he did, her reputation would always be tarnished. But the worst-case scenario that Sally dreaded was that she might be asked to leave the firm. One of them would have to leave; that much she knew. It was her or Harry. She had a feeling Tom would stick up for her, but she wasn't so sure about some of the other partners. Maybe she should have been honest with Tom this morning. She should have told him that she and Harry had been having an affair, but it had been a mutual relationship; there had been no intimidation or coercion on her part. With hindsight, honesty might well have garnered her more of Tom's support in the long term. She saw now that it was probably a mistake to have stuck to her original outright denial.

The best she could hope for was that Harry would decide that he'd gone far enough with his claim, that he had made whatever point it was he wanted to make, and would drop his case against her.

Why was Harry doing this to her? How could he be so cruel when he'd said he couldn't live a day without her? Had he meant any of what he'd said and done?

A tear slid slowly down her cheek. She dashed it away with her hand, determined not to give in to self-pity. Hearing the sound of car doors slamming, she got up from the bed and looked out of the window. Dan and Marcus were on the road standing next to a Honda Civic. They weren't alone. Tatiana Queen of the Bloody Fairies was with them. Marcus was reaching up to kiss her and Dan was ... Dan was doing what, exactly? Waiting his turn to kiss Tatiana?

Watching what happened next – Dan putting his arms round Tatiana and holding her close – sent a roar of fury crashing through Sally's ears. The other night Dan had been so full of self-righteousness, playing to the hilt the part of wronged husband, when all along he'd not been so innocent after all. She's suspected way back in May that there was more than just a work relationship between them; now she knew her instinct had been right.

Furious that he'd played her for a fool, she watched Tatiana get back in her car and drive off, then flung open the wardrobe doors and began chucking clothes onto the bed.

Downstairs she could hear voices. 'Mummy must be home,' she heard Dan say, followed by, 'She's not down here. Let's try upstairs.'

Footsteps approached – one pair light and scampering, the other heavy and measured.

She had no idea what Dan would have told Marcus about her not being at home these last few nights, but she decided to be the one to set the tone and agenda. 'Hello, Marcus,' she said brightly when they came in. 'Come and let me see your chin. I hear you've had quite a time of it while I was away. Fancy falling off Charlie's climbing frame like that! How many stitches did you have put in?'

'Nine.'

'Goodness! And were you very brave when it happened?'

Marcus glanced over towards the door where Dan seemed to be rooted to the spot. 'I wath a bit brave, Daddy, wathn't I?'

'You were extraordinarily brave, Marcus. Much braver than I would have been.' Dan switched his gaze to Sally. 'We've just been down to the surgery for the nurse to check him out. She says he's healing well. The stitches inside his mouth will soon dissolve and his lisp will disappear along with the swelling.'

'And let me guess,' Sally said, 'you just happened to meet your chum from work at the surgery?'

Dan stiffened. 'Don't, Sally. Just don't.'

'You seem to be saying that to me a lot these days. I wonder why. A guilty conscience?'

'My conscience is clear. Can you say the same? Marcus, do you want to go downstairs and choose a DVD for us to watch later?'

'Thomath, Thomath, Thomath,' Marcus chanted as he scooted off happily.

'What have you told him?' Sally asked.

'Oh, the usual, that his mother is busy with work. How have you been?'

Had it not been for the touching little scene she'd just witnessed from the window, Sally might have been tempted to tell Dan the truth. Give him his due, he'd always been a good listener. 'I've been OK,' she'd said.

'If you don't mind me saying, you don't look it.'

'Thanks! But then nor do you.' It was true; Dan did look a mess. He hadn't shaved and he didn't look like he'd slept much in the last forty-eight hours.

She was about to make a bigger effort to ease the hostility between them when Dan said, 'So how's it going with the new man in your life? It must be some cosy love nest you've got going; the two of you spending the day working together and then spending all night together.'

'You disappoint me, Dan. I thought you'd be more adult about this. Resorting to cheap shots really isn't helpful.'

He closed the door – presumably so that Marcus wouldn't hear them – and stepped towards her. 'I'll tell you what isn't helpful,' he said. 'It's you carrying on as if none of this matters. Divorce might be part and parcel of your everyday life, but for me it's near enough the end of the world. So if it's all the same to you, an occasional cheap shot from me is my way of dealing with the unthinkable.'

'Divorce? Who said anything about us getting divorced?'

'Isn't that the inevitable consequence of you falling out of love with me and falling in love with someone else?'

Sally blinked. 'I never said I'd stopped loving you.'

'You didn't need to. Your actions said it for you. And if I'm honest, brutally honest, I don't love you any more. At least, not the woman you've become. I'd have expected that to make the situation more bearable. But it doesn't.' He looked at the clothes she'd thrown on the bed. 'I'll leave you to your packing. Do you have an address you can give me, in case of an emergency?'

Shocked at the cold finality of his manner and his words, Sally said, 'Work. You can contact me at work. And of course my mobile …' She stopped herself short, remembering her smashed phone. 'My mobile's broken,' she said. 'I'll let you know when I've replaced it.'

'Mummy's got to go away again,' Sally said.

His eyes glued to the television screen, Marcus nodded vaguely.

Sally moved so that she was directly in front of his line of vision, blocking whatever it was Thomas and his shunting friends were up to. When she was sure she had his full attention, she said, 'I want you to know that while I'm away, I'll try and ring every evening to speak to you before you go to bed. OK?'

He nodded and strained his neck so he could see the television. He beamed happily at the screen. 'Look,' he said, pointing, 'Perthy'th thtuck in the thunnel.'

Dan helped Sally put her luggage in her car. It was as if he couldn't wait to get rid of her. She wouldn't have thought it possible for him to be so remote and detached. She switched on the ignition and when she looked up after putting on her seat belt, there was no sign of Dan. He was back inside the house, the door closed.

She reversed out of the drive and swerved sharply onto the road. She'd driven no further than the village green when she stopped the car and burst into tears. What was she doing? Why hadn't she told Dan the truth, that Harry didn't want her and that she had nowhere to go? That whatever she'd had with Harry was over.

Go back and tell him, she told herself. Go back and tell him it has all been a terrible mistake. Beg his forgiveness. Whatever it takes.

But her pride wouldn't let her. She just couldn't admit that she'd made such a mess of things.

She lowered her head to the steering wheel and cried harder still, loudly and messily.

A gentle tapping sound on the side window had her nearly jumping out of her skin.

To add to her humiliation, there was Chloe's boyfriend looking back at her through the glass.

Chapter Forty-Eight

Seth was surprised at the way Chloe was treating her friend. He didn't know all the details, but he was aware that their last meeting had been acrimonious and that since then, Sally had confessed to having an affair and Chloe was upset about the effect this was having on Dan.

When he'd arrived outside Chloe's cottage to spend the evening with her, he'd recognized Sally in her car across the road. Slumped over the steering wheel, there was obviously something wrong. Concerned, he'd gone over to see if there was anything he could do to help. He could no more have turned his back on her than he could have ignored a crying toddler on its own in the street. She had been sobbing so violently, he'd insisted he help her out of her car and take her inside to Chloe's.

But now here was Chloe, treating her with brutal contempt. Indifferent to her friend's plight, her arms folded, she was telling Sally she had no one to blame but herself, that she could think again if a few tears would win her any sympathy. 'You should have thought more about the consequences of what you were doing,' Chloe said hotly. 'Have you any idea what you've done to Dan? You've destroyed him. I'll never forgive you for that.'

Sally grabbed a tissue from the box Seth had placed in front of her. She blew her nose loudly. 'He didn't look too destroyed just now when I saw him,' she mumbled.

'He's putting on a brave front for Marcus's sake, of course. Didn't you once think about Marcus when you were cheating on Dan?'

Sally started to cry again.

'Oh, go on, when all else fails, turn on the waterworks. Anything but face up to what you've done.'

'Chloe,' Seth said quietly, 'I don't think this is helping.'

Chloe shot him a fierce look. 'And what would? Telling her she's done nothing wrong and that it'll all come out in the wash?' Chloe turned back to Sally. 'I've had enough of your crocodile tears. Why don't you go and seek solace in the arms of the man who clearly means so much to you?'

Sally started to wail. 'I ... I can't,' she stuttered. 'It's over. He's ... he's not interested in me any more. I don't think he ever was ... And now I have nowhere to go.' She buried her face in another tissue.

'Whoever said bad people don't get what they deserve got it wrong. Wow, Seth, I could almost believe in that God of yours based on this turn of events. Is this what you call biblical justice?'

If Seth had been surprised earlier, now he was shocked. And dismayed. He couldn't believe Chloe's behaviour. 'Could I have a word with you?' he asked, tipping his head towards the sitting room. Alone with her, he said, 'Chloe, you've made your point with Sally, why not show a little compassion now?'

Chloe looked at him with astonishment. 'Compassion?' she repeated. 'You didn't see Dan. You didn't see what she's done to him. Oh, no, if you don't mind, I'll save my compassion for people who deserve it.'

He put a hand on her arm. 'Chloe, she's totally messed up. What's more, she knows it. Don't make it any harder for her.'

'You'll be telling me next to offer her a bed for the night.'

'Would that be so out of the question?'

'You're serious, aren't you? But forget it; I couldn't be that disloyal to Dan.'

'Doesn't loyalty to an old friend mean anything?'

'She's not my friend any more. She's crossed too many lines for me to value what we once had.'

He frowned. 'Surely not?'

'If you'd heard the awful things she said about me, and you, you'd think the same. The last time I saw her she was doing her best to split us up.'

'But you said yourself; she hasn't been herself for some time.'

'That doesn't give her the right to criticize and make fun of you. Or accuse me of only being interested in you because I'm desperate to have a baby. Now if you'll let go of me, I'm going to tell her to leave.'

'Please don't,' he said, removing his hand. 'She has nowhere to go.'

'Not my problem,' Chloe said emphatically.

Disappointed, Seth followed Chloe back to the kitchen where Sally, clutching a handful of tissues, looked at them expectantly.

'Time to bring the curtain down on your performance,' Chloe said brusquely. 'I want you to go now.'

Sally stood up, her shoulders hunched. Seth noticed her hands were shaking. She steadied them by gripping her bag. She was at the door when she turned and said, 'I'm sorry, Chloe. Really I am.' Her bloodshot eyes filled with tears again.

'Me too,' Chloe said off-handedly.

When Sally had closed the door after her, it took Seth all of two seconds to make a decision he hoped he wouldn't regret.

Chloe couldn't believe it. How could Seth have taken Sally's side over hers?

'I can't stand by and not do anything to help,' he'd said when Chloe had tried to stop him. He'd grabbed his keys and then hurried after Sally. 'I'll ring you later,' he'd called over his shoulder.

'Don't bother!' she'd shouted at him. 'I wouldn't want you to take time out from letting that manipulative piece of work cry on your shoulder!'

Left on her own, and with the evening she and Seth had planned to spend together ruined, Chloe shoved the lamb chops she had been going to cook back in the fridge. She stomped round the kitchen, at a loss as to how to rid herself of the fuming indignation she felt.

She didn't know whom she was more cross with: Seth for coming over all holier-than-thou and interfering with something that had nothing to do with him, or Sally for duping him. How could he have been so easily taken in? He'd be singing a different tune if he'd been the one to try and console Dan.

But there was another source of her anger. It was the comment she'd let slip about her being desperate for a baby. Would Seth now wonder if it was true? Of all the things she wouldn't want him to know about, it was that. Nothing would more effectively make a man lose interest in a girl than thinking he was being fast-tracked into fatherhood.

But that all seemed hypothetical now. Did she really want to be involved with a man who could so easily dismiss her opinion and favour Sally's feelings over hers? Did she want anything to do with a man who went out of his way to belittle her and make her look like the villain of the piece? Who did he think he was, some saintly Caped Crusader?

Sally was probably loving it all. Not content with destroying her marriage she was now having a go at wrecking Chloe's relationship with Seth.

Calm now and more in control of herself, Sally looked around her.

The bedroom Seth had shown her up to was what an estate agent would refer to as compact. Seth had called it poky and he'd apologized several times for not having a larger spare room to offer her. From the looks of things, it doubled up as his office. Crammed into the small space was a single bed and a cheap pine desk with a computer and printer on it, along with an anglepoise lamp, two black plastic 'in' and 'out' trays stacked on top of each other, a small clock and a framed photograph. The photograph was of Chloe. On the wall above the desk were two long bookshelves containing a selection of theology books and Bible commentaries. Next to the desk was a filing cabinet and beneath the window was a bookcase, home to yet more heavyweight theology books as well as two Collins dictionaries, one for Hebrew and the other for Greek.

Sally returned her attention to the photograph of Chloe, picked it up and stared at it. The one and only true friend she'd ever had now hated her. Her eyes filled with tears. Yet more tears. Not since she'd had postnatal depression had she cried so much.

She put the photograph back in its place, sat on the bed and thought of Seth's wholly unexpected offer for her to stay with him until she got herself sorted – whatever that was going to turn out to be. Her accommodation might not be up to much, but it had to be better than another soulless, drunken night at the Hilton. With a curate for a host, she doubted very much she would wake up tomorrow morning with another hangover. That had to be a good thing.

Her unexpected host was currently downstairs making them some supper. She could smell onions frying and hear music playing. There was something faintly comforting about the combination.

Buy why? Why was he doing this for her? She was practically a stranger to him. Christian duty, she supposed. This was too good an opportunity for him to pass up, that of playing the part of Good Samaritan. He'd probably boast about his good deed in church on Sunday.

She cringed at the thought. Who'd have thought she would sink so low as to be a charity case? He better not think she was a captive audience for him to hit her with some moralizing, preachy number. One hint of that and she'd hightail it back to the Hilton.

Chapter Forty-Nine

After a good night's sleep and zero alcohol intake, Sally was sitting at her office desk feeling a little more like herself. What that actually meant, she wasn't sure. When was the last time she had felt entirely herself? And who was she anyway? Was she Sally Oliver, wife and mother and respected top divorce lawyer? Or was she Sally Wilson, reckless headcase bent on self-destruction?

In the quiet of her office, she had the sensation of having gone through a prolonged period of madness. She felt exhausted and weirdly disengaged. It was almost impossible to know what was real and what wasn't. Was this how schizophrenics felt?

What did feel real was the certainty that there was no way back. Just as Dan had said in the aftermath of the tsunami, life could never be the same again.

When she'd arrived for work it had been evident that with Harry's accusation hanging over her no one had expected her to show her face. With a demonstration of bravado that surprised even her, she'd fended off the raised eyebrows and whispered comments. But the effort was taking its toll. She jumped every time the phone rang, dreading that it brought yet more bad news. Mostly, though, everyone was leaving her alone. She suspected that could be because she had become the office pariah. The upside was that she was being left in peace to get on with her work. Thank God work had always been her refuge. Without it, she'd be lost.

She'd woken early that morning and, eager not to be late again for work, she'd skipped having a shower, dressed hurriedly and headed downstairs. Seth had beaten her to it. The smell of bacon and freshly brewed coffee welcomed her. 'Nothing like a bacon sandwich to set you up for the day,' he said, poking about under the grill with a fork. His hair was wet from the shower and he was dressed in black trousers, a black clerical shirt and white collar. He made an incongruous, not to say disconcerting sight. He seemed bigger, too.

More imposing. Was that what the armour of God did to him? she'd thought cynically.

They'd eaten in the kitchen, where they'd had supper the night before. And just as last night, his tact was admirable. She'd told him outright that she didn't want to discuss her marriage and to her relief he'd respected her wishes. He'd offered no moralizing advice, only reiterated his invitation for her to stay with him as long as she needed. She really didn't know what to make of his generosity.

'Did you manage to speak to Chloe?' she'd asked him, knowing that he'd tried several times during the course of the previous evening.

'No,' he'd said. 'She's not answering her phone or her mobile. I think ... I think she's cross with me.'

As Sally waited for Murray Adamson to arrive for his appointment, she recalled that hesitation in Seth's reply and felt a trickle of guilt. She thought of the photograph on Seth's desk and hoped that she hadn't caused a rift between the two of them. Surely Chloe couldn't be that angry? But even as she wondered this, she knew that she'd never seen Chloe so furious. Never.

Murray Adamson arrived his customary ten minutes late. Perhaps he'd been held up pressing that immaculate suit of his and dousing himself in aftershave. 'Let's talk business over lunch,' he said. 'I've booked us a table at Heathcote's.'

Sally didn't argue. She was glad to get out of the office.

The restaurant wasn't busy and they had the pick of the tables. Once they were settled and their order taken – Murray having insisted on asking for two glasses of champagne – Sally reached for her briefcase. 'Put that away,' he said.

'But you said business over lunch.'

He flashed her one of his I-always-get-what-I-want smiles. 'I say a lot of things, not all of which I mean. Relax and enjoy the meal. Or at least try to. I've never seen you look so strung out. What's troubling you?'

A waitress, a young Polish girl with a flawless pale complexion, brought them their champagne. 'Well?' Murray said. 'You haven't answered my question. What's wrong?'

'Nothing's wrong,' she replied, annoyed. 'Other than resenting the fact that you've tricked me into having lunch with you.'

'For which I make no apology.' He raised his glass and waited for her to do likewise. 'Cheers,' he said when she'd obliged. 'Here's to the future and a successful outcome to my divorce.' He put his glass against his mouth, took a long sip. 'I sincerely hope you won't try and get me drunk and make me do something we'll both regret in the morning.'

'I can assure you there's no chance of that.'

'Seriously, though, I'd hate to think that you'll disappear from my life entirely when my divorce is final.'

'That remains to be seen,' she said. 'If you marry again and find someone other than your wife irresistible, who knows, you might require my services a third time.'

He laughed. 'Trust me, that won't happen. I intend to find exactly the right woman to be wife number three. I've had it with arm candy and nothing more substantial than candyfloss between the ears. I want a woman with a brain. A woman who's complex and who fascinates me. A woman who doesn't bore me. Someone like you, for instance.'

Sally put down her glass. 'Stop it, Murray. I'm really not in the mood to listen to any of this nonsense. If you can't be sensible I suggest we forget about lunch, return to the office and go through the points I need to cover with you.'

He put a hand out to her, touching her wrist lightly. 'I'm sorry,' he said. 'Forgive me, please. It's just—' His words fell away.

She stared at his tanned fingers and well-manicured nails, then looked up at his face. 'It's just what?'

'I like you. I like you a lot. Surely you must have realized that? But I respect the fact that you're happily married. That's why I've never pushed it with you. You *are* happily married, aren't you, Sally? Sally? Oh my God, I've made you cry. I'm so sorry.'

Two choices, Sally told herself when she accepted that she couldn't hide in the ladies' room any longer. She could either lie to Murray and say she wasn't feeling well, or she could brazen it out, insist they keep their personal lives to themselves and discuss business only. She would have to do it tactfully, of course. She couldn't afford to offend a client like Murray Adamson, not when he brought so much work to the firm. But then the way her luck was panning out, worrying about keeping a client sweet was the least of her concerns. If Harry went through with his threat to take her to court for sexual harassment, she'd be lucky to have a job.

Thinking about Harry was a mistake. The pain of his betrayal ripped through her. What wouldn't she do to ring him and tell him exactly what she thought of him ... But no. She mustn't do that. She must have no contact with him whatsoever.

She wrenched open the door, marched back to the table where Murray was waiting for her and decided upon the latter option. But his anxious expression as he rose to pull out her chair caused her throat to bunch and she slumped into the seat not at all sure she would be capable of ever getting up again. A vision of the *Titanic* sinking slowly but resolutely to the bottom of the ocean came into her mind.

He sat down, slid his chair nearer to hers and placed his hand on her shoulder. 'Sally, can I say something?'

She nodded. Or thought she did. But frankly, anything was possible. This could all be a nightmarish dream and any moment she would wake up at the Hilton with an almighty hangover. Or better still, she'd wake up and that fateful day when Tom had introduced her to Harry would never have happened.

'As someone who cares about you,' Murray said, his voice low, 'I want you to know that you can talk to me as a friend. Nothing you tell me will go any further. I mean that.'

'There's nothing to tell,' she managed to say.

'Is it your husband? Have you discovered he's having an affair? Is that it?'

She closed her eyes at the absurdity of what Murray was saying.

'The man's a fool,' he went on. 'He doesn't realize how lucky he is to have you.'

She opened her eyes. 'Please, Murray, you're not helping.'

'I'm sorry. Do you want to leave? We could find a bar, somewhere more discreet.'

Just as he said this their waitress brought their starters to the table. In her near-perfect English, she apologized for the delay and left them.

Murray looked at Sally. 'Your call. Do we stay or leave?'

'Let's stay,' she murmured.

'Is that because the thought of being somewhere more discreet frightens you?'

'It would take more than that to scare me,' she said more forcefully.

He smiled. 'That's better. A flash of the old Sally Oliver spirit I know and love. Pepper?'

They ate in silence for a while until Murray said, 'I stand by what I said; your husband's a fool. If I was married to you I wouldn't—'

285

'It's not him,' Sally said, 'it's me. I'm the one who's been having an affair. It's over now.' She looked directly at Murray. 'And to clarify matters, I'm not about to embark on another. Especially not with a client.' She shook her head. 'And I don't know why I've just told you all that. Not when I hardly know you.'

Murray put down his knife and fork and carefully wiped his mouth with his napkin. 'In my experience, it's usually easier to confide in someone outside the immediate circle of one's friends. What happened?'

'What do you mean, what happened?'

'Come on, Sally, don't be obtuse. I'm asking you why you had an affair. Was your husband neglecting you?'

'You sound as if you're trying to lay all the blame at my husband's feet. I can face up to the fact that I, and I alone, am responsible for my actions, you know.'

'I don't doubt that for a minute. But what did your lover give you that your husband didn't? That's the sixty-four-million-dollar question. Was it a sense of self? Excitement? Great sex? Or, as I suspect, did you get a kick out of letting down your guard and playing by different rules?'

In spite of everything, Sally smiled. 'I would never have had you down as so perceptive. Or such a relationship expert.'

'What can I say? I've cocked up enough to have learned something along the way.'

It was Seth and Chloe's day off. He'd left countless messages for her to ring him, but he hadn't received a single reply. Whichever way he viewed her silence, it didn't look good.

He parked on the road outside her cottage and with the engine still running and the wipers working at the rain on the windscreen, he stared at her car on the drive and rehearsed one more time what he was going to say. In his head he was word perfect, but he knew the minute he stood face to face with Chloe his script would fall apart and he'd very likely end up saying completely the wrong thing.

He got out, pressed his finger to the front door bell and waited.

Yet more silence.

He tried it again, then gave up and went round to the back of the house. He found her in the garden where, despite the rain, she was digging with considerable energy in one of the flowerbeds. She appeared to be taking on the woody, mutilated stump of some bush or other. The stump didn't stand a chance, by the looks of things.

'Need a hand?' he called out.

She spun round. 'Oh, it's you. What do you want?' She drove the spade into the damp earth, pushing down on it hard with her foot.

'I want to talk to you. Why haven't you answered any of my messages?'

'I would have thought that was blindingly obvious.'

He drew closer to her. Risky maybe, given the lethal weapon in her hands. 'Any chance we can go inside and talk?' he asked.

'No. I want to get this laurel out.'

'Is that what it is? You should have left some of its branches intact. That way you would have had something to help lever it out.'

'Oh, so you're a gardening expert now as well as a marriage guidance counsellor?'

He ignored her sarcasm. 'Why don't you give me the spade and I'll do it for you?'

'No.'

He held his hand out for the spade. 'Don't be churlish.'

'Go to hell! And if you don't mind me saying, you've got a cheek coming here and telling me what to do.'

The rain was coming down harder now. It was drenching them both. Neither of them was wearing a coat. Stick to the script, Seth reminded himself as Chloe continued to glare at him. 'If this is about Sally,' he said, 'you have to understand that I'm not in the business of rubbing other people's noses in their sins. I'm neither condoning what she's done nor condemning her for it. I'm merely trying to help her find a way through the mess she's created.'

'Bully for you!'

'Chloe, please. Don't let a little thing like this come between us.'

'It might be little to you, but it's not to me. You made a choice and it's a choice I can't live with.'

'So that's it? Because I'm trying to help Sally, it's over between us?'

'Looks that way.' She sighed. 'Let's face it, Seth, it was never going to work between us. We're too different. And if you're really honest with yourself, you'd accept that I was never going to be able to live up to the high standards you'd expect of me.'

Shocked how implacable she sounded, he dashed the rain away from his face. 'You don't really believe that?'

'I do, as a matter of fact. I've come to understand that I could never be good enough in your eyes.' Her face, as wet as his own, looked as if it had turned to marble.

'I don't believe you.'

'You're calling me a liar now?' Again the same cold, stony expression.

Suddenly it was more than Seth could take. Anger blazed inside him. He grabbed the spade out of her hands and hurled it with all his strength. It shot through the air and landed with an explosive clatter against the fence at the end of the garden. 'I'm not leaving here until I've made you change your mind,' he shouted.

She took a small step back from him. 'That's never going to happen,' she said. 'For the simple reason that we're chalk and cheese. Our views on life were never going to meet. One of us would have to compromise, and I'm sorry, but I'm not prepared to do that. You have your principles you live by and I have mine.'

'You couldn't be more wrong, Chloe.'

'See! That's the problem between us. You're always judging me. I can't do anything without you telling me I'm wrong.'

'I've never judged you!' he shouted again. 'Not once. Don't you dare ever accuse me of that.'

'You do it all the time. Only you don't realize it.'

'For fuck's sake, Chloe, this is crazy. As far as I can see, the only person judging you is you. Perhaps you ought to ask yourself why.'

As the rain continued to hammer down mercilessly, she slowly turned away from him. In furious disbelief he watched her calmly go and retrieve the spade.

Would it make any difference if he threw his arms around her and told her how much he loved her? Rooted to the spot, he opened his mouth to call out to her, but the words wouldn't come. He blinked as the rain continued to drench him, and then he walked away fast, his footsteps squelching in the sodden grass.

Chloe turned and watched him go. Through the rain and her tears, she swallowed the urge to cry out to him. Come back! Don't leave me!

Chapter Fifty

'You've broken up with Seth? But why?'

Much against her will, Chloe was at Corner Cottage. Ten minutes ago she had phoned Dan to see how he was and when he'd asked if she was feeling all right, she had stupidly, oh so stupidly, burst into tears. Dan had then insisted she come round to talk properly, but she'd said she didn't want to. 'If you're not here in the next ten minutes I'll drag Marcus out of bed and come to you,' he'd said so firmly she couldn't refuse him. Not when it was so late and the rain was lashing down with all the force of a monsoon and the wind had got up. And so here she was unburdening herself to a dear friend who had more than enough troubles of his own to contend with.

Trying hard to hold it together, she said, 'Dan, you have more important things to think about than my silly problems.'

'But Seth was the best thing to have happened to you in ages. You were so right together. I hadn't seen you so happy in a long while. I can't believe you've ended things with him because of Sally.'

She shook her head vehemently. 'It isn't just because of Sally. It's because we weren't right together. Not really. There could never have been a proper future for us. It was that job of his. Let's face it; the Church is no place for someone like me.'

Dan looked at her hard. 'Did you say that to Seth?'

'As good as. But I didn't need to. He knew it, deep down. He might never have wanted to admit it, but it would always have been a problem for us. I could never have shared his world.'

'Would you have had to?'

'I think he would have wanted me to, eventually.'

'I'm not so sure. My understanding of Seth is that he would never have had unrealistic expectations of you, or forced you to behave in a way that you didn't want to. He's too pragmatic to do that. I also think he cared about you too much to do anything that would put him at risk of losing you.'

Chloe turned away from Dan. She should never have agreed to

come here. Ringing him had been a mistake. She didn't need to hear him singing Seth's praises. It only made her feel worse. If that was possible.

As far as I can see, the only person judging you is you. The truth of Seth's words had hit home in a way nothing else could have done. Those few words had shocked her more than even his anger when he'd snatched the spade out of her hands. But it added to her conviction that she had been right to end it. Better that she did it before he turned on her. If she'd learned anything from her break-up with Paul, it was to keep the upper hand.

But what had she been thinking? That she could be with a man like Seth and get away with living a lie? It was easy for him to profess now that he didn't judge her, but if he ever found out what she was really capable of, he would definitely look at her anew. And he had judged her over Sally, hadn't he? He'd accused her of not being compassionate. It was when he'd gone rushing off after Sally that she'd woken up to the reality of their relationship and the fundamental flaw in it. If he could judge and condemn her for siding with Dan, what else could he judge and condemn her for?

With one last attempt to convince Dan that she'd done the right thing, she turned and faced him. 'I know you're trying to help,' she said, 'but the way I reacted to Seth helping Sally is a symptom of the difference between us. If he can't understand that Sally crossed a line with me and that my loyalty to you comes first, then he doesn't understand how the real world works. I can't be with someone who's that naive. What's more, his showy Good Samaritan act blatantly disregards my feelings. You tell me, is that really the kind of man I want to be involved with?'

Exhausted, Dan went straight to bed after Chloe left. The endless, grinding effort to retain an air of outer confidence was getting to him, leaving him drained, with a cold, inner emptiness.

He lay on his back in the dark, his eyes closed, waiting for sleep to come, but knowing it would be some time yet. And because the nightmares he'd thought he'd put behind him had resumed, sleep, when it did come, meant that he was plunged into the familiar circle of hell, caught up in the relentless nightmare of failure. Of failing to save that little boy's life. Of failing to save his marriage.

He thought of Sally. Like tossing a stone into a pool of water, her actions were rippling further and further. Because of her, Chloe had broken up with Seth. Was there no end to the havoc she could wreak?

Sally's actions would have lifelong consequences. Particularly for Marcus. Before too long he'd start asking why Mummy wasn't at home and when the time came to explain it to him, what then? How would he react? More importantly, how would he react when he was older and really grasped the situation? The thought of the years ahead frightened Dan. He wasn't frightened of bringing Marcus up on his own, but what of those dreadful statistics that were routinely trotted out in the newspapers and on the radio and television, that children from broken homes grew up to underachieve, lacking confidence and self-respect. Had Sally thought of that when she'd been throwing herself into the arms of another? Had she thought of anyone but herself?

Or would Sally say that it hadn't done her any harm coming from a single-parent family? She was confident and had achieved all right, hadn't she? She might even argue that it was because of her father walking out on his family that she had striven to get where she was. That she was to be admired for her willpower and determination.

Her single-minded determination was all very well, and Dan had indeed admired her for it, but had it rendered her incapable of caring for anyone but herself?

He gave up trying to understand Sally. He'd already learned the hard way that thinking about her led nowhere but to a place of debilitating anger. He forced himself to think of more practical things instead. Work. He would have to make changes there. If he was to provide for Marcus in the way he wanted to, he'd have to work full time. And not for the trust. They wouldn't be able to afford the level of salary he was now looking for. He'd ring Tatiana in the morning. She'd probably already guessed that this would be the next logical step.

He'd been leaving the surgery yesterday afternoon with Marcus when he'd spotted her car driving through the village. On her way to see a new family the trust was due to start helping, she'd stopped to offer him and Marcus a lift home. She'd been unable to hide the look of shock in her eyes at his appearance, and in as few words as possible, as quietly as he could so that Marcus wouldn't overhear, he'd explained why he looked like hell. When they'd got home he'd hugged her. Big mistake. It had felt good. Much too good. It had also been witnessed by Sally, something he regretted. If he'd been thinking straight he might have spotted Sally's car on the drive.

He hustled his thoughts on. Stick to the agenda, he warned himself sharply. Work. Finding a new full-time job. Which in turn meant finding the perfect childminder for Marcus. The obvious person was Rosie. But would she do it? With a second child on the way, would she take on such a commitment?

He added that to the list in his head of things to do tomorrow. Top of his list was to find himself some legal representation. Should he go for a Manchester firm or find something closer to home?

He opened his eyes. *Legal representation.* Why was he being so coy about it? If it was a divorce lawyer he was in need of, then he should come right out and say it! Why dress up his words in some petty attempt to soften the blow? Was it to kid himself into thinking none of this was really happening? Or that it wasn't too late to stop what felt like an unstoppable force?

As he'd done before, he questioned what he really wanted. Did he want a divorce? Did he want to be the one who instigated the end of his marriage? What if he and Sally talked things over? What if they could turn things around? It was possible. It wasn't unheard of for a marriage to recover from something like this.

For Marcus's sake he could almost imagine trying to do that. It would save his son from so much heartache and confusion. It would give him the stability of a proper family home that he deserved.

But would it be enough for Dan? Would he be happy? Or would he drive himself mad wondering if Sally was being unfaithful to him again?

She'd called him boring. Safe and predictable. Was he? Chloe had said Sally had been talking rubbish when he'd told her some of the things she had said. But maybe Sally was right. Maybe he wasn't exciting enough. If so, that would always be the case. He was who he was. And likewise, Sally was who she was.

A car drove by in the street below, its tyres swishing the puddled wet road. Dan glanced at the alarm clock on the bedside table. He could just about make out from the luminous hands that it was twenty minutes past one. It was going to be a long night.

At the other end of the village, Chloe lay in bed listening to the torrent of water cascading from the blocked gutter above her window. Only the other day Seth had offered to clear out the leaves from it.

Was this how it was going to be from now on? Every little thing a reminder of him?

Only if you let it, she told herself. Only if you're prepared to wallow in self-pity and self-reproach. Only if you're going to regret facing up to the truth. Which is that you always knew in your heart you weren't good enough for Seth, and that you argued with him as a convenient way out of the relationship so he wouldn't discover what you're capable of doing.

She turned over and buried her face in the pillow.

But the voice in her head wouldn't be quiet.

As far as I can see, the only person judging you is you. Perhaps you ought to ask yourself why.

Chapter Fifty-One

Thursday morning and Sally was sitting in her office in a state of numb incredulity.

She had just been told she had been suspended. Suspended for the foreseeable future. Once she had gathered her things, she would have to leave straight away. What's more, Tom hadn't even had the courage to tell her himself. Bill had informed her of the firm's decision. 'We don't have any choice,' he had said, not meeting her eye. 'We've suspended Harry as well, but he's resigned.'

She shouldn't have been surprised by the decision. After all, it was standard procedure in these cases. It still came as a shock, though. Somehow she had convinced herself it wouldn't come to this.

A knock at her door had her snapping, 'Yes!'

It was Chandra. 'I've been instructed not to put any more calls through to you,' she said nervously, 'but Murray Adamson is insisting he talks to you. What shall I do?'

'Put him through,' Sally said with a sigh. 'And don't worry, I'll deal with the consequences if anyone finds out.'

'What the hell's going on?' Murray demanded when Chandra had done as Sally had asked. 'I was told you were unavailable and would be so for some time.'

'I've been suspended.'

'What on earth for?'

'You don't need to know.'

'Sally, I meant what I said yesterday. Whatever you tell me is strictly between the two of us. What's happened?'

She hesitated. Then thought, oh, what the hell! 'What I didn't tell you yesterday is that the man I was seeing was a colleague and now he's accusing me of sexual harassment.'

'The bastard! Has he been suspended as well?'

'Yes. But apparently he's already taken the moral high ground by resigning.'

'And what have you told Tom and Bill?'

'I've admitted nothing.'

'Nothing?'

'In as much as I've categorically denied the allegations.'

'Does anyone in the office know for sure that you'd been having an affair with this man?'

'Absolutely not. I may have behaved recklessly, but I didn't lose all reason. I was still careful.'

Murray was silent. An unusual occurrence. 'In that case,' he said at length, 'seeing as you've suddenly got some time on your hands, are you free to meet for a coffee?'

'I should say no to you.'

'But you won't. Right?'

'I'm in enough trouble as it is. Meeting you might make things worse for me.'

'No point in doing anything by half. Meet me at Harvey Nicks in the brasserie. And then you can tell me the whole story and we'll see if we can't find a way out of it. How does that sound?'

'Why are you doing this, Murray?'

'I told you, I care about you. You're also a damned good divorce lawyer and I don't want some fool taking over my case and cocking things up for me. See you in twenty minutes.'

He rang off before Sally had a chance to agree or disagree.

She packed up her things and went to say goodbye to Chandra. The poor girl looked devastated. 'You will come back, won't you?' she said to Sally. 'Only I don't want to work for anyone else.'

To make her feel better, Sally said, 'Of course I'll be back. Don't worry about it. It'll all blow over.'

Her words may have reassured Chandra, but they didn't make Sally feel any better, and as she crossed the road in the drizzling rain and made her way towards Harvey Nicks, side-stepping the army of *Big Issue* sellers, she knew she had hit skid row in a big way.

How could she possibly defend herself against Harry's accusations? How could she prove their affair had been a totally two-sided relationship, that there hadn't been a hint of coercion on her part? It was her word against his. Simple as that. But thank God she'd never given in to him and indulged in an explicit exchange of texts or emails. The only messages she'd ever sent him were those she'd left asking him to call her after everything had hit the fan. How many had she actually sent? Two? Three? She couldn't remember. If the matter did go to court, the mobile network would probably be instructed to hand over the necessary details, but evidence of a couple of messages at that late stage would prove nothing. It certainly wouldn't prove that she was harassing Harry to do something against his wishes. And thinking about it, she could always claim she had only sent them because of what Tom had shared with her. She could say she was concerned and had wanted to speak to Harry about it.

She was still undecided whether her best chance of surviving this mess was to admit that she'd been having an affair. But if she kept quiet, how could Harry prove that she had? He could refer to the hotel they'd stayed in on two separate occasions, but since she'd enjoyed the subterfuge of not using her real name when they'd checked in, it didn't really help him. Even so, it was a risk to deny it, especially if she had slipped up with something and Harry was able to produce real, hard evidence of their affair. If he could do that, then whatever else she said or denied would be in doubt.

So perhaps she would be better off confessing to the affair. She couldn't lose her job for having sex with Harry, but she would if she couldn't prove it was a mutual relationship. But how the hell did she prove that?

Murray was waiting for her at a table where he was reading a copy of the *Financial Times*. He stood up and kissed her on each cheek. 'Right,' he said when they were seated and two cups of coffee had been brought to them. 'Tell me the whole story. Leave nothing out. I think I might have come up with something to help you.'

She frowned. 'What on earth do you mean?'

'I'll explain in a moment. But first I want to know all the details and *exactly* what you've told Tom and anyone else in the office.'

Sally had no idea why she should do as he said, but the sincerity on his face compelled her to do as he asked. When she'd finished, she felt relief. It felt good to tell someone the truth. Even when she'd been sobbing in Chloe's kitchen she hadn't been able to bring herself to admit that Harry had turned on her in the brutal way he had. She certainly hadn't told Seth. Not when she knew he'd tell Chloe and in turn, Chloe would tell Dan. But then she hadn't actually seen Seth since she'd left the house yesterday morning after breakfast. Last night he'd been out for the whole evening – seeing Chloe, probably. She'd gone to bed early and hadn't heard him return. When she'd got dressed and gone downstairs this morning, there was a note by the kettle apologizing for him not being around, but she was to make herself at home in his absence.

Murray ordered another two cups of coffee and resting his elbows on the table he said, 'So, this is how it currently stands. You haven't admitted anything to Tom and Bill. At no stage did you ever admit there was a shred of truth to the allegations. You've denied everything. Have I got that right?'

She nodded. 'Which, I know, makes me a liar.'

Murray laughed. 'Give me a break; all lawyers are liars. Now listen carefully; this is what we're going to do. And I think you'll agree that as ideas go, it's the sweetest. Together we're going to tuck that Harry Fox up good and proper. By the time we've finished with him, he'll be held up as the poster boy for birth control.'

With the next two days taken up with an ecumenical conference in York, Seth was working at home, trying to squeeze an extra ten hours into his day.

He was also praying for inspiration. This coming Sunday it was his turn to take the family service, and the theme of his sermon – as he'd planned earlier in the week – was forgiveness. His opening line was: '*The unforgivable sin is that of refusing to forgive another.*' As well as being his opening line, it was his only line. He was stuck.

For the last hour and a half he'd been sitting in the kitchen, having set up a temporary office there while Sally was using his guest room. He was staring at the screen of his laptop, trying to think of something insightful and inspiring to say. But his brain was refusing to function. It had shut down, due to his inability to forgive Chloe's coldness towards him. And yes, anyone tempted to point out the irony of this would get short shrift.

It was beyond his comprehension to understand how she could have treated him the way she had. Not only that, there was the manner in which she had turned her back on her old friend so heartlessly. Fair enough, Sally may have made a colossal error of judgement in having an affair, but hadn't Chloe ever made a mistake? He certainly had.

During his first year of working for the vice squad he'd found himself attracted to one of his colleagues. The attraction had been reciprocated and they had embarked on an affair. The fact that she was married hadn't stopped either of them. He'd justified their relationship by telling himself that as long as they were careful no one would get hurt. Not her husband or her three-year-old daughter. And then he'd got caught up in that rail crash and he'd started to rethink his life. When he'd called things off with her, she'd taken it well. Better than he'd expected. Perhaps she too had begun to have second thoughts. The last he'd heard, she was still married to the same man.

So yes, he knew how easy it was to slip into a situation that had WRONG marked all over it. Adultery wasn't an exclusive club with a restricted membership; anyone was allowed in to join the party. The more the merrier.

He would never have thought Chloe would be one of those people who would condemn another out of hand, yet this was exactly what she'd done. What bothered him most were her remarks about her not living up to the high standards he would expect of her, and that she would never be good enough in his eyes. She'd often teased him that he was perfect – something he'd always been quick to refute – but now he was left with the very strong feeling that there had always been more to her comments.

Was it resentment?

It certainly wasn't unusual for clergy men and women to be resented. He knew of three priests who had been attacked in the street for no other reason than their attackers wanted to cut them down to size. They weren't mugged; they were merely informed by repeated kicks and punches that they had no right to set themselves up as being apparently better than anyone else.

In his current mood, he'd take on anyone in the street who wanted to score a point off him. There'd be no turning the cheek.

'Forgiveness,' he said out loud, reminding himself of the task in hand.

But it was no good. The concept of forgiveness had fallen off his radar. He stood up and went to the window. It was raining again, just like yesterday. He thought of his loss of temper with Chloe and didn't feel proud of himself. But would it at least prove to her that he was as human as she was, that he wasn't the plaster saint she'd made him out to be?

He sighed and wondered how much longer Sally would remain here as his guest. He'd hoped that she would open up to him, but so far there had been nothing from her. As yet there had been no mutterings in the parish about him having a lone female guest staying, but it wouldn't be long before word went round. Presumably everyone would leap to the conclusion that it was Chloe. Which meant that Owen would once more take it upon himself to give Seth one of his tiresome little pep talks.

Perhaps he had been misguided to invite Sally to stay, but if a similar situation arose again, he'd do exactly the same thing. Let people leap to their conclusions. What did he care? He'd lost the woman he loved. The woman with whom he'd really thought he could spend the rest of his life. And even after everything she'd said and done, he still felt the same.

The pain of acknowledging this was too much and he made a decision. He would have to leave Crantsford. Otherwise he would go quietly but most assuredly round the bend. By December, he'd be officially out of his curacy nappies and in a position to apply for his own parish. When that time came, he'd pick somewhere as far away from Chloe as he could. He wasn't strong enough to stay here and risk bumping into her at the gym or anywhere else on the doorstep. He needed distance between them.

'What do you think?'

'I think you're mad. Stark raving bonkers. It would never work.'

Murray laughed. 'But you like the idea, don't you? Admit it.'

Sally didn't know what to make of the man sitting opposite her. She'd worked for him long enough to know that he was a risk taker and enjoyed nothing more than getting one over an adversary. But what he was suggesting was breathtaking in its audacity. 'You're not really serious, are you?' she said.

'You bet I am.'

'But why? Why would you go to such extraordinary lengths on my behalf?'

'Harry Fox needs teaching a lesson.'

'And you see yourself as just the man to do it? I still want to know why.'

With what she suspected was practised ease, he slid his hand across the table and touched hers. 'I think you know why.'

With equal ease, Sally slid her hand out from under his. 'You're not expecting something in return, are you? Because I'll warn you now: that isn't going to happen.'

He smiled. 'All I want is for the best lawyer in town to take care of my divorce. I don't trust anyone else. Are we on? Can I talk to Tom, persuade him Harry has no case and that you should be reinstated at once?'

'It may not be as straightforward as that.'

'I shall make sure it is. If they don't do as I say, I shall tell them I'll be looking for a new law firm to handle my affairs.'

Sally chewed on her lip dubiously. 'OK, tell me again how it's going to work.'

'It's quite simple. I tell them you and I have been having an affair since April. Along comes Harry, who makes a play for you. You tell him to back off, but he won't. He starts hassling you, discovers our secret relationship, tries to force you into having an affair with him, says if you don't he'll tell the senior partners about us. When you still refuse to play ball with him, he turns nasty and sends that email to Tom and the rest of the partners, accusing you of sexual harassment.'

'And the reason I never went to Tom and told him what Harry was up to?'

'You were between a rock and a hard place. You were worried how the firm would react to you shagging one of its most valued clients.'

'How about the messages I left on his mobile when I broke my golden rule and tried to get in touch with him?'

'You'd decided you'd had enough and wanted to talk to him about his behaviour or you'd go to Tom and the rest of the partners.'

'And the dates he'll say he and I went away together?'

'We say he's deluded because those were the weekends you spent with me.'

'But what if Harry persists and takes this to court? I can't commit perjury. Do that and my career really will be over.'

'Trust me, it won't go to court. Harry Fox will climb down. I know his sort. He's so low he could look up a snake's arse. Do you really think for one moment that he wants to put himself before a jury and claim that he wasn't man enough to stand up to a woman? No, his game is quite straightforward. He wants to get at you for some reason, to exact some kind of revenge. Can you think of any reason why he'd want to do that?'

Sally shook her head. 'I've thought and thought about it and can't come up with anything.'

'Keep thinking. As I recall you once telling me during my first divorce, it's always an advantage to know the other side's thought processes and motivation.'

'Do you really think Tom and the others will buy our version of events?'

'Completely. I'm one of the firm's most valued clients; they won't argue with me for fear of losing my business. And as I said earlier, it will be me who goes to them with the story. You won't have to be there. That way, it's me lying and not you. Now then, when do you want me to hit Tom with our revelations?'

'I haven't said yes.'

'But you will. Because you know it's your best option.' He pushed the sleeve back on his shirt. 'Let's have lunch.'

'Don't you ever do any work?'

'Plenty of time for that later.'

Chapter Fifty-Two

The next day Sally had no reason to get up early and so she lay in bed listening to Seth moving about the house.

One of the things that surprised her most about his job was how the telephone never seemed to stop ringing. The first night she'd stayed here he'd been up and down like a yo-yo dealing with all the calls. It had been the same last night. 'Is it always like this?' she'd asked him when once again he tried to resume eating the meal he'd cooked for them.

'Pretty much,' he'd answered. 'But my going away for a couple of days does tend to hot things up a bit.'

He'd explained to her about the conference he was attending in York and told her to treat his house as her own during his absence. 'Thank you,' she'd said, 'but I think it's time I was making other arrangements.'

'Do you have anywhere in mind to go?' he'd asked. His diplomacy was incredible. He surely had to be itching to get rid of her.

The ringing of the telephone had saved her from answering him. When he came off the phone ten minutes later he'd thrown the cold remains of his supper in the bin and said he was sorry to be such poor company, but he had to go out.

'Are you going to see Chloe?' she'd asked, suddenly envious of the thought of him enjoying himself, leaving her to worry alone about her future.

His expression had dropped and scooping up his car keys from the work surface, he'd said, 'You might just as well know, I very much doubt I'll be seeing Chloe again.'

'But why? What's happened?'

'Chloe's decided it was never going to work out for us and has pulled the plug on me.' And before Sally had a chance to take the conversation further, he was gone. She had no idea what time he'd come back, but it had to have been after eleven o'clock, which was when she'd turned out her light to go to sleep.

In the bathroom next door to her room, she could hear Seth in the shower. She wondered what made a man like him become a vicar. He seemed so utterly normal. And as loath as she was to admit it, she was beginning to understand what Chloe had seen in him. He wasn't anywhere near as bad as she'd imagined. He wasn't at all sanctimonious or wishy-washy. But then as she'd come to know, she had made some lousy character judgements just recently. She'd got it outstandingly wrong with Harry. And to a lesser degree with Murray. Who'd have thought he would be prepared to help her in the way he'd offered?

Was it cowardly of her to take his offer of help? If it was, she didn't care. Her career was too important to her to throw it away on a shit like Harry. It had taken all of lunch yesterday for Murray to convince her that his desire to help her would not only work but was genuinely offered without any strings attached, other than for her to continue acting on his behalf for his divorce.

But would their story work? Murray was adamant that he could convince Tom that Harry's allegations were unfounded. It certainly worked in her favour that she had told absolutely no one about her affair with Harry. The only person who had an inkling of the truth was Chloe but since Sally hadn't ever confirmed Chloe's suspicions – not even when she'd been sobbing in her kitchen – Murray had discounted that as nothing to worry about. No matter either that Chloe might have shared her suspicion with Dan, it was still no more than supposition and guesswork.

Through the wall, Sally could hear Seth was out of the shower now. She wondered about him and Chloe. Was their break-up really her fault? Had Chloe dumped Seth because she was so angry with him for inviting Sally to stay with him? It'll blow over, she told herself, just as she'd said to Chandra.

She turned her head and looked for the framed photograph of Chloe on Seth's desk. Chloe's smiling face stared reproachfully back at her.

It'll blow over, she repeated to herself, turning hastily away from the photograph and deciding that one of the things she had to do today was find somewhere to live. But where? Where on earth was she going to end up? Should she look for a small flat closer to the office or something near to Eastbury so she could see Marcus without too much difficulty?

Closer to the office might be irrelevant, she thought bitterly. If Murray's session today with Tom didn't work, she would probably be looking for a new job. And, very likely, it wouldn't be in Manchester.

She pictured Corner Cottage and experienced a flash of anger. Corner Cottage was as much her home as it was Dan's. Why shouldn't she return there? She'd moved out to please him, to give him the space he said he needed. Well, maybe it was time for her to assert her rights. She had needs just like Dan. Why should he have it all his way?

But then she remembered why she hadn't wanted to go back; she couldn't admit to Dan that she had been rejected by her lover. It had been different telling Murray about it, because she had been sure he wouldn't fling it back in her face, but with Dan it would be a humiliation too far.

Thinking of Dan made her realize that she had hardly thought of him in the last twenty-four hours. All her thoughts had revolved around her job – perhaps a stark reflection of what was important to her. But why shouldn't it be? She'd worked hard to get where she was. What she'd achieved at McKenzie Stuart was as crucial to her identity as any part of her DNA. It was who she was. Should she have to apologize for that? It was absurd. Like expecting someone to apologize for the colour of their eyes.

So why was she justifying the way she was to, of all people, herself?

Was it because she was a mother? Mothers weren't supposed to think or behave the way she did. Mothers were supposed to feel guilty if they didn't put in the regulation amount of time with their children.

She flung the duvet away from her and sat up. From Seth's desk, Chloe stared back at her again, still smiling, still looking reproachful. Yes, thought Sally defensively, you'd be a much better mother, wouldn't you? You'd never put your career before your child. But we're different, Chloe. You never had to struggle the way I did. If you'd come from the same place as me, I guarantee you wouldn't want to throw it away to stay at home to change nappies and clean up a never-ending supply of sick.

None of this meant that Marcus wasn't important to Sally. He was. He just wasn't the centre of her world, as he was for Dan. Secretly she harboured the hope that one day, when Marcus was older, they would have a very different relationship from the one they had now. She liked to think that they would have more in common and that he would understand the person she was and maybe respect her.

A knock at the door had her getting out of bed, slipping on her dressing gown and opening the door.

'Sorry to disturb you so early,' Seth said, 'I just wanted to let you know I'm going now.' He was wearing jeans and a T-shirt with a loose-fitting overshirt, the sleeves of which were rolled up to his elbows; at his feet was a rucksack. He handed her a piece of paper. 'My mobile number, in case you need me.'

'Thank you. Is there anything I can do while you're away?' she asked. 'Any shopping you need?' She felt Chloe's reproachful gaze boring into her back. 'Or perhaps—' She paused and changed her mind.

'Perhaps what?' he said, with a small, enquiring frown.

She changed her mind again. 'Look, it's none of my business, but I was just wondering, and I know it's a long shot, but if Chloe will agree to see me, would you like me to talk to her? You know, about how she's ended things with you?'

He reached for the rucksack from the floor and hoisted it over his shoulder. 'That's very kind of you, but I think Chloe's made her decision and I have to accept it.'

'Is it because of me?'

She could see he was choosing his words with care. 'It might look that way,' he said slowly, 'but essentially, it's me Chloe's got a problem with and I don't think you can fix that.' He turned towards the stairs, but glanced back at her. 'You'll be all right here on your own?'

'I'll be fine. And who knows, with a bit of luck I might be gone when you return.'

His hand on the banister, he said, 'I hope everything works out for the best for you, Sally. If you ever need anyone to talk to, you know where I am.'

Chloe's first patient of the day was a sixty-two-year-old man who needed a knee replacement. Chloe had been encouraging him to have the operation for fifteen months and finally, now the pain was getting him down, he'd decided to go for it. She said she'd make the necessary referral and teased him that when he'd had the operation she would challenge him to a jog round the village. 'Last one home buys the drinks,' she said as she showed him out.

How she could smile and joke she didn't know. She felt awful.

She'd had a marathon crying session last night. She'd cried so much, her eyes were sore and gritty.

Her next patient was Chelsea Savage. Hugely pregnant now, she looked tired and fed up. Her mother was as vocal as ever and pitching in incessantly. 'Should her ankles be like that? They've puffed up sommat rotten. I don't remember my ankles being like that when I was pregnant.'

'It's quite common at this stage. Is the swelling worse in the evening, Chelsea?'

'Sometimes. Depends.'

'Try and get your feet up as much as you can. Are you still taking the folic acid and iron supplements I suggested for you?'

'Yeah. When I remember.'

'They are important, Chelsea. You really should make the effort to take them. For you and the baby.'

'Yeah. Whatever.'

All during Chelsea's pregnancy, Chloe had seen the girl's emotions go through a series of radical changes. One minute she was looking forward to being a mother and telling Chloe all about the pram she'd ordered and the next she was talking resentfully about how she wouldn't be able to go out at night with her friends when the baby came. It was fear of the unknown, of course, but today the girl's couldn't-care-less attitude infuriated Chloe and she wanted to slap some sense into her. Didn't she know how vital it was for the sake of the baby to take good care of herself? Didn't she appreciate how lucky she was to have this small, precious new life growing inside her? Didn't she know what thousands of women would give to be in her shoes? What Chloe herself would give?

Reining in her anger, Chloe said, 'What about the constipation you were experiencing when I saw you last?'

'Tell me about it! She's in that bathroom for hours on end.'

'Mum!'

'Still having problems, then? Well, try and stick to the list of food suggestions I gave you. Less junk food and more fresh fruit and vegetables. Plenty of fibre, that's what you need. Now, if you'd like to go behind the screen and get up onto the couch I'll take a look and see how things are coming along.'

When Chelsea and her mother had left – not before Mrs Savage had helpfully pointed out that Chloe looked like a wrung-out dishcloth – she wrote up Chelsea's notes, then buzzed her next patient in.

She knew exactly who was next on her list, but each time the door had opened that morning, she had half-hoped, half-feared that instead of a patient coming to share their medical problems with her, it would be Seth marching in to make her change her mind. What she'd do if he did suddenly appear in her surgery she didn't know. But the thought that it was really over between them so thoroughly depressed her that she didn't know what she wanted any more.

She had dreamed of him last night. He'd been holding that dying girl from the rail crash. He was praying for her. Then suddenly it wasn't a stranger in his arms, it was Chloe and he was cradling her with loving tenderness. She'd woken with a feeling of immense loss. She still felt it now.

Since Wednesday she had alternated between knowing she had done the right thing and regretting her decision. When she felt herself weakening – particularly when she recalled the two of them in the garden in the rain and the desolate expression on Seth's face – she had to remind herself of all the reasons why it could never work between them.

When that failed, she had to bring in the heavy artillery and remind herself just how high-handed he had been. It was an echo of how Paul used to treat her and she'd be damned if she would put herself through that ever again.

The door opened and in walked her next patient.

It wasn't Seth.

Seth had attended enough ecumenical conferences to know they all had one thing in common; they were a sizzling hotbed of diocesan gossip. It was usually what made them worthwhile attending.

However, by lunchtime, following two plenary sessions on Inner City Outreach, he was regretting being there. Having looked forward to catching up with several fellow curates with whom he'd studied, he was now wishing he'd stayed home in Crantsford. The ecumenical tom-toms must have recently been given a sound thrashing because he was repeatedly being asked about his new girlfriend. 'Old news,' he kept saying with as much indifference as he could muster.

He joined the lunch queue with Father Jim O'Brien, a rascally septuagenarian from Waterford who, despite – in his own words – having lived as a refugee in Britain for more than thirty years, had lost none of his native wit or engaging brogue. He was one of the speakers for the conference and someone Seth had always admired for his plain speaking. And for his humour. He'd once famously opened a conference with a keynote speech saying he was all in favour of there being other denominations because they kept the rabble out of the Catholic Church.

'So what went wrong, then, Seth? The way I heard it, the parish had not only approved of your girlfriend, but were anticipating wedding invitations.'

Seth pushed his tray along the counter ledge until it was nudging another tray in front of him. 'It's complicated,' he said evasively.

'These things always are. Was it the job? Did she not share your commitment? That can be the devil for buggering up a relationship.'

'Partly.'

'Not much you can do about that. Hang in there, lad. Have you got anyone you can talk to? I can't imagine Owen would be much of a listener in his current state. The word is' – Jim leaned in closer and lowered his voice – 'Owen's had enough and wants out asap. He's not happy with the woolly-minded liberals now invading the Church of England. And you know what that means. Especially as you're due to be fully priested in December.'

A week ago and Jim's words, even if they were based on hearsay, would have had him inwardly cheering. To take over the running of St Michael's would have been exactly what he'd have wanted. But now it wasn't. He needed to move on. And not just inside his head.

'You look like I've just flicked you with a wet towel, Seth. I thought you'd be pleased.'

'Is there a possibility that your insider knowledge could be wide of the mark? Or you misheard?'

Jim smiled. 'Away with you, boy! I may be getting on in years but my grasp of what's going on around me is as keen as it ever was.'

Forcing a smile to his face, Seth said, 'I'm sure it is. But to satisfy my curiosity, from whom did you hear it?'

Jim laughed. 'As an ex-copper you should know better than to ask who my informant is. Now would it help to mend your broken heart if I indulged in some matchmaking? I know of a pretty little curate in Matlock who might be just the thing to lift your spirits. Her name's Eleanor.'

On tenterhooks for the last hour, Sally grabbed her new mobile as soon as it went off. Just as she hoped it would be, it was Murray. 'How did it go?' she asked him.

'Is there any chance you can come into town right away?' he replied gravely.

Everyone at the trust responded with sadness and disappointment to Dan's news that he would be leaving.

'You've made quite an impact here,' Tatiana said when he accepted her offer of a cup of coffee. 'We're all desperately sorry to be losing you.'

They were in her office, the atmosphere between them taut and awkward. He longed for those days when they'd been so easy and comfortable around each other.

He'd been all set to phone in with his news and then follow it up with a formal letter of resignation but had changed his mind when he woke that morning. Having cleaned himself up – shaving and putting on decent clothes – he'd dropped Marcus off at nursery and driven straight here. The trust deserved better than a telephone call from him. Moreover, he needed to get his act together and put a stop to feeling sorry for himself. Hiding at home wallowing in misery and squalor wasn't going to help anyone. Least of all Marcus.

'Thanks,' he said. 'I'll carry on working here for as long as I can. Who knows when I'll actually land a full-time job. I'm sorry for letting you all down.'

'Don't apologize, Dan. Your priorities have changed; we understand that. How's Marcus?'

'He's fine. His mouth's healing well. He'll have an impressive scar to show off to the girls when he's older.' Dan knew Tatiana wasn't referring solely to his son's accident, but he didn't want to tell her that Marcus hardly seemed to notice his mother's absence.

'And you?'

He shrugged. 'Not bad. It's hit me harder than I thought it would. It comes and goes. I'd suspected for a while that things weren't right and initially I felt a sense of relief when I finally knew the truth. But the relief was short-lived. Now I'm angry and can't stop thinking how badly this will affect Marcus in the long run.'

'Don't let it get to you, Dan. My parents divorced when I was very young. I was five at the time. But I like to think I've turned out OK.'

'You seem more than OK to me. You're one of the most cheerful and optimistic people I know.'

She smiled. 'There you go, then. Marcus will be fine. How could he be otherwise with a great dad like you?'

'I haven't been so great lately.'

Staring over the top of her mug, she looked at him with troubled eyes. 'Why are you so hard on yourself?'

'Am I? I didn't know I was.'

'You are.'

Beneath her scrutinizing stare, he shifted uneasily in his chair. 'Perhaps it's because I blame myself. If I'd been a better husband Sally wouldn't have needed to look elsewhere for excitement. She described me as boring and our marriage as stultifying. I had no idea she felt that way. So where does that leave me? Apart from being Mr Boring who doesn't know his arse from his elbow?'

'It leaves you free to get on and make a new life for yourself, Dan,' she said quietly.

They stared at each other in silence. Dan was remembering their last conversation in this very room. *I wish things were different*, he'd said that day. He may have got his wish, and in a way he'd never dreamed of, but he knew it would be a mistake to take things further with Tatiana. Maybe it would never be right between them because they'd both always worry that any relationship they embarked upon would be based on the worst reason of all: him seeking a quick and immediate fix of consolation from her.

But she was right. He did have to make a new life for himself.

Chapter Fifty-Three

On a freezing cold, pale-skied morning in December, Chloe drove to Crantsford. She parked her car at the back of the library and checked her watch. She had an hour to do her shopping before she would have to keep her lunch appointment.

She very nearly hadn't agreed to come but then she had decided that surely it was time to let bygones be bygones. She would at least give him the chance to explain what it was he'd felt so keen to share with her – something he hadn't wanted to tell her over the phone.

Her first stop in her bid to make a start on her Christmas shopping was to call in at the new Waterstone's store. It wasn't her preferred way to spend her precious day off, but it had to be better than braving the busy shops on a Saturday. Thirty minutes later and she was back out onto the street and making for the toy shop where she hoped to find Marcus's present. Wrapping her scarf around her neck against the bitter cold and turning the corner, she collided with a couple coming towards her. She murmured an apology and carried quickly on. But the sound of her name being called had her looking back. 'It is Chloe, isn't it?'

She stared at the man in his smart woollen overcoat, felt hat and leather gloves. It wasn't always easy to recognize her patients when they were out of context. She scanned the woman next to him for clues. There was something vaguely familiar about her.

'Max and Stella Wainbridge,' the man said helpfully. 'How are you?'

'Oh,' she said awkwardly. 'I'm well, thank you. And you?'

'We're not doing so badly,' Max replied. 'We both went down with some bug last week but we've bounced back.'

His wife leaned forward. 'We were sorry to hear that things didn't work out between you and Seth. You seemed so happy together, we really—'

Max shushed her embarrassedly. 'Come on, darling, that's none of our business. These things happen.'

'But you said it yourself only the other day. You said what a shame it was that Seth was working so hard and that that new girl wasn't—'

A young mother with a pushchair was having trouble getting round them. They stepped aside and when the girl had passed, Max terminated their stumbling conversation. 'It's good to see you again,' he said, giving his wife a little tug. 'Have a lovely Christmas.'

Seth hadn't wasted any time in replacing her, Chloe thought when she pressed on towards the toy shop. Be glad for him, she told herself.

With Marcus's Christmas present added to her bags of shopping – some accessories for the pirate ship she knew Dan was buying him – she checked her watch. It was one o'clock.

She hurried off down the street. As she pushed open the door of Café Gigi – his choice – and felt the warm air hit her in the face, her stomach churned with nerves. Bygones, she reminded herself again, casting her gaze anxiously around the busy tables. Be nice to him. No bitterness. No grudges. It's all in the past.

She spotted him at a table on the far side of the restaurant. On his feet, he was waving to her. She went over. He helped her out of her coat and scarf. 'It's so good to see you, Chloe,' he said, making no attempt to kiss her.

'Thanks,' she said. 'And how about that: you've grown a beard.'

'Do you like it?'

'Yes,' she lied politely. It was one of those fiddly beards, the sort that she imagined required masses of careful grooming. 'So what have you been up to since I last saw you?' she asked.

He smiled. It was a smile of pure bashfulness that rendered him suddenly boyish, as if he had a great secret he was bursting to share with her. 'It's been an extraordinary few months,' he said. 'But let's order first and then I'll tell you everything. It really is so good to see you again,' he added happily.

His cheerfulness irritated her. Why couldn't he be miserable like her? When there was nothing for you to smile about, was there anything more exasperating than having lunch with Mr Happy?

The waiter took their order and when he'd returned with a bottle of water and two glasses of red wine, Chloe said, 'Go on then, tell me what's causing you to be so pleased with yourself.'

The boyish eagerness was back. 'I'm getting married.'

'Married!' she blurted out.

'I know what you're thinking. That it's all a bit sudden. I can hardly believe it myself. But when you know it's right, the length of time you've known the person simply doesn't come into it. Don't laugh, but it was love at first sight. I took one look at her and just knew.'

'Congratulations,' Chloe managed to say.

'Do you mean that? I'd hoped that you could be happy for me. But I wasn't sure.' He frowned. 'You and I didn't part too well and I ... well, let's just say I'd like nothing more than to know that we could be friends.'

With a leaden hand, she raised her glass to him. 'Congratulations,' she repeated. 'I think it's great you've found the woman with whom you want to spend the rest of your life. Good luck to you both.'

He leaned across the table and tapped his glass against hers. 'Thank you. You don't know how much that means to me.' He'd no sooner taken a sip of his wine than his mobile went off at his elbow. 'Sorry,' he apologized. Then with a ridiculous grin on his face, after realizing who it was, he mouthed, 'It's her: Anna. Give me five and I'll be right back.'

Chloe watched him walk away from the table and go and stand at the bar to take his call. She had to be grateful that he'd had the decency to take his call in private and hadn't inflicted his mushy endearments to his beloved on her.

She sighed. Who'd have thought it?

Paul getting married.

So that's what he'd been so eager to share with her when he'd called last week. He was obviously so cock-a-hoop with being in love, he wanted to tell the world about it. Oh well, good luck to him. Him and his silly old beard.

He was like a kid with a shiny new toy when he returned to the table, along with the waiter and their meal. 'I dread to think what my next mobile bill is going to be like,' he said, sounding like a man who really couldn't have cared less. 'We're on the phone constantly.'

'Where does Anna live?'

'Skyros.'

'In Greece?'

'She's a local girl I met when Liz and I were running the summer school. Her family own a nearby taverna. Just as soon as I've got things wrapped up here, I'm going back to start my own life-coaching business there. Anna's going to help me run it. We're planning to marry in February. But wait, I haven't told you the best bit. Anna's pregnant! I'm going to be a father. Who'd have thought my life would take this particular turn?'

Chloe tensed. She slowly lowered her knife and fork. Bygones, she warned herself. No grudges. 'A baby,' she murmured. 'How wonderful.' But inside she was screaming: *It's not fair! It's not fair!*

'Her family isn't overjoyed that we've got things a little out of order, they're quite traditional really, but ...'

On and on she could hear Paul twittering away, completely unaware of the pain he was causing her. She couldn't bear to hear another word. She needed to stop him. Either that or she would take her knife to him and shave that preposterous beard clean off his smug face.

'Chloe? Are you all right?'

'We were going to have a baby,' she said flatly.

He blinked. 'What did you say?'

'You heard. And if you hadn't left me when you did, our child would be nearly three and a half years old now.'

He stared. And stared. 'What are you saying, Chloe?'

'I was pregnant.'

'Why didn't you tell me?'

'Would that have made you stay?'

The bitterness in her voice made him frown. He was silent for a moment and then he said, 'Are you saying what I think you're saying? Did you have an abortion?'

'And if I did? What would you have cared? You couldn't get shot of me fast enough when we came back from Phuket. So what if I'd been pregnant? So what if I didn't want your child and got rid of it in the same offhand way you got rid of me?'

'You killed our child? I can't believe it. I can't believe you didn't tell me.' He was struggling to keep his voice low, to stay in control.

'Like I said, would it have made any difference?'

He shook his head. 'I don't know. I don't know what to feel. I'm in shock.'

'Well, don't bother trying to figure it out. It's not worth it. I've had to live with it all this time and I still haven't come close to figuring it out.'

'You regret it?'

'I ... I regret everything.' To her horror she started to cry. She snatched up her napkin from her lap and buried her face in it. When she raised her head, Paul was looking at her in a way she'd never seen before. He looked truly concerned. 'I'm sorry,' she said. 'I never meant to tell you. In fact, I never meant to tell anyone. I'm so ashamed of what I did. And now it looks like I'm destined never to have a child of my own.'

Paul reached across the table and took one of her hands. He was calmer now and looked less angry. 'Tell me about it,' he said. 'Tell me everything.'

She sniffed loudly and took a deep breath. 'Do you mean that?'

'Yes.'

When she'd finished, he said, 'And you've never told anyone this before now? Not even Dan and Sally?'

'I couldn't. Not when Sally was pregnant and Dan was so looking forward to being a father. What would they have thought of me? Then when Marcus was born, I couldn't ever bring myself to admit what I'd done. He was such a beautiful baby. So perfect.'

Tears filled her eyes again. 'There,' she said. 'Now you know everything.'

He looked at her sadly. 'I'm so sorry, Chloe. No wonder you hated me.'

'I hated myself more. I still do.'

Chapter Fifty-Four

Sally hadn't been entirely sure it would be a good idea to come here to Antigua, but now she was glad she had. It was wonderful to exchange the freezing temperatures of winter and pre-Christmas madness for the sun and a steady twenty-six degrees. Better still, and for the first time ever, it was a relief to have left work behind her.

Just as Murray had predicted, when confronted with what he had to say, Tom and the rest of the partners had effected an immediate climbdown and reinstated her. They'd still taken her to task over having an affair with a client, but had said they would let it go in the circumstances. 'That's big of them,' Murray had said to Sally in private. 'The circumstances being that I'd have switched horses in an instant if they hadn't done as I'd asked.'

What happened next had taken them all by surprise. With Harry's claims now officially dismissed as malicious jealousy, Tom had taken it upon himself to do some digging and had unearthed some surprising results. Harry Fox was not the man they'd imagined him to be. His CV proved to contain some highly creative touches. He did have a law degree, but it certainly wasn't a first as he'd made out, nor did he have the exceptional GCSE and A-level exam results he'd alleged. A housemaster at his old school reluctantly admitted that he'd been suspended twice, once for stealing and another time for trying to pass off a dud cheque in the nearby post office. His skill, so it seemed, was for talking himself up in such an impressive way it never crossed anyone's mind to check his CV and thereby he easily gained himself access to the kind of job opportunities his mediocre qualifications would otherwise have denied him. With the right incentive, it seemed he was capable of doing whatever he wanted. And the one thing nobody could take away from him – even Tom admitted this – was that he'd been extremely good at his job. The irony of a low-level fraudster working on important tax fraud cases was not lost on the firm.

Nobody had heard from Harry since his past had been revealed and Sally could almost admire him for his bravado. He'd been so convincing; the execution of his stunt had been flawless. But her admiration soon withered whenever she thought how he had tried to ruin her career and her reputation. She often thought about the dynamics of their relationship. In particular the sexual dynamics. As he'd pointed out, now and then she had enjoyed the novelty of relinquishing control to him. She had yet to fully understand why she had done that with Harry, but never with Dan.

Her marriage was unquestionably over. 'You're better off without me,' she'd told Dan during one of their meetings to discuss the future.

'*I* might be,' he'd said with heavy emphasis and hardly able to look at her, 'but I'm not so sure Marcus will be. Children are better off with both parents.'

'I'm sorry,' she'd said, meaning it. 'But I'm just not like other women. Or other mothers. And I can't pretend I'm something I'm not.'

Sally knew that Dan resented her lack of maternal instinct, but what could she do about it? She was making the effort to see Marcus as often as she could, but with her workload it wasn't easy. He'd spent the whole of last weekend with her in her rented apartment in Didsbury – a temporary measure until she'd decided where to buy a more permanent home – and things had gone far better than she'd expected. It was after they'd watched a couple of the many DVDs she'd stocked up on that they had an interesting and amusing discussion based on the theory Marcus had that shadows were frightened of the sun. She had no idea where this theory of his had come from, but his ability to push home his point with such persuasive argument had impressed her and even left her with a feeling of pride.

She'd been exhausted when she'd dropped him off at Corner Cottage on Sunday afternoon. She had wondered with renewed respect how Dan had managed it full time.

Dan was now working in Manchester – for his old firm again – and she had to give him credit; he wasn't going out of his way to be difficult or unreasonable over the divorce.

Chloe, on the other hand, was being extremely difficult and unreasonable. She had utterly refused to have anything to do with Sally. Losing the only friendship that had ever been important to her upset Sally. But what could she do about it if Chloe wouldn't talk to her, if Chloe still held her responsible for her break-up with

Seth? Sally knew from Dan that Chloe and Seth had never got back together again. And that bothered her. It bothered her a lot.

She put down the book she was trying to read and watched the man who was swimming backwards and forwards across the small bay. She kept on watching him until he eventually emerged from the unfeasibly blue water. For a man of his age he was in pretty good shape. Not quite Daniel Craig in those famously skimpy blue swimming trunks, but not bad at all. Squinting in the bright sunshine, he paused to push his silvery grey hair back from his forehead and walked up the sandy beach to where Sally was lying in the shade of a thatched umbrella. When he was directly in front of her, she lowered her sunglasses and said, 'Good swim?'

'Excellent,' he said. He bent down and wrapped his cold, wet hands around her ankles. 'Have I told you, you have the sexiest legs I've ever had the good fortune to set eyes upon.'

She smiled and tried to kick him off. 'I do seem to recall you mentioning them at some point or other.'

'Good, because I'd hate to think you didn't know just how much I appreciate every little bit of your delectable body.' He started to move his cold hands further up her legs, massaging her calves, then her thighs with a firm, sensual touch.

'I'm warning you, Murray,' she said. 'Behave yourself or—'

'Or what?'

'Or I'll call hotel security and have you thrown out.'

He laughed. 'I do believe you would, too.'

He lay down on the sun lounger next to her and reached for her hand, slipping his fingers through hers. 'I know we only arrived last night, but do you have any regrets about coming here with me?'

'Funnily enough, none at all.'

'I'm so pleased you agreed to come. I'd have hated to celebrate my *decree absolute* alone.'

'I doubt you'd have been alone for long.'

He let go of her hand, raised himself up onto his elbow and turned to look at her. 'I told you before; I'm not interested in anything trivial. I want the real thing. I want to be with someone I can respect and admire.' He leaned over and removed her sunglasses. 'We make a good team, you and me.' He kissed her long and hard.

They had booked separate accommodation for Sally, but that night she didn't sleep in her own bed. She spent the night with Murray in his private villa attached to the hotel. They both knew that she

318

would. It was just a matter of when. The speed with which she'd moved from one relationship to another gave her a few misgivings, but Murray was quite untroubled by it. 'Don't give it another thought, Sally,' he'd said. 'I certainly won't.'

In the morning, breakfast arrived on a large wooden tray and was placed on the verandah overlooking the sea. 'Fresh fruit and a glass of champagne: how else would we start the day?' Murray said.

'It certainly has the edge on driving into wet, dreary Manchester,' Sally said as she watched a hummingbird feeding on nectar from a hibiscus flower in the lush undergrowth. The air was warm and fragrant and the only sound to be heard was that of birdsong and the ocean. 'Work feels a million miles away,' she added.

He passed her a plate of sliced watermelon and pineapple. 'Since you've raised the subject, there's something I want to discuss with you regarding McKenzie Stuart. How would you feel about leaving them and coming to work for me?'

Taken aback, she said, 'I'd have thought you of all people wouldn't want to mix business with pleasure.'

'As I said yesterday, we make a great team. Think about it. Don't rush your decision.'

'I won't, not when I don't know what kind of a job it is you're offering me.'

'I've been thinking of finding an in-house legal expert, an expert I can trust implicitly. You'd be a great asset to my business concerns.'

'But my speciality is family law.'

His eyes danced with amusement. 'Are you saying you couldn't meet the challenge of extending your skills?'

'Don't ever do that to me, Murray. Don't ever suggest or even imply I'm not up to the job.'

He raised his glass of champagne to her. 'I'll take that as a yes, then.'

'Inasmuch as I'll think about your offer. No more. No less.'

'Can't say fairer than that.'

They were halfway through the holiday when Sally did reach a decision. She had spent many hours in the intervening days cross-examining Murray and his motives, as well as her own. She was torn. Half of her saw it as a great move – certainly the salary was tempting enough – but the rest of her couldn't imagine being out of the law firm loop. And what if things went wrong with Murray? She had no intention of becoming his third wife and had told him so. 'You say that now,' he'd said, 'but I sense I'm growing on you.' Really the man was incorrigible.

An abandoned two-day-old tabloid newspaper on the sun lounger next to her caught her eye. She couldn't resist taking a look. Splattered across the inner pages was a series of lurid photographs of a bleary-eyed Darren T. Child leaving a nightclub at three in the morning. Hanging off his arm was a young blonde girl falling out of a chiffon dress that only just managed to skim her bottom. According to the subheadings, she was a member of some girl band Sally had never heard of. The main headline was: *Darren Does it Again!* The article then went on to speculate about the state of his marriage and that this was the fourth time in as many nights that he'd been seen out with a different girl. A close friend of Mrs Child – a friend who doubtless had offered her comment in return for a tidy sum – was reported as saying Darren's latest antics were the last straw and that Mrs Child would definitely be seeking a divorce.

Here we go again, thought Sally, the merry-go-round of marital disharmony. Was that what she wanted to do for the rest of her life? Represent idiots like Darren?

A nasty jolt of reality shot through her, forcing her to accept the unpalatable truth that she, too, had now joined the ranks of those very people she was so quick to despise. What would a tabloid newspaper make of her recent behaviour?

She sat up. Down at the water's edge, Murray was talking into his mobile. Working for him would be a huge risk. She had to consider carefully whether she really wanted to put herself in a position of being beholden to him. But then hadn't she done that already by colluding with his lies over Harry's allegations?

She'd risked so much already for the sake of her career. What was one more risk? Besides, a life without taking a chance would be a life simply not worth living. Wasn't it existing in the safe, risk-free zone of her marriage that had driven her to have an affair with Harry in the first place?

She stood up decisively and went down to the water's edge to join Murray. She had no idea how things would work out between them, but one thing she did know: they were two of a kind. Being here with him, getting to know him properly, she had come to appreciate that he was uniquely understanding of what made her the person she was. She had surprised herself one night when they'd been strolling along the beach by confiding in him about the person she'd been when she was growing up and how hard she'd worked to reinvent herself. She had already shared things with him that she'd never dared tell Dan.

So yes, Murray was right; he had grown on her.

When she was level with him at the water's edge, he turned and smiled. Still talking into his mobile, he put his arm around her. She put her mouth to his free ear and whispered into it.

He immediately told whoever it was he was speaking to that he'd call them back later.

'I won't be able to start for some months,' she said.

'I don't care how long I have to wait,' he said.

She had the feeling it wasn't only work that he was referring to. He took her hand and they stared at the sea and the hazy line of the distant horizon. The water, sparkling in the dazzling sunshine, was calm and benign. It was extraordinarily beautiful.

How could it be so different from the menacing sea that had claimed all those lives almost four years ago, when its savage force had convinced Sally she was going to die alone and terrified in that hotel room? She shivered, despite the heat.

Four years. Was it possible that so much time had passed? Or that her life had changed so dramatically? She thought of Dan back at Corner Cottage with Marcus. When this holiday was over, she would go and see Dan. She would try and explain to him just how sorry she really was. It suddenly seemed important that he understood that none of what had happened was his fault.

Chapter Fifty-Five

There was no mistaking the glint of jittery panic in Lardy McFierce's eye. She looked every inch a woman on the verge of meltdown.

Whatever chaos was about to come her way, Dan reckoned she deserved it. That's what you get for being so high-handed, he wanted to say. That's what you get for putting as many noses out of joint as a heavyweight boxer by wresting full control of organizing the nursery nativity play and the Christmas fair. That's what you get for having scant regard for anyone else's feelings.

Of course, his opinion had nothing to do with Lardy McFierce sending Marcus home the other day with strict instructions that he was to wear a clean and appropriate tea towel on his head today. His attitude had nothing at all to do with her writing a note implying that under no circumstances did she want to see Marcus at St Andrew's wearing the grubby Chester Zoo towel he'd worn for the dress rehearsal.

As tempting as it was to defy Lardy's orders, Dan had toed the line and supplied Marcus with the appropriate headwear and freshly laundered blue dressing gown.

'I know how difficult it must be for you now, Daniel,' Lardy had said when he and Marcus had turned up with Rosie, Dave and Charlie, 'but we can't let standards slip because there are personal problems at home. It won't help Marcus in the long run.' Patronizing bitch!

Her condescension echoed that of Dan's mother. He'd held off from breaking the news about him and Sally for as long as he could, but when he'd eventually got round to it, it had been every bit as exasperating as he'd known it would be.

'I can't say that I'm surprised,' his mother had said stiffly and without the least trace of shock or disappointment in her voice. 'She never struck me as being the kind of girl who'd make a loyal and devoted wife. You're well out of it, Daniel. Mark my words, you'll soon find someone a lot more suitable. Why don't you come down with Marcus for a weekend and I'll organize a bit of a get-together for you. The Irving-Millers' daughter still hasn't married, you know.'

'I'm not surprised,' he'd snapped back. 'She's as appealing as last week's fish. God knows what you think we'd have in common.'

'There's no need to take that tone of voice. I'm only trying to help.'

'You think marrying me off before I'm even divorced is helpful?'

'Life goes on, Daniel. You being alone and miserable won't help Marcus one iota. Will she fight you to have custody of him?' Dan had noted that Sally had been reduced to 'she'.

'I doubt it.'

'I suppose this means you'll have to get a proper job now?'

'That's right, Mum, got it in one; no more lazing around the house watching daytime telly for me any more.'

'I must say, all this upheaval is clearly having an adverse effect on your manners. You could at least try and be civil. Have you thought about boarding school?'

'Don't you think I'm a little old for that?'

'Not for you! For Marcus. Boarding school in a couple of years' time would be ideal for him. It would be a marvellous environment to give him some much-needed stability, not to say the best possible start in life. It would equip him to stand on his own two feet, just as it did for you. It would also free you up to meet the right woman.'

'It would also kill me. Give my best wishes to Dad.' Dan had hung up then, breathless with anger.

Taking his seat in the pew with Rose and Dave and Chloe's parents, he was just about to switch off his mobile when it went off. He hurried outside to take the call. He hoped it wasn't work. He'd left specific instructions that he wasn't to be disturbed this afternoon.

Sliding back into the world he'd left behind to take care of Marcus had not been without its problems. The job itself was fine, and he didn't even object to being treated as a newbie by one or two of his colleagues who were a few years younger than he was. Nor did he have any trouble accepting that he couldn't walk straight back into the role he'd once held, that he would have to take what he was lucky enough to be offered.

What did trouble him was guilt. He felt guilty that he was not only spending so little time with his son, but also depending on Rosie so much. It didn't matter how often she promised him that having

Marcus around made her life easier with Charlie, he still didn't want to impose on her. She'd reluctantly agreed that he could pay her the going childminding rate and for now the arrangement was working like clockwork. What would happen when Rosie's baby arrived was anybody's guess.

It wasn't work calling him; it was Simon Frinley from Frinley and Baker, the estate agents in Crantsford. 'Good news, Dan,' he said heartily. 'I've just received an offer of the full asking price from Mr and Mrs Hughes, the couple you showed round at the weekend. As you might recall, they're currently in rented accommodation with the money in the bank all ready and waiting to go. They seem as sound a bet as we're likely to get. What do you want me to tell them?'

Dan had no need to consider his response or report the offer to Sally for her consideration while she was away on holiday. She was hardly likely to quibble over the full asking price being met. 'Tell Mr and Mrs Hughes that I accept,' he said.

'Right you are. I'll get the paperwork started this end and will be in touch again tomorrow.'

Dan turned to go back inside the church, but was distracted by the sight of a flash of red crossing the road and coming towards the lych gate. It was Tatiana, strikingly dressed in an ankle-length, red Cossack-style coat. Perched jauntily on her head was a black beret. She looked like she'd just stepped out of a Smirnoff advert. Rosie hadn't mentioned that she would be coming, but as Dan waved to Tatiana and waited for her on the gravelled pathway, he couldn't ignore how happy he was to see her again. It was five weeks now since he'd stopped working for the trust. Five weeks since he'd last seen Tatiana. He'd missed her.

She smiled tentatively at him. 'Hello, Dan. How are you?'

He wanted to say *better for seeing you again*, but instead he said, 'I'm OK. You look great. Nice coat.'

'Oxfam's finest,' she said with a light laugh. 'I've had it for years. It's my Christmas coat.'

'It suits you.'

'Thank you. You look very smart.'

He glanced down at his dark woollen overcoat and Hugo Boss suit. 'Work clothes,' he said. 'I came straight from the office and didn't have time to change.'

'How's the new job working out?'

'In some ways it's as if I've never been away.'

'That's good.'

'I suppose it is. How's everyone at the trust?'

'It's our busy time, organizing parties for the families.'

For an awkward moment, with their breath forming in the freezing air, they seemed to have run out of things to say. Until Tatiana, her face flushed with either the cold or embarrassment, said, 'We'd better go inside, or we'll miss Charlie and Marcus's big performance and that would never do.'

Loud, enthusiastic applause rang out.

The play had gone off without too many hitches. The relief on Lardy McFierce's face was plain to see. Only two pieces of scenery wobbled and collapsed, only one of the angels cried – an anxious girl who, Marcus declared with authority, cried all the time – and only one of the three wise men tripped and dropped his wooden chest of gold. Marcus and Charlie spent most of the time nudging one another and grinning inanely at the audience. They really were as good as brothers and Dan hoped that they would be lifelong friends.

Following frequent discussions on the subject, Marcus seemed to have grasped the concept of them moving house and all that appeared to worry him – apart from any of his toys going missing – was that they wouldn't live too far from Charlie. Which meant finding a house in the village. Chloe had offered to put them up if they couldn't find a house immediately, as had her parents, but last week fate had shone benevolently on him in the form of a three-bedroomed semi-detached cottage that had just come on the market. It was a fraction of the size of Corner Cottage and needed a fair amount of updating, but it had a good feel to it and a decent-sized garden for Marcus and Charlie to play in. It was within easy walking distance of Rosie, and Dave had already looked over the house for Dan and pronounced it as sound as a bell. He had also offered to do any of the modernizing work Dan notionally had planned for it.

There had been no urgency to put Corner Cottage on the market, but he'd wanted to get the wrench of moving over and done with. Not for financial reasons, but because he was through with putting things off. He'd done that time and time again with Sally, repeatedly talking himself out of confronting her. He wouldn't ever behave that way again. He'd act quickly and decisively from now on.

He reminded himself of this when he was buying two plastic cups of mulled wine at the Christmas Fair in the crowded village hall. He'd left Marcus and Charlie with Tatiana and she was encouraging them to dig deep in the lucky dip barrel. There was an alarming number of white polystyrene chips being scattered on the floor around the barrel when he rejoined them.

He gave one of the cups to Tatiana. 'Happy Christmas,' he said, raising his voice to compete with the general hubbub of noise, including Roy Wood, who was wishing it could be Christmas every day.

'Happy Christmas,' she replied.

He moved in closer to hear her. 'Are you around during the holiday period?' he asked.

'Mostly.'

'How about Christmas Day?'

'No definite plans as yet. It's always a bit last minute with me.'

'In that case, would you like to join Marcus and me? Chloe and her parents are coming. It'll be a very relaxed sort of day. What do you think? Could you bear it?'

'Are you sure that's what you really want?'

He knew what she was asking him. 'I've missed seeing you, Tatiana,' he said. 'If you're prepared to take things slowly, I'd like to see a lot more of you.'

She gave him a soft, gentle smile.

'So will you come?' he asked.

'Yes. I'd love to.'

Christmas and the run-up to it was the busiest time of the year for Seth. But being rushed off his feet was a blessing. It meant he had little time to torture himself with thoughts of Chloe. He'd tried to push her out of his mind, but the memories of her wouldn't shift. As that cheesy old song went, she was always on his mind. In a relatively short time she had become a fundamental part of his life and nothing seemed to be filling the void she'd left behind.

He missed their long phone calls, especially the late at night ones. He missed being able to share the stresses and strains of his work. He missed her humour and encouragement. He missed kissing her. And the sheer bloody sexiness of her. He dreamed of her regularly. Often it was the same dream; they were lying on a blanket in her garden and he was making love to her. The dream always fractured at the point of him climaxing.

He kept waiting for his feelings for her to change, but they wouldn't. Every day he prayed for some kind of let-up, but God was distant and silent on the subject.

So what could he do, other than throw himself into his work, which was now even more demanding?

Or try replacing her with someone new?

He'd taken up Father Jim O'Brien on his offer to introduce him to the 'pretty curate' from Matlock. Eleanor had been pleasant enough company and they'd had some enjoyable evenings out, but he'd known from the outset that it wasn't going to work between them. She was too serious and intense for him. There was no lightness to her.

He'd kissed her once, mostly because it seemed it was expected of him, but also because he'd wanted to know if he could kiss someone else and not think of Chloe. But he had felt nothing for her. There was no spark, no connection between them. And yes, the kiss had made him think of Chloe.

Shortly afterwards he'd cited the distance from Crantsford to Matlock and their hectic work commitments as an excuse to end things with Eleanor. She hadn't been able to disguise her disappointment, but then she'd shrugged and wished him well. He'd received a Christmas card from her this morning and he took that as a sign that she held no ill feelings towards him.

He wished he could say the same of Chloe. She plainly had no intention of ever forgiving him for helping Sally. He couldn't decide whether to send her a Christmas card or not. Obviously, the right thing to do – the *Christian* thing to do – would be to send her a card, and send it with a generous heart. But he was scared of doing that. What if she didn't return the gesture? There was only so much rejection he could handle.

Chloe was coming to the end of her afternoon round of home visits. Her next one was with Chelsea Savage. Her baby had arrived three days ago and she was now home from hospital.

Chloe parked on the road outside the Savages' house. The daylight was beginning to fade, and the front of the house was lit up with a surfeit of gaudy coloured Christmas lights. She could see flowers and cards on the window sill of the front room as she walked up the short path.

Mrs Savage opened the door. From behind her came the sound of a party in full swing. 'Come in, come in!' the woman bellowed. 'Come and join the fun. It's been non-stop ever since Chelsea got home last night. Friends and neighbours keep calling in to get a look at the baby. And what a looker! She's a stunner all right. Come and see for yourself.'

It was quite a different atmosphere from the one Chloe had expected. Knowing how disapproving Mrs Savage had been about her daughter's pregnancy, this was quite a turnaround. But then, so often, one look at a newborn baby, so small and vulnerable, and the hardest heart could melt.

Chloe caught her first glimpse of Chelsea's three-day-old baby daughter and felt her own heart melt. She was astonishingly beautiful. Swamped in a pale pink babygro, sleeping peacefully in Chelsea's arms, a tiny hand resting against her mother's breast, she could not have been more perfect. It was all Chloe could do not to snatch the baby out of Chelsea's arms and run away with her. How could a baby as perfect as this be created in such a casual, unloving and careless way?

Whatever feelings Chelsea and her mother had experienced throughout the last nine months, Melody-Joy – as Chelsea proudly said her baby was called – was now very much the centre of their world.

After examining mother and child, and politely refusing a glass of sparkling wine to wet the baby's head, Chloe drove on to her last call of the day. She hadn't held Melody-Joy for more than a few minutes, yet she could still smell the milky sweetness of her and feel the comforting weight of her in her arms.

Many times since her lunch with Paul, Chloe had wanted to do what he'd advised. 'You need to talk about this with someone you trust and feel really close to,' he'd said. 'You were always so close to Dan; why not open up to him?'

But whenever she thought of telling Dan, she felt sick with fear. She didn't want him to view her differently, as she knew he would. As a father, he would find it incomprehensible. Hadn't Paul looked at her in horror when she'd told him? He hadn't said it, but the word 'murderer' must have been there on the tip of his tongue. Did she want Dan to think that of her? She'd lost Sally; could she bear to lose Dan as well?

The only person judging you is you. How right Seth had been. But that was only because no one else knew about the abortion.

Paul now knew, and whilst he hadn't outwardly judged her over lunch that day, when his son or daughter was born next year he would. What's more, for the rest of his life, his subconscious would go through the same process as hers; it would mark off the years, silently clocking those milestone birthdays that should have been. Judge her? Of course he would. He wouldn't be able to stop himself.

It would have been the same for Seth. How would he not have been able to judge her? How could someone like him not condemn her for ending the life of a child she'd helped to create? It had been easy for him to forgive Sally's adultery, but forgiving Chloe would be beyond him; she'd taken a life.

As a doctor, Chloe would be the first to point out the obvious: that ethically she had done nothing wrong. Moreover, she would say that she hadn't been thinking straight when she'd anonymously booked herself into the clinic to terminate her pregnancy, that she'd been under a lot of stress, what with coming so close to dying in the tsunami and then Paul leaving her.

It didn't help, though. In fact it made it worse. She should never have taken such an important decision when she was least equipped to do it. All that had been in her mind at the time was the terrible need to be free of Paul's child. Spiteful vengeance, that's what had made her do it. See, Paul, that's what you get for dumping me!

Oh, yes, she'd wanted a child, but she hadn't wanted the child of a man who could treat her so brutally. She hadn't wanted to live with such a cruel and lasting reminder of him.

And yet she had. All this time, whenever she thought of the child she desperately wanted, she was reminded of Paul.

What would Seth say to that? We reap what we sow?

Oh, Seth, she thought with a sudden ache of longing. How different things could have been for us. If only I hadn't ... If only you weren't ...

But what was the point in even thinking that? Ifs and buts never got anyone anywhere.

Her anger for Seth had long since evaporated. She had now accepted that he couldn't help being the man he was and having the beliefs he had. She had been the one at fault. She had known all along that ultimately it couldn't work for them. She had known it from the moment she had recognized him at St Michael's church when he'd been conducting Margaret's funeral. That was why she had refused to see him again. The very nature of his job meant that he espoused a way of life that would hold someone like her in contempt.

How could she be with him when he made her feel the full weight of her guilt? But then she'd ended up falling for him and she'd been so happy she'd kidded herself she could get away with it. As she had so often taught herself, she had managed to block out the memory of what she'd done and allowed herself to dream of a happy-ever-after future with Seth.

But it had all gone horribly wrong. Seth had criticized her for lacking compassion for Sally. Even now that hurt. Because it had shown up her true colours. She wasn't a very nice person when it came right down to it. And who wants to have a truth like that shoved in their face?

Understanding how and why it had gone wrong with Seth in no way lessened the pain of their break-up. If anything, it made it worse because she now realized exactly what she'd lost. That rainy day in her garden, when Seth came to see her, she had been ruthlessly vindictive towards him. She had been trying to protect herself, to push him away. And she had. She had thrown away the love of a truly good man.

Overcome with sadness, she forced herself to think of something else. The memory of holding little Melody-Joy popped into her head. And then she pictured Paul and the look of delight on his face when he'd said he was going to be a father.

By the time she drove up Lark Lane and parked outside Ron Tuttle's cottage, Chloe knew she was in no fit sate to visit a patient. She couldn't get Seth, Paul or Chelsea's baby out of her mind. Round and round the three thoughts went, chasing each other faster and faster, making her dizzy with a feverish sense of despair.

She switched off the engine and recalled Sally crying in her kitchen; it was the last time she had seen her. In all the years they had known each other, other than when Sally had been suffering from postnatal depression, Chloe had never seen her so distraught. She remembered how she had revelled in her friend's tears. She had been so pleased to see Sally get what she deserved. She'd even turned to Seth and called it justice. She blinked away tears of regret at the recollection. How cold-blooded she'd been.

Was it justice that she should now feel so bereft and alone?

She tried to pull herself together. If she could just get this last visit over with, she could then go home and unwind before returning for evening surgery. She was exhausted, that was all. Exhausted and strung out. It was that time of year; everybody was ill right now:

colds, flu, bronchitis, sickness, you name it, someone had it. Roll on Christmas when she could take it easy.

'You look proper worn out, girl,' Ron Tuttle greeted her. 'I reckon I look better than you do, and that's saying something. Now come and sit yourself down while I make us a brew. You look like you could do with a shot of something in it, if you ask me.'

She tried to resist his fussing, but his kindness was too much. 'No time,' she said, her voice strained with wretchedness.

'Nonsense, girl. You're not leaving my house until you've had a cuppa. How about a mince pie to go with it?'

'Ron, please, I—'

He stopped her with a stern look. 'I think the words you're searching for are, thank you, Ron, that would be very nice. Now do as you're told and sit down. And while I make the tea, what's all this I hear about you courting a parson in the summer? I've known you since you were a nipper, so how come I'm the last to hear about it?'

It was no good. He'd worn her down. She had no defences left.

Chapter Fifty-Six

Nothing changes, thought Dan when he heard Sally's car on the drive. Christmas Eve, and she still manages to be late. 'Mummy's here,' he said to Marcus, who was sitting at the kitchen table eating his tea, at the same slotting pieces of a new jigsaw puzzle together.

Marcus looked up, his brows drawn together in an anxious frown. He shook his head. 'I don't want to stay with Mummy tonight. Father Christmas won't find me at her house. She doesn't have a chimney.' He shook his head again as if to underscore his concern.

'Don't worry, Marcus, you're not going anywhere tonight. Mummy wants to see you here.'

He went out to the hall to let Sally in. She still had her own keys to the house, but had tactfully not used them in a long time.

'Good holiday?' he asked, when she was slipping her coat off and hanging it on the newel post at the bottom of the stairs. Her face was attractively tanned; she looked well. He remembered how she always used to glow after being in the sun.

'Yes,' she said without expanding. More tact, he presumed. 'Where do you want me to put Marcus's presents?' she then asked in a whispered voice.

'For now I'll hide them in the understairs cupboard,' he replied, his voice equally lowered. When he'd taken the Hamley's carrier bags from her, he said, 'Come on through. Marcus is just finishing his tea. Can I get you something to eat?'

'No thanks. A drink would be nice, though. But before that, could I ... could we have a talk on our own?' She suddenly appeared ill at ease. 'There's something I want to say.'

'Can it wait until Marcus has gone to bed? Only he probably won't be too accommodating in giving us any time alone before then.'

She glanced at her watch. Dan experienced a spark of irritation. Why did Marcus always have to come such a poor second in her

332

world? 'That's if you have time,' he added pointedly, not caring what reaction he provoked.

'Of course I have time,' she said quickly.

Dan didn't believe her. How could he ever believe anything she said these days?

While Sally was upstairs putting Marcus to bed, Dan tidied the kitchen. The chances of Marcus going to sleep in the next hour or two were slim. It was the first Christmas he had really been old enough to look forward to, and according to Rosie, he and Charlie had been as high as kites for most of the day. She had taken them to the garden centre in Crantsford to meet Father Christmas in his grotto. Both boys had been given a bag of sweets and a jigsaw – the puzzle Marcus had been working on during tea – and when Dan had arrived to pick him up, he'd been beside himself with excitement wanting to tell him all about Santa's amazing grotto. He described the twinkling lights, the music, the dusting of snow – despite it not really being cold – and the pixie who had smelled of Polo mints and had taken their tickets and asked them if they'd been good, because Father Christmas only gave presents to good children. Nothing had escaped Marcus's attention. Dan regretted he hadn't been there to share the moment. Instead, he'd been stuck in a meeting, clock-watching for when he could escape. Everyone else in his team had headed on to a bar in Manchester to get the festivities officially under way, but he'd made his excuses, wished them season's greetings and made a run for it.

With the last of the dirty plates put away in the dishwasher, he poured out two glasses of Chablis and waited for Sally. Just like old times, he thought wryly.

They sat at the kitchen table and seeing the grim expression on Sally's face, he braced himself for whatever bad news she wanted to hit him with now.

'I want to apologize,' she said. 'I've come to the conclusion I couldn't have treated you much worse. You really didn't deserve any of it. I said some terrible things to you and I wish I hadn't. Words can never be unsaid, but I want you to know that I'm sorry, Dan. Truly I am.'

'I don't know what to say,' he murmured, shocked. A repentant Sally was the last thing he'd expected.

'Then don't say anything. There's something else I need to tell you. You might not believe me, but I do love Marcus. Just not the same way you do. I can't help that. I wish I could be more like you, more loving and caring, but it simply doesn't come naturally to me. I did try. And I'll continue to try. But what I found so impossible to live with was the knowledge that I was failing on a daily basis. No matter how hard I tried to be a better mother, the mother you believe Marcus deserves, the more I understood it was never going to happen. The sad truth is, Dan, I can't compete with you.'

He struggled to take in what she was saying. 'Parenthood isn't a competition, Sally. It couldn't be more straightforward. It's about love and wanting to do everything in your power to make your child happy.'

'It might be straightforward to you, but surely you realize that for me, life is one big competitive event. It's not enough for me to take part; I have to win. That's what Chloe and I always had in common with each other: our competitive edge. It was why we became friends. But with Marcus, you beat me fairly and squarely. You did it effortlessly, and I'm ashamed to admit it, I think I came close to hating you for that.'

'You make it sound as if I did it deliberately.'

'Didn't you, just occasionally? Can you put your hand on your heart and say you didn't feel closer to Marcus, knowing that he always behaved perfectly for you but badly for me?'

To his regret, Dan knew there was an element of truth in what she was saying. 'I'm sorry,' he said.

'Don't beat yourself up over it, Dan. I may have given birth to Marcus, but he's always been your son. Every step of the way.'

'It needn't have been like that.'

'We'll never know. But I do know that you're a better person than me. Stronger, too. If only for putting up with me for as long as you did. I'll always respect you for that.' She smiled. 'You know what, you really are a superhero.'

He flinched. 'Don't say that. Please.'

'Too late, I already did.' She took a sip of her wine.

'I'm no hero,' he said, staring down at the table. 'Nothing could be further from the truth. I'm one of life's big, unsung cowards. I've never told you this before, but I still get nightmares about the tsunami. They come and go, but essentially the dream never changes. I'm back there trying to save that boy all over again and then he changes into Marcus and I can't save him either.'

Sally lowered her glass. 'Why did you never tell me?'

He looked up at her. 'How could I, when you'd proved how easy it was to put it behind you? I wanted to be as strong as you, but I wasn't. I thought you'd despise me for my weakness.'

'I would never have done that.'

'But you did. As good as. You accused me of being safe and pre-dictable. You might say now that you think I'm stronger than you, but then you saw me as being weak, didn't you?'

'I told you before, I'm sorry for what I said. I wasn't in my right mind. Do you think you could ever forgive me?'

Noticing she hadn't answered him, he sighed. 'Oh, I imagine so. Not right now, though, Don't expect that of me.'

'Thank you,' she said quietly.

A heavy silence fell on the kitchen. From upstairs came the sound of Marcus singing 'Jingle Bells' – the Batman Smells version. Dan smiled, remembering teaching Marcus the words and how he couldn't stop laughing in the back of the car. He looked at Sally, who was also smiling.

'You know,' he said, 'for two intelligent people, we made a colossal job of cocking it up, didn't we? We survived one of the greatest natural disasters known to mankind, only to fall foul of our own failings. Hard to make sense of it, isn't it?'

She nodded.

Sally drove out of the village satisfied that she had said everything she had planned to say to Dan. Whilst she knew it was early days, she was hopeful that it would eventually help to reconcile them. She really didn't want Dan to hate her, despite him having every reason to do so.

Of course, she hadn't told Dan everything. He knew about Harry's allegations – not surprisingly, rumour and gossip had reached him at his office when he'd gone back to work – and he knew that Harry had disappeared off the face of the earth. He also knew – or thought he knew – just as everyone else did, that it was Murray Adamson with whom she'd been having the affair all along. Not Harry. To add further weight to the story, Sally had had to say that Murray had ended the affair when she'd told him that she'd left Dan – hence her tears at Chloe's and having nowhere to stay. To complete the story she told Dan that Murray had then changed his mind, saying he wanted to continue with their relationship after all. Not only that, he wanted her to work for him.

All in the game, she told herself whenever she thought there was a danger she was juggling one too many balls. All in the game.

Murray called it juggling with octopuses. It wasn't impossible; you just had to have a firm grasp and have your wits about you.

During their flight home from Antigua, in one of his unexpectedly perceptive moments when he was asking her about her marriage, Murray had said that in his experience things invariably went wrong in a relationship when people didn't confront the small irritations. 'The next thing you know,' he'd said, 'those petty little irritations escalate until they are seemingly insurmountable. You must tell me when I start irritating you,' he'd added.

'What do you mean, when you *start* irritating me?' she'd replied with a smile.

What Murray had said wasn't exactly revelatory, more like basic common sense, and yet with all her experience dealing profession-ally with the fallout of countless domestic irritations, she had made the same mistake as countless clients: she had failed to act. Would she have behaved differently had someone put a mirror up to her marriage and shown her what was really going on?

She stopped to fill up with petrol and had driven only a short distance when her mobile went off on her dashboard. Her first thought was that it would be Murray checking she was on her way.

Caller ID proved otherwise. Not recognizing the number, she answered cautiously.

'Is that you, Sally?'

She nearly drove off the road with shock. *Harry!*

'I'll take that stunned silence as a yes,' he said. 'How are you?'

'You've got a bloody nerve ringing me.'

'I like to call it spirit. Or chutzpah. Something you're not short of yourself. That's why we were so good together.'

'We were never good together, you little shit!'

'Oh, don't be like that. You're not going to say I meant nothing to you, are you? Don't say that, not after all the fun we had. And it *was* fun, wasn't it? God, how I enjoyed playing you. I made you want me so badly, didn't I? One little hint of denial and you were practically on your knees begging for it.'

Suddenly fearing that Harry might be recording their conversation, Sally put her guard up. Better still, why not cut him off? No, she couldn't do that. There was something she had to know. Something only Harry could tell her. She turned off the dual carriageway

336

and brought the car to a stop in a layby. 'Why did you do it?' she asked.

'What? Ring to wish you a happy Christmas?'

'I'm talking about you trying to destroy my career.'

'Oh, that,' he said airily. 'Well, let me tell you something, Sally. I did it to teach you a lesson.'

'But why? What did I ever do to you?'

'The fact that you even have to ask the question disappoints me. Cast your mind back to my first day at McKenzie Stuart, then focus particularly on the way you treated me. You treated me like dirt, like I was beneath your consideration. You thought you could put me in my place, didn't you?'

Sally thought back to that fateful day. She hadn't treated him like dirt, but yes, she had tried to put him in his place. She'd even boasted to Chloe about it. But he'd deserved it. He really had. 'I don't understand,' she murmured. And choosing her words carefully, just in case he was recording their conversation, she said, 'I thought we'd put that misunderstanding behind us.'

'You might have done. I didn't. From the moment you didn't take me seriously, I knew how I'd go about teaching you a lesson you wouldn't forget.'

'You mean, based on my not wanting to be eyed up as a bit of office fluff, you set out to destroy me? How pathetic you are, Harry.'

He laughed. 'Don't you realize, Sally, it's always the littlest things that cause the most trouble in life. By the way, nice move bringing in Murray Adamson. Presumably you traded with him; sex for a few lies. Nice touch. You're a real pro, Sally.'

'Goodbye, Harry. I hope I never have the misfortune to meet you again.'

'You probably won't. I'm giving law a break and moving to France.'

'One more question,' she said. 'Why did you ring me?'

'Tis the season for goodwill to all men, and since I knew you'd be tearing yourself apart wanting to know why I did what I did, I thought I'd put you out of your misery. Call it a Christmas present. *Au revoir!*'

The line went dead.

Sally thought about what he'd said. You didn't call to put me out of my misery, Harry, you called because you needed to brag about what you did. You wanted to show off how clever you think you are.

She made a mental note to change her mobile number after Christmas and drove on to Prestbury, where Murray would be waiting for her.

Chapter Fifty-Seven

'Why is it that Christmas Eve always makes me feel about ten years old?'

Chloe laughed and flicked a handful of soap suds at her brother. She was so glad he had decided to come home for Christmas, bringing with him Madeleine, his latest girlfriend.

'Could it have anything to do with the fact that we're both sleeping in our old bedrooms and have been banished to the kitchen to do the washing-up just as we always used to be?' she said.

'With the prospect of no presents in the morning if we don't do the job properly. Or worse, no Christmas pudding.'

'You always did look forward to that bit of the meal most, didn't you?'

'Sweets for the sweet, I always say.'

She snorted. 'Excuse me while I quietly guffaw.'

'Go right ahead, little sister, and mock me. But you know I can't help being so damned irresistible. Just ask Madeleine.'

As a guest, Madeleine had been let off washing-up duty and was upstairs wrapping some last-minute presents. 'Not that you need my approval,' Chloe said, 'but I really like Madeleine. Is she likely to stick around long in your life?' Nick had a history of cutting and running if things started to get too serious. He liked his freedom and his own space.

'She might do,' Nick said casually. Then he smiled. 'I hope so.'

Chloe smiled, too. 'Then just you make sure you treat her nicely.'

'I fully intend to. And since we're having a cosy share and tell moment, why did things go wrong between you and the guy you were seeing in the summer? I got the feeling from Mum and Dad that it was all ticking along quite happily. He'd certainly won their approval. Especially Mum's. Was it the whole churchy thing that you couldn't cope with?'

She rummaged around in the washing-up bowl for the last of the silver cutlery that couldn't go in the dishwasher. It would be so easy to say yes to her brother and leave it at that. But ever since she'd broken down at Ron Tuttle's, she had wanted to pour her heart out. She desperately wanted to tell someone how much she still loved Seth and how she wished she hadn't been so cruelly hurtful to him. She had even promised herself that if he sent her a Christmas card, she would get in touch with him to try and explain her behaviour. Not because she thought he would want her back, but because she owed him an apology. And maybe apologizing, face to face, would start the healing process for her.

But there had been no card from him, so she had kept her apology to herself, deciding that he really had moved on. After all, he had that new girlfriend Max and Stella had mentioned. There was no need to put herself through the anguish of baring her heart and soul to a man she was no longer involved with. Or likely to see again. Her gym membership had run out in November and she had decided not to renew it. Her trips to Crantsford were infrequent enough to convince her that the risk of bumping into him was minimal.

Whenever she remembered how she'd fallen apart in front of Ron, she despaired of ever making a full recovery. If only Ron hadn't been so nice to her that day. 'You shouldn't be around clumsy folk like me,' he'd said gruffly. 'I'm always putting my size ten right in it. That's what my wife used to say. "Ron," she'd say, "you're a meddler. Keep your nose out of other people's lives." How about a little nip of whisky in that tea for you? That'll see you right.' She had managed to resist his offer and had been grateful that he had eventually let her escape without having pushed her for the reason she was crying.

'Houston, we have a problem. The lights are on but there's no-body at home.'

'Sorry, Nick,' she said. 'It must be my age; drifting off without answering a question.'

He looked quizzical. 'Either that or I prodded where you don't want to be prodded. Do I let it go, or bravely press on and risk you telling me to mind my own business?'

'It's OK, I don't mind telling you about it. It wasn't anything Seth did; it was me. I turned into a monster when I was with him.'

Nick stopping drying the large dish in his hands and leaned back against the work surface. 'I find that hard to believe.'

'Believe it, it's true. I was horrible to him.'

'But why?'

Chloe had always been close to her brother; rarely as children had they kept secrets from each other. When she'd got into trouble at primary school for swearing, it was Nick she'd confessed to. When she was sixteen and had sat in Dad's brand new car, started the engine and lurched violently against the garage door, knocking the bumper off, it was Nick she'd confided in. Nick had even covered for her. He'd told their parents that he'd opened the garage door from inside, forgetting that the new car was parked on the drive. He'd lied for her because Mum and Dad would have gone mad if they'd known she'd been messing about in Dad's new pride and joy, whereas Nick was currently in their good books for having just passed his A-levels with straight As. Also, the previous week, Chloe had covered for him over something. She couldn't remember now what that had been, but that wasn't the point. The point was that they'd always been there for each other.

So was Nick the person to whom she could unburden herself? Could she risk telling him everything? 'If I tell you something I did, something I regret, will you promise not to think badly of me?' she asked.

'I could never think badly of you, Chloe.'

'Just say you promise. Please.'

Frowning, he said, 'OK, I promise.'

She moved away from the sink, dried her hands and took a deep breath. She told him everything.

When Chloe had finished, Nick said, 'You couldn't have been harder on yourself, could you? Don't you think we'd have all supported you in whatever decision you wanted to make?'

She reached for a tissue and blew her nose. 'I thought Mum would be so keen to be a grandmother that she might persuade me to keep the baby.'

'I very much doubt she would have done that. Do you miss him?'

'Who? Paul?'

'No. Seth. Do you still think about him and wish you could turn back the clock?'

'I'm trying to cut down how often I think of him. I've got it down to a mere every other minute now.'

'You don't think it's worth telling him what you've just told me? I'm sure he'd understand.' Nick hesitated. 'He's not a red-hot pro-lifer, is he?'

She shrugged. 'That's what I'm afraid of. I do know he was keen to have children. It was something we discussed very early on in our relationship.'

Nick went quiet. 'I still think you have to risk talking to him,' he said finally. 'If he practises what he preaches, then he should be able to forgive you. And when it comes right down to it, what have you got to lose?'

'Even if he could forgive me, I think it's too late for there to be anything between us again. I heard recently that he's started seeing someone else.'

'Classic rebound behaviour,' Nick said dismissively. 'It won't mean anything.'

'I wouldn't count on that.'

'Come on, Chloe, where's my tough little sister who once threatened to break the arm of one of my friends when he came to stay?'

She cringed. 'That was because he'd been trying to spy on me in the bath.'

'Who's spying on whom in the bath? And who's for a glass of devil juice before we go for the midnight carol service?'

It was their father. Standing in the doorway, he was dangerously armed with a bottle of sloe gin. Last Christmas morning they'd all woken late and with hangovers due to polishing off a bottle of their father's homemade liqueur. 'I think I'll pass, Dad, if you don't mind,' Chloe said.

It was as well she did, because when they were putting on their coats, gloves and scarves to go to St Andrew's, Chloe made a split-second decision. 'I'm not going with you,' she said.

'But you always come with us,' her mother said.

'It wouldn't be the same without you,' her father said. 'Who's going to sing off-key with me?'

'You can't stay at home all on your own,' Nick said, helping Madeleine with her coat. 'That's not allowed. First no sloe gin and now this. Next you'll be opting out of playing charades with us tomorrow.'

'I promise I'll never do that,' Chloe said with a smile. 'Not when I know I rule when it comes to charades.'

'But what will you do instead?' her mother asked.

'I'm sure I'll find something to do. Now go! Or you'll be late.'

*

Thirty minutes later, Chloe hurried up the path towards the church. Lights blazed at all the windows and the loud, robust sound of 'Hark the Herald Angels' met her ears.

She was nervous. Petrified would be a more apt description. This could turn out to be the worst night in the history of worst nights for her. But she had to do it. Nick had been right. She had to take the risk.

It was always possible, though, that he wasn't here.

She pulled open the heavy door and stepped into the small porch. She helped herself to a hymn book and a carol service sheet, and pulled open a second door. Greeted by a brightly lit interior and a packed church, she spotted an empty seat right at the back. She squeezed in next to an elderly couple. Behind her was a soaring Christmas tree; the air was fragrant with the smell of pine. Just as she got herself settled, the singing came to an end and the congregation sat down. She was so nervous her hands were shaking and she dropped her hymn book with a noisy thump. People around her turned to look, but she didn't register their expressions, she was too busy bending down to retrieve the book. When she straightened up, she searched the front of the church for Seth.

Oh, God, there he was! Her heart crashed against her ribs. She slumped as low as she could in the pew without attracting unwanted attention or losing sight of Seth. Fully robed up – fancy, embroidered stole over a white surplice – he looked well. What was she saying? He looked amazing, just as he always had. His hair was longer than when she'd last seen him, but maybe that was how his new girlfriend liked it. On second thoughts, perhaps he did look a little tired. Who didn't at this time of year?

So lost in scrutinizing him, she hadn't realized that the service had come to an end and that everyone was on their feet. A procession of choir boys and girls was making its way along the nave of the church. At the rear came the choir's older members and then ... and then Seth was following behind. He was smiling and shaking hands with members of the congregation, wishing them a Happy Christmas.

He was five pews away from her.

Chloe's knees began to shake.

Four pews away.

Her mouth was dry and the shaking had spread.

Three pews away.

Her knees were about to buckle.

343

Two pews away.

Oh, God, she was in real danger of cardiac arrest.

One pew away.

She hoped they had a defibrillator here.

Was there a chance he wouldn't recognize her, all bundled up in her hat and scarf? Was there a chance he would pass by and not even notice her?

He turned, his hand already outstretched, the warmth of his smile aimed directly at her.

He stopped dead. The smile vanished. There was shock in his face. Confusion, too. Was she imagining it, or was there regret in those blue eyes of his?

His hand finally made contact with hers. 'Happy Christmas,' he murmured. She held his gaze, her cheeks burning.

And then he was gone. Swept away on a tide of high-spirited well-wishers.

She stayed in her pew, alone and trembling. Her plan had been to wait until Seth had finished shaking hands with everyone in the porch and then ambush him. It had seemed reasonable enough back at home when the idea had occurred to her, when she'd suddenly thought how good it would feel – and symbolic – to wake up on Christmas morning knowing that she'd found the courage to speak to Seth.

But now all she could think of was how depressed she would feel tomorrow morning if he refused to talk to her.

A team of men and women were tidying up the pews, putting away hymn books and Bibles, straightening kneelers. 'Are you all right, dear?' asked a woman with a small, festive pine cone pinned to her coat lapel. 'Only we'll be locking up in a minute.'

'I won't be long,' Chloe said, as if she'd come here for some late-night shopping. The woman smiled and went about her business, just as Chloe caught sight of Max and Stella walking towards the porch to join the exit queue.

When she was sure Max and Stella had gone, Chloe got up. To steady her nerves, she walked the length of a side aisle, and went and looked at the nativity scene. The usual suspects were in evidence, their painted plaster faces serene and full of humble adoration. Surrounding the model of the lowly cattle shed and figures were pots of poinsettias and homemade Christmas cards. She picked one up. A child's wobbly hand had written the words: *Congratulations Reverend Seth, love from Tabitha (aged six) and William (aged three)*.

Inside another card that was sprinkled with glitter, a slightly more sophisticated hand had written: '*Congratulations Reverend Seth, you're the coolest! Luv from Tess.*'

She put the cards back and wondered what Seth was being congratulated for. Then it hit her. He'd got engaged! He was due to be married!

No wonder he'd just looked at her the way he had. Perhaps his girlfriend – his *fiancée* – was here with him.

Oh, what had she been thinking in coming here? But how to escape without causing him any embarrassment?

From behind her, she could hear what sounded like the last of the goodbyes being said.

Then she heard the sound of a heavy door closing.

Then the main lights were being turned off.

Filled with panic, she wanted to run and hide behind the nearest pillar.

Which, unbelievably, was exactly what she did.

Chapter Fifty-Eight

'Chloe?'

The sound of Seth's voice in the empty church caused Chloe's heart to leap.

'Chloe?' he repeated, his footsteps advancing towards her. 'Where are you?'

He was closing in on her. Reason finally took hold of her and not wanting to appear any more foolish than she did already, she stepped out from her hiding place.

'There you are,' he said. 'I was beginning to think I'd imagined seeing you.'

'Would you be happier if you had?'

He frowned and looked at her as if he hadn't understood. 'Shall we sit down?' he said. He pointed towards the front pew of the side aisle. 'Or do you feel uncomfortable being here? Would you rather we went somewhere—'

'Please,' she interrupted him, 'don't be so considerate. I don't think I could cope with that.'

They sat down, side by side, each staring straight ahead. She removed her hat and loosened her scarf, her nervousness suddenly making her feel hot. 'I'm sorry I missed most of the service,' she said. 'It was a last-minute decision to come. Owen not here?'

'He's gone. He retired a couple of weeks ago. St Michael's is officially my first parish, for which I'm solely responsible. We had a party here last week to celebrate my new position.'

Did that explain the cards? Chloe wondered. 'Congratulations,' she said.

'What made you come?' he asked.

She turned at his question, found herself looking straight into his intensely blue eyes. Her pulse quickened. 'Selfishness, pure and simple,' she said. 'I wanted to see you, to tell you something. It won't undo what I said or did, but I'm hoping it might help you understand why I behaved the way I did. Do you remember that day when you came to see me, the last time we spoke? You said the only person who was judging me was me? Do you remember saying that?'

He nodded.

'You were right.'

'I'm sorry. Nobody likes a smart arse.'

'Actually, it's the truth we don't like, and I was doing my best to keep that from you. It was my reaction to your comment that I should show some compassion towards Sally that did the damage. I know you probably didn't mean it, but your words were like a judgement of me and I knew then that I couldn't live up to your high expectations. I also felt that if you could judge me over something like that, what else would you judge me for?'

He frowned severely. 'So what is it that you're so frightened I'll judge you for?'

'When Paul left me, I discovered I was pregnant. I hated him so much for leaving me the way he did that I didn't want to keep his child and so I secretly had an abortion. It won't surprise you, I'm sure, but it wasn't long before I hated myself more than I hated Paul. It seemed a cruel twist of fate that I'd got rid of the one thing I then longed for most: a child.'

'Who did you turn to for help and support?'

'No one. Not my parents, Dan or Sally. Certainly not Paul. I hadn't told them that I'd been pregnant. Not until recently. I finally confessed to Paul what I'd done. And then tonight I told my brother about it.'

'Either one of them judge you?'

She shook her head.

'But you thought *I* would? Because of this?' He indicated his robes. 'You think I'm so perfect it gives me the right to attack others for their flaws? You didn't know me at all, did you?'

'I was frightened of losing you. I was jumping the gun a bit, I know, but you were everything I wanted in a partner. I could see us having a real future together. Except deep down I knew it couldn't be possible because of what I was keeping from you.'

'So instead of sharing any of this with me, you destroyed that future?'

'I didn't want your condemnation. Not when I cared about you the way I did.'

'Better to condemn me then?' His voice was edged with bitter sadness.

347

A long and heavy silence passed between them. Chloe broke it by getting to her feet. 'I've done what I came here to do. I wanted you to know that it wasn't anything you did or said; it was entirely me. It was me who messed up our relationship. I wish you luck with your new girlfriend. I hope she treats you a lot better than I did.'

He stared at her, his head tilted, his eyes dark. She thought he'd never looked more handsome. If nothing else, she would have that memory of him, a snapshot to treasure. But then she ruined it by picturing him kissing his new girlfriend, imagining him caring for her the way he'd cared for her. Her heart skittered.

'What new girlfriend?' he asked. He was standing up now.

'The one Max and Stella told me about when I bumped into them a couple of weeks ago. As I said, I wish you all the best.' She started to walk away. Fast. The reality of Seth being with someone else was too much for her. She had the awful feeling she was going to lose it if she didn't get out quick.

She'd got as far as the middle of the nave when she felt a hand on her arm. 'Chloe,' he said. 'Please don't rush off. At least not until I've had a chance to say something.'

'It's late,' she croaked, her words trapped in her throat. 'You need to go home.'

'Don't tell me what I need, Chloe. Not when I know my own mind so well.' With a swiftness that took her by surprise, he took her in his arms and kissed her. He kissed with such passion that when he released her she swayed in the firm circle of his embrace. 'I must be hallucinating,' she murmured, dazed and breathless. 'I can't really be standing in a church being kissed by a vicar.'

'It's real enough,' he answered, 'and before you ask, there is no new girlfriend. I saw someone a couple of times, but it was never going to work. For the simple reason I couldn't get you out of my head. I still love you, Chloe.'

'How can you, after all the things I said?'

'God only knows!' He let out a short laugh. 'But the fact that I do only goes to show how strong my feelings are for you.'

'I don't know what to say. I never dreamed you'd still feel the way you do.'

'Then say you'll give me two minutes to change and lock up and then come and have a drink with me.'

'But everywhere will be closed. It's well past midnight. And haven't you got to be up early in the morning?'

'I doubt I'll sleep much tonight. Come home with me, Chloe.'

Christmas morning and Seth woke late, a little after nine o'clock.

After checking that last night hadn't been a dream, he allowed himself a small smile. A smile that soon developed into a hopeless, mile-wide grin of euphoria. He felt he'd been given the best Christmas present of his life. It was a gift he had no intention of ever letting slip through his fingers again. There would be no more secrets between them. No more unspoken concerns or misunderstandings. No more destructive misplaced guilt.

He should have known there was more to their break-up than just that business with Sally. But an abortion. And one that she regretted so deeply. He would never have guessed. It saddened him to think that she had carried such a dreadful weight on her shoulders for as long as she had and that she'd suffered so much for it. He hoped he'd convinced her that he would never judge her for what she'd done. What right-thinking person would?

How glad he was that Chloe had come looking for him last night! What courage that must have taken. He was glad, too, that his request to be moved to a parish as far away from Crantsford as possible had been turned down. He'd approached the bishop at a seminar in Chester last month and had been informed that there were already plans in place for him. Father Jim O'Brien's prediction, based on ecumenical gossip, proved to be bang on the money; Owen did indeed want to retire, which meant Seth was the ideal person to take over from him.

But it was what else the bishop had in mind for Seth that had clinched matters. A new scheme backed by the Church was being set up in the New Year to help young offenders, and given Seth's background, it had been suggested he was the perfect candidate to take an active role in the initiative. He was to be attached to the police station in Crantsford as of the middle of January and he was looking forward to the challenge.

He lay as still as he could for a further ten minutes, staring up at the ceiling, then gave in to temptation. What man wouldn't?

He turned over, gently lifted Chloe's hair away from her cheek and kissed her. When her eyelids fluttered open and she smiled sleepily at him, he kissed her again. 'Happy Christmas,' he said.

'Happy Christmas to you.' She sighed and stretched languidly, then put a hand against his chest. 'You OK this morning? Any regrets?'

He raised her hand to his lips. 'None at all. You?'

'Only that I wish I had a present to give you,' she said.

'You've given me more than I ever expected. Although there is one other thing you could give me.'

'Name it and it's yours.'

'Give me your trust,' he said, still holding her hand. 'Trust and believe in me when I say that for as long as I live, I'll never want you to be other than the person you are, that your happiness is more important to me than my own. Can you do that?'

'Already done,' she said.

'Good.' He stroked her cheek. 'But as much as I wish I could lie here all day making love to you, I'm afraid I must tear myself away and have a shower. Family service is in less than an hour.'

'Would you like me to join you?'

'In the shower? You're more than welcome.'

'At church, silly.'

He smiled. 'Only if you want to.'

'I want to.'

'In that case, we'd both better get a move on. Max and Stella will be pleased to see you.'

Max and Stella weren't the only ones to be pleased that Chloe was making an appearance at St Michael's. Before setting off to walk the short distance to church, Chloe telephoned her parents to tell them she'd be home later than planned that morning. She'd called them late last night, just to put their minds at rest that she hadn't been abducted by a mischievous Santa, and her mother had been ridiculously overjoyed at the latest development. 'Bring him back with you tomorrow,' she'd said, making Seth sound like a new toy Chloe had just been given for Christmas. 'I'm sure Dan won't mind an extra one for dinner. We can always rustle up some extra food to help out.'

She sat in the second row of seats from the front with Max and Stella. They'd greeted her warmly and insisted she sit with them. She watched Seth conduct the service with pride and happiness. It was obvious that he loved what he did and that he was good at it. Equally obvious was that his congregation loved him and held him in high regard. Would their opinion of him change if they knew that he hadn't slept alone last night?

He hadn't needed to, but Seth had explained they would have to be discreet. He'd said he didn't mind people drawing their own conclusions as to what they may or may not be up to – after all, most of his congregation was aware of his views on sex; that what was important was that it took place within the context of a committed relationship – but to flaunt the fact blatantly that they were sleeping together was a different matter. Apart from anything else, the bishop might feel compelled to say something if it were brought to his attention.

Not so long ago Chloe would have been compelled to say something about it, too. Such as wasn't this a classic example of Church of England hypocrisy? But for Seth's sake she would keep quiet.

She watched and listened to him as he gave his sermon, which he'd assured everyone would be quick and painless. He didn't use the pulpit or any notes. Instead he moved about at the front of the church, his body language relaxed and expressive, his face animated. It was difficult for Chloe to concentrate on what he was saying, though. Her thoughts had drifted elsewhere, to making love with the Reverend Seth Hawthorne, the vicar of St Michael's.

The juxtaposition of Seth the Man of God with Seth the Dynamic Lover would take some getting used to. When she'd said this to him in the shower earlier, he'd laughed and said there was only one way for her to get used to the idea and that was to indulge in as much sex with him as possible. After last night, she certainly had no problem with that!

He'd asked her to trust him and she did. She really did. Her love for him was deep and aching and she knew that at last her heart was connected to him in a way she'd never allowed to happen before. He'd shown nothing but kindness and understanding after her confession about the abortion she'd had. There had been no condemnation. No criticism. Not a single word of censure. Only love and acceptance.

In front of her, she sensed that Seth was bringing his sermon to an end. She sat up straighter and paid more attention to what was going on.

St Michael's wasn't as packed as it had been last night, but there was still a good-sized crowd. Everyone was very smartly dressed, including the children. They looked like they'd been scrubbed within an inch of their lives and were doing their best not to wriggle too much. Each and every one of them was guarding a wrapped present on their laps. The significance of this became clear when Seth called the children up to the front of the church and explained that they were going to distribute the presents randomly to everybody in the

351

congregation, along with the ones he had in the sack he was holding up.

The distribution started in a quiet, orderly fashion, but rapidly gained its own momentum as presents were opened and members of the congregation began expressing surprise and delight. Laughter broke out when Max stood up to show off a pair of comical spectacles complete with furry eyebrows and mini windscreen wipers. Stella was given a book of jokes, the pages of which she immediately began flicking through, and the couple in the pew behind them were given a box of chocolates and a coffee mug.

Just as Chloe was thinking that she was the only one with nothing to open a small, dark-haired girl handed her an envelope with her name on it. Touched that she had been included, she opened the envelope and pulled out a card; a printed watercolour of St Michael's on a snowy day.

'What have you got?' Stella asked, leaning over to get a better look.

'Yes,' joined in Max, 'no keeping it to yourself.'

Chloe opened the card, then snapped it shut. But not before Stella saw what was written inside and let out a small gasp.

Her heart racing, Chloe glanced up and saw Seth at the front of the church. Surrounded by happy, laughing children, he was staring directly at her. He looked unbearably anxious, like a man dreading bad news. How could he think she would say no? She smiled at him and nodded, very slowly, but very surely. His handsome face was instantly transformed and he smiled back at her.

The rest of the service passed in a blur.

Afterwards, when they were alone in the vestry and Seth was changing out of his robes, he admitted that it had been the same for him.

'I can't remember a single word of what I said in the remaining minutes of the service,' he said. He came over to put his arms around her. 'Did I tell them at the end to go in peace and serve the Lord? Or did I blurt out that I couldn't hang around as I had a pressing engagement in bed to fulfil with the girl who'd just agreed to marry me?'

'Oh, it was definitely the latter. That's why they were all smiling so much.'

Chapter Fifty-Nine

Boxing Day.

Dan had it all planned. Or he hoped he did. It had taken very little effort or persuasion on his part, which only added to his conviction that he was doing the right thing.

The idea had come to him yesterday afternoon. It was opening the door to Chloe and her family and seeing Seth standing at the back of the group that had started him thinking. If one reconciliation was possible, why not another?

Seth had apologized for gatecrashing lunch, but had said that Chloe had wanted to surprise him. Graham and Jennifer had brought extra food, just in case, but he'd prepared more than enough for everyone, having already adjusted things when he knew that Nick and his girlfriend would be joining them.

The best part of the day had been when Chloe, pink-faced and grinning, had tapped her knife against her glass and announced she had something important to say. 'This morning Seth asked me to marry him,' she said, her face growing pinker, her grin widening, 'and I said yes.' They all went a bit crazy after that: lots of whooping, kissing and hugging. Another bottle of champagne was opened and through all the toasts and general mayhem, Marcus sat on Tatiana's lap, asking her to explain why everyone was making so much noise.

It had been one of the best Christmas days Dan could remember. Which was why he was determined to make today a day to remember as well. It was senseless not to try. They had too much history not to put the last few months behind them. After surviving what they had, exactly four years ago, surely they could do this one little thing. If they'd learned anything from that experience, surely it was that life was too short and too precious to do otherwise?

Sally was perplexed. When Dan had phoned first thing this morning and invited her for a drink at Corner Cottage, she had agreed because it would have been churlish not to.

It had seemed odd not to spend Christmas Day with Dan and Marcus, but spending it quietly with Murray had been a very pleasant experience. They had shared the cooking of lunch – something she and Dan hadn't done in years – and she had surprised herself by how much she had enjoyed the day.

At the back of her mind was the worrying thought that Dan might have an ulterior motive for inviting her to Corner Cottage. What if he was hoping for an outcome to their meeting that she knew wasn't possible? He'd sounded oddly upbeat on the phone and she really hoped she wasn't going to have to disappoint him. Relations between them had been going well recently and she didn't want anything to jeopardize that.

She knew that her actions had cast her in the role of hard-nosed bitch, if not for Dan, then without doubt for Chloe, and if she had to shatter Dan's hopes of a reconciliation she would be stuck with that label for ever. But how could she let him down gently? Hadn't she hurt him enough? Why did he want to put himself through yet more unhappiness?

Dan and Marcus opened the front door to her. Marcus was wearing a pair of light-up reindeer antlers and the new outfit she'd bought him from Gap. Presumably that was a tactful gesture on Dan's part, suggesting Marcus wear the new clothes for her visit.

With his usual high level of enthusiasm, Marcus grabbed her hand and said, 'Mummy, Mummy, we've got a surprise for you. Come and see! Come and see!'

She looked at Dan. Was it her imagination or did he look worried? Dear God, surely he wasn't going to ask her to come back in front of Marcus? He wouldn't do that to her, would he?

She allowed herself to be dragged to the sitting room. Standing at the shut door Marcus suddenly turned and said very solemnly, 'Close your eyes, Mummy. Then the surprise will be even better.'

She did as he said and let him lead her into the room, willing herself to keep smiling, no matter what.

'*Ta daar!*' Marcus sang out after she'd heard him turn the door handle.

She opened her eyes, and … and there was Chloe. 'Happy Christmas, Sally,' she said. 'Dan decided it was high time we settled our differences. I think he's right, don't you?' She smiled. 'After all, he knows us better than anyone and knew we'd never put our stubbornness behind us without help.'

Stunned, Sally glanced back to where Dan was hovering in the doorway. He still looked anxious. But she now understood the cause of his apprehension. That he could have thought to do this for her and Chloe touched her deeply. Overcome with emotion, her voice tight, she said, 'I don't know whom to hug first.'

'But Daddy, why are they crying?' Marcus said, his little brow puckered. 'Didn't they like our surprise?'

Out in the kitchen, Dan got down on one knee in front of his son. He knew that Marcus didn't fully appreciate the reasons behind bringing Sally and Chloe together this way, so all he could say was, 'They loved it. That's why they're crying. Grown-ups do that. When something really nice happens, we sometimes cry.'

Marcus didn't look convinced. 'That sounds silly.'

Dan wrapped his arms around Marcus and held him tightly. 'One day you'll understand,' he said. 'One day you'll realize just how silly we really are. And the really silly part is that sometimes we get so much wrong we forget just what we get right.' He tilted his head back so he could look into his son's face. Straightening Marcus's reindeer antlers, he said, 'And the best thing I ever got right was you.'

Marcus frowned. 'Now *you're* crying, Daddy.'

'Because I'm happy.'

'Really?'

'Yes. Really.'